The laws of human attrac

I'm breathless.

Just before I walk into the classroom, I glance over my shoulder. Lo's eyes are deep and piercing. I feel the weight of them hovering, watching. Holding me motionless as time, too, stands still. I force myself to peel my gaze away from his compelling stare, making my feet obey weak commands to enter the classroom...one in front of the other, like a drone. Something hot pulses across the back of my neck, racing across my body, and I can't even think.

It's not Ehmora who will be the death of me.

It's this boy.

WATERFELL

AMALIE HOWARD

HARLEQUIN®TEEN

Recycling programs
for this product may
not exist in your area.

ISBN-13: 978-0-373-21105-0

WATERFELL

Copyright © 2013 by Amalie Howard

This edition published by arrangement with Harlequin Books S.A.

For questions and comments about the quality of this book, please contact us
at CustomerService@Harlequin.com.

® and TM are trademarks of Harlequin Enterprises Limited or its corporate
affiliates. Trademarks indicated with ® are registered in the United States Patent
and Trademark Office, the Canadian Trade Marks Office and in other countries.

Printed in U.S.A.

For Cam, who never stops believing.

Prologue

Shivers race through my veins like gilded fireworks. The covers are twisted, matted like the hair on my head, and the room is filled with an eerie green glow. For a split second, it feels like I'm still asleep, half out of a leftover nightmare but not quite awake. My fingers are bent and curled like gnarled branches, and the sweat feels clammy against my skin.

The green light flickers, and I blink.

Get up.

Complying with the fierce voice in my head, I shrug off the blankets with a rough kick, and for a minute everything glows in a haze of gold, green and pink, as if the northern lights have just taken up residence in my room. I am no longer sleeping but wide-awake—I can feel myself breathing, hear the night's sounds outside my window. But the lights are still there, beaming off the walls and every piece of furniture, as if I'm captured in some kind of glittery prism.

Panicked, I throw an arm toward my bedside lamp and freeze.

My hand is glowing.

I look down. My entire body is glowing, like the iridescent

scales of some fantastic creature shimmering down my limbs in bands of colored light. All my cells tingle, hearing the call, responding to it just as my people had known I would. *Too soon,* I think. *Too soon.* I'd been promised four years. It had been only two.

My confusion spirals as the electricity builds and the room is nearly blindingly gold. Tiny pricks pepper along my spine and the sides of my neck, and I'm thrashing around in bed like a fish out of water. A huge rush of energy slams into me and the light turns into a white-hot dazzling force. Struggling to breathe, I hear the voice. My father's voice.

Run, Nerissa, run. *All is lost. Never return.*

1
Unmasked

"Run!" the voices scream. "RUN, RISSA!"

I can barely hear them over the pounding of blood in my ears as my feet skim over the grass. I'm winded but can sense the others on my left flank, already closing in. I push my feet faster—I must get there before they do or we are lost. In the past few seconds, white netting looms in front of me like a spidery haze, just as a heavy shoulder jolts like a ton of bricks into my side. The breath is knocked out of me as over a hundred pounds of muscle collides into my side with the force of a speeding train. Adrenaline jerks along my limbs and I kick out, blindly swinging the wooden pole in my hand with all the force I can muster. There's nowhere to run, nowhere to go.

It's now or never. I have to strike first or the moment's gone.

The silence stretches into eternity as the momentum of the assault makes me keel backward, my shoulder dangling limply, and then there is nothing but the feeling of falling until the ground rushes up to meet me with an unforgiving crunch. The only sound around me is the rasp of my own labored groans combining with the wheeze of my opponent's. Her eyes are as fierce as mine.

Either way, it's over.

"GOAL!" the crowd cheers wildly just as the buzzer goes off, signaling that it's halftime. It's been one of the most intense games we've played all season. Bishop's is the top-seeded field hockey team in Southern California and if they beat us, we're out. Going into the second half of the game one goal up on them means everything. I roll to my knees, gasping as my cocaptain, center midfielder and best friend, Jenna Pearce, throws herself on top of me, screaming in unbridled delight.

"I don't know how but you did it!" she shouts in my ear. "Getting us ahead at the last minute like that. I love you so hard right now."

"Nice goal, Riss!" someone else yells. "Way to bring the fire!"

The ten-minute halftime in the guest locker room goes quickly. Coach Fenton is pleased that we're ahead, but things can change on a dime especially with a team as aggressive as Bishop's.

Coach clears his throat. "Okay, listen up. First off, great teamwork out there! Offense, follow your striker. Marin's calls on the field and her shot on goal got us here. Let's keep that drive going. Defense, you've been like a vise, let's keep that up. Pearce," he says, glancing at Jenna, "outstanding job manning the midfield line. Smith," he snaps at a tired-looking brunette. "You've been letting your opponent get ahead of you the entire first half. Get your head in the game."

"She's too fast, Coach."

He studies her, frowning. "Then Andrews is in."

Jenna pokes me in the side and raises an eyebrow. Cara Andrews—second-string right forward, former friend and my current archnemesis—has been warming the bench the entire game. She used to be starting striker on the JV team freshman year until I got bumped up from right forward sophomore year. Now she's been relegated to second string on the varsity team. I'd prefer to keep it that way, but it's the coach's call even if Jenna and I are the captains. I grit my teeth and keep my eyes on the coach. Cara's presence on and off the field makes no difference to me.

Coach Fenton takes a long look around at all the sweaty, tired faces in the room. "Keep the momentum going, you earned it with blood and sweat. Don't lose it now. We have a thirty-five-minute half to prove ourselves—show this team that the first half was just a taste of what we can do. Don't take on any bad fouls and play a clean game. We're the underdogs. Let's own it. Come on, everybody hands in! Bring this home! Fighters on three—one, two, three…"

"Fighters!" we all yell in unison.

We troop fiercely onto the field, pumped full of adrenaline and courage. But by the time we're three-quarters of the way through the second half, I'm so winded that I can barely breathe, and that's saying a lot for me. The score is still one–zero with less than a quarter regulation time to go. We have to hold them off for seven more minutes. I glance down the field where Jenna and the center midfielder from Bishop's are faced off in a bully. They thump the ground, then tap their sticks against each other and it's on.

"Kate," I yell to my left forward. "Watch your mark! If the ball comes to you, pass it to me or back to Jenna."

"Got it."

Jenna wins the ball and passes to one of her wingmen, who takes it up the right side of the field. Keeping my eye on my opponent, I charge up the middle just as my teammate passes Kate the ball. As instructed, she sends it my way, but within seconds, I am stormed by three defensive players from Bishop's in some kind of blitz attack.

Dimly, I hear Coach Fenton screaming at me from the

sidelines. "Pass it to Andrews, Marin! Andrews is wide-open! Marin, ANDREWS!"

Cara is indeed wide-open, but hell will freeze over before I pass her the ball. I can get the shot without her, even with the blitz. Ignoring the shouts from other teammates and my coach, I shove through the defensive line with otherworldly agility. They're on me like glue and Cara is still open, but I've got the shot that will seal our victory.

My triumph is short-lived as one of the midfielders on the other team sweeps the ball out from under my nose and drives it back up the field, striking it down to her offensive line. Our collective breath stops as their striker takes her shot on goal with seconds to spare before the end of the game. If they score, our chances of holding them off in overtime are slim.

The ball flies through the air as our goalie makes a super-human dive to the right, taking the hit on her right shoulder and deflecting the shot. Relief floods through me as the buzzer sounds, ending the game. High-fiving Kate, I turn to face a furious Jenna.

"What the hell was that?" Jenna hisses.

"What?"

"Out there with Cara. You nearly cost us the game. If it were any player but her, you would have passed the ball, and you know it."

"I had the shot," I say, ignoring my sudden surge of anger.

"You didn't have a shot."

"We won, didn't we?"

"That's not the point, Rissa. We play as a team. And everyone saw what you did out there."

"No one cares. We won."

But someone does care. I feel the weight of Coach Fenton's stare all the way through the handshakes with the other team. He's not happy that I ignored him, but it was my call on the field. I stand by it. He doesn't say anything as I raise my chin in a half-defiant gesture and walk past him to hug our ecstatic goalie.

With a twinge, I see that she clutches her right shoulder on contact. "You okay, Sarah?"

"Best case, bruised. Worst case, dislocated. But either way, totally worth it."

I meet Jenna's eyes, the question in them clear. *Was it?*

Shrugging, I turn away and, in the next moment, Sarah and I are both picked up and carried along in a tide of girls toward the sidelines, where the bus is waiting to ferry us all back to school. The cheering is deafening for the ten-minute ride and continues into our own locker room. The only girl with a scowl on her face is Cara, but I refuse to let her ruin this moment for me.

"Nice job, Fighters," Coach Fenton says after we shower and gather in the middle of the outer room. "That was close, but you did it. You stayed strong and won us the game. And that kind of teamwork is what makes us Fighters." He doesn't make eye contact with me, but for the briefest of seconds I feel that the last part of his sentence about teamwork is directed my way. I shake it off as a new wave of cheering and hollering makes its way around the room.

"Have a great weekend, team," Coach Fenton says. "You deserve it. See you at practice on Monday."

Grabbing my gym bag on the way out, I join in the whooping as the revelry spills into the hallway. Even with the near-miss, you couldn't wipe the smiles off everyone's faces—making it to the semifinals is a huge deal for a prep school that hasn't been in the Spring Hockey Tournament playoffs for more than a decade. I'd been recruited into the game during my second day as a freshman at Dover Prep. As much as I hate to admit it, I have Cara to thank for that. Back when we used to be friends, we'd been joined at the hip and she'd insisted that we try out together. We'd both made the JV team—she as striker, and me as right forward. To me, it'd been a way to pass the time.

The plain truth is I can't participate in any competitive water sports, even though swimming is more my thing than hockey. My guardians warned me about that, and at the time I'd yet to figure out what else I might enjoy. Field hockey fit the bill as well as any other sport, and two and a half years later, I'd become quite good.

More than good, a sneaky inner voice whispers. Starting striker on the varsity team as a junior is pretty much unheard of.

I acknowledge it with a smug grin. My natural athleticism isn't a curse—it's a gift. As long as I'm careful and don't draw undue attention to myself, it's a bonus. And it isn't like swimming where I can clock a fifty-foot pool in less than ten seconds, almost half the time of the Olympic world record for freestyle, or hold my breath indefinitely. A smile curls my lip upward—technically I'm not holding my breath, but nobody really knows that.

"Riss," a male voice says from behind me as I reach the parking lot. An odd magnetic feeling, as if someone has placed a wet cloak over my skin and is tugging on it at the same time, stops me in my tracks. I turn toward the pull automatically, my body registering its owner a half second before my brain does. Sure enough, the owner of the voice—and the sensation—is a tall skinny boy with a shock of blond spiky hair and moss green eyes, holding a skateboard under one arm.

The smile on my face slows and stops altogether as I spot the familiar critical look in his eyes. I sigh. Speio and I used to be so close, but lately, everything I do seems to piss him off—field hockey, my friends, school, all of it. I can't do anything right, and it's getting to the point that he's becoming the nagging older brother everyone assumes he is. I know he means well. After all, his parents are tasked with keeping me safe, but it's not like that's *his* job.

"We need to talk," he says, and grabs my arm to pull me to a bench across the street. He's barely six months older than I am, but he's strong and his fingers dig painfully into my upper arms.

"Ouch," I mutter, pulling away and rubbing my already reddening skin. "What the hell, Speio?"

"What do you think you're doing?" he says in a low voice.

"What? You mean the game?" I can hear the defensive tone in my own voice as he nods. If Speio called the shots, I would be the kid who sits in the back row at school and never answers any questions or sits in the library all day…under a protective tarp in flame-resistant gear. "You followed me to the game at Bishop's?"

"I have to keep an eye on you," he says. "And I saw you. I saw what you did at the end with the three defenders."

"What did I do, Speio? Move a shade faster than normal?" I say as a wave of irritation replaces my earlier defensiveness. "Besides, what does it matter? Your parents are Handlers here. Not you. You don't have to watch me every ten seconds!"

Speio flinches as if I've struck him, but then brushes it off. "I just don't get it. Why do you try so hard to be like them?"

The soft comment strikes an unexpected nerve. "You know why, Speio," I snap more harshly than I intend. "I have to fit in."

My words are sharp but true. I've spent almost my whole life studying the other side, trying to understand humans and learn everything I could about them. And now, living here as a human, I've had to put theory into practice. As a student, I've absorbed everything academic they've thrown at me. As an athlete, I've enjoyed all the games, using my legs to run and my arms to swing a stick—things I'd never before experienced. Here, I've felt free for the first time in my life. Unfettered with who I am.

Now, a year after my father's cryptic message, it seems that I'm only delaying the inevitable—facing what is left of my legacy. The truth is, I don't want to think about any of it. So I'll pretend that what I'm doing is still the same, until someone tells me it's time to go back. And if that day never comes, maybe I'm fine with that, too. I'd rather be here, pretending to be young and carefree, instead of there, where everyone will look to me for the answers I don't have.

My family's legacy and my royal duty.

Speio stares at me. "But that's just it. You don't have to, because we don't belong here. We've been here three years already, and you don't even talk about going back. Waterfell's your home. You have everything there, can't you see that?"

Not anymore. I shake my head firmly. I may have been born in Waterfell, but my father was clear that I should never return—someone else was the ruler of our undersea home now. I grit my teeth, raising cold eyes to Speio. "I'm here to learn—this is part of my initiation cycle. You know that. And until I come of age to rule, we stay."

"And then what?" Speio presses. "We go back? You won't even talk about going back, and that's what scares me. Because you don't want to go back, do you?" His eyes widen at my expression. "That's the truth, isn't it? I can see it written all over your face when you're with the humans. But you're not them. Don't you get that?"

My blood rushes in a slow surge at his rising tone. "Careful, Speio," I tell him.

"Why?" he shoots back. "For being honest? You're so selfish, Nerissa."

"I'm selfish?" I repeat carefully, unable to keep the anger from seeping into my voice. Speio is only here because his parents, Echlios and Soren—both Handlers—are sworn to safeguard me. There's nothing he can say that will make them break their blood oaths. It's a fact, but still, something in his last words sneaks under my skin, unsettling me. Maybe because there's truth in what he says or maybe I'm still rattled from Jenna's accusations on the field. "Why am *I* selfish?"

"Because this is all about you," he says. "You don't care about anyone but yourself."

I glare at him, a thousand fiery emotions running through my brain. "It is about me. And yes, I'm the one who's decided to stay here. But you're free to go back if that's what you want. Go, and be one with the home none of us have anymore." Speio's eyes widen, but I don't stop. My words slow and become more enunciated, exhibiting the fact that English is not my native tongue. I hate the way the words taste in my mouth, so clipped and guttural. I also hate the way the commands come so quickly to me as if being a ruler is an inborn trait.

Because it is.

No matter what I look like, I can never escape who I am.

So I become the monarch. I become the royal with the clipped tones and the icy, immovable face. "You weren't told because I didn't want you to know. We don't have a home anymore, Speio. The Gold Court is finished. Wake up." He flinches at the cruel whip of my words. "We're never going home. Do you understand that? We have nothing to go home to." I gesture madly to the people walking around us and to the school behind me. "This is our home now. Accept it."

"But you're—"

"But nothing. I'm nobody." I lower my voice, forcing a smile to my lips even though all I want to do is scream… scream all the pain and anger and loss seething through me at his naïveté. Speio's expression is scared and confused. I gentle my voice. "Ask your parents. Get them to tell you the truth." I pause and press my hand to his shoulder in a comforting gesture, an apology of sorts, but he shakes my arm off like it's a snake. "Tell them that I commanded it."

I walk across the parking lot without looking back, and jump into my car. My hands are trembling with emotion and my throat is dry like sandpaper. I gulp and lean my head against the cool window, heaving breaths into my lungs, hoping to staunch the tide of helpless anger that's threatening to overwhelm me. But it's too late. I need to get out of there before I do something ridiculous like throw up all over the floor of my Jeep. Flooring the gas pedal, my tires burn a black path across the asphalt as I peal out of the lot, gasping for air and heading blindly for the shoreline. I need to get to the ocean.

The drive seems endless even though it's only a few minutes before I see blue on the horizon. Then I'm out of the car and running on the sand as fast as my legs can take me despite my exhaustion from the earlier hockey game. I don't care. If I stop, I'll break…I'll collapse and never be able to get back up. My face is wet as the taste of salt dips into my mouth, making me ache even more. Driven by pain, my vision spirals into the raw memory.

Days after my father's warning, Speio's father, Echlios, came back from a brief trip to Waterfell to see me. He was different that day. I'd never seen a Handler express emotion, but he did. He repeated exactly what my father had told me, but I already knew. My father never would have risked contacting me otherwise.

"Your father is dead," he said. "The High Court has been taken by Ehmora."

"Ehmora?"

Echlios nodded. I wasn't surprised. Queen of the lower

Ruby Court, she belonged to one of the stronger families, always opposing my parents, always scheming to replace the Gold Court with the Ruby Court. She'd never been content to stay hidden. She wanted it all—the waters, the lands, every last bit of it. And now that she'd displaced my father, she'd do anything to take control of the High Court.

And once I came of age at seventeen, I'd be the rightful heir. No wonder my father had urged me never to return. Leaving Waterfell was a part of my grooming—a necessary part of my training to understand the world in which we lived, to share the lives of humans, before I assumed the position I was born into just like all the heirs before me. But my training turned into something more with the death of my father. Without a home to return to, I took refuge in the human world.

"How?" I asked.

"It looked like a hunting accident," Echlios said, his face shadowed. But I knew better. My father was murdered.

"My father's advisers? What of them?" I asked him.

"All missing, presumed dead. My lady, it's not safe for you here. Ehmora's spies will no doubt have told her where you are."

I shook my head. If what Echlios said was true, this was the only safe haven I had left. Running meant I'd always be on the run, and I'd never give Ehmora that satisfaction. "No running. This is my home now. What does she want, Echlios?" I asked him, and then frowned. "What's to stop her from just killing me, too?"

"She needs you."

"Why?"

But I already knew why. Rule of the High Court in Waterfell was determined by succession of birth, unless there was no direct heir. Then each of the lower courts—Ruby, Emerald, Sapphire and Gold—could present a challenger. Whoever won would become the next king or queen, and their court the new High Court. Since I was the only living heir to my father's throne, once I came of age, the High Court would rightfully be mine. But the truth was, I didn't want it.

"Well, she can have the throne," I said dully. "I don't care."

The thought of returning to Waterfell was a bitter one, with my father gone. All his people—my people—would be looking for someone to lead them, and I wasn't that person. To them, I'd been a frivolous child who'd shirked every form of royal responsibility and been indulged by a doting father. They'd loved him but only tolerated me. They'd be better off with Ehmora as queen. I said as much to Echlios.

"You don't mean that," he said.

"I do. I belong here now. I'm never going back."

As the memory fades, I'm hissing the word *never* through my teeth just as the smell of salt hits me like a rolling wave, and I pump my legs faster, stopping only to throw my backpack on the side of the pier and to kick off my shoes. Self-disgust pours through me in violent waves. I hate feeling so power-less. I hate the way that Speio looks at me as if I'm a loser...a coward who's taking the easy way out. But it's not like I have much of a choice, do I?

In seconds, I fling myself off the edge of the pier in a grace-ful swan dive, letting the icy water envelop every part of me, and suddenly I can breathe again. I ignore the startled glances of the surfers clad head-to-toe in wet suits and churn my arms in a strong front crawl that takes me effortlessly past the break-ers. The water is cold for February, but it feels balmy against my bare skin as I duck underneath the last of the breaking waves to make my way underwater to where the ocean rocks with a gentle wide roll.

I'm careful to control my reaction to the water—it's like life energy to me—and it takes work to stay focused and make sure I don't transform when every part of me wants to give in to the magical pull of the sea. But I relax enough to let the cold salty water do what I came here for. I let it soothe me, fill me, pass over and through me until I am nearly faint with it.

Until I am calm once more.

It has been only moments but it feels like days. The arms of the water will always be my home, up near the surface or down in the deep.

Floating on my back watching the popcornlike clouds sail across the sky, I don't immediately notice the surfer paddling toward me. Or maybe I do and hope that he will go away, but I can feel the changes in the water that tell me he's coming closer.

"Hey, you okay?"

I turn around with a flippant remark on the tip of my tongue that gets stuck as I make contact with a pair of the oddest-colored eyes I've ever seen—a bottomless blue, as if he'd leached the color straight from the depths of the ocean. The eyes belong to a boy not much older than me. He paddles closer.

I must have imagined the strange, nearly navy color, or it must have been some trick of the sunlight, because on closer inspection, his eyes are more dark than light, almost blue-black. His teeth flash white at my look. Flushing, I realize that I've been ogling him for the better part of a minute.

"I'm fine," I manage, tearing my gaze away from his odd eyes.

The boy shoots me another knowing glance before his gaze dips to my bare arms. "Um, you're not wearing a wet suit. Aren't you freezing?"

"I'm fine," I repeat, a little irritated by his smile and the fact that my private moment of bliss has been interrupted by what seems to be some annoying local—even if he does have amazing eyes—one who probably doesn't even go to school and spends all his days tanning and surfing. "Look, thanks for your concern…"

"Lo," the boy supplies helpfully. At my blank look, he clarifies. "Name's Lo."

"Well, thanks, Lo. See you around."

I duck-dive and swim a few lengths underwater before resurfacing several feet away. He hasn't moved and is still staring at me with those strange dark eyes. Lo shoots another irritatingly white smile in my direction, a knowing grin as if he's far too used to having that effect on girls. No effect whatsoever on me, of course. I'd been overemotional and caught by surprise.

"Catch you later, then," he says loudly.

I watch him as he deftly paddles to catch a wave, his body sleek as a seal's in his wet suit. He rides the wave expertly, skimming along the foamy lip of its crest to curl across its open face and twisting his body like a whip to bring the board up and around.

Lo's a pretty good surfer, I admit to myself.

Then again, he probably surfs every available hour out of every day like half the other kids carving it up out there. He's just another boy with a board, and I've certainly seen my share of them showing off their tricks, especially living in San Diego. Jenna's boyfriend, Sawyer, is captain of the surf team at Dover, the reigning state champions. We'd always joked that if she and Sawyer ever had kids, they'd be born All-Star All-Americans just from the gene pool. Jenna likes her boys talented and driven, just as she is. It is one of the reasons I like her so much—she gives everything her all, from sports to studies to her relationships. She never shies away from anything.

Typical surfer-boy bravado aside, for some reason, I can't tear my eyes away from Lo's lithe form. He moves as if he is one with the wave, a part of it instead of riding on top of it, in some kind of fluid symmetry. He surfs like how I like to surf, something that Sawyer calls Zen-surfing.

As if sensing my stare, at the very last minute on his final turn, Lo rips backward on his surfboard to make eye contact with me one last time—a look that I can feel even as far away as he is—and winks before somersaulting backward into the surf.

I feel that last glance of his all the way to my toenails. Not even the icy touch of the water can calm the deep flush that tunnels its way through me.

2

Clouded Waters

"Miss Marin, kindly report to Principal Cano's office."

Even though all the stares of the students in the room suddenly converge upon me, my second-period Spanish teacher doesn't look up from the pile of papers on his desk. I shrug, grinning at the kids in the front row, and sport a sneaky thumbs-up to Jenna and Sawyer sitting in the back next to my empty desk. Jenna rolls her eyes in an exaggerated movement as if I've just gotten off scot-free from a fate worse than death, but she's kind of right. Anything's better than verb conjugations in Spanish class, even if it is facing the resident dragon-lord of Dover Prep.

The outer office is empty except for a familiar face. Cara ignores me, probably because she's still mad about the match, or it could be that she's just being Cara. She's the principal's niece, so she basically thinks that everyone at Dover is there to be at her beck and call. According to Jenna, the school is divided into Cara peons and Cara crap-ons. I'm definitely in the latter. Cara and I used to be friends—best friends even—but things had ended after a boy she'd liked asked me out, and I'd said yes. Apparently I'd broken a cardinal rule of girlhood, but technically, I didn't steal anything that didn't want to be stolen. And then when I took her place as starting striker on the JV team sophomore year, that'd been the clincher.

I shrug and look around. Normally the waiting room has a couple students standing around but it's empty so I sit after checking in with Cano's receptionist. Pushing aside the stack of college brochures on the table next to me, I thumb through the only magazine I can find and nearly snort at some of the articles. Flipping through one about "Ten Ways to Talk to Your Teen About Sex," I can't stop myself from bursting into laughter despite the immediate quelling look from the receptionist. I can't imagine any parent who would use a cucumber as a prop in any kind of meaningful conversation.

"What's so funny?" a voice behind me asks. The smell of salt and sand fills my nostrils, and I swing around. It's the boy from the beach.

Lo.

He's wearing a wool hat and black T-shirt with cargos instead of a neoprene hood and wet suit, but those eyes are unforgettable.

I slam the magazine shut, feeling a slow flush crawl up my neck and around the back of my ears. "Stalk much? What are you doing here, anyway?" I snap, noticing the golden sand grains covering his flip-flop–clad feet.

"Not stalking. I'm new here."

"Sure you are." Considering he isn't wearing the Dover Prep required uniform, I'm pretty sure he's taking me for a ride. I turn my attention back to the magazine, opening its pages and pretending to be absorbed in reading. A low chuckle alerts me to the particularly large headline entitled "Embarrassing Medical Problems." I feel my skin getting hotter and toss the offending magazine to the table, turning to confront Mr. Nosypants.

"Why don't you go back to surfing or tanning or whatever it is that you beach boys do?"

Lo smiles. I force myself not to notice that his teeth are whiter than I remember or to acknowledge the tiny response that makes my ears feel like they're melting into unrecognizable nubs.

"I thought you were watching me surf the other day," he says with a grin.

"Hardly," I shoot back with feigned nonchalance. "Couldn't have picked you out from the lineup of identical surfing doppelgängers if I tried."

"So that wasn't you out beyond the breakers staring at me like I was a frosted cherry smoothie?" Lo's smile turns impish.

"What?" I splutter. "I was so not. I hate cherry." I can't exactly control the flush that seeps through my skin. I snap my lips shut, aware that I'll only make it worse if I say anything more, especially in response to that annoying, knowing look on his face.

"Hi, Lo," Cara says in a breathy voice, walking past us on her way out of the office. "Nice to see you again." Once more, it's as if I'm invisible, but no surprise there. Lo has obviously qualified for the peon list. I snort and turn back to studying the other brochures on the table before selecting one on making informed college choices.

"Hey, Cara," Lo says to her with a smile that could melt butter, and then stands to move past her and sit in the empty seat next to me. With a death glare in my direction as if his actions are somehow my fault, Cara tosses her hair and stalks off. "So what's your name?" he asks me.

Despite giving him immediate brownie points for blowing off Cara, I'm still trying to think of a snarky comeback in return for his earlier comment. Just then Principal Cano himself walks out of his office. He heads over to his assistant, holding a file in his hand. Cano is a tall swarthy, stern-looking man whose presence will make any classroom fall into immediate silence. It's no different in the office. Well, except for Lo.

He stifles a laugh and whispers against my ear, "That guy is a dead ringer for Borat. If he has an accent, I think I'll die."

"Shut up," I hiss back, leaning away from Lo's warm breath. "So not funny. He's Albanian and he's a huge fan of detention, so keep talking if that's your thing. Your funeral."

In the same breath, I have to bite the smile trying to break across my face because Principal Cano is the butt of much Borat-related humor at Dover, all, of course, expressed in secret. A couple years back, one student actually posted a photo of the offending infamous green mankini on her blog with Principal Cano's face, and she'd mysteriously disappeared within the same week. Rumors varied from she'd been expelled, to her family had moved to the other side of the country, to she was being held in Cano's garage to be tortured for eternity.

I, of course, know better. Speio—who seems to somehow know everything that goes on in school—told me that there had been a very private lawsuit and an even more private settlement. So I know that it was definitely the second one, but who am I to curb the fun of speculation? Still, Cano is not one to be messed with—he takes his job as school principal seriously. Supposedly he used to be some kind of big-time molecular scientist in Eastern Europe and published several books on DNA research before he had a breakdown. I can't imagine anything worse than managing a school full of hormonal teenagers, but different strokes for different folks.

"Ah, Ms. Marin," Principal Cano says in a thickly accented voice. Beside me, I feel Lo's indrawn snort and I bite the inside of my cheek even harder. I paste my best impression of a cheerleader smile on my face and lean so far away from Lo that I'm nearly out of my chair. "Congratulations on the game last week. Coach Fenton said that you were instrumental in the win."

"Thank you, sir," I say. "But it was a team effort."

"That's the spirit," he agrees. I notice that he hasn't acknowledged Lo but, new student or not, beach-bum surfer-boy is hardly my problem. "Come on in."

As I stand to follow Principal Cano to his office, Lo winks at me and sprawls in the chair as if he's in his living room. He picks up my discarded magazine and flips through it, raising his eyebrow and pointing overtly at the embarrassing-moments article. Unable to help myself, I roll my eyes at him. He's a piece of work, that one.

Despite the pretense with the magazine, I feel his eyes on me all the way into the principal's office. I say hello to the guidance counselor, who's sitting in the second chair on the outside of the wide mahogany desk. Mrs. Leland is a tiny bird of a woman with dark hair always combed back in a bun, and a quiet demeanor. I smile at her and she congratulates me on the game as I take the seat to her left.

Luckily, Principal Cano only wants to talk about college choices, something I haven't even started to think about. I still have a year of high school to go, but for some reason, it's on his list of priorities. Jenna had told me he'd had a similar conversation with her about sports schools and sports scholarships. She'd mentioned something about it looking good on Dover's—and by default Cano's—record so he always took a vested interest in any potentially promising students, which apparently included me. But Cano has always seemed to be interested in my progress at Dover, so his attention is nothing new.

Lo catches my eye through the blinds of Principal Cano's office. He's staring at his phone, completely uncaring of any the rules governing visible cell phone use in school areas. I nod at the appropriate intervals, pretending to listen to Cano but surreptitiously studying the boy sitting outside. Something about him tugs at me. I don't know if it's the whole lonely-boy slash bad-boy vibe, but there's something there that just gets me.

It isn't about his physical looks. I mean he's okay, but nothing spectacular. His tanned face is all hard angles and hollows, and his almond-shaped eyes make him look almost feminine. He's not bad looking, that's for sure, but *cute* isn't a word I'd use to describe him. More on the slender side than bulky, there's something resilient about him. I didn't get to see that much of him in the wet suit, but I'm sure he's in great shape if his surfing is any indication. He's strong. I see it in the sharp curve of his jaw and in his long slender fingers tapping away on the phone's screen.

Suddenly, my own phone vibrates in my pocket as a smile curls the left corner of Lo's mouth. He doesn't look up, just continues to stare intently at the device in his hands. I frown. Coincidence? It buzzes again and, this time, I can't help myself.

"Excuse me, Principal Cano, sorry to interrupt but I think I forgot to turn my phone off this morning. I just want to make sure it's not on." Cano tosses a benevolent smile in my direction as I slide out my phone with a quick glance at the offending messages. I don't recognize the number but the words are more than maddeningly identifiable.

Still enjoying that cherry smoothie, I see. BTW, you didn't tell me your name.

I'm so hot with delayed embarrassment that it feels like I'm going to melt into a puddle on the floor any minute. Lo hasn't looked up but that smirk is still lurking around the corners of his mouth. I'm itching to slap it off his face and figure out at the same time how he got ahold of my unlisted number. I shove my phone back into my pocket.

Tearing my glance away from the annoyance on the other side of the window, I focus on Principal Cano, who is now looking through my file. Boring. Not much in there other than the usual—transcripts, grades, notes. On paper, I'm an exemplary student, never drawing unnecessary attention to myself.

My gaze spans the desk, and suddenly, my boredom disappears. Next to a heap of files on Cano's desk is another open file far thinner than mine. The photo of an arrogant but familiar face is clipped to one corner.

Lo's file.

I bolt upright and forward in my chair, curiosity peppering my brain. It would be so easy to glimmer over the desk without anyone being the wiser. Curiosity gets the better of me, and maybe a little desire for payback. The need to see what's in that file becomes insistent. In a world governed by paperwork, his file is even thinner than mine, which makes him very interesting.

Lo obviously has money; otherwise, he wouldn't be here. Not that it matters, but Dover is a snooty private school that isn't exactly known for giving free rides. As a student with a royal trust fund and a generous long-standing alumni grant, I had no trouble getting admitted. Dover has been my family's alma mater for centuries.

My real family...the nonhuman one.

Who wouldn't exactly approve of what I am about to do. Especially my Handlers.

Shoving the thought of them away, I focus on the task at hand. Glimmering isn't expressly forbidden so I'm not doing anything too untoward, but it is frowned upon because of the potential exposure. I'll be careful so there won't be any risk.

Taking a breath, I shrug off the nerves, feeling the water inside my body press against my skin in immediate response as a round weightlessness forms in the middle of my chest. I extend the glimmer-shadow outward like a ball of water, hovering over Principal Cano's desk as he's speaking and gesturing at some notes in my file.

From any outside perspective, I'm sitting in my chair and listening intently to what Cano is saying. But for my own purposes, my glimmer-self can now see the pages on the desk as easily as if I were sitting on Principal Cano's lap. Which is a pretty gross thought.

Focus, I tell myself, and push slightly to the right.

The glimmer-shadow almost breaks but I pull it together with a long, slow breath that slivers through my teeth. Glimmering is a delicate business that involves manipulating minuscule amounts of water in the air and connecting those to the source in my body. The technical term for it is *hydroprojection,* which basically means controlling the energy of moisture to project an invisible extension of myself wherever I choose. But I like the word *glimmer* better because that's what it looks like if anyone were to ever envision it.

As expected, the pages in my file are boring, basically showing my transcripts from my last school, my current grades, my extracurricular activities and all the usual stuff. I'm not interested in any of that. I am interested in the Annoyance. Hovering over the second file, I glance at the sparse notes. Lo is a C student. No surprise—I could have called that just from his don't-care attitude. Did four sports at his last school including swimming and soccer, and is a Junior State Surf Champion. No surprise there, either. I just don't get why he's here and why he had transferred to Dover in the middle of his junior year, from Hawaii of all places.

A note in red on a yellow Post-it catches my attention on the corner of the manila folder. The words *Under Observation* are underlined several times. It's stuck above a newspaper clipping. I almost lose hold of the glimmer at the horrific mangled photo of a boat. Nearly his whole family was killed in a sailing accident during a freak storm. His foster father survived but is on life support in some private hospital in Australia, and it appears that Lo was sent here to live with his biological mother, his only remaining family.

A pang of pity spirals its way through me, becoming more intense as it touches my glimmer-self, so much so that it ripples outward. Of their own volition, my eyes turn to the boy sitting in the waiting room outside and connect with a pair of liquid blue ones. He's staring right at me.

I dissipate in an instant, broken apart by the fierce vulnerability in that look. Or maybe he looks that way because of what I've just read. Either way, I feel guilty for my spying even though he couldn't possibly know what I'd been doing. There's no way he or any other human would be able to see anything—glimmers are invisible, undetectable to human eyes. Only the Aquarathi—my people—can sense a glimmer, not humans. And Lo is not one of us. If he were, I would know him in an instant.

As an Aquarathi heir, my blood commands any of my kind to declare themselves to me, and it isn't like they have control over doing so; their bodies respond. It's complicated to explain, but we work in the same way that water bonds to water. A single drop is but a part of the whole.

Principal Cano's voice snaps me back to reality.

"Sorry, sir?" I say, momentarily disoriented.

"He asked if you could send Mr. Seavon in on your way

back to class?" Mrs. Leland, who is standing next to him, has picked up Lo's file.

At my blank stare, Mrs. Leland gently clarifies. "Lotharius Seavon. The boy in the waiting room whom you were speaking to earlier."

Lotharius? I nearly giggle out loud but compose myself. We do live in California, after all, where people name their kids after colors and adverbs and feelings. There's even a kid called Happy on the surf team at Dover. Lotharius is tamer than most. And for some reason, it suits him, probably more so than "Lo" does. Maybe it's his exotic looks, but "Max" or "Tony" just wouldn't seem fitting.

"Oh, of course," I say just as Mrs. Leland hands me another pile of college brochures. "Is he new here?" I can't help myself but after seeing Lo's file on the desk and having him brag earlier that he was a student, I have to know for sure.

"Yes, today is his first day, and he's a junior like you." She stares at me with a thoughtful look, tipping her little bird head to the side. "Actually, Ms. Marin, perhaps you could help to show Mr. Seavon around at lunch. Help him get his bearings a bit." I want to kick myself in the teeth for even asking about Lo…now I'm going to be stuck with the annoying creature. I make a mental note to try to fail my next English exam just get my name off Cano's "promising students" list, but with my luck, I'll get hauled in twice as often.

I smile graciously through my gnashed teeth. If there's one thing I've learned in my world, it's that etiquette and flawless courtesy will get you anywhere, especially as a teen. It's as if the adults don't expect it. "Of course," I say sweetly. "It would be my pleasure."

"Thank you, Ms. Marin," Principal Cano says, parting his lips in an odd grimace that barely passes for a smile. "As always, it's been wonderful talking with you. Keep up the good

work and be sure to let Mrs. Leland know if any of those—"
he nods toward the brochures in my arms "—strike your fancy,
and we can take it from there." He presses a button on his
desk phone and speaks into the handset just as I'm exiting the
office. "Lori, we're running a little behind. Can you readjust
my schedule after Mr. Seavon? Thank you."

Outside, Lo stares at me with the ever-present smirk on his
face. His eyes, so vulnerable before, are now unreadable. The
furrow speeds across my brow and is gone before I can process
why his moodiness is even a blip on my radar. I don't care.

A twinge of something slices through me as I think of all
the tragedy in his life, but I'm not here to fix anyone, especially boys who obviously don't want to be fixed. And I'm sure
he'd be pissed if he knew that I'd looked at his file.

Guilt stabs me and I stare at him, inexplicably annoyed.
"So…after you're done, I have to, um, show you around later."

Lo laughs, the sound of it rich and deep, and crinkling the
outer corners of his eyes. The smile softens his entire face,
transforming it from sharp to almost pleasant. I pretend not to
notice. "Whoa, try not to sound so ecstatic! New-kid baby-
sitter, the job you've always wanted."

I can't help but return the smile at his sarcastic comment.
"Well, I don't like to boast but they do call me the new-kid
whisperer."

"That must be pretty special."

"So special," I say with an exaggerated eye roll.

As we stare at each other with tentative smiles on our faces
and laughter in our eyes, something strange flowers in the
middle of my chest. It feels like a glimmer, only more tangible with its butterfly touches extending along my arms and
legs, as if everything inside of me is responding to someone
else's glimmer call.

It's not like I haven't crushed on boys before, but this feels different than any of the other times. The unfamiliar feeling is climbing into my neck and making my blood race. I'm breathless and scared, but still want to sink feetfirst into it, letting it fill me up. For a second, I wonder if this is what Jenna feels whenever she talks about the butterflies she gets with Sawyer.

I've never had a real boyfriend, and I've definitely never been in love—it's almost impossible for an Aquarathi to feel a connection with a human the same way we do with one of our own kind. It's not an abomination or unnatural or anything outmoded like that; it's just weird, like two pieces working fine together but not really perfectly matched.

"So what are you here for?" I say into the suddenly weighted silence stretching between us. "Orientation?"

A wicked grin. "Nope. Had that last week."

"So you're here voluntarily because…?"

"Not voluntarily. Detention," he says with a wink.

"On your first day?" I gasp, shaking my head at his cavalier expression but struggling not to burst out laughing. There's something about him that is so irritating yet appealing at the same time. It's exasperating. Lo stands, swinging his backpack to his shoulder. He's far taller than I expected, but then again I was practically immersed in water the first time we met. I fight the urge to step back at his sudden nearness and the smell of salt that I can almost taste on my tongue. "So what'd you do?"

"Cut class to go surfing." He throws a hand out, gesturing at his clothing, but I keep my gaze planted firmly on his face. "Got caught trying to sneak in and get changed. No biggie."

"Wow, all on your first day—first period, no less. That takes a certain kind of stupid," I say.

"I don't like to be confined. Or being told what to do."

"I can see that, but you know, this is a school," I say in a mocking tone. "And at school, there are these things called rules. And if you break them, there are consequences."

Lo's smile turns cool, very unlike his earlier ones. The air between us becomes heavy with sudden tension. "Well, guess I'll know who to ask when I need a refresher on how to be perfect."

"Says the guy heading for detention," I snap back, stung by his taunt even though I'd just done the same to him. I'm not perfect—I just don't act out as he obviously does. There's a huge difference between the two. I can't afford to call attention to myself, and I'm there to educate myself, not push the boundaries. I don't know why I'm letting myself get so rattled by someone who doesn't factor into my existence. "Whatever, I couldn't care less what you do," I say, stalking out of the waiting area.

"Sure you do. See you at lunch, Nerissa."

3
Irritations

"Ugh, I can't stand him!"

"Can't stand who?" Jenna says through a mouthful of cheeseburger.

"Lo. Lotharius Seavon. The new kid. I'm surprised you haven't seen or heard him yet, he loves himself so much." I can hardly keep the venom from my voice. Two class periods later and almost halfway through lunch and I'm still flustered by our earlier exchange. And by the fact that he hasn't shown up at the cafeteria, where we were supposed to meet. I saw him in English but he didn't even look my way, and now I'm supposed to be nice to him and give him the grand tour? I mutter an expletive under my breath and poke viciously at my salad.

"Wow, that bad?"

"Jenna, you can't even imagine how bad," I seethe. "He honestly thinks he is God's gift or something. I mean, I swear he has rocks for brains. First of all, who would cut their first day to go surfing and show up not in uniform and make fun of Cano almost to his face? An idiot, that's who."

"I'd cut to surf," Sawyer interjects, his streaky brown hair falling into his eyes. "I mean, I wouldn't get caught, but yeah, not like I haven't done it before."

"Yes, but it's not the same thing," I argue hotly. "And if you got caught, wouldn't you at least act sorry? You know, have some remorse or something? It's not like he even cares. And then to tell me that I'm so perfect because I follow the rules, what does that even mean?" Jenna is staring at me with a weird combination of hilarity and disbelief, her cheeseburger lying forgotten in her hand. I'm on a tirade now, so much so that I don't notice the sudden wide-eyed look on Sawyer's face. "Who does he think he is, anyway?"

"Talking about me again?" Lo's voice over my shoulder is tinged with amusement. "You know, I'm going to start thinking that you have a crush on me."

"What?" I splutter, every cell inside of me freezing in response. "As if I would ever be interested in you in a gazillion years!"

"That long?" Lo's reply is mocking, but even my rudeness doesn't stop him from sitting down at the table and smiling winsomely at Jenna, who has a very odd look on her face. She's staring from me to Lo and back again, as if she's seeing something fascinating. Fighting my stupid reaction to his buttery voice, I still haven't looked at him, keeping my eyes averted as if that'll make him disappear.

"Hey," she says with a grin. "I'm Jenna, the snarky one's best friend, and this is my boyfriend, Sawyer. I take it you're the Antichrist or something."

"More like the 'or something.'" Lo's laugh must be infectious, because everyone at the table is laughing. Well, everyone except me.

Forcing myself to look at him, I notice that even though he's dressed in the required school uniform, Lo still manages to look as comfortable as he did in the hoodie and flip-flops earlier in the office. I also can't help but notice that the navy blazer brings out the bluer flecks in his eyes. He grins and throws his arm across the back of my chair. "So you like my new look?"

I glare at him, my gaze sliding over his artlessly styled sandy hair, and shove my chair—and his arm—back from the table, my usually calm exterior surprisingly ruffled. "The one that screams Justin Bieber wannabe? Sure." My sarcasm isn't lost on Jenna, who is watching me carefully with an amused look on her face.

"I meant the clothes, but thanks for noticing the rest."

"Look, let's just get this over with before lunch ends. You coming?" I say to him, rolling my eyes skyward. Jenna is wide-eyed, staring at me now with something bordering on delight in her expression. My glare spins to her, but instead of quailing, she collapses into a fit of giggles. "What is your problem?" I snap. "Cano told me to show him around."

"Nothing," Jenna says, grinning. "Nothing at all."

I ignore the fact that "nothing" in Jenna-speak means the exact opposite. I hate the fact that I'm so frazzled. Must be a combination of what happened with Speio and all the thoughts that have resurfaced about my family. I'm just not myself. Later, I'll have to explain that to Jenna instead of letting her go on thinking that some new guy has me in a tizzy. Which, of course, he doesn't.

"So, are you coming or what?" I say to Lo, who still hasn't moved from the table. "Or maybe we can get Cara Andrews to take over as the official tour guide of Dover Prep. She's only been staring this way for the past ten minutes like a lovesick puppy."

Lo turns those dark eyes on me, amusement still flickering in their depths, but there's something else there, too—a glint of disappointment, as if my earlier words had bothered him somehow. That makes no sense, I know. Lo doesn't care what anyone thinks of him, far less me. It's more likely his pride's been injured or something.

"Sure, lead on. I am at your bidding," he says, standing and ignoring my dig about Cara. My gaze flicks to his, but there's nothing that reflects the slight mocking tone I heard in his voice. "Nice to meet you guys," he says to Jenna and Sawyer.

"Yeah, definitely see you around!" Jenna singsongs with a grin at me that makes me want to throttle her.

"So obviously, you know that this is the cafeteria," I say over my shoulder on the way out, throwing a murderous glare at my best friend. As we walk by Cara's table, I can't help noticing that her lovesick glances have now evolved into full-on venom directed at me. I sigh. Just great—all I need is to get in a war with an ex-nemesis over some guy prize that I don't give two hoots about. She can have him for all I care. I'm just about to offer her the tour task—and simultaneous peace offering—when I notice that Lo's already at the cafeteria doors, staring at me with an arrogant, challenging expression as if he's expecting me to do just that.

Am I that predictable? I sigh and head toward him.

In the hallway, I walk briskly but Lo has no trouble keeping up with those long legs of his, not that I'm noticing that he has long legs. He's just tall, I tell myself, and then realize that I'm having an internal argument about Lo—the thorn in my side—and his legs, which I now inexplicably feel like breaking.

"Cara's got the hots for you," I remark, angry with myself for letting him get under my skin. Again. "She'd do a much better job at this than I would."

But Lo doesn't answer, just continues to wear the same amused smile as if it's his customary expression—or maybe it's his expression around me. I must be so amusing to him. My leg-breaking thoughts return in full force.

"Lockers," I snarl, throwing my hand to the side and gesturing needlessly to the metal-lined hallways. "Gym's down that way, also pool, tennis courts and sports fields."

"Where you play field hockey?"

"What?"

A smile. "I heard you were cocaptain. Plus, everyone's talking about that game you guys won last week. Kind of hard to ignore." Lo pauses to look at me, tilting his head and chewing on the corner of his lower lip as we're walking. I look away quickly, enflamed again. "So, field hockey, huh? I just don't see it."

"See what?" I snap back, irritated for feeling so flustered around a stupid boy. I quicken my step, wanting to get this tour over with so I can get as far away from him as possible. "Down there's the music hall and the auditorium."

"You look more like a swimmer to me."

"I hate the water," I say without thinking. "Student center is down there."

Lo's chuckle is long and deep. I sprint up the stairs at the end of the hallway. "Didn't look like you hated the water the other day."

Crap, crap, double crap. "I meant I'm allergic to chlorine so I hate pool water."

It's not that I'm entirely allergic. Chlorine in intense concentrations can be irritating to our internal tissue, but it isn't toxic or anything. I can swim in a pool fine, but the chlorine excuse works well as a response to anyone suggesting that I try out for the swim team, which Speio would likely have an aneurysm over.

"Interesting."

"What's interesting about that?" I can't help myself but Lo's quiet response bugs me.

"It's too bad. You're a strong swimmer."

Confused by what sounds like a sincere compliment, I duck my head and then smile. "Hmm, thought that was you watching me before, like a—what were your words again?—oh, yes, a cherry smoothie," I jibe, mimicking his words from that morning.

Lo winks. "Strawberry's my favorite, but who's checking?"

My breath hitches in my throat at his obvious admission, my words tumbling out past it. "Principal Cano's office is down that hall, as you know. Plus, all the other admin offices and the faculty lounge. Media room over there down the same hallway. Art studio's on that side. Classrooms. They're pretty much the same, you know, the usual." I turn toward him, still flushed at his casual admission of staring at me on the beach. "Look, this is pretty much it. Like every other high school."

"I wouldn't know. My last high school was twelve rooms."

"In Hawaii?" I blurt out, and then kick myself. "I mean, Mrs. Leland mentioned that you were a transfer. From there."

Lo throws me a long measured look. "She did?" I nod. "What else did Mrs. Leland say about me?"

"Not much, just that you had transferred because…" I trail off, unable to finish the sentence or find a quick enough substitute for *because your family burned in a horrific accident.* My immediate rush of pity is no surprise, nor is the sudden reaction to it on Lo's face. His hard expression hits me like a bucket of ice water. "I'm sorry, I didn't mean—" Every muscle in that angular face snaps to attention, his eyes becoming cold and unreadable.

"Thanks for showing me around." Without another word, Lo stalks off in the opposite direction just as the bell rings. Flustered by his sudden departure, I retrace my steps to my locker to get my history books.

In class, I find myself unable to concentrate. Caught in the crossfire of Speio's pointed looks, Jenna's raised eyebrows,

Cara's demon scowls and the fascinating topic of the Bill of Rights, all I can think about is Lo and my hideous faux pas of alluding to his private secrets. From the look on my face, he'd guessed that I'd somehow found out about his family, and now I feel terrible for spying in Principal Cano's office. I kick myself mentally for the nineteenth time.

"Class, please open your textbooks to page one hundred and eleven, and read the rest of the chapter," Mr. Moss says. "Then pair up and work on the quiz questions at the end. There will be a real quiz next class."

Amid the groans in the classroom, mechanically I do as requested, but I can't even focus to get the right answers. Jenna glowers at me.

"What's with you?" she whispers.

"Nothing. Just not feeling that great."

A wicked grin. "Anything to do with loverboy? Did you make out on your tour?"

"Gross. I don't know what you're talking about. And I'm not into him, so forget whatever it is you're plotting about in your head, okay?" I say. "I don't want to talk about Lo."

We both jump at Mr. Moss's voice. "Ms. Marin and Ms. Pearce, I expect that you two are discussing the quiz and not something unrelated to history."

"Um, yes, sir," we both say. Jenna leans in again once Mr. Moss's piercing stare has moved elsewhere. "So is he single?"

"For the love of…" I grumble, irritated. "I don't know, Jenna."

"I wonder where he is," she stage-whispers. "Bet he's with Cano for new-kid stuff. Look, if this guy's our year he has to be in Bio next period. You can make your next move then!"

"Will you stop with the plotting?" I stare at the practice quiz, ignoring her attempts to get my attention and silently hoping that she's right—that he'll be in class next period.

But Jenna is wrong. Lo isn't in Bio. I know I shouldn't care but I feel responsible, as if I'm the cause of him not being there. It seems as if I have an unerring, magic ability to ruin the lives of everyone around me. Even people I don't know.

Some queen I'd be.

Beating myself up for the rest of the day and feeling more and more guilty with each passing second, I'm literally out the door before the last bell has stopped ringing. Ignoring Jenna's reminder that we have hockey practice, I mumble something about having an appointment and race to the south parking lot.

There's someone leaning against my Jeep. My stomach sours.

"What do you want, Speio?"

"So who was that guy you were talking to at lunch?"

I stare at him. "A new kid. A transfer."

"From where?"

Speio's twenty questions undermine my rapidly failing composure. "What, are you my keeper now?" I snap, moving to unlock my door. Speio blocks my way.

"No, Nerissa, I'm your Handler, right?"

I freeze at the sarcastic accusation in his voice, recalling my command for him to speak with Echlios. "No, Speio, you're not," I say gently. "Your parents are. What did Echlios say?"

"That we were stuck here forever. When did you decide?"

"A year ago," I say tiredly, not wanting to bring up my father, how everything had changed since then. "Speio, can we talk about this later? I can't do this right now."

"It's never a good time, is it?" he shoots back. "No, Nerissa, let's talk about this now. I knew something was wrong when you started devoting all your time to hockey practice. We were supposed to go back, and my father just kept telling me to be patient, that we would return in due time, when you were ready. That was all a lie, wasn't it?"

I swallow and lean against the car door. "I'm sorry, Speio. What do you want me to say? That it's true? That I can't face Ehmora? I can't be who everyone wants me to be. My father was king, not me."

"So what?" Speio spits, eyes flashing. "You're the heir. It's your duty to protect your people. The whole kingdom is falling to pieces without you."

"You don't get it. She makes a better queen than I ever could."

His expression at my clipped words goes from frustrated to furious. "So you give up, just like that? Let the person who killed your father take your place? What about our families, Nerissa? They're still there."

I think about saying that he has family there, that mine—at least my immediate family—is gone. But I can't get the words out of my mouth.

"You know what Ehmora is capable of, and yet you turn your head the other way. She cares about power, not the people. Anyone loyal to your father has gone into hiding, hoping that you will come back to help them," Speio seethes, digging his fingers into the metal bars of the Jeep so deeply that it buckles beneath them. "But we've stayed here and done nothing while so many died, and all you want to do is forget about who you are, to become like these insipid humans. You're stupid and blind. And selfish."

"Don't you speak to me like that!" I hiss. "I am your—"

"My nothing," Speio says dully, his eyes wet with tears, gesturing to the landscape around us. "You are a princess of nothing. A princess of rocks and mud and death."

My hand cracks across his face, and not even the angry red mark tempers my rage. I shove at his chest, my speech becoming more formal and clipped in my native language. "Shut up! You don't know anything, you stupid boy."

Speio's fingers slide along the imprint of my fingers on his face. "Better a stupid boy than a coward."

"You are out of line," I whisper, sliding down against the side of my car. But Speio's right. I can hear my own voice breaking, as his words strike more deeply than my hand did against his face. I am a coward, because I've done nothing to avenge my father, to protect my people or, for that matter, the ocean I love. I've hidden here with my head stuck in the ground like one of those ridiculous giant birds, refusing to accept the legacy I was born into. "You don't know anything!"

He stares at me. "You're right, I don't. I'm bound to you here on land by your command and your cowardice. No one bothered to tell me that we would never be going home. Or that we didn't have a home. I can't do this anymore." Speio turns and walks away. He stops at his car at the edge of the parking lot, his fists clenched, before turning around. "You think you're safe here? That she isn't coming after you? She will. She wants you dead, just like she wanted your father dead. And she'll kill us all when she's done with you. I'm not sticking around here for that."

"Who told you that? Your parents—"

"—are trusting fools," Speio finishes. "Isn't that why you didn't tell me in the first place? Because you knew I'd call you out on it?"

"No. I did it to protect you."

"Keep telling yourself that," Speio seethes. "You and I both know why you wanted to keep this from me, because you knew I'd never let you. You're a coward, plain and simple, and that's the truth. Well, I'm not going to die here. Unlike you, I'd rather take my chances where I belong. Down there. And if I get that chance, I'm taking it. With or without you."

I don't even notice when it starts raining or how long I've sat against the side of my car. But when I open my eyes, mine is the only car in the lot. I can feel pain tearing its way through me like lightning bolts. I've known Speio pretty much my whole life. He's been my confidant, my best friend, the one who'd never desert me in a million years, and now he's going to do exactly that.

The rain mixes in with the salt of my tears, running like a salve on my molten emotions. The cool water soaks into my skin and I turn my face upward, watching the darkened clouds move across the sky, fading in and out and being ripped into jagged edges by streaks of lightning. The storm is an echo of the one inside of me...because of what I am.

A monster.

I glance upward as a jagged streak of lightning rips the sky to pieces. The storm will only get worse if I don't do something to banish the tornado brewing inside of me. Brushing my wet hair from my face, I stand. My mind races from the keys in my hand to the thick brush of woods beyond. I need to move, to run, to scream. It's the only way the storm will subside.

Without a second thought, I throw my bag into the car and race into a nearby thicket, following a running path strewn with leaves. I don't stop until I come to an open spot, my chest pounding and my breath catching in my throat. The storm is still raging above, but I stand in the middle of the glade with my arms lifted toward it, embracing the bulletlike drops of rain pelting down on me. I spin, my arms out wide, sending the rain in the reverse direction back up toward the skies until the air around me shimmers with suspended droplets. Slowly, I pull the drops into me, like the arc of a fountain, feeling them pass over and inside my flesh, and out to the ground below.

Water is cleansing.

But not as forgiving or forgetful.

The storm inside of me spills over, black thunderclouds

forming almost instantly in the sky. I've betrayed them all—and everything that I am, I have betrayed by pretending to be something I'm not. I'm not human.

I'm Aquarathi…even if I don't want to be.

I shove my arms upward, the strength of my will creating an invisible ceiling until all the water pools on top of it in midair, and then I release it. The force of it knocks me to my knees but it's still not enough. Speio is right. I am a coward who does nothing but care about herself.

I must be punished. Harder.

Lightning staggers down around me through the rain into the ground beside me, blistering the skin of my body through the earth. Speio once called electricity our Kryptonite—the one substance that can stop us in our tracks. Even though the bolts are barely touching me, they are near enough that my human skin is scorched, and I'm almost senseless from the pain of it dispersing into my cells.

I barely feel the body crashing into me, slamming us both to the ground and breaking my terrible connection with the sky and the earth.

"What are you doing, my lady?" Echlios's face is horrified. But I can't even speak. All I can do is cry against his chest and choke on the bitterness that's killing me. Echlios embraces me tightly, funneling the water that's around us through his body and into mine and healing the singed areas. After a while, when everything inside of me calms, the storm ebbs until the rain is but a light shower. "What were you thinking?" he says, rocking me back and forth.

"I'm a fake—" I begin.

"No, you are not. Come, let's get you home."

I let Echlios take me back to my Jeep and he drives us home, leaving his own car in the parking lot. On the way, I stare out the window, watching the ocean glint in the distance as if it,

too, is reproaching me. A critical part of our human acclimatization means taking steps to ensure that the humans are
focused on taking care of the oceans and marine life. I have
done none of that. I'd turned my back on it—all of it, not
just my family and my people, but my home. I'd pretended
to be human because it'd been so much simpler to be nobody
than to fight to be somebody. I'd even refused to continue
my combat training with Echlios and Speio, to do anything
Aquarathi-related. Instead, all I'd done was run away from
who I was. And my people had paid the price—Speio, Echlios
and Soren most of all—when Ehmora had stolen the throne.
Because the worst possible thing that could happen had happened, and I'd chosen to let it.

"There has always been dissent between the courts," Echlios
had told me. "Your father said it wasn't our place to interfere
in the affairs of humans. But Ehmora had other ideas, and
she has the support of the Emerald and Sapphire courts. She
believes that Earth is our shared home and we must step in
to prevent the death of the oceans. That as a species, it is our
duty to alter the course of the future if necessary."

"You mean, reveal ourselves to the humans?" I said,
shocked. For millennia, we've lived in secret and in symbiotic
harmony with the human race, either blending into human
life like Echlios, Soren, Speio and I have during a human
initiation cycle, or lying hidden in the depths of the oceans.

"No, but nudge where needed to prevent future disaster,"
Echlios said. "It is the reason the alliance between all the
courts was formed. We intervene where we have to in order
to preserve our own future. Ehmora believes this is our world,
too, regardless of what the humans do. So the royal heirs are
sent here for the human cycle to learn…and to act in our interests."

"But Father always said that Ehmora wanted to control the humans."

A sad smile. "She does. Your father knew that Ehmora wouldn't stop at a nudge or two. She wants more. She wants all of it. Your father only sought to protect us, to avoid war with the humans. Don't you think if they knew about us, they would hunt us down? We're so few compared to them."

My father was right. Everything we knew about humans suggested they would stop at nothing to analyze, conquer or kill us. It's in their nature. But a part of me also agreed with Ehmora. After all, I'd known no home other than Earth. It stands to reason that we should protect our planet, even if the humans don't know about our existence. But my father's belief that Aquarathi should remain in the shadows was rooted in the cautious thinking of our ancestors, as they had done for centuries. He wanted to keep us unidentified and alive, and as king of the High Court, his word was law. He'd gone against Ehmora.

And he had been murdered for it.

Echlios carries me up to the house from the car, bringing me back to the present. One of our neighbors waves with a concerned look, and Echlios explains that I took a tumble during a run. Technically he is my Handler, but he is also my legal guardian, the closest person I have to a parent in the human world. Although the house is mine, we have to keep up the appropriate human pretenses. I manage a feeble wave on the way inside.

"My lady," Speio's mother and my guardian "mom" says, her voice full of concern as Echlios helps me hobble through the door.

"It's okay, Soren, I'm fine, just a minor disagreement with a thunderstorm. I need to be alone right now. Please?" I ask weakly. She exchanges a worried look with her husband, but steps back to let me pass.

My room is as I left it—untidy, vibrant and colorful. Unlike the somber hues of the rest of the house, mine is more like my true home. The one I'd sworn never to return to. I stare at the brilliant pieces of sea glass coating the shimmery indigo ceiling, all the bits that I'd found on the beach over the years, and the stained-glass windows I'd made Echlios install above the French doors. I'd painted the walls myself in all the shifting blue hues of the ocean—cerulean, azure, cobalt, navy, sapphire and aqua. When the sun hits the stained glass just right, it's an explosion of magical color that can only be rivaled in one other secret place, a place I haven't seen in nearly three years.

Waterfell.

I can almost hear Speio's voice in my head asking if I hate Waterfell so much, why the minishrine in my room? But I don't hate Waterfell. I just hate who I'm supposed to be when I'm there. A child princess they all look at with a mixture of contempt and pity; contempt because I'd always done what I wanted when I wanted with no care for my father's wishes, and pity because it was a grave I'd dug for myself. In the end, my father's advisers had been elated when my initiation began and I was out of sight.

Out of mind.

With a painful gulp, I open the sliding-glass doors to the patio and step outside. In the backyard, shielded by the house on three sides and the beach on the other, I shed my clothes and dive into our deep saltwater pool, swimming down until I'm at the bottom. The skies have gone from an angry gray to a dark blue tinged with pink and gold. The Aquarathi, particularly the royals, have always had a tumultuous relationship with weather. Storms at sea are often caused by our emotions, even as deep down as we live. At least the myths of old have gotten that right—sea monsters are synonymous with storms.

The dark blue color of the sky reminds me of Lo's eyes, and for a second, I realize that I haven't thought about him since I left school. A twinge of guilt seeps through and I know that Lo is the least of my worries for all the people I've hurt or disappointed. The water ripples above me and I see a shadow standing at the edge of the pool. I nod, and there's a splash as someone swims down toward me.

I'm sorry, Speio mouths, sinking down to the bottom. "I was out of line," he says in our language, little more than a series of clicks and sharp pulses underwater. His blond hair fans around his face and I grasp his hand in mine.

"I'm sorry, too," I say, gripping hard. He grips back just as tightly. "We'll figure this out, Speio, I promise. I can't just hide here and I know that now. I'm sorry I didn't tell you. You were right. I was afraid of what you'd say."

Together we lie back on the bottom of the pool with the water undulating above us, and watch the last afterglow of day give in to the darker demands of the night. There's barely any moon, but we don't need the light in the growing darkness. The shimmer of green and gold dancing beneath my skin is just as mesmerizing as the one of turquoise and silvery white beneath his. I close my eyes.

We could almost be back home.

4
Bonding

"You're asking me out?"

I stare at Lo incredulously in the cafeteria. He hasn't spoken to me in days, and apart from seeing each other in class over the past week and a half—and awkwardly ignoring each other—we've been like a couple of ships passing in the night. In fact, with the exception of Sawyer, he seems to have gravitated away from my group and toward Cara's—which has me experiencing polar-opposite feelings that I have no intention of analyzing. For all I care, he could be any other boy floating along the school hallways.

Only Lo doesn't carry himself like every other high school boy. He walks with a curious nonchalance, an easy arrogance in his step and exuding confidence. Sawyer told Jenna that it probably stemmed from him living abroad for so many years. For some reason, the two of them—Sawyer and Lo—took an immediate liking to each other, probably via their mutual love of surfing. Once, during lunch, Sawyer mentioned that Lo was widely traveled and had lived practically everywhere. I snorted and replied snarkily that life as a pampered prince must be tough for some, but shut up immediately when Jenna stared at me like I'd grown two horns on my head.

So right now, with Lo standing in front of me, I refuse to even look in her direction because I'm positive that she'll have some ridiculously giddy I-told-you-so expression on her face, especially because said boy is asking me out.

"Like on a date?" I say.

"Yes. Is that so hard to believe?" Lo says.

"A little," I say, frowning. "I mean, you don't like me, and that's fine because I don't like you, either. Plus, you've been marked as Cara's property, so yes, it is hard to believe."

Lo smiles evenly at me. "First, I'm not anyone's property. Plus, I didn't think we had a chance to get to know each other, so I'm trying to fix that."

Despite my secret thrill at his words about Cara, going on a date with Lo is not something I'm interested in doing. At all.

"Why?"

"Why not?" he counters.

"I don't think it's such a good—"

But Jenna cuts me off, her face a ferocious glower that fuses the rest of my sentence to the roof of my mouth. She's made it pretty clear that I owe her for covering for me earlier in the week when I ditched practice because of a complete emotional breakdown that I could never tell her about. Obviously, she's calling in the favor.

Smiling sweetly, she says, "Why don't we make it a double date?"

"Jenna," I whisper in warning, but as usual she ignores me, plowing through.

"It'll be fun. Tomorrow night after the surf meet. We can go to the Crab Shack—they have a great Saturday two-for-one special." She stands, tucking her bag under one arm and kissing Sawyer on his head. "Look, I have to run, guys. Have to talk to Leland before class. But tomorrow, perfect!"

And just like that it's over. I watch in stunned silence as Jenna makes her way out of the cafeteria. Lo has a similar dazed look on his face, and Sawyer can't stop laughing at both of our identical expressions.

"Is she like that a lot?" Lo asks in a bemused voice, as if he isn't quite sure what's happened.

Sawyer grins. "You've just been Jenna-rolled. You know, she's like a human steamroller. I find it easier to just let her go when she gets an idea in her head." Sawyer laughs again. "Comes from a good place, though, and hey, at least she helped your game." He nods at Lo and winks as if I'm not sitting right there next to them. "So how were the waves this morning, bro? I missed out, had to work an early shift before school."

They start talking about surfing, and I zone out. As I finish my sandwich, I surreptitiously start studying Lo…the guy I'll be going on a date with thanks to Jenna, which I still think is a bad idea. He leans back in his chair with his arms crossed over his chest, listening to Sawyer ramble on about low tide, agreeing with a nod. He seems so guarded, except when he's with Sawyer or surfing. He doesn't trust easily, that's for sure. Even though I can't get a good read on him, he and Sawyer seem to click, and Sawyer isn't the kind of guy to make friends easily, as Jenna pointed out to me. But even Sawyer's obvious approval of Lo as a person doesn't help my weird paranoia where Lo is concerned. Not that I am paranoid about him, I just don't know him.

Not that I want to, of course.

Lo laughs at something Sawyer says, throwing his head back and raking a hand through hair that's the color of sand. When we first met, he was wearing a wet suit hood and then a beanie. I assumed that he was dark-haired, given his dark eyebrows, but instead he is more on the blond side. The lightness makes his eyes seem almost black in contrast.

Lo's gaze slips across the table toward me, and I duck mine hastily and pick at my food. I hardly want to be caught staring at him, especially with Cara sending incineration-size glowers toward our table. Lo has been sitting with them at lunch, so it must be killing her that today he's at my table. I'm not usually one to give in to petty rivalries, but Cara's been getting under my skin lately as if she has some kind of point to prove, with Lo especially. The thrill that runs through me at the thought of what she'd say if she knew about the date has me grinning—a grin that draws Lo's attention like a spark. So when I see Speio waving at me from across the cafeteria, I grab my tray and excuse myself.

"As much as I love hearing you guys gab about how surfing is the answer for world peace, I gotta run. Catch you later."

"Aw, don't be hating, Riss," Sawyer says with a teasing grin. "It's all good. Haven't seen you on the waves lately. You forgot how or what?"

"I just don't want to show you up," I joke back.

"You surf?" Lo's voice is quiet but surprised.

"Sometimes." I would never tell either of them that I surf mostly at night when no one else is in the ocean…when it's just the waves and me. Plus, it's dangerous, especially if either of them chooses to come along. The sea is full of dangerous predators after dusk—sharks, to say the least. They keep a healthy distance from the Aquarathi, but for humans they probably wouldn't be so charitable. "Haven't been lately, though."

"You should come after school today," Sawyer says. "High tide's at four. You in?"

With a glance at Lo, I shrug. "I'll think about it. Jenna wants me to go shopping with her so we'll see. Later."

"I'm looking forward to tomorrow," Lo says. I ignore the

low burn that his words cause deep in the pit of my stomach, and choke back my automatic sarcastic response. Jenna'll kill me if I ruin her grand plans for my love life. Instead, I try to smile and look enthusiastic, but my effort is poor at best. Lo grins as if he can see right through me.

On the other side of the cafeteria, Speio seems to be in a good mood despite the still-shaky fallout from our fight. Although we had talked about everything, things between us are not as easy as they used to be. I still don't have any answers with respect to the situation with Ehmora, so for now, we have to wait until his father can find out more about Ehmora's motives from his remaining connections.

I mean, she left me alone for an entire year after my father was murdered, so it stands to reason that she has what she always wanted, control over the High Court. After much discussion, I realized that Echlios and Speio were right and, regardless of what happened, I can't hide forever. I'm the only living heir to the High Court, and as much as I love living in the human world and the anonymity it gives me, the responsibility I have to my people weighs on me. Am I scared? Sure. But leaving people in the hands of a false queen with a crazy agenda is far worse than the alternative.

Echlios's spies told him that many of those who were loyal to my father—and still are—are being imprisoned and eventually exiled or executed for fictitious crimes against Ehmora. There has been a systematic cleanse of anyone who could ever oppose her, a vicious act that only I can put an end to once I come of age. And so, we've formulated a loose plan. I'll continue to participate in my cycle of human adaptation, while Echlios engages his allies in the High Court or any of the other lower courts.

Despite my command to do nothing after my father's death, he'd been intent on protecting my interests—both here and in Waterfell—a fact that I'm now very grateful for. Without him, I'd probably have *no* allies. Speio will continue to be an extra layer of security at school, and for the moment, it will be business as usual until we regroup and come up with a more solid plan of action.

"So the new guy seems to be getting close to your circle," Speio comments through a mouthful of chocolate brownie.

"Gross, Speio. I can see into your stomach from here. And no, he's not a part of *my* circle. He and Sawyer are having a surf bromance. We're all going to the Crab Shack on Saturday if you want to come," I say in a nonchalant voice. Speio swallows and watches my face carefully as if trying to assess my words for truth. I widen my eyes and paste a sardonic expression on my face. "Your brain's going to explode if you keep trying to mind-meld me."

He grins and resumes chewing. "So what do you know about him?"

I lean forward with a conspiratorial look and whisper, "He's a Death Dealer who moved here from Hawaii. You know, a secret lycan-killing vampire machine. We need to be super careful around him. He's out for blood, I can feel it."

Speio rolls his eyes, relaxing. "Ha, ha, very funny. And seriously, quoting from *Underworld?* You could do so much better in the realm of vampire cult movies. Kate Beckinsale is weak."

"Kate is awesome," I say. "One day, I'm going to rock a pleather cat suit just like that one. Think I can pull it off?" I gesture at my torso and Speio shakes his head, grinning at me.

"Nope, you can't."

I grin back and shove him in the shoulder at the insult. We burst out laughing together.

I'm still giggling as my eyes connect with a pair of amused blue ones from the lunch table I just vacated, and the laughter flies from my lips. Lo has turned his chair so that it's sideways against the table and his feet are propped on the one beside him, one arm resting along the table and drumming with his fingertips. He holds my gaze effortlessly, a whisper of a smile playing about his lips. There's something there I can't place, the pull of something magnetic...like water to water. I'm only able to drag my eyes from the spell of his at Speio's voice.

"What?" I mumble, suddenly disoriented.

"Sure looks like he's in your circle." This time, I can't help the dark flush that seeps up the back of my neck and into my cheeks. I glare at Speio and keep my eyes firmly on the table, embarrassed to have been caught in a weird eye-lock with some boy.

"Look, he's just a new kid. Check him out if you have to, I don't care."

But I do care. A part of me wants to know everything there is to know about Lo. I want to know why my heartbeat trips over itself every time I think about him, or why his name makes me breathless. Even if it means getting Speio to do it.

"I can introduce you after school," I offer.

I glance at Speio and chew on my bottom lip, trying to think through whether adding Speio to the mix would be a smart decision. I sigh. I'm already going to the Crab Shack with Lo, so Speio'll have to meet him sometime—it's one of Echlios's few rules: anyone who comes close to me has to be thoroughly checked out. Even Jenna was subject to scrutiny once we started hanging out together regularly, and then Sawyer because he was Jenna's boyfriend. I joked once to Speio that he was my Aquarathi Secret Service. Let's just say he wasn't as much a fan of the acronym as I was.

"Surf session after school," I say. "Want to come with?"

"Surfing? During the day?" I nod. "You're going to have to tone it down, you know. It's a full moon in a few days, which means you're going to have to be extra careful with the water…and the other things."

"I know, Speio."

A shiver races up my spine at the thought. Speio means the fish and other sea creatures. Around full moon, they tend to get a little crazy around us, which is why I don't go swimming then if I can help it. They aren't dangerous. They're just more aggressive so they draw too much attention. Soren told me once that it had something to do with us glimmering in response to the moon. Full moon is a very uninhibited time for my people—apparently Aquarathi pheromones are a pretty powerful thing—and we are apt to get a little moon-crazy.

It gets worse until we bond with a mate, which usually happens soon after we mature into adulthood in a coming-of-age transition called Dvija. Most Aquarathi experience Dvija between fourteen and nineteen, so it's unusual for any of us to go beyond our teen years without bonding with a mate. I'm almost seventeen and still haven't experienced Dvija. Speio has, but living as humans, neither of us has had the opportunity to think much about bonding.

"What are you thinking about?" Speio asks, interrupting my train of thought.

"Dvija and bonding," I admit. If I can't talk to Speio, who else can I talk to about the ins and outs of who we are? Echlios and Soren, as much as I love them, are way too much like parents for me to be comfortable bringing up something so awkward.

Speio's eyebrows shoot into his head. "Um, okay. That's weird."

"Don't you ever think about it? I mean, you went through Dvija two years ago. What does it feel like?"

"Wow, time and place," Speio says, glancing around, and

then pauses, watching me and leaning across the table. "Riss, where is this coming from? Are you okay?"

I feel myself blushing. I refuse to let my eyes slide to the boy sitting at the edge of my peripheral vision. Why would a human boy make me think about bonding? It isn't like it would be possible with one of them. Although in human form we're physically compatible with humans, bonding is altogether an entirely different matter. For the Aquarathi, it's a connection at the most basic molecular level—the core of who we are, of everything we are.

"Never mind. It was just something Soren mentioned," I say quickly, and change the subject. "So about surfing, I'll be careful, I promise. And if you come, you can keep an eye on me."

"Sure, I'll be there," Speio says, looking incredibly relieved that we've veered away from the bonding subject. His grin widens into something roguish. "Those friends of yours better be ready for a schooling."

The rest of the afternoon passes in a blur, and apart from a few speculative glances from Lo during English whenever he thinks I'm not looking, it feels like I'm back in my groove. I've taken more detailed notes than usual but it's either that or obsess about why Lo keeps sneaking furtive looks in my direction. I'd rather write a thousand pages of notes than tie myself up into knots about what some human boy thinks about me.

I'd also told Jenna before class about the impromptu surf session but she doesn't seem too upset about postponing our shopping date.

"Sawyer said it would be good practice before the surf meet," she says. "And we know I'll do anything for that boy, including not shopping. That's true love for you."

I shake my head at her lovesick face, studiously ignoring her suggestive glances that swing in Lo's direction and then back to me. I know exactly what she's hinting at but it's not going to happen. Double date or not, getting to know a boy who already makes me jumpy—or makes me think about bonding—is a definite no-no.

"Stop," I tell her when she starts making smoochy faces.

"Come on," she whispers. "He's hot."

"There's far more to life than hot boys," I whisper back. Although my sneaky inner self doesn't dispute that Lo is hot in a sexy, two-dimensional kind of way—like one of my favorite anime characters, Eiri from *Gravitation* or Noctis from *Final Fantasy.*

"Not much more," Jenna says, waggling her eyebrows comically. We burst into smothered giggles until our study hall teacher glares us into silence.

After school, we split up in the parking lot. Jenna is riding with Sawyer since his boards are already in his truck. Speio and I head to my Jeep. Lo's driving himself in a tricked-out truck that looks more like beast than car. When I stare at it, he shrugs. "Gift from my mom. She overcompensates a lot."

"So where are we going? Black's?" I ask, pulling up alongside Sawyer. Black's is a tricky break with perfect conditions because of an underwater canyon, though it's usually crowded.

"No, too many nakes," he says. I snort. He's referring to the nudists. Black's used to be known as a nude beach, and even though nudity is outlawed, put it this way…if you want your eyes to bleed, you go to Black's.

"Aw, nudies need love, too," I shoot back, grinning.

Since Speio and I have to swing past the house to pick up my board, we all decide to meet at Lower Trestles, which is about an hour's drive north of where we are. It isn't a gentle surf spot but I assured an overconfident Lo that he didn't need to accommodate any groms. He grinned and told me that he hadn't expected any less.

Once our boards are strapped up top, Speio and I don't talk

about anything other than classes and the weather…pretty much as mundane a conversation as you can get. Neither of us wants to acknowledge the giant gorilla in the backseat, which I'd inadvertently brought up at lunch.

Bonding.

But I can't get it out of my head. I can't stop wondering what it would feel like to let someone into you so much that you can think and feel as one. Even thinking about it is secretly thrilling.

It's for life, Soren had explained to me once years ago during one of our training sessions that she still took very seriously. As much as Echlios was responsible for my physical development, Soren saw to my grooming and preparation as High Court heir.

"As a species, we don't bond more than once," she'd told me.

"How come?"

"Too painful. When you become a part of someone else, and they a part of you, bonding with another would be too complicated."

"But what if one of us dies?"

"Then a part of you dies, too."

It was as simple as that. The thought of it terrifies and excites me at the same time, and the older I get, the worse it becomes—the heavy sense of anticipation, knowing that a part of me is out there somewhere, waiting for me as much as I'm waiting for it.

With me, bonding would be so much more than it'd be for any other Aquarathi. If I had returned home, my Dvija would have been celebrated with all kinds of ceremony, because any partner of mine would become my royal companion. But since my father's death, everything changed. There was nothing for me to return to—no crown, no ceremony and no family.

My mother died when I was very young, and for years it was just my dad and me. As a child, I'd been willful and stubborn to a fault, always getting into trouble and disappearing.

"There are better ways to get attention," Soren had said to me after an ill-advised disappearing act during an important court banquet in Waterfell. "Like being a daughter and princess he can be proud of. You should have been there today. Your absence was noted by many."

"I don't want to be a princess," I'd said sourly. "And I don't care."

"You can't keep running from who you are, Nerissa. One day you will be queen."

"I'd rather live in a cave full of vomit."

Looking back, I was far more trouble than I was worth. Our people faulted him for being so indulgent and not taking a firmer hand with me, saying that if he couldn't control his own child, how could he control his people? Put it this way—when I left, no one missed me. After all, as the humans say, no one mourns the wicked. Without my father, the thought of returning to Waterfell alone was—and still is—terrifying.

"What's wrong?" Speio asks, sensing my change in mood.

"Nothing. I was just thinking about…my father," I say after a few seconds. "At least you still have Echlios and Soren, even if we aren't there. My father's gone, and I'll always be a constant disappointment to the Aquarathi." Speio doesn't answer right away, but I can see a sudden tightness at the corner of his mouth and in his fingers on the steering wheel. My voice fades to a whisper. "How can I face them? They only remember a silly child."

"The people will give you a chance. You're the heir," he says. "Look, you're almost seventeen. Dvija's bound to happen soon. When you come of age to rule in a few months, everything will change."

I glance at him. "Spey, does it hurt?"

"Does what hurt?"

"Transitioning. Dvija."

"A little." Speio's voice grows as tight as his fingers. "It's more like you feel everything, like everything is heightened, all emotions." He shoots me a look. "Riss, you know all this, how we work, how all of that sense of awareness goes away once you—"

"—bond," I finish, hesitating before I ask the real question. "But what if we never do? What happens then?"

"If we stay human," he says quietly, "it hurts less."

"Oh." Which explains why Speio very rarely accompanies me on my occasional deep-sea jaunts when I transform into Aquarathi form for hours at a time. "One more question, and I'll shut up, I promise."

"You can ask me anything, Riss, you know that."

"Can we bond with a human?"

I already know the answer, but I risk the sudden sharp look that Speio launches in my direction because I want to hear him say it. I need to hear him say it. I need to know that the butterfly sensation in my chest caused by this human boy means nothing.

"No," he says, his green eyes searching. "But it doesn't mean we can't love them."

"Did you ever? Love one of them?"

"No. It's just not as real for me. No matter how much they love you, or you them, you will always want more. You will always search for the missing part of yourself." He pauses. "And that can never be a human."

We don't speak again until we pull into the deserted stretch of gravelly road. The others are already there and getting changed. It's a bit of a hike down to the beach so the plan is to gear up first and walk down. I pull my hair into a ponytail and shrug out of my jeans to pull on a shortie wet suit over my bikini—it may be spring, but the water is still chilly, and even though water temperature doesn't affect me, I need to keep up appearances.

"Hurry up, slowpokes," Sawyer yells, already dressed and heading down the path.

I notice that Jenna isn't changing. "You're not surfing?"

"Here? No way. It's like overhead out there, if you haven't noticed. I prefer the baby waves." She thrusts a camera in my face. "I'll just take some shots of you guys. Looking good, Lo," she says loudly with an exaggerated wink.

I try to force myself not to look at him but it's too late. My eyes connect with a killer six-pack made even more killer by the ridge of black neoprene riding low on a pair of very lean hips. With a sharp intake of air and scolding myself in the same breath for even noticing, I tear my eyes away. What's wrong with me? It's not like I haven't seen tons of showboating surfer dudes flaunting their chiseled bodies all over La Jolla. I make myself look up, keeping my expression nonchalant.

But Lo makes no such effort. He's staring at me with a look of blatant appreciation on his face, and this time I can't stop the blush that rises like an answering tide through me, nor the feeling of complete dissolution taking hold of my body. I barely even notice Speio's frown or Jenna's ecstatic face.

I know one thing's for certain.

It's not the butterflies I need to be worried about.

5
Taking the Drop

Out here, the ocean is vast, like a glittering surface that stretches to meet the sky, dipping and rolling in constant movement. In the distance, the edges of Catalina break the line of the horizon. With the sun making its way down, everything is dusted in a golden tinge—a sea and sky of molten gold. This is my favorite time of day, just before the sunset shimmers into red and orange, when the world is at its most perfect.

Breathless, I lie on my board way past the lineup where the ocean is only a gentle swell, dangling my arm into the water and feeling the fine layer of salt crusting on my face. I'm not tired, but it has taken more effort than usual to control my impulses. On top of my volatile feelings with Lo, I know I'm playing with fire because being in the ocean this close to the full moon is risky, when the call of the sea is so strong.

The others are still going strong. I can see Speio in the distance doing a sharp cutback on a wave and Sawyer paddling out to the lineup. I don't see Lo. I've done everything possible to stay out of his way, especially after that moment up top. I need time to process what this thing is—if anything—between us. Speio, thank goodness, hasn't said a word to me about the earlier interaction but I'm sure he's saving it for the ride home.

Great.

Staring down into the blue depths below me, I want to dive down and keep going until I meet the ocean bottom. The pull of the deep is as seductive as the sea salt on my skin. Maybe I can cheat just a little. There's no one out here, anyway. I wiggle my fingers under the water and relax, letting the ocean seep past my human skin, watching as tiny rivers of gold-and-green light shimmer up my wrist and my arm. The feel of it is drugging, making me light-headed and dizzy.

I close my eyes only to have them snap open at the feel of steel fingers digging into my upper arm.

"What are you doing, you idiot?" Speio mutters, wrenching my hand out of the water. I didn't even hear him paddle out to me. "Get it together!"

"I'm sorry—"

"Nerissa, I warned you that you had to be careful. I felt it the second you let go," Speio says, looking around us nervously. "Other predators will, too. And we're around people."

"I know. I said I was sorry, and it was only for a second," I say, rubbing my tingling arm with my other hand. My skin still glows a little, but nowhere near as brightly as when it had been submerged. "I couldn't help it. The call was impossible to resist. I wanted to, just for a second." My voice is beseeching.

Speio's stern face relaxes. He straddles his board, sitting upright, and reaches across to place his fingers against my skin. Almost immediately, I can feel the sharp tug of the ocean, only through Speio's body. It's nearly violent. My eyes widen.

"Feel that?" he asks gently. When I nod, he says, "That's what I have to deal with being in the water, worse when I sense another like me. In this case, you. That's Dvija. Every part of me is open and calling out to that missing piece. You asked me about it earlier at school. It's this—one part pleasure, a hundred parts pain. Even as a human. And it's a thousand times worse in Aquarathi form."

"Oh," I say, stricken. "I didn't know. How can I help? What can I do? Do you want me try Sanctum?"

When I was younger my father told me that part of the responsibility of being an Aquarathi leader is being able to preserve our people's well-being, by emotional intervention if necessary. He called it Sanctum, and I only ever saw him do it once. I still remember the feeling of bliss emanating from every Aquarathi around him. His power and reach were awe-inspiring.

"Thanks, but it's too dangerous in human form. Plus, you're not a queen yet." Speio smiles a wistful smile. "Bonding makes all the pain go away."

Speio's reality hits me with the force of a sledgehammer. My voice wavers as I put two and two together. "So because of me, you have to deal with feeling like this anytime you're in the water. Or around me. That's why you got so angry before when you found out that I'd never planned on going back."

"Sort of."

"I'll fix this, Speio. I promise."

My throat is constricted. Speio is right. I've been more selfish than I could have ever imagined. I had no idea of the pain he was in every time he was in the water or in proximity to me. And that night in the pool must have been torture for him, but he still stayed there.

To earn my forgiveness.

Suddenly, I feel so small and powerless, even though I'm supposed to be the one with all the power...the one they're all supposed to come to for strength. I'm utterly useless. Speio's words in the parking lot at Dover were hurtful, but nothing he said was untrue. I am weak and self-seeking. I am stupid, blindly so.

A tear slips down, tracking its way through the salt on my face, and I grip the sides of my board until my fingers go numb. I hate feeling sorry for myself more than anything. Speio hunches over and presses his forehead to mine. "Stop," he whispers. "You'll make it worse if you cry. It'll be okay."

"What if it won't?" I sniff. "What then?"

"We'll deal with that if we have to," Speio says against my hair, and then yanks a fistful of it and shoves me off my board into the water with a playful grin. "Now if you want to stop being such a sniveling baby, maybe we can get a few more waves in."

Drenched and spluttering, I glare at him and climb back on my surfboard. "I wasn't sniveling. I was crying in a perfectly dignified manner."

Speio makes a noise that sounds suspiciously like a snort and rolls his eyes. And snorts again. In the next second, I'm laughing so hard that my sides are aching and good tears instead of sad ones are pooling in my eyes.

"You're so dumb." I giggle.

"Hey, you two. What's up?"

Lo. My entire body tenses and flutters at that velvety voice. I try to hide my immediate visceral response but it's like trying to stop a freight train with a feather. Speio's expression stiffens, the levity between us disappearing in the wind.

I'd forgotten.

With the water channeling between us, he can feel whatever it is that I'm feeling. *Everything* that I'm feeling. Blushing furiously at the thought of anyone—especially Speio—knowing what this boy is doing to me, I force myself to control my body's responses, severing any link with the ocean and Speio, and reinforcing my human shell. Almost immediately, the connection weakens until there's nothing but a shimmer of wind between us.

Oddly, I feel a sense of loss. I liked being linked to Speio— it made me feel less alone. Without a word, Speio sends a dark scowl in Lo's direction, then spins on his board and paddles off. Obviously, he felt the same.

"What's his problem?" Lo asks, his voice husky.

"Nothing. He's just…protective."

"Of you?"

"I guess. We've known each other a very long time so it comes with the territory," I say, noticing that the fading sunlight makes his wet hair look like burnished metal. His hair is such an odd color. It's not reddish-blond like mine, but it's not gold or silver, either. It's more of a mix of the two. The only thing I can think of to describe it is wet sand.

"Why are you staring at me like that?" Lo asks, tilting his head. "Like I have seaweed on my head or something?"

I flush and tear my gaze away. "You have strange hair."

"Um, thanks. I think," Lo says, and then chuckles. "Made it myself."

"No, I meant. It's a nice color. I like hair," I finish lamely, and want to kick myself. I like hair? Could I be any more of a loser? "I mean, I don't like hair."

Shut up, shut up, shut up!

"So do you or don't you?" Although his face is deadpan serious, I can hear the thread of amusement in his voice and I feel myself bristling. "Like hair?"

"Could we just drop it, the hair thing? You have nice hair. Happy?" I snap, and start paddling back into the lineup.

At least I've worked out that when Lo opens his mouth, it's a great way to keep me aggravated enough with him so that the other things, like the annoying treacherous butterflies, cease to matter. Despite the physical attraction, which

I admit is there, I could never fall for a boy like Lo. He's too self-confident and too amused all the time, like everything is part of some big joke.

"Come back, Nerissa. I'm sorry," Lo says, keeping pace with me easily, his arms cleaving through the water like pistons. I'm just about to tell him where he can stuff it when I notice his eyes widen at something behind me. I glance over my shoulder, but all I can see is a ripple on the water as if something had just clipped the surface and then resubmerged.

"What the hell was that?" Lo says. He noticed, too.

"I didn't see anything." But just as I say it, something heavy brushes against my right arm dangling in the water, and a jolt staggers through me at the contact of flesh on flesh. Speio was right. My reckless little dance with the ocean probably summoned the thing.

"There it is again! You see it? A fin?" Lo's voice has now turned wary and I bite back the urge to laugh at the nervous look on his face. It could be a dolphin, not a shark, even though I'm guessing it's the latter. Guys—they can be so macho all the time, and the minute they see a fin it's all over. I don't blame them, though. Sharks are terrifying. I've seen fifty-foot ones that look like prehistoric monsters down in the depths of the ocean, but I can never tell anyone that, of course.

I press down onto the tip of my board so that my head and chest submerge along with it and nearly swallow a mouthful of water. My eyes widen and I pull my board back up. It's no dolphin. And it's no shark, either.

It's lots of them.

Their gray shapes are murky dark shadows, milling in the darkening waters, and I know that more of them will come. Even though Aquarathi pheromones are pacifying, all it will take is one drop of our blood to whip things into a violent food frenzy. Not that I'd be at any risk, but all of the others would be…including Lo. So the sooner we get out of there, the better. I look around for the others. Jenna and Sawyer have their arms around each other on shore. Speio, standing near them, is glaring at me.

"No, I don't see anything," I lie to Lo, paddling away from him with deft strokes. "But it could be a dolphin or a shark. It's nearly twilight, feeding time, after all. Think you can make it back without falling and being fish bait?"

My grin is challenging. To my surprise, a slow smile breaks across Lo's face at my dare. It's such a swift change from the wariness that it confuses me. Isn't he afraid? Or have I misinterpreted his expression about the shark?

"You in?" I ask with a raised eyebrow.

"See you on the beach, surfer girl."

Digging my palms into the water, I paddle as fast as I can to get ahead of the next building wave but Lo is right there with me. Exhilarated, I watch him stroke alongside, keeping up with no trouble. His face is determined, but I know that mine is, too.

"Don't you dare drop in on me!" I yell, grinning.

"You have to catch it first for me to drop in," he shouts back. "Or do I need to school you on wave etiquette?"

"Just try to catch me!"

We're neck and neck as the wave fattens, taking both our boards with it in unison as we furiously paddle to keep up with the wave's speed. Out of the corner of my eye, I see a silvery shimmer on top of the water to my left near Lo just as the wave begins to crest, but it's gone before I can even blink.

The wave's pressure builds beneath me, picking up momentum in a matter of breaths. Gripping the sides of my board, I hop to my feet and angle my surfboard across the wave's face, only to see that Lo is in the exact same position, with a huge grin on his face. Just a few feet apart, we're flying at the speed of the wind on the same wave, and for a second, we share an incredible moment of perfect synchronicity.

Then the lip of the wave curls over us and we are inside a shimmering tunnel, the outside world visible only through the sheer wall of curling water. I can hear the tremendous roar as seconds merge into one another and time slows to a trickle. Suspended in a moving bubble, we glide along the wave, nothing between us but water and the swell beneath our feet. Every cell in my body is responding to the water rushing around me, so much so that it's hard to control my Aquarathi instincts, to pull myself in…to not give in to the ocean's insistent call. I'm tingling from head to toe.

Lo's eyes catch mine and everything inside me electrifies.

And then the tingles are everywhere, spreading to the tips of my fingers, my neck, my ears, my spine. Frowning, I look away with effort, digging my toes into the deck of my board and leaning forward to skim past his board. I gasp as the front lip of water curls into my neck and my board glides scant inches from his, but then I'm past him and flying upward to rip a cutback along the top of the wave.

When I glance back over my shoulder, he's still staring at me, a sliver of a smile on his face. His eyes are dark and knowing as if he senses the effect he's having on me. I turn away, breathing harshly, focused on getting to the beach. I can't get far enough away from this boy who makes me feel so disconnected, like I'm nothing but liquid around him.

I don't even care about the threat of the sharks below us. I'm more afraid of Lo than anything else…of the way he makes everything inside me react to him like I'm some kind of puppet on a string. Even now, I can feel him behind me, his presence like a tangible force drawing me to him. For a second, I wonder whether Speio and all the others feel the same way when they have to reveal themselves to me, like the pull of something formidable.

It terrifies me.

It's kind of absurd that I want to escape the ocean more than anything right now, when it's been my safe haven forever, just to get my feet on solid ground. There, I won't be susceptible to the lure of the sea or its gilded fantasies where Lo is concerned. I'm letting the full moon and the embrace of the ocean affect me more than they should.

I let the wave take me almost into the beach to where the others are waiting on the sand, watching over my shoulder as Lo paddles out for another. Avoiding the death glare on Speio's face, I grab my board and head toward where Jenna is sitting next to Sawyer, looking at the photos she'd taken of him on his last ride.

"Nice pipe," Sawyer says, high-fiving me. "Amazing that you two were in it at the same time! Sweet!"

"Yeah," Jenna echoes, waggling her eyebrows and snapping a photo of my face. "Sweet." I shoot her a nasty glare as I undo the tie from my ankle and wrap it around the tail of the board.

"I think I'm done," I say.

Sawyer flashes me a disbelieving look and chugs a bottle of water. "Really? One good wave and that's all you got?"

I nod and lie back on the sand. Better out here than in there. The sharks will move on once they realize I'm gone. Plus, being anywhere near Lo is not a good idea. I can still feel the way his body moved next to mine, see the expression in the endless depths of his eyes...the pull of them like the ocean, compelling and deep. Lo makes me feel more alive than I've ever felt. And it scares the heck out of me.

Sawyer looks to Speio. "You in, bro? Come on. Don't leave me hanging."

"Sure," Speio says, grabbing his board and shooting me a

look that clearly says I should stay put. I roll my eyes but I have no plans to move. Leaning on my elbows, I watch the boys paddle out, but Lo catches my eye as he rounds the crest of a particularly large wave. Just as he pops up on the board, my heart stops in my chest as the wave starts to close out almost immediately. Even though he's a capable surfer, nothing but glue or a miracle can keep him upright as the force of a barreling truck bears down on him, throwing him off the board like he's a piece of lint.

"Ouch," Jenna says. "Wish I'd gotten a shot of that." She stares at me with a grin. "Or the look on your face when he fell."

"Why don't you shut it and go do something useful?"

"Why so grumpy?"

I shoot her a glare that could incinerate ice, but she ignores me with a wink, walking down the beach to snap some more shots. Scowling, I reach into my backpack for a bottle of water. The wind threatens to rip some of my papers from the top of the bag, and I just manage to grab hold of an escaping flyer that I'd tucked in there the day before. Taking a swig of water, I study the flyer fluttering beneath my fingertips on the sand. It's from the San Diego Ocean Foundation for a marine conservancy drive event.

I should have been involved in something like this from the day I stepped onto land, but I've been so caught up in escaping who I am that I've ignored my real responsibilities. Instead, without a care in the world, I've enjoyed everything human youth had to offer…while my people paid the price for my freedom. At least now, I can do something worthwhile. I can try to ensure that those who are left in Waterfell have a future.

"Hey, Jenna," I yell out. "Can I talk to you about something?"

She stops snapping pics and walks over to sit next to me cross-legged on the sand. "Sure. What's up?"

I don't need her help, but it would be fun to do it with someone else. "Check this out. There's an ocean conservancy drive happening in a few weeks, and I want to get involved."

"Since when are you interested in ocean conservancy?" Jenna's words aren't sarcastic, they're curious, but I can't help the immediate pang in my belly. She's right. I haven't been, when it should have been the one thing that I was interested in. My father had said to stay away, and that's what I've done, playing hockey and pretending to be human here on land. I've shirked every responsibility ever given to me and forgotten about the ocean. It's the only home the Aquarathi have, and all I've done is turn my back on it...and on my people. And who knows what Ehmora is planning, now that my father is out of the picture.

"I'm interested now," I say.

"But what about hockey and practice? It's not like you have a ton of free time."

"It won't interfere, I promise." I stare at her. "I really need to do this, Jenna. It's important to me. And I'd be so happy if you wanted to do it with me, but I totally understand if you have too many things on your plate." I pause. "But I need to."

"How come?"

"It's kind of a family thing. Complicated."

Jenna shoots me a look. She knows that I don't really talk about my family so she doesn't press the issue. Her expression turns thoughtful. "Okay, I'm in."

I can't believe how easily she gives her friendship, incorporating my needs with hers as if she doesn't even question whether I'm worthy of it. It's humbling. For about the five hundredth time, I feel like I want to return the favor and tell her everything. Confide the truth of who I am and everything else that I've hidden from her for so many years. The Nerissa she knows is a mere shadow of who I really am. But I can't—revealing who we are to humans is against all of our laws, an offense punishable by death, even for me.

"Text me the details, okay?" she says, and stands, dusting the sand off her shorts. "Oh, here comes your boyfriend. I'm going for a walk."

"No, wait—" I begin, but it's too late as a long shadow falls over me and I look up, shading my eyes with one hand. Lo dumps his board facedown on the sand and collapses next to me, breathing hard. He runs a hand through his damp, wind-blown hair. His cheeks are red and his eyes are glowing. Every part of me comes alive in response to his nearness.

"Hey," he says, his dark eyes searching. "Why'd you come in?"

"Tired," I say tersely.

"Me, too," he says, touching the side of his head. "Got worked on a big one, though."

"Sorry." I manage to keep my voice cool, detached.

"You okay?"

"Fine."

"Okay," he says with a puzzled look, but falls silent.

Lo is trouble. I can feel it in the way my pulse races at the mere presence of him, the way my breath takes on a shaky cadence. I have to pull it together and end this growing in-fatuation, which is all it really is—a crush.

I take a deep breath. "Look, I know I said I'd go with you to the Crab Shack, but I can't. It's…complicated." Complicated is beginning to define my life.

Lo shoots me a look, as if he can see right through me. "What are you afraid of?"

"I don't know what you mean," I say.

"Yes, you do." My answering flush is immediate. I hate the

way he can see right through my bluster. It's a perceptiveness I usually see in Jenna, and while it's a cool trait with her, it's maddening with him. I take a deep breath.

"Lo," I say. "I don't want to play any games with you. I mean, I'm not interested in dating anyone. I can't."

"Why?"

His quiet directness is disconcerting. "Because I have too many things going on—school, hockey, family—to get involved with anyone." I'm aware that my reasoning is flimsy but I can't seem to put two coherent thoughts together when he's staring at me with that knowing look in his eyes.

"Nerissa—" the delicious way he says my name sends a shiver through my entire body from tip to toe "—I like you. You're interesting. I want to get to know you. And I want to know the real reason that you don't like me."

"I don't," I blurt out, ignoring the fact that he just admitted he liked me. "I mean, I do like you fine as a person." *I like you too much, that's the problem.*

Once more, I'm struck by how different he is from other boys. No boy I know at Dover, or any other school, would flat-out up and admit they liked a girl, or lay out perfectly logical reasons on why they should get to know each other. His quiet self-assurance throws me.

"So what's the problem, then? For us to hang out? As friends."

"Cara thinks you have enough friends." I don't even know where the words come from, but they're out of my mouth before I can stop them. Lo's expression doesn't change but I can see the slow lightening in his eyes. It's worse than an actual smile.

"She's just someone who befriended the new guy."

The way he says it makes me feel awful, like I'm some sort of pariah who thinks she's too good for everyone else. Maybe I used to be like that, but I'm not anymore, and certainly nothing like Cara, who has her own hidden agendas. But it's the opening I need. So even though my body feels otherwise, I stand, grabbing my board and bag.

"Good. Then you don't need me," I say softly. Lo's reaction takes me by surprise. This time, he smiles and lounges back on his elbows, stretching his sand-crusted legs out in front of him. I frown, recognizing his grin as the same one from earlier when we'd been competing for the wave. "That's not a challenge, if that's what you're thinking."

"Okay."

"Okay, what?" I say, exasperated.

"Not a challenge, I get it," he says, and nods over my shoulder. "Here comes your warden."

I glance down the beach to see Speio walking toward us from the water with the familiar stormy expression on his face. But instead of being angry, this time I'm grateful for the interruption.

"Catch you later," I say to Lo, and walk toward Speio.

"Definitely," Lo says.

The single parting word curls around me like velvet, leaving me in little doubt of his intentions.

6
Warfare

"Terrific game, Fighters!"

The metal bleachers around the field are packed and full of screaming supporters. We just took down the number-three seeded girls' hockey team in Southern California and are now in the finals. Although my head wasn't completely in the game, I'd used the field as a way to get rid of some much needed aggression. I'd played better than I'd hoped, scoring two out of the four goals. Jenna shot the winning goal in the final six seconds of the game.

As usual, Speio was sitting in the stands with a huge scowl on his face—and was the only one scowling when I scored my goals. He still thinks I'm wasting my time playing hockey, but there's no way I will give up on my team, not after walking away from everything else. They need me. In any case, Lo's enthusiastic cheering made up for Speio's complete lack of school spirit. Not that I noticed, of course. I found it interesting that he showed up for the game.

Again, not that I cared. Much.

"You were on fire today, Riss!" Jenna screeches in my ear as we join our teammates walking back to the locker room.

"Says the girl who brought the fire," I yell back, grinning. "You cleared, like, half the field in three seconds for that last goal. Just brilliant!"

"Thanks!"

We dump our gear and head for our lockers, sweaty and jubilant. Getting to the finals took a lot of hard work and many a long practice, but seeing the faces of my teammates—even Cara, who'd sat on the bench for most of the game—was worth every grueling second.

"So where's the victory dinner?" It's one of the defensive players on the team, another junior, Mary.

"Think Coach said the Crab Shack in an hour. You guys in?"

"I can't," I say quickly. "I have a ton of homework, and I have to head over to the Marine Coastal Center for a bit. You guys have fun."

"Party pooper!" Mary says, sticking out her tongue at me. She grins suddenly. "Sure you don't want to? Heard your boyfriend's going to be there. The lovelicious Lo." She draws out his name suggestively and waggles her eyebrows.

"What?" I sputter, glaring at Jenna.

"Don't look at me," she says, throwing her hands in the air. "As much as I'd like to claim I do, my many talents don't extend to controlling the rumor mill."

I turn my glare to Mary, whose grin widens at my red face. A door slams at the far end of the locker room and I notice that Cara is missing. "He's not my boyfriend, regardless of what he or anyone says. I don't even like the guy."

"Great, so he's up for grabs, then?"

"Sure," I say, ripping off my uniform with more force than necessary and jerking my head toward the toilet stalls. "But I think Cara has dibs. Don't say I didn't warn you."

"Noted," Mary says with a grin, fluttering her eyelashes. "She doesn't have a chance in hell."

For a second, I envision myself smashing Mary's pretty face in, but the feeling dissipates as quickly as it comes. Even when he's not around, that boy has an atrocious effect on me. I avoid Jenna's gaze like the plague because I can sense her studying me and coming to obvious Jenna-like conclusions in her head. I'll only make it worse if I say anything, so I snap my mouth shut and strip off the rest of my gear.

"Well, I guess I'll see you later, then?" she says to me after a while. "Oh, Sawyer wanted me to ask you. You're going to the surf meet next Saturday, right?" I notice that she doesn't say anything about Lo even though he's on the team, too. "There's a bonfire on the beach afterward. Thought we could all hang out. Feels like it's been forever with school and practice since we've done anything fun. You know, just us."

Although ten different reasons that I shouldn't go jump to my lips, I nod. Sawyer has been my friend for years, and just because he is now friends with Lo doesn't mean that I have to give up my support and friendship. Plus, Jenna hasn't quite forgiven me for bailing out of the double date, so I owe her. "Of course. Tell him I wouldn't miss it for the world."

"Cool, I'll let you know when he finds out more about the times for the heats," she says with a glance. "Sure you don't need me to come with to the marine center? I don't really care about the Crab Shack thing."

"Only if you want to," I say, and I mean it. I was glad Jenna had agreed to volunteer with me at all. "I mean, I don't have a shift or anything. I was just going to do homework and see if Kevin needed any help."

"You know what, I'll come and if Kevin doesn't need anything we can do the Crab Shack."

After showering, we walk out to the parking lot together,

and I make the requisite call to Echlios, letting him know where I'm going to be. The truth is, I'm happy to sit around and do my homework at the marine center. Already, I've spent the past week there and feel more at home than anywhere else. A part of me wonders why I waited so long. It's also part of the reason that I want to go over there instead of going out with the rest of the team.

I need to go there.

I don't know if it's the sense of purpose or doing something... anything...to help, but for the first time since I've been here, I feel like I'm in the right place at the right time. At the center, I'm involved in many of the ongoing projects that affect marine life—urban sewage runoff, pollution, toxicity, beach cleanup, reef regeneration—but my favorite is working within the Marine Protected Areas, which helps the protection of coastal ecosystems. The underwater state parks are beautiful.

"Hey, Kev," I say to Kevin, the bearded guy who's the youth program director for the center, at the front desk. "Any more news on those poachers near San Clemente Island?"

"Hey, guys," Kevin says with a thoughtful frown at Jenna and me. "You have a shift today? Thought you weren't back until next week?"

"We had some free time," I say, throwing my backpack on the floor behind the desk. "You mind if we hang around for a while? Help out?"

"Actually, it's good that you're here. Need a favor. We have a new volunteer and it would help me out a ton if you guys could show him around outside. I've already done the tour in here, so just the beach and a couple of the main MPAs? Take the boat," Kevin says. Grinning, I roll my eyes at Jenna—seriously, I must have Tour Guide tattooed on my forehead. Kevin nods to someone behind us. The smile freezes on my face the minute I turn around.

"What are you doing here?" I say.

Kevin looks from me to Lo and back again. "You guys know one another? Great! Jenna, Rissa, Lo will be doing some community service with us."

"Community service? What'd you do, rob a bank or something?"

"Detention," Lo drawls, and nods at Jenna, who for some reason turns a dark shade of red and mumbles something about getting changed before taking off. "Cano thought since I love cutting class so much to go to the beach, I should make up the time doing something worthwhile. I'm here every day after school for the foreseeable future."

I glare at him, regretting that I gave up the team dinner only to be stuck with Lo of all people. I refuse to even think about him being here every day and ruining my sanctuary. "Seriously, you know this is taking it to a whole different level of stalkerism, don't you?"

Lo pastes an innocent look on his face, widening his eyes— as blue as the ocean—in mock horror. "Cano sent me here."

"Sure he did."

"Actually, it was Leland but they sort of do things together. The dynamic duo, I like to call them." I don't know why Lo is trying to make small talk. Maybe it's to impress Kevin but I don't care. I'm stuck with him once more for touring duty. As if reading my mind, Lo grins widely. "Lead on. I am at your bidding," he says, repeating his mocking words from our first day of school.

"Glad you find this amusing," I snap, grabbing my backpack. "Because it's not the least bit amusing to me! I'm hardly the local tour guide."

"You talk like a grown-up, you know that," Lo remarks.

"Well, most of us juniors aren't children like people think we are," I say with as much snark as I can inject into my tone.

"Unlike you." I smile sweetly at Kevin, who has a bewildered expression on his face. "See you, Kev." I turn back to Lo, my smile fading into a blank expression that barely hides my aggravation. "Well, come on, then, if you're coming."

Grabbing the keys to the ATV, I head through the front office doors and down the hall. Not looking back at him, I jab a finger down another hallway. "I'm sure Kevin told you the men's bathroom is down there. Meet me out back in five. Five minutes, Lo, or I'm gone without you."

"You're so bossy," he throws back, but I refuse to engage and walk away in the opposite direction.

In the women's bathroom, my aggravation is unleashed on Jenna, who's staring at me with a guilty look on her face. She pulls on a pair of cargo pants over her swimsuit. "Seriously, all I ask for is a moment where that guy isn't stalking me for ten seconds."

"Did it ever occur to you that he may be into you?"

"That's just it. I'm not into him," I snap, shrugging out of my school uniform. "And I've told him so. He just won't take no for an answer. And plus, what's with the Cara thing? Did you see them? They were practically canoodling after the game. And she's a total psycho freak." I know I'm ranting now but I can't help myself. "I mean, the fact that he likes her and me in the same universe makes absolutely no sense. It's kind of gross, really. And what's with the lie about detention? Everyone knows that Cano likes the standard study-after-school detentions."

"Cara used to be your friend, remember?"

"Used to, as in past tense, Jenna. She's a bitch."

She stares at me. "You kind of both were."

"Wait, what?" My hand stalls at the folds of my T-shirt.

Jenna sighs. "Freshman year, when you guys were friends. Rumor is you sort of took over and shut her out. Put it this way—if I hadn't transferred in, I probably wouldn't have wanted to be friends with you back then. Plus, look at what happened with the game against Bishop's. You made a bad call because you don't like her."

"I thought we were past that," I say in a defensive voice. "And being better at hockey doesn't make me a bitch."

"Or prettier or smarter or naturally better at everything than she was." She spreads her palms at my look and takes a deep breath. "Look, you're different now. We all are, but you can't really blame Cara for resenting you now. I mean, come on, even Cano told her to be more like you." She pauses. "In front of everyone."

I stare at her as I recall a vague recollection of Cano—Cara's uncle—telling that to his niece in the school parking lot in front of half the school. I shrug. Cara's family issues weren't mine then, and they aren't mine now. I narrow my eyes a fraction. "And that's my fault how?"

"I don't even think this is about Cara at all," Jenna shoots back smoothly, refusing to be cowed or drawn into an argument. "I think a boy likes you and you're afraid that you like him back. And maybe he's telling the truth about detention—"

"Are you kidding?" I interrupt, ignoring the first part of what she'd said. "That guy wouldn't know the truth if it hit him in the ass. He's so self-absorbed, it's insane. He practically followed me here after the game."

"You don't know that."

"What does everyone see in him? Just tell me." This time Jenna doesn't answer me. She knows me too well, when I get into one of these moods. I don't want an answer because anything she says will probably make me crazier. I sigh, shooting her a look. "Sorry," I say. "I'm not myself today."

Dressing quickly and suppressing the urge to break things, I stash my backpack in a locker. There's no way that Cano or

Leland would just get an idea to let a student do community service at the Marine Coastal Center. I'm positive that it's all Lo's doing and part of the whole challenge thing. It's like I can't get away from the guy—no matter what I do, he's always there…watching and smiling that stupid, mocking grin of his. He's getting under my skin like sand in the lining of a swimsuit, chafing and annoying.

"What a piece of work," I mutter, twisting my hair into a ponytail.

"Look, here's my two cents as your best friend. I know you're going to do what you're going to do, but listen to yourself for a minute," Jenna says. "You're losing sleep over a boy you claim to not be interested in, and this isn't like you. You're bringing up old stuff with Cara, of all people, because it's bothering you that he hangs out with her for ten seconds after a game or stops to talk in the hallway at school." I'm shaking my head in denial but Jenna continues, her blue eyes sincere. "Yes, it is. Thing is, you need to figure out the real reason why you don't want to give him a break."

Stumped, I stare at her for a minute, her face assessing but sympathetic. Jenna's right as usual—I am being completely irrational. There's no logical reason that I can't be friends with Lo or work with him at the center. Plus, the more hands we have, the better. I just have to keep him at a distance. That shouldn't be too hard, should it?

"Fine. You're right. I don't know why I get so irritated." Jenna grins, looking like she wants to say more to answer my rhetorical question, but I stall her with a glare. "Don't even go there," I warn. "I'm okay with admitting I'm not being entirely fair to him, but that's it."

Jenna throws her hands in the air. "Look, I don't want you to marry the guy, just give him a chance, that's all. Sawyer really likes him, and you know Sawyer, he barely says a word to anyone."

"Okay, I'll try…just for Sawyer's people spidey-sense," I say, rolling my eyes and glancing at my watch. "Crap, I told Lo five minutes. It's been fifteen!"

Lo's waiting outside, and raises an eyebrow, tapping the face of his watch. I feel myself color immediately but Jenna jumps in to diffuse the situation.

"It's my fault. Sorry," she says. "Had to talk to my mom."

"No worries," Lo tells her with an easy smile, and for a moment, I feel peeved that he is so laid-back with her as opposed to how punchy he is with me. If I'd said anything, no doubt he would have provoked me more and things would have escalated from there. "So we ready?" he asks, and gestures at his clothing. "This okay?"

He's dressed in boardies and a dark blue T-shirt. For early spring, the weather is in the high sixties so it's not that cold. Still, I don't know why it irks me that he looks entirely too comfortable. "It'll be colder on the boat," I warn him.

He shrugs, glancing at me dressed in cargo shorts and a long-sleeved shirt. "I'll be all right."

"If you say so."

"You sure you know how to drive that thing?" he asks warily as I jump into the four-seater ATV. Jenna straps herself into the backseat and I can't help grinning.

"Scared, princess?" I taunt, turning over the engine, my grin morphing into something wolfish. "Come on, you'll be as safe as kittens. Right, Jenna?"

"Um, sure?" Jenna says.

"It's not the ride I'm worried about," he says with a teasing smile, and all of a sudden, all of my bravado leaves my body in a whoosh. He swings in on one of the upper rails, and I pull off so quickly that he snaps backward in his seat and grabs for his seat belt. A small twinge of satisfaction seeps through me.

Riding down the sandy trail at the back of the Marine Coastal Center, we head down to the beach. The boat is docked at the far end of the shore, and I make certain to ride over every sand dune that I can at the highest speed. We're practically flying over some of the dunes and coming down hard. By the time we reach the opposite end, Lo is a few shades paler than normal, clutching the sides of the ATV in a death grip. Jenna isn't new to my driving, but even she looks a little shaken.

"You have issues, I hope you know that," Lo tells me, hopping out on shaky legs.

"That was for stalking me."

"Look, I'm not stalking you," Lo protests in earnest with a sidelong look at Jenna. "To tell you the truth, I was just leaving Cano's office the other day, and Jenna'd suggested to Leland that the center needed extra hands."

Jenna freezes, her face indignant. "That's not how it happened. Leland asked me about my extracurricular activities for the college apps, and that's what I said. I totally didn't invite him to have detention here!" She punches him in the arm. "Thanks for throwing me under the bus, Seavon!"

Seavon?

Why's she calling him by his last name like they're best buds? I frown. My throat is so tight that all I can do is glower. Oh, she's so dead later. I'm so mad, I can't even speak and I can feel my face getting redder and redder. Jenna rushes to thwart the impending outburst.

"Riss—"

But Lo diverts the fire. "Trust me, if I'd have known Nerissa was going to be here…"

"Then what?" I burst out.

A wicked grin. "I would have cut class every day and gotten detention sooner." Jenna snorts and bursts into giggles.

"You're impossible," I say, blushing through an imperceptible snort of my own. The corners of my mouth twitch at his cheek, my anger deflating like a receding wave. I shake my head, face flaming. "A real piece of work. Come on, help me with the ropes before that mouth of yours gets you into trouble."

Lo's grin widens to show his evenly spaced white teeth, his eyes dipping to my lips. "Really? What kind of trouble?"

It's all I can do to contain the rush that invades my body at his words. Instead, I start pushing the open-top white thirty-foot boat off the edge of the dock. Jenna unties the last rope and jumps in after us, heading up top to the bow. She tosses me a surreptitious wink but I ignore her, flushing even more and welcoming the blast of wind against my hot face.

We're already heading out into open water before I realize that being in this close proximity to Lo on a boat in the middle of the ocean probably isn't the best idea. Shoving the disturbing thought from my head, I point out some of the protected areas.

"Where'd you learn to boat?" Lo shouts over the roar of the wind and the engines.

"Echlios—my guardian—taught me. You know Speio?" Lo nods, his eyes shooting skyward. I ignore the gesture meant for Speio. "Well, he loves boating and we have these family… diving expeditions. He actually has his own boat docked near our house on the shore."

"Speaking of your shadow, I'm surprised he's not hot on your tail." Lo peers under the side rails. "Or is he hiding here like a silent ninja somewhere?"

"Speio's fine," I say. "He's just—"

"—protective, I know," Lo finishes. "How come, if you

don't mind me asking? You in some kind of witness protection or have a secret identity you don't want found out, or what?" I can't help myself. I start laughing so hard that the boat lurches sideways and spins into a half circle before righting itself. Lo can't imagine how close he is to the truth. "What's so funny?"

"Nothing. I'm not in witness protection," I say, still laughing. Jenna makes her way back at my laugh with an irritating, self-satisfied smirk on her face. My laughter snaps off like a switch. "Anyway, back to the tour—over there are the kelp forests. Interesting to swim through but not if you get tangled. It's all part of the La Jolla Underwater Park."

"Underwater park? Sounds awesome."

I glance at him but he looks honestly excited about it. Jenna chimes in. "Yeah, it's pretty cool. You scuba?"

"Yep, got certified a few years ago."

"In Hawaii?" I blurt out, and then curse myself as Jenna's eyes widen. I hadn't meant to bring up a sore subject. But Lo only nods, his eyes unreadable and smiling a tiny smile that makes my heart lurch in response. I chew on my lower lip and stare at the water.

"So you surf and scuba. What else do you do?" Jenna says with forced joviality as I maneuver the boat around La Jolla point to the adjoining cove.

"Those are my two favorite things," he says. "I love the ocean, always have. My…foster dad and I ran a marine wildlife support organization back home. We once took care of a baby dolphin for a whole year. I don't know why I feel more comfortable with fish than people but I just do. Go figure, right?"

"Really?" I interject, trying to erase the sad look in his eyes. "I mean, weren't you terrified of a leopard shark surfing the other day?"

"One, I wasn't terrified. And two, it's a shark. They eat people."

"Not leopards," I toss back with a grin.

"Well, I'm not taking any chances with the rulers of the ocean. They have long memories, sharks," Lo says in a confident tone.

"Where'd you learn that?" Jenna asks.

"Google."

Jenna snorts again and, this time, I can't cover my own laughter at his comical expression. I glance through my lashes at Lo, who leans in to hear something Jenna is saying about the underwater canyons. His face is flushed from the wind and fresh air, and he looks happy. It's obvious he enjoys being on the water and hanging out with the two of us. Maybe Jenna is right. I haven't really been all that fair to him. I should give him another chance. After all, he is funny and sociable when he chooses to be, and anyone who loves the water as much as he obviously does can't be that bad. I'm so caught up in my intense scrutiny of him and subsequent self-assessment that I don't realize that Lo is talking to me.

"Like what you see?" he repeats amused.

"What? No. I was looking through you," I splutter, rattled and mortified that he'd caught me staring at him like a love-sick puppy. The humiliation makes my words far sharper than they should be, demolishing all my good intentions. "For your information, not everything is all about you. Can't you take the hint? Some people just don't like you."

"Like you?"

"Especially me," I say tightly.

Jenna shoots me a disappointed look and moves away, but Lo just stands there, silent, watching me. I don't know why I let him get me so riled up, but it's like I can't control myself. A part of me wants to apologize, to take back my throw-away comments, but instead I keep my eyes averted, feeling slightly ashamed but mostly furious with myself as I steer the boat back to the dock.

As if he, too, wants to get as far away from me as possible, Lo follows Jenna to the front of the boat, where she's pointing out some of the landmarks on our way back. I don't blame him, but I feel the loss of his presence like something tangible. Lo looks back once in my direction, his lower lip trapped between his teeth, something thoughtful flitting across his face before he turns his attention to Jenna.

I stare blindly at the ocean, considering all the reasons that I don't like him. I hate the way he looks at me as if he knows me, when he knows nothing about me at all. I hate the way he talks, and the way he looks, and the fact that everyone— including my own best friends—seems to adore him. I hate the way he smiles so easily at anything Jenna or Cara says, when all he can do is snap mocking comments at me. I hate the way he makes me feel with one glance as if all the water in my body is electrified and I can't breathe. I hate how he surfs, and how his lips curve into a lopsided smile when he's happy. I hate everything about him, especially his stupid lips.

Ignoring the tiny shiver coursing through me at the thought of Lo's lips, I sigh and swallow past the knot in my throat, watching him laugh easily at something Jenna says. Suddenly, I realize that I'm envious because, deep down, I want him to be that way with me.

Effortless.

And then the truth hits me like a curling wave.

I don't hate him at all.

7
Sanctum

I'm concentrating on holding the shape of the tiny drop of water on my finger in study hall when I feel a gentle tap on my shoulder. Speio slides in beside me. The drop dissipates into my skin and I slam my notebook shut hastily. The last thing I need Speio seeing is the insensible doodles I've made while staring at Lo across the room. I've seen him a couple times at the center after school, but we're never on the same shift. I don't know if it's just fate, but a part of me knows that he's avoiding me like the plague. Not that I blame him, but I feel compelled to say something. Although, I'm not even sure what I'd say if I got the chance.

Hey, Lo, sorry for being an ass. I'm just socially incapable of interacting with boys who show any interest in me. And by the way, guess what? I like you, too.

Not likely.

He'd probably walk away laughing his head off. Even I'm not so obtuse that I don't know that boys can only take so much. So it's over before anything can even start, which is probably a good thing in the grand scheme of things. At least, I keep telling myself that.

Even Jenna hasn't spoken to me for a couple days following the boat tour. It still stings something fierce that she told me in the changing room afterward that, deep down, maybe I haven't changed so much since freshman year, that maybe I am the same egoistic girl with a giant chip on her shoulder. I know I'm not that girl anymore, but everything about Lo makes me feel like a loose cannon. No one has ever made me feel as inside out as he does...like all my secrets are exposed to him, and it's making me crazy. It's not an excuse, but Jenna's right—this isn't like me.

Between feeling incredibly guilty and the voice of my princess alter ego, who coldly asserts that I shouldn't care what any humans think about me, I feel like my head is going to explode. I want to sink to the bottom of the ocean and sleep there for a week before having to deal with any of them again.

Especially him.

The boy with the eyes of my home's darkest depths.

The boy who barely deigns to look at me.

The boy who hates me.

"Did you talk to Echlios?" Speio whispers, interrupting my pity party.

"No. I left this morning without seeing him. Soren said he was out. Why? Did something happen?" I ask, watching the creases on his forehead deepening. At least whatever he says will take my mind off Lo.

"Not here," Speio whispers as the bell rings, signaling the end of the period and the school day. "Too many people. Five minutes outside."

Grabbing my backpack, I walk with Speio to my locker in silence. I barely notice any of the other kids—all I want is to know why Speio looks so cagey. He looks downright panicked. Someone from the hockey team shouts something to me about a party but it sails over my head, lost in the usual Friday afternoon chaos.

Jenna walks by with Sawyer but her face is still stony. Clearly, she hasn't forgiven me yet. A twitch at the corner of her mouth barely resembles an acknowledgment as we make brief eye contact. Sawyer shoots me a resigned smile—he knows better than to come between the two of us until we're ready to admit we're both bullheaded idiots.

My inner turmoil bubbles, human conscience and alien indifference battling. The words are on the tip of my tongue but I can't bring myself to say them as she pauses for a half breath, the invitation slim, but still waiting for my apology. But I can't give it. I can't admit that once more I've overstepped the boundaries of acceptable behavior over a ridiculous boy. I can't admit that he gets to me that much. And as guilty as I do feel, I'm sick of apologizing for a human shortfall that shouldn't even factor into my existence. Alien indifference wins out for once.

I bend to no human. Not even one who is my best friend.

Turning away to stash my books in my locker angrily, I wait until she and Sawyer have passed by before dragging Speio outside to a gnarled maple tree in a less crazy corner of the quad. I fold my arms across my chest.

"Fine, we're alone," I say, my irritation from the nonscene with Jenna laced through my words. "What's going on? What did Echlios say?"

"Ehmora is on the move. Up," Speio says with a surprised look at my tone.

"What does that mean?" I gasp, all the anger draining out of me along with my breath. "She's leaving Waterfell? Why?"

"You know what she wants, Riss. You're still the only living heir to the High Court...and you're going to come of age soon." Speio's gaze slips away from mine. "I don't think you're safe here anymore. I don't think any of us are."

"We can go deeper inland," I suggest. "Where she can't come after us." But I know the immediate horror on Speio's face is reflected in the halting nature of my words. Being apart from the ocean will kill us. Slowly and painfully. "Spey, at least we'll be safe, and if we disappear somewhere in the Rockies, maybe we'll have half a chance."

"We don't have a chance away from the sea, Riss. We'll be half alive, half dead." Speio leans in, his voice low. "I've heard stories of Aquarathi going inland and never being heard from again. Because they shriveled to nothing and died. Think about what you're saying for a second. If you get upset, where are you going to run to? A swimming pool? For how long? Our bodies can't exist away from the sea, you know that."

"I know. It was a dumb idea. I'll talk to Echlios and see what he says later," I say with a shiver as something cold and featherlight slips across my neck. All the cells in my body spin toward the sensation, like a touch of something liquid on my skin. "Did you feel something just then?" I ask Speio.

"No, why?"

"It's nothing," I say, doubting that I felt anything in the first place. "I must have imagined it. It felt like a pull of one of us, but not really. It was weird."

Speio flushes and mumbles something unintelligible. Out of the corner of my eye, I notice that Lo and Cara and the rest of her minions have made their way outside. They are laughing loudly and talking about going to the beach. I force myself not to react. Whatever—or whoever—Lo does is no longer of any concern to me.

I face Speio, commanding my gaze not to wander. "Sorry, what did you say?"

"I said it could be me," he repeats.

"What do you mean?"

He eyes me, his skin turning dull red. "Lately, I've been feeling tons of these random flashes. Soren told me that it's part of Dvija, because I haven't bonded yet. Maybe that's what you felt."

"Oh," I say, my attention now well and truly fixed on him. "Is it worse than what I felt before, that time at Trestles?"

"No, the same. Just more of it." He shrugs and takes a deep breath, rubbing the back of his neck with one hand. "It'll get less as I get older or go away eventually. As they say, right now, I am in prime Aquarathi breeding form."

"Eww! TMI," I say, and then laugh out loud.

At the sound, I sense someone's stare from behind us fall onto me like a solid weight. I glance to the side but it's not Lo, it's Cara, her pretty face spiteful. Lo is not even looking in my direction; he's talking to one of the other girls. With a flip of her hair, Cara throws her arm around Lo's waist but he dips down in the same second to tie his shoelace. I can't help my sense of immediate gratification at the look on her face as her hand flutters in midair like a lost appendage, only to fall lamely down to her side. I grin widely, ignoring the look of pure venom on Cara's face, and turn back to Speio.

"It's not TMI. It's just the way it is with us. We're not like them," he says, waving a hand at the kids milling around us. My grin fades away at the thought of Speio missing out on what should be his right—if we weren't stuck here because of me. He should be in Waterfell finding his mate. Instead, he's here as my companion because his parents are my Handlers.

"Spey," I begin thoughtfully, "could we…I mean, you and me…" I trail off at the violent color that surges in Speio's cheeks.

"No!" he says, and clamps his mouth shut as if he's trying

not to throw up. I try not to look too insulted even though the slap of his rejection is sharper than I'd expected.

"Wow, that's harsh, even for you, Speio."

He reddens to an almost neon hue, shaking his head wildly. "That's not what I meant. I mean, I don't think of you in that way. I mean, I like you and I feel the connection because you're our next queen, but it's not...you know...that."

"Thanks a lot," I tease, relaxing at his obvious discomfort. For a second, I feel that odd touch of water again on my skin like a sliver of cold in a warm pool. But this time, I figure it's definitely Speio, considering how flustered he is. "You sure know how to make a girl feel good. But what if I felt that way toward you? I mean, would you resist me then?"

I burst into laughter at the shocked look on his face. I'm joking by this point, my initial hurt fading to nothing, but Speio's response is serious. "No. I wouldn't be able to resist you, and you already know that. If you commanded it, I would have no choice."

"Jeez, Speio, I was just kidding," I say. "Relax. I would never make you do anything you didn't want. You know that I think of you as a brother. I was just joking. How could you even think I was serious?"

"It's not a joking matter."

"Okay," I say. "I get it. Don't offer to lessen best friend's pain. Fine."

Speio's face softens at my words and he reaches out his fingers to touch the back of my hand. It's an innocent gesture, but one that opens the floodgates to everything Speio is feeling inside...and everything he's fighting. Like the last time, his light touch morphs into something electric, slamming into my body like a jolt of pure energy. Everything he senses is echoed and magnified through the thin barrier of our human skins. My back arches against the tree behind me and I gasp aloud as blood thunders in my ears, a wave of desperate long-ing surging through me.

Not mine. Speio's.

He moves to pull his fingers away, but I flip my palm up-ward and grasp them tightly. I have to do something. I don't know if it's even possible in human form. I've certainly never done it on my own, but it's as easy as doing a glimmer, I tell myself. Only I'm pushing a part of me into someone else.

What's hard about that?

Closing my eyes and taking a deep breath to filter out the voices all around us, I find the calm spot deep in my center and thrust some of the stillness pooling there toward Speio, imitating the form of a glimmer-shadow. I have no idea if it's going to work, but I try, anyway. I'm careful to make sure it's just serenity and not any other emotion before I press the glimmer forward and into Speio. After a few seconds of feel-ing like a complete charlatan, his fingers grip mine tightly, his eyes widening.

It's working!

Through the glimmer, I can feel Speio's negative energy evening out. The pressure increases as I feel Speio sucking my energy into him, and suddenly, in the space of one heartbeat, I'm fighting to close it off before he drains it all out of me. I rip our fingers apart, my skin stinging as if the first layer of it has been peeled away. Speio jerks back a couple steps, breath-ing hard.

"What'd you do?" Speio asks in a dazed whisper, clutching his own hands to his chest.

"Sanctum," I gasp, bile churning in my stomach.

"Riss, in human form?" he whispers. "We don't even know if that's safe. Why would you do something like that?"

"I couldn't let you suffer any more because of me. Did it help?"

Speio stares at me with an undecipherable expression on his face. Then he smiles a small but sad smile, and leans forward to pull me into a hug. "Yes. It did, you crazy fool."

When he releases me, I slump back against the tree and slide to sit on the grass with my eyes closed, drained from the effort of what I've done. I open my eyes and look up and across the quad, my gaze of its own volition crashing into a dark navy one. Lo is studying me intently, his gaze not wavering when I meet it. Frowning, I feel the urge to spin around, because it's as if he's looking through me to something over my shoulder. But I know there's nothing there but a tree.

"What's wrong?" Speio says, noticing my frown and moving to squat beside me. He follows my gaze and turns back to me. I blink, and Lo is bending to listen to Cara as if he never looked over here in the first place. "Oh, I get it."

"No, it's nothing. It's complicated." I sigh, breathing heavily, my vision starting to spin. "Wow, Sanctum really packs a punch. I feel like I just swam a thousand miles in ten minutes." Speio's face tightens and I reassure him hastily. "Don't worry. I'm fine, just tired. I'm just glad it worked."

Speio stares at me for a second but doesn't push the point. "Well, in other news that may help certain things be less complicated, Echlios seems to think Lo is harmless, so you can do the girlie thing if you like. Lo checked out." Speio is actually embarrassed, but I'm too tied up in knots at the sound of Lo's name and too drained to tease him about it. By the "girlie thing" he means that I can consort with Lo or any other approved boy, should I so choose. "Just be careful. They can fall hard for us," Speio warns, and pauses as if he wants to say something more, his mouth opening and closing like a fish.

"What?" I ask.

"And you should know that Sanctum can work on them,

too. They're very susceptible to us and to our emotions, so be careful."

At Speio's words, I feel a slow flush invade my body at the thought of meshing any part of myself, human or otherwise, with Lo. "It's okay, you don't have to worry. I don't think he and I are going to be friends, anyway," I say, suddenly breathless.

"Why? I thought you were head over heels for him?" Speio says with a surprised look. "Wasn't he the one you were getting all wired about when we were talking about bonding?"

I'm mortified that I'd been so transparent to Speio. "No, he wasn't."

"Riss," he says gently. "I felt it in the water that day, remember? You don't have to hide your feelings from me. It's okay."

I sigh, my voice a whisper. "It doesn't matter, that's all done now."

"Well, maybe it's for the best," Speio says, watching me carefully. "He doesn't seem like your type, anyway. Way too arrogant."

I'd thought the same thing, too, but ever since voicing it to Lo that day on the boat, I'm not sure that *arrogant* is the right word to describe him. He's plenty confident, which makes him nothing like most boys his age, but he's more self-assured than anything.

"I don't have a type," I tell Speio. "And he's not arrogant. I think it's a front to cover something else." Like the loss of his family or having to move to another state. Self-disgust pours through me at how I'd treated him, even knowing the details of his private life. "And what do you know about types, anyway?"

"I know that someone like that isn't the right guy for you," Speio answers honestly. "Even if he got cleared by Echlios.

There's something strange about him, and maybe the arrogance is a part of that. He's too…quiet."

Quiet? That's a new one. I wouldn't exactly peg Lo as quiet, but I can see where Speio is coming from. Lo is very still. He studies people from the sidelines. He rarely rushes anywhere and even his speech is perfectly modulated. Like he's in stealth mode all the time. Oddly enough, I enjoy that about him. The stillness. It makes me think of calm water with not a single ripple on its surface, deep and full and infinite.

"I don't trust him," Speio is saying.

I stifle a grin, glancing at the group of them hooting loudly over something Lo had said. His own laugh is distinctive, pulling at parts of me I don't recognize. I shiver a little.

"Speio, you don't trust anyone," I say with a wry look.

"And for good reason."

"Like I said, you have nothing to worry about," I say, forcing a smile. "I'll see you at home for dinner, okay? You know how Soren wants us all to be at the table on time. Last time, you got grounded for being late." Speio and I exchange an amused look. Soren's notorious for her human rules—like sitting down to dinner like a normal human family and talking about our days, or doing human household chores like laundry or dishwasher duty, my nemesis. "I need to swing by the marine center first to change a shift."

"You sure you're okay to get home?" he asks. I nod, and he rumples my hair before standing and stretching. He stares at me with an awkward expression and shoves his hands in his pockets. I wait silently, knowing that he has something else to say. "Riss? Thanks for what you did. I know it took a lot out of you, but it means more than you know that you would do that for me."

I smile, a real one this time. "Don't waste it. Go on a date or something."

Speio snorts, grinning, and walks away. I watch his tall, lanky form disappear around the corner to the parking lot, his white-blond hair blowing into his face. For a second, I wonder why I can't be interested in Speio. He's not a bad person, and I know he cares about me even if it isn't that way, as he so succinctly put it. It would make everything so much easier— for him and for me, especially when Dvija happens, which for me will be a hundred times worse than Speio's. And if worse comes to worst, he said I could command him. I blanch at the thought. I could never compel someone to love me, no matter how desperate I get.

Most of the students have left, including Cara and Lo, and as much as I want to sit there for the next hour, I need to get myself somewhere safe. I need to get home or to the ocean… whichever comes first. Standing on shaky knees, I grasp the rough bark of the maple tree for support as hot white dots fill my vision. The earth beneath my feet is tilting as if I'm standing on a surfboard, and I'm desperately trying to keep my balance. Taking a deep breath, I focus on my Jeep and getting to it.

But I've barely taken ten steps before the ground starts to feel as if it has the consistency of a fat marshmallow. I grab the side of a nearby lamppost for support as my knees buckle underneath me. I should have gone home with Speio, but it's too late now. There's no way that I can drive myself, so I dig into my pocket for my cell phone to call Echlios, but my fingers are oily with sweat, slippery and unreliable. The phone slides from my fingers.

Darkness hovers at the edges of my vision as I sink to the lawn, trying to find my fallen phone. The white dots take over, and suddenly, I can't even breathe. Not caring who's watching I splay my palms over the lush green grass and start to suck the moisture out of it into my body until nothing but brownish-yellow patches remain beneath my hands. It's still not enough.

The skies are clear with not a rain cloud in sight. Commanding clouds would take too much energy. Water must call to water, and I barely have enough to keep my body from failing completely. I glance at my fingers through blurred vision.

Sanctum in human form had drained me more than weeks without the ocean would have. The skin of my hands and forearms is already flaking and taking on an odd gray-green color, with tendrils of black curling upward through it like poison. For a second, I wonder what I'll look like if I die. Would my human skin slough off completely? Would I shrivel to nothing? Would my remains be sent to a lab for dissection and study? Would I endanger those I love and leave behind?

That's the thought that forces me into sluggish action.

Desperately, I reach for the phone lying on its face at my side but I can't even see to dial the number. The greenish pallor of my arms is spreading, the black lines spiraling upward. I need more water. But making one last effort to take from the life around me is futile—even the air is as dry as bone. My fingers curl into stone claws and I close my eyes, struggling to swallow my congealing saliva.

This is it, I think. My last stupid decision will have cost me my life.

"Riss? NERISSA!" The voice sounds like it's coming from everywhere at once. It's loud, stabbing into my head like needles. "Oh, my God, what happened?"

Through the slits of my eyes, all I can see is a dark shadow blocking the fading light from the skies. The voice is an echo of an echo. My brain won't even process the identity of its owner. An arm slides under my head and the voice speaks into a phone. All I can hear are the words *emergency* and *school parking lot*.

Slow-motion panic. No, no ambulance, no hospitals, I want to say but my mouth refuses to cooperate. I don't want to die, but I don't want to be locked up under a microscope, either. What kind of life would that be? I crack open my mouth and pain rockets through me. Warm salty brine trickles into my mouth. I've ripped the skin off my lips.

"Try not to move. It's okay," the voice says, pressing something cool against my burning mouth. Warm fingers wind into the crooked numbness of mine. "Everything's going to be okay. I won't let anything happen to you."

It's the last thing I hear before I give in to the darkness.

8
No More Secrets

My head feels groggy. My lips are dry and crusted with salt, but I can move my tongue and I can swallow, albeit painfully. Drawing my lower lip between my teeth, I wince at the sting and the sour salty remnants of dried blood.

I'm alive. Somehow.

I'm in my own room, a warm rush of air flowing in through the open French doors. Bright bits of colored sea glass spatter the ceiling, making me blink against the orange sun reflecting through them like jewels. I look outside. The sun is just setting over the tops of the palm trees and I can see the pool gleaming golden just beyond the steps of the patio. I want nothing more than to hurl myself into its comforting arms, but as I heft myself to my elbow, I realize that there's someone else lying next to me in the bed, covered head to toe beneath the sheet.

A warm rush invades my body. I know it isn't Speio, because if he had been the one to rescue me last night, I would have sensed him instantly. No, my savior had been someone human, but someone who'd thought to bring me straight to Echlios and not to a hospital. My belly plummets immediately.

Please don't be him, my inner voice is screaming.

I tug on the edge of the sheet, my stomach clenched in a grapefruit-size knot, and I'm wishing with everything inside of me that it's not who I think it is. I'd take anyone—even Cara—over Lo seeing me in the feeble state I was in.

And so obviously not who I'm pretending to be.

My skin would have been spongy and wrinkled, the consistency of a dehydrated jellyfish. And I don't even want to think about what my eyes would have been like uncovered, with their startling, scary irises. At that stage of dehydration, I wouldn't have been able to control the protective camouflage over them, the one that mimics the appearance of human eyes. It would have been a dead giveaway that I'm not anything remotely human.

The sheet slips back in response to my gentle tug and I'm holding my breath. But it's not sandy hair that greets me, it's a tangle of glossy auburn. Jenna. I exhale with a curious mixture of relief and disappointment, which bothers me because I don't know what I would have done if it had been Lo in my bed. But my bittersweet relief is short-lived as reality hits me.

Jenna...

She is a gazillion times worse than Lo. I don't even know how I would begin to confess the truth about myself or that I'd lied to her for so many years. Most humans don't take well to deceit, I learned early on, especially those of the best-friend variety. I wonder how much Echlios has told her. He must have said enough for her to allow her to stay with us. But then again, Jenna isn't exactly clueless—she is at the top of our class with an above average IQ. It's one of the reasons I gravitated to her once I got over myself sophomore year. She isn't vapid like most of the girls in our class who have money and good breeding in spades but not brains.

Which means I can't fake my way out of this one.

Sighing, I shimmy my body with tiny movements to the edge of the bed. With some luck, I can avoid any discussion until I've had the chance to think things over, or at least to talk to Echlios. I'm just swinging my legs over the side when I feel the mattress dip behind me.

"Hey," Jenna says sleepily. "You're awake."

"Yes." I don't want to face her but I do. I'm not sure what I was expecting but her face is the same as it has ever been… like an open book, no judgment, just compassion. "So you found me yesterday?"

Jenna throws me a groggy, confused look. "Yesterday?"

"At school?"

"Riss, that was last week." Her voice is quiet but her eyes become more alert as she sits up and props herself up on two pillows, watching me intently. "How much do you remember?"

I shake my head, frowning. "Not much. Voices. Yours, I guess, until just now when I woke up. Exactly how long was I out?"

"Five days. It's Wednesday."

"And you've been here this whole time?" I ask, frowning.

She nods and yawns. "Sort of. I stayed the first night, and I came back this afternoon after school. It was pouring rain and Soren didn't think I should drive home, so she called my mom and I guess I fell asleep. Don't worry, everyone thinks you're sick, and I've been helping out."

"And Echlios and Soren are okay with that?" I ask.

Jenna's face twists into an all-too-familiar stubborn expression and I have to force myself not to grin in automatic response. "They had to be," she says. "I wouldn't take no for an answer. Speio tried to remove me bodily and I was forced to retaliate. With my hockey stick." She grins at my gasp. "Let's just say that we're barely on speaking terms but he backed off."

"You hit Speio?"

"Well, I didn't actually connect, but he got the message," she says. "He's got pretty fast reflexes, that kid. Kind of like you." Her voice trails off, this time her eyes dropping to the bed as if she suddenly can't look at me.

"Like me?" My words are barely whispers in the sudden sticky silence.

"Yes." I remain silent, unsure of what to say...of what she wants me to say, so I wait instead. Jenna raises her eyes to mine, the words flowing out of her like hot unwanted lava. "I'm glad you're okay. Echlios said you were going to be, but when I asked him what happened, he said that you had to tell me. That he didn't have permission to reveal anything on your behalf," she says with a lingering look at my face and arms, which makes me desperate to cover myself under the sheet once more. "So you want to tell me what kind of secret rock royalty you are? The love child of Steven Tyler and Lady Gaga, mayhap?" she asks.

Laughter bubbles out of me at her wry expression and I fling myself back across the bed into her arms. "Have I told you just how awesome you are?"

"Yeah," Jenna says, hugging me back tightly. "Which is why you're going to tell me everything. Starting right now."

Sitting back on my haunches, I make a sad face. "How about some food first at least? Nearly dead girl is starving."

"Okay, fine. But no more delays," Jenna says. "And we should probably tell the others that you're awake."

"They already know."

"What? But—"

I smile. "They would have known the minute I regained consciousness. Soren's already got something to eat for us outside. Come on. I'll tell you everything you need to know. Or at least put your wildest imaginings to rest."

"They're pretty wild," she warns me. "I mean, your eyes a week ago were like something out of *The Exorcist*." Jenna makes a face at my snort. "Seriously, I almost took you to a priest instead of to Echlios."

My reunion with Echlios, Soren and Speio is quiet but I can see the relief in their expressions, especially Speio's. I'm not sure he would have told them about Sanctum, which was risky on my part, but Echlios is far from foolish. It would surprise me if he hadn't already guessed. I'm sure I'll get the lecture later but at least he won't say anything while Jenna is there.

I make a sound that is like a high-pitched pulse followed by a low chirp and some clicks. Echlios returns a similar sequence and Jenna stares at us with wide eyes. I smile reassuringly in her direction and usher her out to the patio table.

"What was that?"

"A kind of language," I say, sipping on a glass of water and chewing on a piece of yellowtail sashimi. "Want some?"

"Oh." Jenna takes some of the sushi and stares at me uneasily.

We eat in silence until the sun has completely disappeared and the twilight sky is flickering with starry dots. I'm a little blown away by Jenna's reserve. If the situation were reversed, I'd be jumping down her throat and demanding that she confess everything to me at once. A small part of me recognizes that, despite her bravado, Jenna may be terrified.

I push my plate away and slide my chair back. In seconds, a silent Soren is there to clear away the remaining food and our utensils. Jenna's eyes flicker again with an undecipherable expression, moving from Soren to me, and then back again.

"What's with them?" she asks.

"What do you mean?"

A curious frown. "The way they treat you with complete

deference. I never noticed before. Like you're their boss or something."

"Something like that," I say gently. "Join me at the pool?"

I don't go in but sit on the edge to dangle my bare legs into the warm water. Jenna sits next to me, and even in the shadowy gloom I can see the tension her profile. I like the dark—it will make it easier to tell her the truth about myself. And I don't want to look at her reaction. I don't want to see just how scared she is of me.

"First of all," I say with a small laugh. "I'm not demon-spawn with triple sixes tattooed on my head."

"Good to know," she says. I can hear the smile in her voice and breathe a sigh of relief.

"Second of all, I'm Nerissa, your friend." I need her to understand that most of all. "And I'm a girl. Like you."

"Well, not exactly like me."

I shoot a look in her direction but she's watching the water, swishing her feet back and forth. "No, not exactly."

"Look, Riss," she says. "Stop beating around the bush and trying to figure out a way how to say this gently because you're trying to protect me. I saw you. I saw your weird freaky-looking eyes. I felt your boneless body. I saw you change before my eyes. I know that you're not…just a normal girl. Are you some kind of witch? A fairy? A shape-shifter? I promise you I'll be fine. Just tell me what you are so I can stop driving myself crazy trying to figure out why my best friend is not normal!"

I can hear the violent edge of tears in her voice, and that's what shakes me. I don't know what I am so afraid of. Jenna isn't going to run away. She's already stuck around after seeing my entire body collapsing in on itself.

Then why am I so afraid that I'm going to lose her once she knows the truth?

"I'm not a witch," I say softly. It would almost be easier to lie. People in this world choose to believe in odd supernatural things. "I'm not a fairy, either. Those things don't exist, Jenna, and I wish it were that simple. The truth is, I'm not like you. I'm not human at all. I'm...something else." I almost choke on the last word, but I force it out. "Alien."

Jenna turns toward me. "Alien as in extraterrestrial or resident alien from Chimichanga in some undiscovered country?"

"The first one."

Now I have her full attention. I can feel her eyes on me like lasers in the shadows. "What? You mean like the kids from the *Roswell* reruns?"

I want to laugh at her connections but that's as good an example as any. I chew on my lower lip. "Sort of, but they were humanoid. And they're actors on a TV show. We're not."

"We?"

"Me, Echlios, Soren and Speio."

Her gasp is loud in the silence. Slipping back the lens film over my eyes, I can see the expression on her face as if it's bright daylight. One of the benefits of being Aquarathi—we see in pitch-black darkness. "So are you guys more like the alien visitors in *V,* then?"

"Seriously, Jenna," I say. "What's with the obscure television series?"

"They're my only points of reference," she says, making wild gestures with her arms. "It's not like I've seen an actual alien in real life. And now you're telling me that you're one. That you're all freaking aliens." Her voice is shrill. "Do you know how crazy that sounds?"

"Jeez, stop swinging. You're going to punch me in the eye," I say, grabbing her wrist gently. She jerks her arm out of my grip as if my touch is acid and studies her wrist carefully in an almost scientific manner. I try not to let her rejection sting but it does. My tone is sour. "What are you looking for, anyway? My touch isn't going to hurt you all of a sudden, Jenna. You're not going to melt into a pool of your own bones."

"What? Can you see me in the dark?" My silence is my assent. "Christ, you can totally see me in the dark. Is that one of your alien abilities?" She peers at me, her expression amazed. Her voice takes on an excited edge. "Your eyes have gone all glittery. What else can you do? Can you read my mind like Edward Cullen?"

I roll my eyes. We've moved from TV to *Twilight*. Awesome. A part of me would have preferred for her to be freaked out instead of so logically curious. "Come on. Now you're just being theatrical. No, I can't read your mind. I'm only a different species, not some paranormal creature that doesn't exist."

"Only a different species…" she splutters. "My best friend is an alien. It sounds like some B-movie title." She shakes her head as if the truth of it is suddenly hitting her. But she's seen me. Her brain can't dispute the evidence she's seen with her own two eyes.

Despite her curiosity, I know that my admissions have to be overwhelming for her. We've always known about the existence of humans. After all, our histories tell the stories of how our ancestors fled to this world from our dying planet. But the humans don't know about us.

"I'm still your best friend. That's not going to change," I say. "And, Jenna, you can't tell anyone. Not even Sawyer."

A sniff. "I know."

"You okay?"

"Yes. Just trying to process it all," she says. "So I'm guessing you guys like water."

"More like need it," I say.

She studies the water in the pool. "Echlios told me you were suffering from something called hypertonic dehydration. But

I'd never seen or heard anything like that so I looked it up on Google. It's a combination of extreme water and salt loss." She turns to look at me, and even though I know she can't see me, I keep my body very still. "They had you in the pool for a lot of the time. Like the bottom of the pool. I was so confused the first time that I jumped in to get you out." Her confession startles me. "But Soren stopped me, saying that it was the only thing that would save you. That's when I faced the reality that you were...not you."

"But you still stayed."

"You're my friend, no matter what," Jenna says, her voice a soft whisper. "Anyway, after the pool situation, Echlios said he didn't have permission to tell me more than he did. They're not the same as you are, are they?"

"Why do you ask?"

"Just observation from watching Soren before. And the fact that they all looked terrified when they came to get us at the school. And Echlios kept saying 'my lady,' which still makes me want to crack up." Jenna snorts.

I laugh and swirl my feet in the water. I can feel my skin sucking in the salt like a greedy sponge. "Don't worry, I feel the same." The silence stretches into an awkward heaviness between us. It's a first for the two of us—we never have any kind of silences, awkward or otherwise. Knowing that I can see her, Jenna stares in my direction with an expectant expression on her face. "Okay, my turn, I guess, but first, one last question. Are you sure you're...truly okay with all of this?"

"Yes. I'm sure," Jenna says. "I'm not going anywhere, Riss. And you have my word—I won't say anything to anyone. I promise."

I take a deep breath, knowing I'm breaking one of my father's hard and fast laws: humans must never know about us. In fact, any one of my people caught breaking the law will face exile, which is a death sentence. Exile from the trench where we made our home on Earth means fair game to other ocean predators…ones far worse than we are. And any humans who have the misfortune to see us in our true form must be killed. I shiver at the thought.

But this situation is different. Jenna saved me. Surely that has to mean something.

After a searching look, I begin to speak. "My people are called Aquarathi. We came to this planet thousands of years ago when our own planet was destroyed. It was called Sana, and it was a planet similar to this one with immense oceans and slivers of land, only in a different solar system. What's wrong?" I ask, noticing her face.

"Nothing," she whispers. "I mean, you have no idea how outlandish this all sounds."

"I know," I say gently. "You sure you want to do this now, Jenna? We could wait…talk later or something."

"No, I'm fine. It's just so insane, the whole different solar system thing. I mean, it's not like I don't believe there isn't intelligent life out there but seeing it—you—in the flesh right in front of me is mind-blowing. Like I'm going to blink and wake up in my own room kind of mind-blowing," she says. "Keep going, I'll be fine. I want to know everything."

"Okay. Do you understand how evolution works?" I ask her, and she nods. "Okay, so evolution suggests that all living things evolved from one single common ancestor, with billions of years between us, and that we are all connected. Right?"

"Yes."

"Well, on Sana, there were two main sentient species—the tetrapods that evolved into hominids, and the chordates— aquatic vertebrates—that evolved into us, the Aquarathi. The hominids, like you, occupied the land bits, and we coexisted with them for many years. But things began to change as the hominids got greedy. They wanted to control us and we resisted, so they poisoned the ocean, thinking to enslave us. Hundreds of thousands of Aquarathi died."

I pause to take a breath, knowing that what I've just told her is a lot to take, but despite her earlier interruption, Jenna is listening intently, her face animated. I continue. "But the people were stupid because when the waters started dying, so did the lands. A few insurgents were on our side, but it wasn't enough to stop the tide and the spread of toxicity. Even the air turned poisonous." My voice is thick. "Sana is a dead planet now."

"What did you do?" Jenna whispers. "I mean, you're here so you must have gotten out."

"The people working with us located a few planets with a similar topology, but none of them could support life, none with oxygen. According to our historical scrolls, all the probes they sent out came back with negative data. But in the past few days when we were on the brink of extinction, one probe came back showing a planet with suitable oxygen levels." I gesture with my arm to our surroundings.

Jenna fills in the blank. "Here."

"Yes. There weren't many of us left, barely a few hundred. And even less of the hominids. The reigning Aquarathi king at the time taught the remaining survivors how to morph into a humanlike form to make the journey. And that's how we were able to come here."

"In a spaceship?" Jenna asks hoarsely.

"Yes, millennia ago. We made our home down in the deepest depths of your oceans. Unfortunately, the people who escaped with us didn't survive long. They couldn't integrate with the land dwellers of this world, and in the end, the levels of carbon dioxide, though minimal, were enough to kill them all. The Aquarathi, however, adapted to survive. And we stayed hidden for thousands of years."

"But you're here," Jenna blurts out. "And you look totally human to me."

"Our ancestors didn't want to make the same mistake they made on Sana. They had to be involved, but only from the sidelines, just to make sure that we would be safe as a species. We've chosen to remain in hiding because of what happened before, but each heir is mandated to learn about your culture during a four-year initiation cycle in human form."

"Heir?"

This is the part I'm uncomfortable with. I'm trying to think of the best way to say it to Jenna when I hear—sense—someone approach behind us. Echlios, Soren and Speio have all been listening intently, and I can feel their collective distrust that Jenna knows our secret. But it was my call to reveal it, not theirs. I nod imperceptibly to Speio that it's okay for him to join us.

"Hey, Jenna," Speio says in a soft voice. At his voice, Jenna jumps nearly a few inches into the air, a fair feat given the fact that she's sitting. Speio slides down to sit next to her. In the darkness, I see her eyes widen at Speio's nearness, now that she knows that he, too, isn't human. Her fear is evident without seeing it reflected in her expression—I can sense it from the water rushing around in her veins.

"Hi," she manages after a second, struggling to compose herself. She glances quickly in my direction, as if recalling our conversation about my ability to see in the dark, but I look away hastily. "So what were you saying about the Aqathi heir?"

"Aquarathi," Speio corrects gently. "And Nerissa is the heir. She is the next queen."

"What? Queen?" she splutters, mouth agape, glaring at me. "You're a queen? And you didn't say anything?"

"Yes. Or I will be, if and when I return."

Jenna doesn't miss a beat. "What do you mean *if?*"

I ignore Speio's warning glare across the top of Jenna's head. I know that he thinks I'm revealing too much, but I trust Jenna. She's the only human I've ever trusted, and she deserves to know the truth. All of it.

"My father was killed for his throne."

"Omigod, Riss. I'm so sorry!" Jenna says, hugging me with one arm.

"Before he died, he sent a message for me never to go back there. So I've been here this whole time." I pause. "I didn't want to go back, so I stayed. Speio and his parents, too, because of me." I smile sadly in the darkness, my voice soft. My words are more for me than her. "You were right when you called me selfish. More than you know."

"I don't believe that for a second."

I smile at her fierce loyalty but shake my head. "Thanks, but it's true."

Jenna stands and walks to the edge of the patio to turn on the fairy lights decorating the trees at the edge of the property. She stops for a second to stare at Echlios and Soren, who are both in the kitchen, being very careful about not looking in our direction. Quietly, I hear Soren whisper in our language, asking whether I'm okay. The sound of it is the whisper of a pulse on the wind, and nothing that Jenna or any other human can hear. I click back that everything is fine just as Jenna turns around and makes her way closer to the pool. She doesn't resume her position between Speio and me, but instead leans against a table a few feet away on my left, studying us in the light.

"So my best friend is an alien sea princess," she says in a soft voice, "who transforms into human form but can't go back home just yet." I recognize the tone of when she's in hunker-down, game-face mode, and I bite back a grin. She'll assess the facts logically, as impossible as they may sound, no matter what. "Where is home exactly?"

"Ever heard of the Mariana Trench?" I ask her, and she nods. Of course she has. She's Jenna, *Jeopardy!* champion of the world. "Well, it's the deepest part of your oceans. We make our home there…where we're safe, untouched by humans."

"But you come here to learn about us if you're the heir? Like you did."

"Yes. To not make the same mistakes of the past."

"But you're stuck here because your father was killed," Jenna says.

"Yes."

"Are you're not going back?"

"I don't know," I answer honestly. "I have people there still, but it's complicated. There are others who want us all dead. Speio and his family most of all, because of their loyalty to me."

Jenna gulps, glancing at Speio, but he's staring at the pool surface lost in his own thoughts. She moves to sit again next to me at the edge of the pool, crossing her legs beneath her. Her eyes narrow as she studies my face, fascinated. Belatedly, I remember that the protective film is no longer over my own alien eyes, so I blink to engage it. It's kind of like the nictitating membrane of a shark that goes over its eyes when it's in attack mode, only ours is more of a defense mechanism to protect us from discovery.

"No," she says. "Leave them the way they are. Please."

I comply but frown. I know what she's seeing—the pale gold sclera, normally the white part of the human eye, and the larger than normal multicolored irises rimmed by an electric gold ring. Does she want to remind herself that she's not talking to something human? Will she look at me differently now that she knows what I am? Aware that I'm second-guessing the actions of my friend, I silence my inner demons.

"They're beautiful, your eyes," she whispers after a while. "But definitely not human. Anyone could see that. But even so, you could be wearing psychedelic contacts or something. I mean, you look so normal otherwise." Her gaze flutters to my arms, torso and legs. "I've seen you in the locker room after hockey games. You look just like me. Just like all the other girls."

"We mimic," I say. "To blend in."

"Mimic?"

"I can manipulate the water in my body into any form I wish, for short periods."

"Any form?"

"Yes, but human is the simplest."

Jenna tips her head to one side, chewing on her lip as if scared to ask the question lurking on her lips, but eventually she does. "What do you really look like?"

"Are you sure you're ready to see that?" Speio's voice is cool. He doesn't trust that Jenna won't go running to the local authorities and out us all. But he doesn't know her like I do. Every drop of water in me knows that I can trust this girl.

"She's ready," I say, meeting Jenna's eyes. Speio sucks air through his teeth, a disrespectful gesture that I ignore, and stalks back into the house. But it will be better without him. I stare at Jenna, and she holds my gaze without flinching.

"He doesn't like that you told me, does he?" she asks. I shake my head.

"Do you trust me?" I whisper.

She nods. I meet her eyes for a long time before I decide both our fates—hers for knowing, mine for telling. Then I slip into the water, feeling the weight of human bones inside of me dissolve into water and then elongate once more into the delicate skeleton that shapes my Aquarathi form. Like humans, we are more liquid than anything else but our spinal column is similar to humans. That's where the similarity ends. The rest of our skeleton expands outward like coral webbed fins, hard but soft at the same time.

My bones strengthen, cracking into place under skin that's transforming into something hard and brilliant. The shape of my face twists outward, my limbs bending inward as my hide pulls and tightens over sleek muscle, shimmering into scaly, impervious existence.

I no longer resemble anything human.

9
True Forms

"Holy shit!" Jenna mutters, her eyes wide, stepping back until she's pressed up against the sliding glass doors leading out of my room to the patio. "You go big."

Taking up half the pool, my metamorphosed bulk is five times as large as a standard human male…the size of a small whale. Only I'm no whale. I glimpse my reflection in the mirrored glass that Jenna is pressed against.

A creature with an elegantly curved neck cresting above a torso covered in burnished golden scales, each the size of a silver dollar, stares back at me. Its eyes are glowing multicolored orbs, the pupil barely a black fang slicing through the middle. In the mirrored glass, the creature is so bright that it appears to be glowing.

I tilt my neck, stretching upward, and the reflection follows.

My body is muscular but slender, with a thin iridescent purple-finned membrane that is interspersed with spines extending along the entire ridge of my back to a fanlike tail. Two wide, lustrous fins extend on either side of my upper torso, bearing down into clawed forearms. The shorter spines along my back lengthen on my head and curve backward in a circular fan, while shorter ones dot my pointed nose with frill-like tendrils on either side of my snout. A ridge of sharp, coral-like thorns crowns my brow...the mark of an Aquarathi heir.

Jenna still hasn't moved but I keep my jaws tightly closed—no need to frighten her more than necessary. I want to encourage her to come closer, but my mouth won't allow me to form any human words so I click for Soren. She appears immediately, glancing from me to Jenna. Her eyes are guarded but, unlike Speio, she knows her place with respect to my decisions. I speak again directly to Soren, and although I know Jenna can't understand our language, I see her frowning, trying to separate the sounds.

"She says to tell you not to be afraid," Soren says, making Jenna jump. "And to come closer when you are ready. She won't hurt you."

"I know she won't," Jenna says bravely, but I can still hear the nearly inaudible waver in her throat. She's terrified.

And rightly so—after all, I'm what most humans would call a sea monster. I'm the sea serpent that historians have written about for years, the fiend that has capsized whole ships and devoured sailors by the mouthful.

Well, not me, but certainly others like myself.

Like any existing species, we have our rogues and our rebels, the ones who blatantly go against the orders of the High Court. It's the only thing that Ehmora and my father had agreed on—the rogues had to be controlled. There haven't been any recent attacks, but still, human history has enough accounts and sightings for us not to disappear into oblivion.

Some of us can't help it—by the very nature of what we are, we draw the unsuspecting to us. Fish, animals, even humans. Any invertebrates. We are predators and they are prey. And if humans see us, they have to be dealt with.

But not Jenna, she's different.

I wait, watching her carefully even though I'm starting to get a little claustrophobic. In my true form, I don't enjoy being confined in a four-walled pool. I needed to be in the open ocean, unconstrained. I flex my fins, making the line of multicolored membrane ripple along my back like a cat arching. Jenna jumps and flees backward about three feet.

I shoot her what I think is an apologetic look but her eyes widen to the size of saucers and she edges back even more. Turns out my look of apology has more of an effect like "you look delicious" instead of "I'm sorry." I sigh and click to Soren.

"Come," Soren tells Jenna gently, leading her to the side of the pool. Never a coward, Jenna steps forward despite her fear, her eyes on mine the entire time. This time I remain perfectly still and don't attempt any human expressions.

"Your eyes were beautiful in human form, but now they're like giant jewels," Jenna murmurs, standing close. "Does everyone like you have eyes that color?"

I respond to Soren, who translates. "She says no. You must put your hand against her hide," Soren says. "She can speak to you directly with a physical connection between you."

Gamely, Jenna stretches out a hand to touch the glistening scales of my side, barely grazing my purple-and-gold-striped underbelly. Her fingers splay against my scales.

"You're so warm!" she blurts out. "I expected you to be cold with the scales and everything."

"We run to hot temperatures," Soren offers. "That's why we choose to be so close to the planet's core, where it's the hottest. We like heat."

"Oh."

I push the water in my body toward Jenna's fingers, feeling the water in hers pulsing against her fingertips. Her eyes widen as her fingers seal like magnets to my skin. She moves to pull away but Soren stalls her with a gentle palm placed atop her own.

"It's only a water connection," she says to Jenna. "It won't hurt you. It's so she can speak to you."

Can you hear me?

"Yes," Jenna breathes, her voice full of wonder. "It's like hearing you underwater. Sort of muffled but I can still hear you. Weird. How do you do that?"

I cock my head at her. *Sound comes from vibration. In Aquarathi form, I just manipulate it via the water in my body to your body.*

"Wow, I didn't know you could do that."

Well, humans couldn't but water responds to us differently...and to me in particular.

"Because you're a queen?" she says.

Yes.

Jenna slides her hand slowly against my side and the sensation is oddly comforting, like a human hug. I've never let a human touch me while in Aquarathi form before, and as soothing as it is, it makes me uncomfortable. The darker, alien part of me views any human touch on my Aquarathi skin as threatening. Without thinking, I make a hurried flutter of clicks and pulses in Soren's direction.

But before Soren can react to my commands, Jenna's eyes bug out of her skull as she tears her hand away from my side to cover her ears and falls to her knees clutching her head. With a sound like a snapping rubber band, I transform deftly back into human form and climb out of the pool soaking wet to crouch beside Jenna. She's staring at her palm that's smeared with red. A thin stream of pale red liquid is trickling from one of her ears.

My voice is a shriek as I reach for a nearby towel to cover myself. "Soren! What's wrong?" I glance at Soren, who is dabbing at Jenna's affected ear with a piece of tissue. The fluid is watery and has already stopped trickling but my voice grows even more shrill. "Is she going to be okay?"

"She'll be fine. Her eardrum couldn't take the vibration of our language. I think it's only a rupture that will heal on its own in a few weeks, but I'll get her something for the pain." Soren looks at me gently. "You couldn't have known, my lady."

Soren's wrong. I should have known and I should have been more careful. I chew on my lower lip, biting hard so that blood fills my mouth. "Jenna, are you okay?" I whisper. "I'm so sorry. I didn't realize the connection would amplify the sounds of our language. I thought the frequencies were different."

Stricken, I fold my best friend into a hug. Jenna hugs me back even more tightly. "I like you better human," she says against my hair. Her voice is strong but quiet. "I mean, you're beautiful the other way, too, but I like you this way. I'm fine, Riss. Don't worry. Not much worse than getting clocked in the ear with a hockey stick."

"You sure?" I ask, pulling away to look at her face, doubtful. "Are you really okay?"

"I'll be fine. It was weird, like a popping sensation, but the pain isn't so bad anymore. I have sensitive ears, anyway. Plus, I've had worse scuba diving. Riss, it's okay. Trust me! Anyway, I really want to talk about you." Now Jenna is trying hard to comfort me, which only makes me chew my lip harder. But I take her words as they're meant.

My smile is tiny. I blink. "You probably won't be able to dive for a few weeks."

"All for a good cause," she says with a shaky grin. "Your eyes are back. I like your real ones but they're a bit freaky. Psychedelic!" Jenna runs her fingers down my arm. "Your skin even feels like skin. I mean, it's so weird seeing you like this and knowing that you're not really human. Do you have blood like we do?"

"Not really," I say. "Aquarathi blood is an oily fluid, far thicker than blood. It's the reason my skin is so glowy sometimes, especially if I'm happy. You know like when I get too much sun, and you always ask whether I put on bronzer? That's the real reason for it."

Jenna laughs, shaking her head. "You're unreal. I mean, it's all unreal. You look just like us, but underneath, you're... something else."

I smile wryly. "Like the aliens from *V,* right? What were they again? Reptiles under human skin?"

"But you're not a reptile. Right?"

I shrug. "Depends on your definition of reptile. We're not cold-blooded."

"Isn't that an oxymoron? A warm-blooded reptile?" Jenna says with that look on her face as if she's searching through her Rolodex of a brain for the answer. Sure enough, her eyes light up. "Wait a sec! I think I do remember reading in *National Geographic* a couple years ago that some extinct marine reptiles were warm-blooded." She frowns. "Mosasaurs, I think. Serpentine prehistoric creatures."

"Honestly, you're like a walking encyclopedia, Jenna." I roll my eyes.

"That makes sense," she continues, more to herself than to me. "I mean, based on what you were saying about branches of evolution earlier, maybe your species evolved differently in your solar system. Unlike the mosasaurs, you didn't go extinct where you came from—instead, you evolved to the intelligent and transformative state you're in now." She studies me with new eyes. "Just amazing," she breathes.

"Okay, Einstein, slow down," I say, glancing over my shoulder to see if any of the others are in hearing distance. "Hence the reason no one can know about us. We'll be hunted to the point of extinction here if humans find out we exist. You can't say anything to anyone, Jenna, I mean it."

"I know, Riss."

She holds a tendril of my hair in between her fingertips. "Now that I know what you really look like, I see that your hair is the same color as your—" She breaks off awkwardly.

"It's okay, you can say it...scales," I say. "It's our identifying marks. See how Speio's hair is white-gold? His body is that color with emerald-green fins. Like his eyes."

"Wow, that's cool." She glances inside the house, thinking for a second. "So Echlios would be dark brown with silver fins?"

"Close, his body is actually a flame red, but that color hair would be too attention drawing. His hair is dyed brown. Soren is a lighter gold than I am, with green fins like Speio's."

Jenna grins widely. "So I guess if I were Aquarathi like you, I'd have a dark red body and light blue fins? That just sounds pretty!" She stares at me for a second. "Do they have the same eyes like you do? With the film thing?"

"Yes. Our eye color is too bright, too jewel-toned with the weird irises. Plus, we need the extra layer of protection from your sun's light." At her look, I clarify my statement. "Down in the trench, it's pretty dark, which is why I was able to see you in the darkness before. But in the underwater caves where we make our home, the cave walls are lined with different minerals that glow off our bodies so there's plenty of light to see. But still, it's not like being exposed to direct sunlight."

"Like your room!" she says brightly, and then her voice turns wistful. "It sounds beautiful."

"It's home," I say simply.

"I noticed when you changed back into human form that you were kind of glowing a little bit."

I grin. "You mean like this?" Stretching out my hand, I make the bluish-green fireworks burst along my forearm under my skin, and watch Jenna's eyes go wide until she, too, is grinning as widely as I am.

"That's wicked cool," she says. "What is that?"

"You mean you don't know?" I tease her. "The technical term for it is bioluminescence. Nearly all deep-sea marine creatures can make some kind of neural light, and it's no different with us. You know that blue-green glow you see in the water at night sometimes?" Jenna nods, completely entranced by my showy display. "Well, that's us sometimes. Other bioluminescent microorganisms in the water switch on in response to us like electricity. Pretty cool, right?"

"Are you kidding me? It's more than just cool, it's freaking awesome!"

Jenna's voice is as animated as her face, and now I know for sure that the worst has passed. She's more interested in functional capabilities, which means she has accepted the fact that she's in a house full of migratory aliens from another galaxy who are living on her planet and pretending to be human. And that makes me incredibly relieved, because if she hadn't been able to accept my secret, she would have had to die.

And that's one thing that I wouldn't have been able to circumvent, not even for her sake.

"So what other awesome things can you do?" she asks, suspending the dark turn of my thoughts.

"Not much else," I say with a modest smile. "I'm not allowed to be on the swim team for obvious reasons. Let's just say I can beat the world record twice over." Jenna laughs out loud, her eyes bright. "Same goes for surfing. So recreation only."

"You are such a charlatan," she squeaks. "I totally believed you when you said you were allergic to chlorine."

"That wasn't entirely a lie," I say, waving over Speio, who has been watching us from the living room at the far side of the pool, hovering with a tense expression on his face. I need him to be comfortable with the fact that Jenna knows about our family—about who I am—and not consider her a risk or, worse, a threat. "We don't mix well with chlorine. With extended exposure, it can actually choke us, just like fish. Irritates their gills."

"So wait, do you guys have gills?" Jenna asks, glancing from me to Speio, who has reluctantly joined us at my silent command, and peers at our necks. "I mean, I didn't see any before when you were...the other thing."

I nod. "You can't see them with your eyes but they're there."

"Far out." Jenna leans back on her haunches, her eyes assessing. Speio remains silent but I've already warned him to restrain himself. I know he doesn't agree with what I've done, but he is not the regent. I am. At least Echlios and Soren are staying out of it, and unlike their son, they're keeping their opinions of my actions to themselves. "So, Speio, is that why you aren't on the surf team, either?" Jenna asks.

"Yeah," he mumbles, and falls mute. I glare at him until he shifts uncomfortably and stuffs his hands in his pockets. He sighs and sits next to us once more, answering Jenna's question. "We're so in tune with the water that I would command the wave without knowing it. So Riss figured it would kind of be cheating." He glances at me, his face relaxing.

"It is cheating," I say to him.

"I disagree, of course, but what our fearless leader says, goes." To this, I punch him playfully in the arm and shake my head. The truth is, being perfect at anything draws attention. And worse, using any Aquarathi power, even unintentionally, out in the open ocean is a risk that we can't take. I can see the headlines now—Rogue Sharks Gone Wild During Local Surf Meet. Um, no thanks.

"So what do you mean, you command the wave?" Jenna says, banishing the gruesome image in my brain. Speio looks at me first for approval before he answers Jenna. This one is a little sensitive but I'd rather be honest with Jenna after everything. We're all in now. And she's probably going to need to protect herself from us if word ever did get out about what she knows. I dip my head slightly.

"Water responds to us," Speio says. "Most Aquarathi can command the water around us and inside of us to a limited degree. So in terms of surfing, I can manipulate the wave to crest perfectly, which is why Riss thinks it's cheating even if it would be completely invisible to anyone else." Speio snorts. "I call it technical advantage."

I snort back. "Don't think Sawyer would see it that way. Part of the beauty of surfing is the unpredictability of the wave. If we manipulate that, it's wrong." It feels good to talk about something as mundane as surfing rules and etiquette, and I run with it gratefully. "Right, Jenna? I mean what's the point?"

"Yeah, I guess," she says dubiously, staring from me to Speio. "But I agree with Speio, too. I mean, if any human had a talent, they'd make use of it, especially in competition. So why shouldn't you?"

"Um, because it's an alien talent as opposed to a normal human one, and that totally changes the playing field," I say. "Honestly, Jenna. I thought you were a stickler for the rules. And now you're bending them because some cute alien boy has put the ridiculous notion into your head." I make a tsk-tsking noise and shake my head.

But my choice of words is poor. Jenna has gone all deer-in-headlights again. Her face is panicked, her eyes widening into terrified orbs as she stares at Speio, who for his part has an indescribable expression on his face. Jenna's voice is a squeak. "What do you mean put something in my head? Is he mind-controlling me?"

"Don't be ridiculous," I say hastily. "I meant the normal power of suggestion, not mind control. First of all, no species has the ability to control another. That's science fiction. We're not in your head, okay?"

"Says she who can do exactly that," Speio mutters.

"Speio, not helping," I hiss to him before turning to Jenna, my tone careful. I choose my words with wisdom. "As his queen, I can command him, true. But that is within our species, and it's not something I do in general, especially to humans. You do not have anything to fear from us." I lean forward slightly to meet and hold her gaze. "I need to know that you at least understand that. I would never hurt you. You know that, don't you?"

"Yes," she says after a few seconds. Her voice is unsteady but her eyes are unwavering. It's enough for me. A sharp tinny bicycle-bell sound chimes through the air, making us all jump, but it's only Jenna's cell phone. "It's my mom." She answers. "Hey, Mom….Yes….No, I'll be home soon….Yes, she's much better," she says into the phone with a glance at me. "She's going to be fine….Okay, I'll tell her. Love you." After she hangs up, she slides the phone into her back pocket. "Sorry about that. She says to say she's happy you're feeling better. She wanted to know if I was staying over but I think it's best if I head home tonight."

Jenna stares at the watch on her wrist and then back at me, the silent question in her eyes. As much as I want to keep her next to me for the foreseeable future, I made the decision to trust her and now I have to live with that. I'd hoped to ask her to spend the night once more, but it's obvious she needs space to decompress and process everything that I've told her. And she can't do that here with me breathing down her neck like some kind of alien sea monster. Cue self-deprecating laughter here.

"It's okay," I tell her. "You should go."

Her face is torn. "I want to stay, really, I do, but Dad's away at a sales conference, and you know how Mom gets…" She trails off, unable to meet my eyes, but I still give her a reassuring smile. "And I still have homework to finish for school tomorrow. You're going to be at school, right?"

"Yep. Business as usual."

"Okay, well, I'll see you." We embrace each other tightly in silence. She says goodbye to Speio and stands. "And, Riss, thanks for telling me. I know that you didn't have to but I'm glad you did. And you can trust me, too. I hope you know that."

"I know," I say softly.

But I don't really know. Instead, I hope. I watch as she says goodbye to Soren and Echlios with the same warmth as she would have in the past. It's a good sign. She's come to love them, too. She won't betray us.

She can't.

Or she'll have to die.

10
Human Nature

Hot white light creeps into the corners of my eyelids, and the feeling of warmth spreads like butter across my human skin. I wake to a balmy morning, a flutter of a breeze winking across the surface of the pool.

After Jenna left last night, I stared up into the night sky for hours, my eyes burning and throat parched. As much as I'd felt the human inclination to cry, my body wouldn't spare the water. I'd understood that I'd not been quite recovered from the earlier ordeal with Sanctum, and opening up to Jenna had pushed me over the edge. I fell asleep under the stars on a chaise longue outside, which isn't uncommon for me, especially when I'm feeling out of sorts.

I still am.

I stretch my body and slip into the water, letting it soothe away the aches and pains of the confinement of my human body. Everything aches in an odd way—my mind as much as my body. Trusting someone with everything you are— especially when you're an entirely different species—is incredibly traumatic. On top of that, revisiting my history had made me miss my father something fierce. I wish he could see me as I am now, and not the selfish girl he'd sent away to find herself. I want more than anything to be worthy of his legacy, worthy of him.

I sigh and float, sensing Speio walking toward me. He crouches at the edge of the pool. "Did you sleep out here?"

"Yes." I stare into the pale blue haze of the morning sky that's still tinged pink with the first blush rays of the sun. "You ever think about it, Speio?"

"Think about what?"

"Last night, I fell asleep watching the stars," I murmur. "They were so bright—all shiny white dots on this unending blue-black background. It was so beautiful." I pause, a wry smile twisting my mouth. "It's not even our solar system, but I felt a pang of nostalgia so strong that it felt like someone had punched me. I don't know where it came from but it was so unexpected...." My voice trails off.

"I don't get it," he says. "You were feeling nostalgic about the stars?"

"No, not the stars. Sana. I had this weird feeling. Must have been from talking about everything. I missed our planet, as strange as it sounds."

"That is weird, considering you've never been there," he says. Speio's voice has a slight edge and I can tell that he hasn't forgiven what he probably considers to be unforgivable trespasses— in other words, trusting a human. But it was my call, and it's done now so there's nothing to be said for it. "Plus, it's not exactly our home. This is."

"Maybe it's a memory, from one of my father's stories or something. You know, Speio, sometimes I wish we were there instead of here," I confess. "Where we didn't have to stay hidden all the time."

"They had different troubles, Riss. The grass isn't always greener."

"I know."

"You think Jenna'll say anything?" he asks, dipping his feet into the water. "Now that it's morning and she can see everything in the clear light of day?"

"I don't know."

"You don't know?" he repeats. His voice is a sneer and I feel myself bristle in response to his tone.

"No, I don't know. And if she does, then you can kill her," I snarl back, drawing myself out of the water with one hand and walking past him. "Is that what you want to hear me say, Speio?"

Speio's eyes are cool against my back. "No, Riss. If she does, that girl's death sentence is all on you. I want to hear you say that you'll take care of it."

I don't answer him as I shut the glass door to my room and draw the curtains across it. After a while, I sense him walk back inside and I slump to the floor. Speio's right. Everything is all squarely on me now. I'd made the decision to tell Jenna, to show her what we were, to break one of the laws that had kept us safe for millennia.

I'd given up the keys to my kingdom to a teenage girl. A clever and mature teenage girl, but a girl nonetheless. I had to hope my faith in Jenna is as strong as her faith in me. Otherwise, this will be an experiment gone horribly wrong, and I'll have to take care of any fallout, which is something I don't even want to think about.

With a shiver, I dress quickly, throwing on jeans and a sweatshirt before dragging a comb through my salt-crusted hair and giving up halfway to tie the snarls into a loose knot. My backpack is untouched from the week before and I cringe at the thought of having to catch up on a week's homework. Despite my considerable otherworldly abilities, I still have to put my nose to the schoolwork grindstone and study as hard as anyone else. Too bad my alien powers don't include a photographic memory.

In the dining room, I can hear my family moving around, but they're not alone. Soren is concentrating on a newspaper, and Speio is now glowering at me like I'm some kind of slimy traitor. I ignore him, my attention now focused on the tall, thin man speaking to Echlios just out of sight in the hallway. Sensing my presence, he turns toward me. Not a man, after all. On cue, the wet cloak sensation envelopes my skin as his essence bows toward mine, all of the water in his body making his identity known to me instantly.

Aquarathi. Eron. Ruby Court Royal Guard.

His face shimmers fleetingly, telltale reddish lights flickering along his near-translucent neck as he extends it toward me in a gesture of allegiance. For a second, I wonder why Echlios would be speaking to a member of Ehmora's old court, but I acknowledge him in silence, and the connection between us dissipates. The blood recedes from the surface of my skin, once more at rest, as the man takes his leave.

I pour myself a cup of hot tea, ignoring Speio's glower from across the table. Besides Jenna, I have other things to worry about. Like the usurper Aquarathi queen who wants to kill me.

"A Ruby Court spy?" I ask Echlios as he walks into the room, and he nods. If Echlios trusts him, then I have no reason not to. "Did he bring any more news on the situation with Ehmora? Have we figured out what her plan is?"

"Eron has confirmed that she has left Waterfell, but from what he's telling me, it seems like she's waiting."

"Waiting for what?"

"For you to come of age, I expect. She's nothing if not calculating. And clever. As long as I have known her, she has always had some ulterior motive."

Thinking back to what I know of her, I realize that Echlios

is right. I met Ehmora once, when she visited my father to discuss the chaos between the lower courts. She was queen of the Ruby Court, and one of the most powerful rulers with the most influence. The kings of the Emerald and Sapphire Courts followed her lead more often than not.

My father respected her but had never trusted her.

She had been beautiful and icy. It'd been whispered that Ehmora and my father had been more than acquaintances at one point, but I'd never believed it. My father could never love a creature so cold and untouchable, and in the end, he'd chosen my mother, Neriah from the Gold Court, and that had been that. Among the Aquarathi, Ehmora was known for her biting intelligence and her unforgiving temperament.

During the visit, I was awed and a little cowed in her presence, hiding behind my father. In Aquarathi form, she was formidable—all burning ebony scales with bloodred fins. Her gaze was one of deep red fire that pinned me against the cave wall as if she could see right past everything inside of me. I'd never been so terrified in all my life.

I shake off the dark memory and focus on Echlios. "And our people? My father's advisers? What did Eron say of them?"

His face darkens. "Some are still alive. Captive."

I frown, a tremor of unease sliding through me. "Wouldn't she want to get rid of any of our people who were loyal to my father? I mean, it's a classic coup maneuver."

"I don't think that that is Ehmora's end game."

"What do you mean?" I say casually, eating a piece of sashimi and trying not to be disturbed by the weird twist of Echlios's mouth, as if he's working out how to say something awful to me. Mentally, I prepare myself. "She has the High Court now. What else does she want?"

"You're still the true heir. Even if she has temporary control of the High Court, Ehmora can never be accepted as its queen. Our rules of succession are clear. If there are no direct descendants who are of age, only then can a new regent be chosen via challenge. But you're still alive, yet she hasn't officially challenged you. I think she has other plans," he says after a minute.

"You mean to kill me, too?"

"That's just it," Echlios says with a glance at Speio. "She can't—she'd be executed. Your father's death was accepted as an accident, but yours would not be. It's too risky. Eron thinks she wants you to come back, but to rule under her thumb."

"I'd never be her puppet."

Soren shoots Echlios an insistent look. "Tell her," she says to him. "She needs to know now instead of later. She can't have her head in the sand, pretending that she and Ehmora aren't going to come face-to-face at some point. It's leverage, and Nerissa needs to know."

"What's leverage?" I say. Echlios's face becomes even more pained, his internal struggle clear. I eye him, letting the waters in my body surge to the surface of my skin and bend his to my will. "Tell me."

He sighs. "Your mother is alive. Ehmora has her. Captive." I almost throw up the piece of food in my mouth as all the air is thrust out of my lungs in one heaving breath at his words.

"What do you mean my mother is alive?" I sputter, everything inside of me wild and uncontrolled. "My mother is dead. She died a long time ago. My father—"

"Wanted to protect you," Soren says gently. "Lady Neriah isn't dead, love."

"Then where is she?" I whisper on a half-broken sob as Soren channels her thoughts directly to me. My mother is alive...captive all these years somewhere in Waterfell by Ehmora.

"How could you keep this from me?" I choke out.

"We were bound not to tell you, my lady. By your father."

My heart feels like it's separating into a million icy droplets, each sinking into my body like glass shards. "Why?"

"Perhaps he did not want to cause you pain."

But the pain is already making itself felt in violent, heaving waves. Why would my father have lied to me? Why would he have told me she was dead when she's alive? Launching to my feet, I'm prepared to run out of the house and swim straight to Waterfell.

Echlios stands to grab my arm with gentle but firm restraint. "You can't just run out of here, Nerissa. That's what Ehmora wants—you for her. That's her bargaining chip. Her leverage."

"Release me," I say, my jaw clenched. Echlios complies, his hand falling to his side. "We have to go. I don't have a choice. I'd trade me for her any day. It's my mother." I don't even realize that I've fallen back into my natural language, the flow of clicks and pulses so quick it's falling out of me like brittle staccato notes.

"There's more," Echlios says. "Lady Neriah is not in Waterfell. Eron has new information that she's being held captive here on land."

"Where?" The desperation coating the fleeting edges of my thoughts translates into sound. I can barely get the words out. "Here? In San Diego?"

"Maybe. Ehmora has many friends and spies across the United States." He squeezes my shoulder. "But it makes more sense that Ehmora would choose to be close by...closer to you."

"We have to find her, Echlios."

"We will," Soren says, wrapping her arms around me. I don't want to be touched but I accept the comforting gesture nonetheless. Swallowing past the acid in my throat, I squeeze her back. She has been a capable guardian and is the closest thing I've had to a mother over much of my life, but she could never replace my mother…whom I'd thought dead for so long.

My voice is a threadlike whisper. "Do we have anything else from Eron to go on? Anything at all?"

"I'm working on it, my lady."

"Thank you, Echlios," I say with a deep, drawn-out breath. "What can I do? I can't just sit here."

"For now, that's the best thing you can do…just continue your day-to-day activities. Ehmora doesn't know that we know about Lady Neriah, and right now, that's our only advantage to try to find her. Which means we need to be extra careful at school and anywhere near the ocean where Ehmora can get you alone. It may make sense for you to curtail your duties at the marine center, at least for now."

"No, I can't do that. They need me and I need them," I say quietly. "I'll be careful, Echlios, but I don't think that changing everything I do is the answer here. If she wanted to capture me, she had more than enough opportunity in the past two years after she killed my father. And if she wants to play her new trump card about my mother, then she'll just have to come find me."

"Nerissa," Soren says softly. "Remember our lessons—stop and think. Remember who you are, and promise me that you won't do anything rash on your own. We will find your mother, but we have to do it together without compromising your safety."

"Of course, Soren. I'm not stupid." I glance over at Speio, who hasn't said a word since we'd started speaking. He seems shocked at Eron's news but it's not like he's got my back anymore. He's probably gloating that he'd been right all along when I was pouring my heart out to Jenna. "Plus, I've got Speio to make sure of that, don't I?" My tone is bitter but I can't help myself. I raise hard eyes to Echlios, my words clipped. "Contact me the minute you find anything. Understood?" He nods, his lips a thin white line and his eyes shadowed. Echlios is a master of his emotions but he is as affected by this as I am.

Perhaps even more so because of my father's demands.

Leaving the house without waiting for Speio, I jump into the back of my Jeep and floor the accelerator. He can get himself to school just fine without me. Although I'm calm on the outside, on the inside I'm seething. I can't believe that they kept such a terrible secret from me. A quiet part of me argues that they were doing it at my father's behest, but I shove it away. They should have told me after he died that I still had a mother. Instead, they'd let me believe that I had no one left... that I was alone.

I pull into an empty parking space and fall into the sea of students entering the school building, trying to calm my frazzled emotions. The stakes have gotten a lot higher. On top of it all, the knowledge that Ehmora has human allies is terrifying, if only because I can't sense them as I can other Aquarathi. Anyone could be a threat, even right at this moment.

Stepping out of the Jeep, suddenly I wish that I had Speio at my side even though I'm still furious with him. Maybe he would have told me, but things have gotten so strained between us, first with the arrival of Lo and then my big reveal to Jenna. The sour thought of what could happen if any of Ehmora's spies figure out that Jenna knows about us weaves its way through my brain. Now, because of me, Jenna could be in very real danger. No wonder Speio had been so cagey.

Someone bumps against my side and my heart jumps violently into my mouth. But it's only two students pushing past me in the parking lot. I haul a deep, calming breath into my lungs, my fingers tightening on the strap of my backpack. I remind myself that Ehmora is not going to attack me in public. I hope.

But that doesn't mean that she isn't watching.

Ignoring the shiver that climbs up my spine, I walk into the building and head toward my locker. Jenna is waiting next to it, so I wipe the worry from my face and paste a bright smile on it instead.

"Hey, Riss," she says in an overly cheery voice.

"Hey." I stuff my backpack in my locker and pull out my history books. "What?" I say, noticing her wide-eyed expression.

"You're so normal. I mean, so you."

I can't hold back my immediate eye roll. "What did you expect?" I ask. "Random fins sticking out of my head? Shark teeth?"

"Wait, what? You have shark teeth?"

"Seriously?" And then I take in Jenna's own exaggerated eye roll, and we start laughing at the exact same moment. "Careful, or I may have to show you my real teeth, and trust me, they're way worse than any shark's." I bare my perfectly normal human white teeth to her, still grinning. I'm starting to feel a whole lot better as my anxiety slips away for the moment.

"Ooh, I'm so scared," Jenna shoots back.

"Scared of what?" Sawyer says, throwing his arms around Jenna and giving her a big sloppy kiss right in front of me.

"Really, you two?" I joke. "I just ate breakfast and now it's in my throat. Get a room or something."

"Riss thinks she's so tough," Jenna says to Sawyer when their lip-lock comes to an end. "But I think maybe we need to find her a boyfriend of her very own to soften her up."

"I don't do boyfriends," I toss back, raising my eyebrows meaningfully. "And now you know why."

Sawyer perks up immediately. Seriously, the guy is like a male version of *Gossip Girl*. "Why? You don't like boys?"

"No. I mean, yes, I like boys," I say, flushing. "I just don't like relationships. I'm young. I want to have fun. Keep my options open."

"Way open," Jenna quips. I glare at her but it doesn't stop her. "More fish in the sea, that kind of thing?" she says with an innocent look. I want to kick her in the shins but can't stop the grin cracking the corners of my lips. At least she hasn't lost her sense of humor.

"Exactly right. More fish in the sea," I agree.

Sawyer shakes his head. "You know, Riss, I never thought you were that kind of girl, otherwise I'd have dated you instead of No-Fun over here." That comment earned him a well-deserved punch in the arm from his girlfriend.

"You have a lot of fun," Jenna says indignantly, dragging Sawyer's face down to hers until she breaks away breathlessly. "Are you having fun now?"

"You know I'm just kidding, babe." Sawyer grins and kisses the top of Jenna's nose. "But Riss is kind of hot."

I snort. "Eww, you're like a brother to me. So not my type."

"Sawyer, heads up!" Jenna and I practically dive out of the way as Sawyer makes a photo-worthy lunge across the hallway to grab a neon yellow flying disc. "Nice catch," a voice shouts from behind me.

At the familiar tone, it's impossible to stop the tingling that starts at the base of my ears. Turning in slow motion, I meet Lo's gaze and my breath stops. His hair is still wet from his surf session and his skin is glowing, making those eyes of his seem even more bottomless. It's been over a week since I pretty much made it clear that I wanted nothing to do with him…a week since my collapse, which thankfully he—and anyone else—wasn't around to see.

I try to say hello but the word sticks in my throat on its way out so I stare at my shoes instead, which only makes my gaze jump to Lo's sand-flecked feet as he stops to retrieve the Frisbee from Sawyer. Inwardly I grin at the flip-flops—an obvious act of rebellion on his part considering they aren't part of the Dover Prep uniform. It's one of the other things I like about him. Not his complete and blatant disregard for the rules but that he doesn't compromise himself and who he is. There's a strength in that.

"So mono, huh?"

I realize that Lo's talking to me after Jenna nudges me with her elbow.

"What? Sorry, yes." Glaring at Jenna in belated understanding that she'd told everyone I'd had mono, I nod without looking at Lo. Couldn't she have picked something a little more dignified like a broken arm or an amputated appendage or something? Mono. Just gross.

"So…been kissing a lot of guys?"

Like a bomb, even though it's a joke, there's sudden dead silence. Sawyer laughs nervously, and if Jenna's eyes get any bigger, she's going to look like more of an alien than I am. This time, I do look at Lo, whose face is deadpan until the corner of his mouth curls upward along with his eyebrow. His eyes soften. Something in them throws me, making my legs feel like they can't hold me up any longer. Every drop of water surges within me toward him and I'm flailing inside like a fish out of water.

"Not going to kiss and tell?" Even his voice shifts to a lower cadence to match the expression in his eyes, and the only thing I feel is panic.

"Where's Cara?" I blurt out.

I could kick myself. Repeatedly.

Lo's lips twist into an oddly wry expression and a shadow

crosses his face. The softness I'd seen in his eyes vanishes in a blink as if it had never been there. He was flirting. With me! He offered me a truce and I stupidly said the first dumb thing that came to my mouth. *Where's Cara?* Idiot.

"Where's Speio?" Lo returns coolly, and pats Sawyer on the back, stepping past me. I deserve that, I know. Jenna doesn't say anything and busies herself with her locker, knowing better than to say anything to me especially about Lo. Taking a minute to compose myself, I snap my own locker shut.

"See you guys in class," I say to no one in particular, and walk past Sawyer and Jenna without looking at Lo. It's magnetic—and maddening—the way each cell in my body wants to throw itself into him, and the farther away I get, the more I feel him pulling me back. I wonder if this is what Jenna feels whenever she's around Sawyer. The laws of human attraction are new to me. For some reason the thought of Dvija races through my brain, and I'm breathless. I realize now that the intense longing I'd felt via Speio is pretty similar to what I'm feeling right at this moment.

Only it's for a human boy, and it's not like I've gone through Dvija or anything.

Just before I walk into the classroom, I glance over my shoulder only to have the breath stolen from my lungs. Lo's eyes are deep and piercing. I feel the weight of them hovering, watching. Holding me motionless as time, too, stands still. I force myself to peel my gaze away from his compelling stare, making my feet obey weak commands to enter the classroom…one in front of the other like a drone. Something hot pulses across the back of my neck, racing across my body, and I can't even think.

It's not Ehmora that will be the death of me.

It's this boy.

11
Connections

The ocean is cool and dark and mesmerizing. Its arms are wide and ever reaching, gathering me close in cool undulating swatches of navy and midnight-blue. A silver flash catches my eye as a shoal of fish rush past, the reflective surface of their scales catching the shimmer of light piercing into the deeper water. My eyes follow as they swim upward, where the navy transforms into shades of aqua and turquoise. Shapeless waves rock me tenderly, cradling my body in a mother's liquid embrace.

I could rest there forever. Or dream it, anyway.

Instead of my blue paradise, I'm sweating it out in a classroom and wishing for the second when I can leave to get to that exact place in my mind. The place where I can let it all go if only for one minute—Jenna, Ehmora, my mother, Speio and, most of all, Lo, whose glances I can still feel fluttering over me like mist.

If I didn't know better, I'd guess that he's studying me... trying to work me out or something. His face, when I occasionally glance to the side of the room where he is sitting, is thoughtful and serious. Any other guy would have been history by this point—boys aren't interested in girls who humiliate them. He must be a glutton for punishment or have some secret stalker issues that no one knows about, unless he's shooting for some kind of revenge angle. But Lo doesn't strike me as that type.

Cara, definitely, but not him. I notice her eyeballing me and I glare back. Lo isn't her property even if she thinks he is. He's clearly not mine, either, but I'll be damned if I let her intimidate me. Raising my eyebrow in silent challenge, I let my gaze slide to Lo, who is sitting in the desk to her right. Given our history, it's not exactly the nice thing to do, but I do it, anyway, watching as Cara's face turns a splotchy shade of pink.

Oblivious to our little catty byplay, Lo leans back in his chair, his lower lip caught between his teeth, studying the chapter on European colonization that we're supposed to be reading. He stretches out his legs and crosses them, pulling the textbook to his hips. He has long slender fingers, I notice. Hands are one of my favorite things about being human. I find them beautiful and graceful, even the short stubby kinds. Lo's are noticeably well-groomed.

A lock of sandy hair curls into his face and he swipes it away with a quick swish of his fingers. He sure is easy on the eyes, I'll give him that. I don't know if I'm getting softer or he's getting cuter or if I'm just pretending to put on a good show for Cara, who is growing redder by the second. But the growing ache in my chest suggests otherwise.

I can't seem to let him go.

Cara slides a note across to Lo and he reads it. They both look at me, her face full of malice, and his blank. Caught staring, I can't hide the answering flush that rises up my neck as I stare blindly at my own textbook. Fighting the sick urge to shape a glimmer to read whatever's in the note, I study the page in front of me until the text starts to blur. I read the same passage fifteen times before the heat making my ears feel like they're on fire starts to recede. I don't care what's in the note.

Sure you do, a sneaky inner voice taunts.

I've half made up my mind to do it when Mr. Moss raps on his desk and announces a pop quiz for the last few minutes of class. A collective groan makes its way across the classroom as Mr. Moss passes out the sheets. I'm not worried—human world history is my strong suit, given I'd had to learn it when other human kids were learning their colors and shapes.

"When you've finished, hand in your answers and you may leave," Mr. Moss says.

I mark the answers quickly and wait a couple minutes before turning in my paper. Jenna and Sawyer are not too far behind me, and catch up to me at the lockers.

"Want to ditch study hall with us?" Sawyer whispers. I stare in shock at Jenna—she's the last person who'd ditch any classes whatsoever. She frowns on it something fierce whenever Sawyer skips school for surfing.

"Big week," she says a trifle defensively. "I need some downtime."

"We could get in serious trouble if we get caught," I say.

"Got it covered," Lo says, walking over to us. "My car is parked outside the service entrance behind the cafeteria. And if anyone asks, Principal Cano needed to see us."

"Cano?" I say warily. "You're playing with fire. He hates ditchers. How?"

"Cara's got it."

I don't even hide the skepticism on my face. "Cara? She'll throw us under the bus the first chance she can get. You can't trust her."

"She's my friend. And you can trust me."

"Exactly," I say. "She's *your* friend. Not ours. And she kind of hates me, so maybe I should just bail."

"Are you kidding?" Sawyer says. "If there's one time you have to cut last period, it's today. The tide's in and the waves are magic. Double overhead from that storm swell forecast. You've gotta come with!"

"Trust me on this, okay?" Lo says.

Despite my misgivings, I follow them down to a side exit in the back end of the cafeteria. I don't know why I agreed. Maybe it was the expression in those liquid blue eyes, or maybe it's the thought of finally being in the ocean. Or maybe it's the fiery feeling still licking through my entire body at Lo's nearness. Either way, nothing inside me puts up a fight, and the truth is, I want to go.

Lo's car is parked where he'd said and to my surprise I see my big-wave board in the back of the truck, along with Sawyer's and Lo's. Even Jenna's gun surfboard is there, and I shoot her an accusing glare that she pretends not to see. I can't even believe that Jenna is in on it—she hates when Sawyer cuts class to surf.

"Did you guys plan this?"

"What's any break-out-of-school expedition without planning?" Sawyer says with a wink. "We need to think in advance. Where have you been, anyway? Under a rock? This storm has only been the topic of conversation every hour for the past week. First time the La Jolla Cove is breaking in, like, years. We have to go."

I roll my eyes in Jenna's direction. "I was under a rock. Had mono, remember?"

"Oh, right. The kissing queen," Sawyer quips with a snide look at Lo, who is suddenly busy strapping the boards down in the back of the truck.

"Shut up," I say, and climb into the truck. I try not to be affected by Lo's proximity on the far end.

He shoots me an apologetic look. "This truck's plenty big

with room for three across but it's going to be a tight squeeze with the four of us."

"Is this even legal?" Jenna asks, squashing in next to me. I don't answer. I can't even talk now that Lo's entire right side is in firm contact with my left. I can feel the warmth of his skin through his uniform and smell the salt still on him. I try not to breathe as Sawyer tucks in on the end, shoving Jenna and I across until I'm well and truly sandwiched between Jenna and Lo.

"Sorry," she says.

"You two can share the middle seat belt," Lo tells us in a weird, tight voice. "We'll take the back roads just in case."

"This is totally illegal," Jenna mutters again.

"What's a breakout without some illicit action?" Sawyer chimes in loudly, making us all jump. I inch my way closer to Jenna but nothing stops the warmth of Lo from leaning into me. He is holding himself rigidly, and as he starts the engine his arm brushes past mine.

"Sorry."

"It's okay," I manage.

Lo puts the truck into gear and we pull out of the parking lot. For one moment, I think I see Cara's face in the second-floor study hall window but I'm sure I'm imagining it because when I crane my neck over Jenna to see as we drive past, there's no one there. My nerves must be kicking in.

The ride down to the beach is quick but feels like forever. The tendons in the back of my neck are aching from holding myself perfectly still. Every time Lo pulls on the steering wheel or accelerates, his arm or leg shifts against mine. The friction is unbearable on so many levels. By this point, I can feel Lo's heartbeat pounding against the bare skin of my arm, and my own pulse has unconsciously aligned itself with his. It's torturous and magical at the same time.

I glance over at Jenna, who is practically sitting in Sawyer's lap and looking pretty happy about it. Between Lo and I holding ourselves like pieces of clay and those two lovebirds nuzzling into each other like baby kittens, the tension in the truck is so thick that it's nearly solid. I lick dry lips and feel Lo's gaze flutter over them before he drags his attention back to the road. The tension jumps up another notch and not even the wind blowing in from outside can dissipate it. I hold my breath and count to a hundred in my head, my eyes fixed on a tiny chip in the windshield.

"You okay?" Lo asks.

My nod barely qualifies as movement, but Lo takes it as an answer, anyway. I count from a hundred back to one but it's useless. My attraction to this boy is skyrocketing with each passing second and the attempt to calm my nervous energy is only making me focus on it more. The water in my body is rushing around like a reverse waterfall, up and back over my limbs, into my chest and head like wildfire just from his nearness. I can hardly contain it.

I force myself to think of math homework, running my brain through countless complex equations. Then I define and spell every single SAT word I can think of that we've covered over the entire year. I'm so desperate for mind over body control that my next step is French conjugation.

"We're here."

I don't think I could have made it a single minute more. And who knows what that might have turned into—me climbing on top of Lo and having my way with him or punching Sawyer in the face just to get out of the car. Or maybe something even worse, such as my skin lighting up like the sky on the Fourth of July? That would have been pretty…and pretty hard to talk my way out of.

Grabbing my wet suit, which Lo has thoughtfully provided

alongside my board—I don't even want to know what he told Soren to get it—I make my way to the women's bathroom at the end of the pier.

"Riss, wait up!" Jenna shouts, running to catch up, her own wet suit and swimwear in hand. "Hey, you okay?" she asks when she catches up to me. The bathroom is empty so we don't bother to use the toilet stalls. Instead, we head over to a bench next to the pay lockers lining the wall.

"I'm fine," I say. I throw my gear into one of the open lockers and strip.

"You don't look fine. You look worked up. And red."

"Red?" I ask, pretending to tug on the leg of my wet suit. I know exactly what she's going to say.

"Your face looks like it's going to explode," Jenna explains. "And in the car, your heart was racing so fast, I thought you were running a marathon. You sure you're all right?"

"Yes," I snap, and then recoil at the look on her face. Other than stating the obvious with Lo, I tell her the only other thing that's still bothering me. "Sorry, I'm just worried about the whole ditching thing and…I still feel weird around Lo. I mean, you remember what happened on the boat and everything.…"

Jenna stares at me, her eyes widening with delayed understanding. "You like him." I nod slowly, my eyes dropping to the floor. Her face screws up and she shakes her head. "But I thought you didn't—I mean, you gave up a date with him. You told him to back off."

"I know what I said, Jenna," I reply. "I thought I did want him to leave me alone, but it turns out I don't. He makes me feel confused and fluttery and tongue-tied all in the same moment. I mean, he's still arrogant and obnoxious, but sometimes I think that's all a front. But it doesn't matter, anyway. I really screwed up and he's with Cara so what's the point?"

"You need to tell him."

"Why? He's not interested, anyway." I pull the strap that connects to the base of my zipper and snap my suit shut.

"What about the...other thing?" Jenna says slowly. "Can you...be with humans?" I want to laugh but it's not funny. Something that has always been amusing to me is not so much anymore. There's nothing humorous in how chaotic I feel whenever I'm around Lo. And I hate the way my stomach dipped when she'd said the word *be* with him, because I do want that, too.

"Yes, I'm like you, remember?" I say, cheeks burning at my inner admission.

Jenna sends me a sidelong glance, eyes narrowing at my flushed face. We're the same as we've always been—two best friends, only now with a huge secret between them, one that will always factor into the way she thinks about me. "On the outside," she says. "But what about on the inside? I mean, you're not exactly like us. Right?"

"What're you asking me, Jenna?"

"Can you hurt him? Unintentionally, I mean."

"No more than you can hurt Sawyer."

"But the other day, with my ear..." She's fighting for the right words, and I can see the tears welling in her eyes even as what she'd said cut me. "You didn't mean to and you did."

"I'm sorry—"

Jenna grabs my shoulders. "I'm not saying that to hurt you or for you to apologize. I just don't want another accident. Or people asking questions about you, because that could be bad, right?" Belatedly I realize that she's only trying to protect me. It has nothing to do with Lo at all. Or any fear of me for that matter. It's fear *for* me.

"The thing with you happened because I was in my other form. I won't hurt him, or anyone else. Don't worry." I force a grin to my face. "Plus, like I said, he's not interested so he's off the hook from Nerissa's terrible tentacles, anyway."

"That's just it, Riss," Jenna says. "I think he is. He stares at you all the time, in the cafeteria, in class, in gym, with these really weird intense looks." She frowns. "It's kind of creepy actually. Half the time, I wonder if he's daydreaming, because that stare of his is borderline stalker."

"He stares at me?" I say, my heart aflutter.

"All. The. Time."

"If that's true, how come I never see him do it?"

"Because you stare at the ground whenever he's around, remember?" she says dryly. "Come on. Hurry up before they send out a search party." Jenna pulls on her swimsuit and then her wet suit. I hadn't thought she could actually go in the water so soon after the ear thing.

"Are you going in?"

At my worried look, she smiles. "It's all good. The doctor said that I have a minor perforation, and I could put some special ear putty in there if I want to go in the water. I'm on antibiotics for any infection," she says. "Totally minor," she adds hastily. "Told the doc that I got hit with a hockey stick during practice. He went for it. We're all good."

"Hey, you two," Sawyer shouts. "Move it! This is surf time, not lady chat time."

"Coming!"

Grabbing our boards from the back of the truck, we follow the boys down the trek to the beach. This is a reef break and can be of the more dangerous surf breaks in San Diego, especially when the surf is as big as it is. Sawyer wasn't kidding when he said this break only happens every few years. Jenna carries her seven-foot surfboard herself, refusing any help from Sawyer, and I tuck my board under my arm.

"How are we going to find one another?" Jenna says, staring at the crowded lineup—guess a bunch of other hardcore surfers are as excited about the storm swell as we are. "There's like a hundred people out."

Sawyer consults his watch. "I say we check back here in an hour. Sound good?"

Walking down the beach, Sawyer says hi to half a dozen people, most of them locals and far older than we are, as well as a few others familiar faces from school. People love Sawyer— he's naturally outgoing, and being an amazing surfer on top of that makes them like him more. He's also a local, which means he has a ton of beach credibility. Oddly enough, Lo doesn't say hello to anyone, but I expect that that's because he's still relatively new here. I still can't look at him, especially after what Jenna said in the bathroom, and keep my eyes on the horizon counting the incoming sets.

On the beach, I tie my hair into a ponytail and strap on my leash before I paddle out to the lineup. Guilt flashes through me as I remember Echlios's warning about not leaving school without Speio, but I shrug it off. It's not like Ehmora or any of her henchmen can attack me with this many people around. The full moon has come and gone, so fish attacks are low probability. And I'm in the ocean—if worse comes to worst, I can defend myself with the best of them.

Duck-diving beneath a set of gigantic waves, I kick out strongly and paddle hard through the white water, trying to make the most of the slim window between sets to get as far out as possible. Despite my strength, my arms are aching with the strain of it already. It's tiring but in a good way. The ocean is something I can fight and pit myself against while embracing it at the same time.

After several minutes of hard paddling, I pull myself into a sitting position. I'm barely winded, but then again, I can breathe underwater—one of the many perks of being me. Lo pulls up alongside me and sits on his board. He, by contrast, is breathing hard, his neoprene-clad chest rising and falling rapidly. His face is flushed and his eyes sparkling.

"Hey," he says. "That was gnarly."

"Gnarly?" I ask with a grin. "Catching up on your West Coast surf lingo?"

"Figure it's universal." He glances behind us to the waves crashing onto the rocks. There's already half of a yellow board smashed on top of them. "What do you think, twelve feet or so?"

"Just about. Those rocks look wicked. You nervous?"

His wide grin makes my chest constrict. "No way! See you on the flip side."

I watch as Lo takes off, barely catching the lip of a massive wave. He disappears on the other side, then pops up with a cut-back to do a floater across the top that takes him a few inches off the wave itself. There's no doubt about it—he's a class-act surfer. He has so much natural talent that I don't think even Sawyer is as good as he is. Or maybe I'm just biased because I think everything he does is amazing.

Shaking my head at my unnatural girlie thoughts, I grin and start paddling. But before I can grab my wave, a grayish-brown fin catches my eye.

My heart sinks. Already? Usually they don't show up for an hour or two, after I've surfed and am too tired to hold on to my human armor. I look around but don't see anything. Maybe I'm imagining things, or maybe it isn't here because of me. I wait for a few more minutes just to be sure, but the surface of the ocean is glassy with no sign of a shark. Paddling for the next wave, I catch it easily, gripping my rails and hoisting myself to my feet as the board's nose dips downward. My toes grip the wax on the deck of my board and I'm flying across the gigantic face of the wave.

As the wind whips into me, nothing can take away from this moment. Nothing, not even the black shadow that follows me on the inside of the wave. I sense the shark before I see it on a reverse cutback that brings me nearly nose to nose with its ten-foot bulk. Although they can't hurt me, they can do a lot to everyone else. And it will be because of me.

Noting the swarm of people surfing, my sense of responsibility kicks in. With a flush movement, I detach my leash to release my surfboard and dive into the face of the wave, facing the creature head-on. It veers away, sensing that I am a far bigger predator than it is, but I need to make sure that it heads back into deeper water...away from the cove. Breathing through my gills, I swim easily after it, allowing a fine sheen of webbing to connect my human fingers and toes together so that I can swim faster. It's not a full-morph but just enough to help me keep up with the monster. No doubt my slight transformation will draw other things, but I will be out of the water long before that happens.

The shark swerves deeper and suddenly I lose it in a bed of long kelp. Disoriented, I twist around. Somehow, I've lost my bearings. But I don't have a second to lose worrying about where I am because I'm face-to-face with a creature that looks like some sort of ancient Greek monster. The bottom half of her body is that of some kind of sea eel while the top half is that of a striking woman with long black hair. Her face is a perfect oval covered in tiny fins, her eyes crimson pools. I've never seen this half woman half creature before, but I would know her anywhere, in any form.

Ehmora.

But it's not really her. It's a glimmer. I know that because she would never face me directly. As the only living heir of the High Court, in person, I can force her to yield to me. She's not that stupid.

Several lethal-looking black sea snakes flutter at her sides, two near me. They're highly venomous, I know, and unlike many other poisonous species, they can control how much venom they inject into their prey, causing anything from localized numbness to death in seconds. A brief childhood memory of one of the Sapphire Court's Aquarathi dying from an attack of a swarm of sea snakes floods my brain. Their venom had killed him instantly. Although Ehmora is a glimmer, the snakes aren't. I hide my fear behind a show of bravado.

"It was you," I say in our language. "Your snakes killed Renza from the Sapphire Court, just like you killed my father."

Ehmora smiles but it is a dead smile, a crack in her features, nothing more. "Ah, yes, that one." She waves a hand at the snakes around her. "They are good servants. But there's one thing that they love more than the taste of Aquarathi. Human flesh." Her threat couldn't be more obvious. "And your father, well, the rumors are he got himself entangled with a bloom of box jellyfish while hunting. How unfortunate."

I ignore her taunt about my father. "You think I care about these humans?"

Her smile distorts into an ugly grin. "Of course you do. I've been watching you with them, but I know you know that already. Your best friend, Jenna, perhaps?"

"What do you want, Ehmora?" I ask, despite the churning in my stomach at the sound of Jenna's name on her lips. I don't deign to address her formally as queen. She is a traitor of the worst kind. Her face twists at my deliberate slight. "Are you going to kill me, too?"

"No, darling. I need you. But once more, you know that already, don't you?"

The woman studies me, bending her head to one side. This time her smile is real and predatory, flashing white through the glassy water. It chills me to the bone, as if I'd just been measured and found to be a larger threat than she'd expected. Good. I thrust my chin out in defiance of her and her stupid pet snakes. Her expression turns stony.

"I will never give in to you," I shout, my anger pushing the frond of iridescent thorns on my forehead—my crown—outward. Her blood-colored eyes flash fire but her face remains perfectly composed.

"You will."

"I'll die before that happens."

"That can be arranged, but I have other plans for you," she says quietly. "But first, you need to be taught a lesson in humility." She nods at the snakes and then the glimmer vanishes.

The sea snakes don't, however, and they crowd around me, their jaws open to obey her last command.

12

The Gauntlet

I'm looking into the jaws of death. Several of them.

At least a dozen of the sea serpents circle me, their eyes as red as their master's. One drop of the snake's neurotoxin can kill three humans and would likely make me lose focus. But they can dispense up to eight drops at a time. Twelve of them with eight drops each add up to a number that I can't afford to mess with.

Glancing down, I see only murky depths both beneath and above me. There's no sunlight where we are, which means we are deep. Way deep. I have no idea where I am in relation to La Jolla Cove, but I have no chance against the snakes if I don't change back. From what Ehmora said, they won't kill me, but there's no way I'm playing nice and taking a willing beat-down.

I'd kill them all for Renza.

My bones elongate under my human skin with little provocation, following the crown of bones that already shifted onto my very human head. It's not painful but as my skin modifies into scales that stretch over its new frame and sleekly defined muscle, I feel the pinch of it like a rubber band against my senses, snapping and lengthening. Fins push out wide—fluid rushing around inside of me and expanding outward.

I flex curled talons and whip my tail. The serpents swim backward to compensate for my new size but don't flee. Their queen has given them a command and they must obey. Gold-and-green fireworks shimmer along my limbs and torso as I send five glimmers out at once like silent golden shadows. Unlike any other Aquarathi, my glimmers can touch. They can inflict pain…all with the power of my mind. Five of the snakes sink into the murky depths beneath us as the force of my water invades and collapses their brains.

Spinning, I dispatch three others with the barbs at the end of my tail. Four left. With no concern for their fallen brothers, the remaining serpents attack me at once, and it's all I can do to not let their teeth get anywhere near my exposed under-belly. But that's exactly where they go—where they've been taught to go, I realize.

Twisting to the side in a rage, I snap my jaws shut on one of the snakes, feeling its soft flesh give way like putty between them. A sour taste fills my mouth but I swallow the rest of it whole. I shred another in half with a swipe of my hind claws. The other two brush against me but I dive downward, my finned tail propelling me like a torpedo.

The remaining two follow me but I'm hoping to outma-neuver them. I flip myself backward, catching one of them in the head with a well-aimed tail strike, and the last one gets a glimmer-death of epic proportions.

Exulted with my victory, I shift back and swim for the sur-face only to find that my brain feels fuzzy. Twisting around to examine my body, I see the faint trail of iridescence leak-ing out from twin holes near my lower belly. Crap, one of the suckers got me. I swim harder but it's no use—I'm no-where near the surface before my vision starts to blur. I can already feel the onset of muscular paralysis. I won't die but I'll be knocked unconscious way before my body can eliminate the toxins.

Crap. Double crap.

White stars explode and then the blackness takes over.

Voices surround me. Human ones. Hazy shapes of bodies are moving as my eyelids flutter open. I can't quite see but I raise a hand tentatively. They're fuzzy human hands. My relief is tangible.

"She's fine!" Jenna's voice is shrill. "Just give her some space."

"Why is she naked?" That one is Sawyer's voice.

"Riss?" Jenna says, leaning down, tugging into place a towel she threw over me after I moved my arm. "I called Soren. They're coming for you but you need to be still. I got your clothes from the locker. Can you shimmy into these?"

"What happened?" I ask hoarsely, pulling on the T-shirt and underwear that Jenna hands me awkwardly beneath the towel. My movements are stilted and painful. My entire body—although human—feels battered and bruised. I remember what happened with the snakes but I want to know what Jenna thinks happened, and how I even got to the shoreline alive when I should have been miles away.

"We regrouped as planned, but you didn't show," Jenna explains. "And then Sawyer saw your board cracked on the rocks and we…" She trails off, leaning in down to my ear. "Everyone thought the worst when we couldn't find you. What happened down there, Riss? Did you…change?"

"Yes. Later…tell you later," I gasp. But the truth is, I don't know what happened down there, especially after the last snake got in its bite. Something or someone found me and dragged me to shore. Was it someone like me? One of us? A friend? Ehmora herself? She said that she didn't want to kill me.

I have no idea what happened and it scares the hell out of me. Closing my eyes, I take a deep breath to make my Aquarathi blood flush out the rest of the toxins. It's more condensed in human form so it should work faster. Theoretically.

"Here, I got a blanket from the first-aid kit in my truck." My eyes snap open. The voice belongs to Lo. "How is she?"

"Awake," Jenna says, tucking the blanket over me.

"Hey." Lo's eyes are as blue as the place I just came from, and full of something I can't quite place. Concern. Maybe something more. "You okay?" he asks me, and I nod. "Do you remember anything? Anything at all?"

My eyes slide to Jenna and she tips her head forward. She'll back up anything I tell Lo. The words fall out of me like rehearsed lines. "I was surfing and thought I saw something. I panicked. I remember falling and then I saw the wave coming down on top of me." I stop, improvising madly. "I must have gotten dashed on the rocks because my wet suit was ripped, and the water getting in there was freezing. I figured I'd die of hypothermia if I didn't at least get to shore. I found a towel and got undressed. Then I passed out. That's all I remember."

"You took everything off?" Sawyer interjects from behind Jenna. She shoots him a glare that he pretends not to see. "Seems a bit much."

"I thought I'd been bitten," I say quickly. "And my swimsuit was in shreds, anyway. Sue me, dude, I was delirious with cold and pain."

"Sorry. Just saying," Sawyer mutters. I meet Lo's eyes. His expression is the same as before, only a corner of his lip is tugging upward as if he finds something amusing.

"What?" I ask him.

"Nothing, just that Sawyer finds your state of undress so

interesting." He smiles, his teeth a fine white line. For some inane reason, I think of Ehmora's perfect smile earlier and I shiver. "What's wrong?" Lo asks, noticing the look on my face. There's nothing similar about their smiles other than the flawless whiteness of them, or maybe Lo is just the first person to smile at me since my interaction with Ehmora. Either way, my stomach sours.

"Just cold," I say.

Lo leans in, his eyes warm. "Do you mind?"

"Mind what?"

But before I've even finished the sentence, he has pulled my entire body against his. He's so warm that it's all I can do to cuddle in against him, seeking heat and comfort. Jenna is smiling and I wrinkle my nose at her. She winks and takes Sawyer's hand, leaving us alone for a minute.

"Thanks for the blanket," I say against his chest.

"My pleasure," he says. We sit quietly, the murmur of voices around us fading now that the almost-dead girl is alive. "So… all your clothes?"

I can hear the laughter in his voice and I shove him in the arm with my free hand. He grabs it with his right and intertwines our fingers. Breath forsakes me as something unfurls deep within my stomach, something raw and beautiful. It makes my heart race and my chest feel like it's going to break apart from the sheer force of it.

His light touch moves to caress my palm and then slides upward again to wrap his fingers between mine tightly. "You have beautiful hands," I murmur. "Like a pianist, long and slender."

"Thank you," he says. "You are beautiful, too." I flush at the look on his face and the feel of his hands closed against mine, reinforcing the sound of his words.

"Don't you mean 'yours'?"

A smile. "No."

"So you don't hate me?" I ask, my own voice tremulous. The heat of him reaches through the thin wool of the blanket, and of their own volition my waters beat against my body with insistent demand.

"No," he says again. "How could I? You're you."

Perhaps it is my tiredness or my own weakness, but for a second, I let myself imagine what it would be like to be with Lo, human or not. If I weren't already lying down, the weakness in my legs at the mere thought wouldn't be able to hold me up. They feel about as strong as kelp fronds. A jittery feeling takes hold of my entire body, and suddenly, I'm the one with the unsteady heartbeat.

"I thought I'd pushed you away," I say inanely.

"You tried." Lo's hand releases mine to move a curl of hair that had fallen out of my ponytail into my face. His fingers trace a pattern on the side of my forehead down my temple to my cheek, and I almost melt with the tenderness of it. "But you didn't succeed."

"I'm glad," I murmur, and blush.

"Me, too."

His voice is so quiet that I have to strain to hear him so I look up. He's staring at me with the most intense expression in his eyes and everything around us stops. The hand that's resting against the side of my face slides around my nape into my hair, his thumb resting against my chin, and I realize that he's waiting for permission.

Permission to kiss me.

I've never wanted anything more than this moment. I smile and he does, too. He bends toward me, his fingers pulling upward, drawing my face toward his. Lo smells of salt and sea, and everything else that I love about the ocean. His eyes are open and are a deep mesmerizing blue, staring deep into mine as if he's searching for something other than my consent to kiss me. I don't know what it is but his gaze makes me feel like I'm made of tingles and air.

At the last minute before his lips touch mine, his eyes flutter closed.

The kiss is a shock of images and smells and feelings, hitting me all at once—my home, my friends, the ocean, the land, beauty, chaos, life and this strange, infuriating, lovely boy. Everything about him flashes into me, and then there's nothing else but Lo.

His lips fit mine as perfectly as our fingers did, and his mouth is as warm as the rest of him. My own hand is splayed against his cheek, holding him to me, as caught as I feel. I've kissed a few boys but nothing came close to the feeling of Lo's lips against mine, and I don't want it to end.

But it does, when I hear Speio's anxious voice.

"Where is she?"

Lo and I pull apart. He leans in to kiss my cheek and then my nose, brushing my hair back with one hand. "You're going to be fine, Nerissa."

I smile at the soft words. He's the only human who calls me by my full name. I like it. I like the way it flows over his lips and sounds like a caress instead of just a name. My gaze falls to his lips at the thought and I flush. I want him to kiss me again. He reads me easily.

"I do, too," he whispers.

"You do what?" I ask, confused.

"Want to kiss you again."

This time my flush invades every part of my body until my ears feel like they're going to melt off. I drag my eyes away and stare at the sand, thinking of Speio and Echlios and how angry they're going to be when they find out.

The tingles flee, replaced by a coil of nervous energy rippling through me. I don't even know what I'm going to say to them. I've never lied to Echlios but I'm considering it. He would flip his lid if he knew that I'd confronted Ehmora alone. And been bitten by a sea snake. And passed out in the middle of the ocean.

"Where is she?" Echlios's voice this time.

"She's over there, by the rocks," I hear Jenna telling him just as he, Soren and Speio come into view, pushing past the group of surfers still standing around.

Lo stands, holding me in his arms, and I'm stunned by his strength. I'm no lightweight but he's carrying me as if I weigh nothing. I long to run my fingers along the sleek bulges of muscle at the edge of his T-shirt but resist the urge with Speio now staring daggers in my direction.

"What happened?" he demands.

"I'm fine, Speio," I say, swinging my legs down and telling Lo that I'm okay to walk the rest of the way. Speio's lips are a thin white line. I can't imagine the trouble he must have been in when he went home after school and had to explain to Soren and Echlios why my Jeep was still in the school parking lot…and why he had no idea of my whereabouts. Echlios's face is a wooden mask. Soren's is full of concern. At least I'll have her on my side if push comes to shove.

"Good," Speio bites out. "Glad you're fine."

"Hey, man," Lo say gently, still holding my arm. "Lay off. She's been through enough today."

"Lay off?" Speio seethes. He's on a short fuse, I can see that now. He's totally furious and looking for a target—one that Lo provides easily. "Who do you think you are?"

"I'm her friend."

"She has enough friends. And she doesn't need any that force her away from school to break the rules. My parents were very worried."

Lo's eyes narrow. "I didn't force her to do anything, bro."

"I'm not your bro." It's obvious that Speio's spoiling for a fight, so I step between them, physically restraining each of them.

"Stop," I say. "It's not his fault, Speio. I wanted to go with them." I glance at Echlios, who still hasn't said a word. He's a master at controlling his emotions, but even I can see the slow tic in his jaw. "I'm sorry I didn't call or text."

"Are you okay, my la...darling?" Soren asks, nearly calling me *my lady* in front of everyone but correcting her slip at the last moment. Her eyes are worried, falling to my side immediately. She can sense the ache where I'd been bitten. I've never been able to hide any injuries from Soren—she's so tied in to me that she feels them as if they are her own. I pulse to her about the sea snake venom and see her eyes widen. She stares meaningfully at Echlios and he steps forward to take my arm, steering Speio out of the way at the same time.

"Thank you," he says to Lo. "We'll take it from here."

I glance at Lo but his face is once more unreadable. He confounds me so much, this boy. One minute he's like an open book, and the next he's a blank slate. He smiles but it's nothing like the one before. This one is reserved and formal. For a second, it throws me, but then I realize that he's meeting my "parents" for the first time. That's enough to put any boy on the defensive.

"Echlios and Soren." I rest my fingers on Echlios's arm and he stops instantly. "This is Lotharius Seavon. He's my friend from school. Lo," I say, looking at him, "these are my guardians, Echlios and Soren. And you know Speio, of course."

"Pleased to meet you," they both say. Speio scowls and walks away.

"A pleasure," Lo says, his smile deepening, although still not quite meeting his eyes, but he's much more relaxed than just a minute ago. He turns to me. "I'll call you over the weekend. Get some rest."

After telling Jenna and Sawyer goodbye, we head home. In the car, Speio is still sulking and not even looking in my direction. His attitude is blatantly disrespectful but I cut him some slack. After all, he's in a boatload of trouble because of me, and even if I am the regent and can do whatever I want, it doesn't mean I should...especially if it makes people I care about take the fallout for me. Finding the balance between queen-to-be and teenage girl is more work than I ever thought it would be.

I sigh and lean back against the car seat, staring out the window and trying to figure out the best way to tell them what happened. I literally have half an hour before everything goes atomic in my house, because when Echlios finds out about Ehmora, he is going to explode. Queen regent or not, I'm in for it in spades. We pull into the driveway and I sigh again, getting out of the car.

"I like your young man," Soren says, interrupting my thoughts.

"He's not—"

"Come on." Speio cuts me off, his voice brittle. He slams the car door. "Everyone on that beach saw you making out with him."

"What is your problem?" I snap, going red at the thought that everyone saw our very public display of kissing. At the time I wasn't even thinking about where we were. "If you're mad at me, take it out on me, not him. Besides, I thought you said he was cleared? Echlios?"

Speio doesn't wait for his father to respond. "He is cleared. I told you, I don't like him, that's all. Something about him just rubs me the wrong way."

"Enough!" Echlios says, glaring his son into silence. But

that doesn't stop me from responding—Speio's irrational anger toward Lo is upsetting to me. Didn't he tell me to date Lo in the first place? He even told me to be careful.

"What, Speio? What exactly rubs you the wrong way? That he didn't ask for your permission before he forced me to cut school to go surfing today? That he didn't ask you to tag along? That he didn't ask you if it was okay to kiss me? Which is it?" My voice is shrill by the last question, and even Echlios is frowning at me from where he's standing at the front door.

"All of it," Speio spits back. "You don't care about anyone else but yourself. Not even your own mother."

I step forward, cracking my palm across Speio's face. Soren gasps at the sound, but not even that is enough to stop the flood of tears from bursting out of me—pain at what Speio has said, regret for what I've done and how my people have suffered, sorrow for not knowing about my mother when I should have known, guilt at undermining Echlios and Soren. I crumple to my knees, my remorse all-consuming, screaming my grief into my wet palms.

"I'm sorry, Riss. I didn't mean—"

"Speio, go inside," Soren tells him, and crouches down beside me. "Nerissa, let's get you inside and into some warm clothes. All will be well, come with me."

Still weeping, I let Soren lead me inside, where I shower and get changed into sweats. In the mirror, my eyes are puffy and bloodshot. Flipping back the protective covering from my human ones, I see that my real eyes are even worse, my pupils dilated and threaded through with fine red lines. The neurotoxins from the snakebite packed a punch. I take a deep breath and dust some concealer on my face. Gripping the sides of the sink, I stare at myself.

"You're an Aquarathi princess. Daughter to a murdered father and heir to a stolen throne," I tell myself harshly. "What you did is done, now take responsibility. Be the queen you're supposed to be…the queen your mother needs you to be."

My family is waiting for me in the living room. Speio's face is still stony but his eyes match mine beneath the concealer, as if he, too, has been crying. Something inside me softens. Our relationship is marked by highs and lows, but despite the rough patches, we have never lost our friendship. Even though his words have cut me deeply, I know he didn't really mean what he said. He was angry and upset because of what I'd done.

As always, Echlios cut directly to the chase. "So what really happened?" I clear my throat and recount in a few short sentences exactly what took place. I leave nothing out because I know I can't, not even to protect my own ego. Speio's words, though cruel, put everything in crystal-clear perspective.

My mother's life is on the line.

And I can't jeopardize that. Not now, not ever.

Their faces become identical masks of shock. Neither Echlios nor Soren will publicly berate me. They may talk about my idiotic risk-taking in private, but I know they won't say anything to my face. They are way too dutiful for that, unlike their son, who takes more liberties than he should. He, for his part, is quiet, his mouth hanging open—hopefully at my bravery instead of my stupidity.

Soren is the first to speak after a long and awkward silence. "A dozen sea serpents," she murmurs. "It's a wonder you were able to take them all on alone. How are you feeling? Still woozy?"

"I'm fine," I tell her. "But I don't think they were fighting to kill. Ehmora's glimmer told them to teach me a lesson and I guess that's what they managed to do."

"Who found you again?" Soren asks.

"I don't know," I say. "One minute I was spiraling downward and the next I was on the beach with Jenna. Someone did, though. Maybe another surfer or a diver."

"Did Ehmora say anything about Lady Neriah?" Echlios asks in a choked voice.

"No, and I didn't give anything away, either." I pause. "What could she have meant, you think, by she has other plans for me?"

"Maybe she means to challenge you in front of the other courts," Speio suggests. "That's how it used to be, remember? In the old days?"

"Yes," Soren says. "But our laws of succession are governed by birthright, not challenge. Nerissa could simply refuse to accept the gauntlet. She is the true heir."

But I'm shaking my head, mulling things over in my head. "No, I think Speio's onto something. I mean Ehmora has my mom, right? So technically she could trade my mother's life for me accepting her challenge. And I'd do it. There'd be no decision. I'd have to do it."

Echlios is nodding. "Speio's suggestion is sound."

"I could do it," I say. "Face her in battle."

"My lady, Ehmora is nearly a century old, cunning and strong. She has years of experience on you."

"And I have youth on my side," I counter. "Plus, I have the one thing she does not."

"What's that?" Echlios asks.

"I have you." I stare at him. "You were my father's best and trusted protector. You're trained in all of our fighting strategies. And he sent you here with me, to protect me, to train me. I'm the one who chose not to learn." I pause, taking a deep breath before blurting out what I'm proposing. "I'm ready now, Echlios."

Speio leans forward, his eyes bright. "She's right. She should have been training with us from the start. We need to make up lost time." I'm so grateful for his support that I shoot him a thankful look.

"This is nonsense," Echlios says. His mouth is tight and he has that stubborn look on his face that says he won't bend to anything I have to say. I've never made him do anything, and always deferred to his lead as my guardian in the human world, but I will if I have to. I know I'm right and that this is the only way. If I agree to her challenge, I will have to fight.

"It's our only option and you know it," I say firmly. "I'm asking you, Echlios, for my father. And for my mother. But if you won't agree, we both know that I have the power to command you to do so as your liege. I don't want to do that, so I'm asking. I am going to fight with or without you. Will you train me?"

Echlios doesn't answer for a long time but I can see his red Aquarathi colors burning scarlet beneath his skin and I've never seen him lose control of himself, ever. Soren reaches her hand across the table to take his. She stares at him and nods just once, and as much as Echlios makes the daily decisions, I understand that Soren makes the big ones. Almost immediately, Echlios's skin settles back into its normal hue but his mouth remains a hard, uncompromising line.

"Fine. I'm not promising that it will be easy. You'll bleed and you'll hurt."

I meet his steely eyes. "When do we start?"

"Right now."

13
Things Are Blooming

A sharp poke in my upper arm jolts me awake, and I wipe the drop of drool pooling at the corner of my mouth.

"Wake up, or Marsden's going to see you," Jenna hisses in my ear. A greenish blackboard swims into view along with the glare of my English teacher, who is heading right for me. I force my eyes open and try to look attentive.

"I'm good, I'm good," I whisper back, rubbing my arm. "What'd you poke me with? A knife?"

"A pencil. Pay attention."

Concentrating on the blurry sonnet text in front of me, I pinch my legs to stop my eyes from going back to sleep and try to focus on what Cara is reading aloud. It's some love sonnet by Shakespeare that she's obviously reading to Lo in an affected voice that makes me nauseated.

"'Love is not love, which alters when it alteration finds...'"

Blah, blah, puke.

No wonder I'm passing out. I should be irritated at her overt flirtation with my sort-of-soon-to-be-but-not-really-boyfriend, but the truth is, I'm so worn out from Echlios's coma-inducing training coupled with intense workouts that her heartsick voice and googly eyes to Lo don't even register on my annoyance scale.

"'That looks on tempests and is never shaken…'"

I do notice that Cara's nearly in Lo's lap at this point but I can only roll my eyes and slouch backward into my chair. Even with recent developments over the past couple weeks, I don't own Lo. We only kissed that one time on the beach, and a few conversations since then does not a boyfriend make.

Still, he did call as promised over the weekend, and since then, we've spoken nonstop into the wee hours of the morning every night, which likely accounts for a large part of my sleep deprivation. We aren't officially dating, but we are getting to know each other. I like that he wants to get to know me, and even though, for obvious reasons, there's a lot I can't tell him, I can still pretend to be a normal teen for a few hours. My secret bliss has only been marred by Echlios's death training every other waking hour. So between school, Echlios and hours of night talk with Lo, I'm practically a walking zombie.

Another poke in the arm. My eyes snap open. "Easy," I hiss, glaring at Jenna.

"Loverboy's staring at you again," she whispers.

"Huh?" I say, peeking over at Lo. "No, he's not. Googly-Eyes's poetic laments have totally hypnotized him. I mean, who wouldn't be brain dead by now?"

"Look again, he's watching you. He's doing that weird I'm-watching-but-really-looking-elsewhere thing that he does. It's actually kind of adorable."

I glance over again but am distracted by Cara's antics. She's nearly done and has started fluttering her eyelashes to the point that it looks like she has something caught in her eye. I hide my snort with a cough. Jenna is right, though—Lo's face is intensely focused as if he is somewhere else. I shrug. "I don't think he's looking at me, but can you blame the guy? I'd be screaming for mercy if I were in his shoes."

Something wet tickles the back of my neck and I frown at Jenna. "Cut it out."

"What? I didn't do anything."

"Ms. Marin and Ms. Pearce, if you have something to say, please do share it with the class," Mrs. Marsden says loudly. Every single head turns toward us, including Cara's furious one for stealing any of the slightest bit of her thunder.

I freeze like a deer in headlights but Jenna interjects smoothly with an earnest smile, "We were only just saying how lovely Cara's poem is, and we'd love to hear her read more, Mrs. Marsden."

"Yes, yes," I agree fervently. I can't get detention. Not only is it one of Echlios's rules, but it'll also cut into training time and we don't know how much time we have left. "We'd really love to hear some more." My emphasis on the word *love* is so effusive that even Mrs. Marsden looks a trifle suspicious.

Marsden's face is skeptical but she nods at Cara to continue. Cara's fury has morphed into complete saccharine sweetness now that the spotlight is back where it belongs. She's an unpredictable bundle of awesomeness, that one. I'm not really looking forward to the day when Lo makes his intentions toward me public and Little Miss Shakespeare goes postal. A part of me secretly hopes that we can keep it quiet, but in a small school like Dover that's near impossible.

Cara's overhoneyed tones are enough punishment. "'Rough winds do shake the darling buds of May…'"

Thankfully, the bell puts us all out of our Cara-induced misery, and I grab my stuff with a smothered groan. Even walking is painful. Echlios is a slave driver. Not only does he have us doing deep-water fighting sessions, he also has us training in human form, which makes no sense to me. If I face Ehmora, we'll be in Aquarathi form. When I voiced my opinions, he shut me down by saying that our core strength is the same, regardless of external shape or stimulus. I guess he has a point.

"Why're you walking like you just got off a horse?" Sawyer asks.

"Because I just went horseback riding," I say, stuffing my books into my locker.

"What? Where?"

"Be nice," Jenna says, shoving past Sawyer to her locker. "Don't lead him on. You know how literal he can be. Now he's going to be asking about horses all day long." Sawyer turns red at Jenna's teasing, belatedly realizing that I, of course, was being facetious. He grins good-naturedly.

"Asshat," he says to me.

"Yeah, well, Cara brings out the snark monster in me. Anyway, I've been working out with a personal trainer," I tell him as we walk together to the cafeteria. I look around for Lo but don't see him. I don't want to be too obvious about seeking him out, so I keep walking. "Have to lose a few pounds and get into shape for next summer."

"Why?" Sawyer asks, frowning. "You're ripped. If you need to get in shape, then the rest of us are hosed."

"She's training for a triathlon," Jenna says to Sawyer, and I send her a grateful glance. She always knows exactly the right thing to say that will make sense and not sound like an outright lie. She's the only one who knows the truth about what Speio and I are doing with Echlios. I can use all the help I could get, even from a human.

Contrary to what Speio wanted, I decided to trust Jenna with everything…down to what happened with Ehmora and the snakes. She was horrified, especially to learn about my not-dead mother, but agreed with my plan to train just in case our suspicions on Ehmora's end game were correct. Jenna will also be a good cover if anything happens at school, or within our circle of friends.

As she's being right now.

Not that I only need her for that. I love being able to have someone to talk to who isn't Speio or Soren. Someone on the human side who gets that girl side of me, because she exists, too, right along with my Aquarathi side. I can't discount that part of me. And who knows, maybe that will help me against Ehmora.

"Cool," Sawyer says, looking at me with new respect, piling food on his tray like he hasn't eaten in a week. "How long's the bike piece? I didn't even know you liked riding. We should go this weekend. I know some great trails."

"Um—"

"One-mile swim, twenty-mile bike ride, five-mile run," Jenna supplies, once more to the rescue. She's a master strategist, that one. "And she can't. She has training 24/7." We carry our trays over to an empty table and sit down. I look again for Lo but still don't see him. I don't see Cara, either, which starts to grate on my nerves.

I bite into my fish and chips, and notice Jenna staring at me. "What?" I ask with a mouth full of food.

"You're eating fish?" Jenna whispers into my ear.

I stop chewing to stare at her and nod. "You saw me eating sushi at home, remember?"

"That's kind of cannibalistic, don't you think?"

"It's the law of the jungle." I swallow and answer. "Or the ocean in this case. Bigger fish eat little fish. We're king of the aquatic food chain." I grin and smack my lips. "Normally I like my meals way less cooked than this but when in Rome…"

"Eww, gross!"

"What's gross?" a male voice interjects. Lo slides in beside us to sit next to me, facing Sawyer across the table. His smile is incendiary. I try not to notice the brightness of it—or any of the unhidden feeling behind it—and stare at my food after returning a tiny smile of my own.

"Riss is into raw fish, that's what Jenna thinks is gross," Sawyer offers. "Rabbit food, I say. Give me a cheeseburger any day."

"I like burgers," I protest. "I just like fish more. And who doesn't like sushi?"

"I like sushi, too," Lo says. "I know a great place. We should go one of these days, if you like."

"Like on a date?" Jenna can't help herself, but Lo takes it all in with good humor, smirking at her obvious ploy.

"Sure, a date sounds good," he says, totally playing along at my expense and winking at Jenna. Her expression is gleeful. "When do you think she'll prefer to go? Friday or Saturday?"

"Definitely Saturday," Jenna says.

"Um, guys," I say. "I'm, like, right here. And as empty as my social calendar may be, I'm not that desperate. I can make dates for myself. Plus, I can't Saturday. I have training." I sigh, cursing my stupid idea of training with a certified masochist. "For the foreseeable future, I am on lockdown."

"You can't go out to eat?" Sawyer says.

"Nope. School, homework, hockey, training. This is my life."

Underneath the table, Lo's hand slips into mine, and for some reason it reminds me of our kiss on the beach. His thumb circles in the inner part of my palm, and every part of me is consumed by warmth. With each move of his fingers, my pulse spirals. If my skin gets any warmer, I'm going to burst into flames. Everything else—Cara, dating, training—takes a backseat to the tingles taking over my entire body just from Lo's light touch.

"Riss!" Jenna is yelling over the table. "Hello?"

"What?" I say, blushing and ripping my hand out of Lo's.

"I've only been saying your name for the past ten minutes," she says, shoving something in my face. A newspaper. With an article about an ocean disturbance last Friday just before the big storm, something about phytoplankton. "Did you guys see this?" She stares meaningfully at me, glancing away quickly when she sees Lo looking at us.

Grabbing the paper, I read a few lines only to have my stomach sink. The storm had blown in on Saturday as predicted and the pictures showed some of the oversized swell, but that wasn't all. My fingers clutch the newspaper as dread pools in my stomach. I didn't know about this, though—this one is all me.

Lo leans in and scans the headlines quickly. "Cool, I love plankton, amazing creatures. Something must have disturbed them."

"What's it say?" Sawyer asks, looking over the top. "I surfed one time at night during the Red Tides and it was magic. I was like a fairy surfer with a trail of blue pixie dust."

A snort from Jenna has Sawyer going pink. "'Cause that's exactly what you want to be, a fairy surfer. You're lucky I'm madly in love with you with the things you come up with."

"Fairies are cool. Especially badass boy ones," Sawyer retorts. "Come on, Riss, ignore my unimaginative girlfriend and read."

I read out loud. "'Experts are baffled by the localized appearance, commonly called a bloom, of greenish-blue phytoplankton—early for this time of year—two days ago about forty miles northwest of San Diego. Marine biologists at the San Diego Marine Center claim that the odd cluster of the organisms must have been preceding the famous Red Tides, which periodically affect the

California coastline, turning the waters an electrifying blue at night.'" I pause, the weight in my stomach rising into my throat.

"Keep going," Sawyer insists, his eyes wide.

"There's not much more," I say. "Just a comment from Kevin at the center that phytoplankton is usually blue, and this one was an anomaly that looked more green and yellow instead. They're saying it was a marine abnormality because it only lasted a few minutes and it was during the day. And they plan to learn more with some expedition to capture data." I can't read any more, and I shove the paper toward Sawyer. "Here you go. Knock yourself out."

My belly feels like there's a black hole in the bottom of it that's sucking me in. The bioluminescence reported in the paper was obviously me, when I'd been fighting off Ehmora's serpents. We must have been closer to the surface than I'd thought for any of it to be visible. The plankton had been a lucky dodge, but I know that Echlios will only be more on edge if he knows that any bioluminescence—particularly mine—is the subject of potential discussion and research at the marine center.

"As much as I love plankton, I gotta run," Lo says, pushing his chair backward and standing. "See you in Calc," he tells me. "Have to see Cano."

"What's up with Cano?" I ask, forgetting about the article.

"What can I say? No one's immune to these charms," he says with a deadpan look, and I burst into laughter. "Plus, he likes to think that he's in control. You know, running the school like it should be run, and he wants to make sure I'm toeing the line. Didn't exactly get off on the right foot, if you remember."

Meeting Lo that first day seems like aeons ago. We had a spark from that very first day, only I was too blind to see it. Or maybe I did see it, and was afraid of what it would mean for me. Either way, I know that I can never ignore what I feel for Lo, even if it won't last because of who I am. And with everything moving so quickly with Ehmora, my time here is limited. For all I know, she could challenge me on my seventeenth birthday, the minute I come of age.

"I remember. See you later."

"I'll catch you guys later, too," Sawyer says. "Need to talk to Coach for a second. Wait up, Lo. I'll walk part of the way with you."

Jenna sighs and falls back into her chair. "I thought they'd never leave. Sorry about the newspaper. I brought it from home and had to show you."

"No, I'm glad you did. I'd rather know than not know."

"So I take it that was you?" I nod. "I figured after what you told me. The distance sounded right. Will they be able to trace anything?"

I shake my head, toying with the French fries on my plate. "No, because it's not plankton. But I'm going to need to find some, and fast."

"What for?"

"Hello! Unexplainable phenomenon, curious scientists, ZERO plankton—what do you think would happen?" I nearly screech, letting my bubbling panic rise to the surface.

"Riss, calm down," Jenna says in an even-toned voice. "They're scientists, not the FBI. They'll put it down to a jellyfish bloom or something like that. Come on, it's the ocean. Things move quickly, you know that better than anyone. Relax and don't go hunting down any plankton, for heaven's sake."

"Right." It's the only word I can manage, because, of course, she's right. She's always right. "I swear to God, you are one of the smartest humans I have ever met, and we think we're way more evolved than you are."

Jenna grins, her face wreathed in mock shock. "You're a fish, an überevolved fish, I'll give you that. But more evolved than humans, come on!"

"Girlfriend, I can transform from this form to another. Evolve that."

"No fair! That's biological evolution and nothing to do with intelligence." The bell rings, interrupting our sham power struggle, and Jenna shoots me her game face. "Species intelligence showdown, my house, after school."

Laughing, I completely forget about the stupid article and all of my worries. I love that girl so much. "Can't. Have training after school. But definite rain check, Miss Brainy-Pants."

The rest of the day passes by quickly. I might have fallen asleep a couple times but no one noticed and I didn't get the pencil death jab from Jenna, so win–win all around. Sawyer and Lo took off with the surf team right after school and Jenna had to meet her mom in town. I'm on my own, but not really because I get to go play Torture-the-Princess with Echlios. Yay, me.

Oddly enough, I haven't seen Speio all day. I know he's at school because we drove here together, but I haven't seen him lurking around the hallway or the cafeteria like my second shadow as he usually does. It's not like me not to notice his absence but I've haven't exactly been on my game most of the day.

I pull out my phone to see if I have any texts as I'm walking to the parking lot, and notice that Speio's waiting, leaning casually against the Jeep. "Were you at school today?" I ask him.

"Sort of."

"What kind of answer is that? Either you were or you weren't."

He shrugs. "I was, but then I wasn't. Had to do something

for my father," he adds when he sees my look. "Something to do with jellyfish. A whole bunch of them."

My heart sinks. "He saw the newspaper article."

"It's all good. Fighting for your life against a psychotic rebel queen wannabe qualifies as a hall pass on this one." Speio jumps into the passenger's side of the Jeep. "He isn't mad, he just wanted to make sure that you're covered, given all the attention. You know, just in case someone talks to someone else who lets something slip, and then they find out you're really an alien giant sea creature pretending to be human. And then the Men in Black show up and we're all toast."

"You watch way too many movies," I say, starting the engine. "And you know that Jenna would never say anything, slip or not. She's like a vise." Speio quirks his eyebrow and I drop the subject. "So how'd you get them? The jellyfish?"

"Pheromones." I almost choke at the word. "And it wasn't easy. You totally owe me by the way," Speio says. "First of all, I had to swim nearly to China to find the right kind of jellyfish with green bioluminescence to match yours, and then I had to get them excited enough to follow me back here. No small feat, I assure you." He pauses, his face completely serious. "Just so you know, I now have a harem of Aequorea Macrodactyla of my very own in the bay, so watch out."

"Aequo-what?"

"Jellies with green light." He pats himself on the back with a smug grin on his face. "Thank you, Speio. You are so awesome, and what would I do without you?" he says to himself with a meaningful look at me. I repeat his words, with admiration written all over my face. His mouth screws up slightly. "I do have to admit that it was kind of gross, though, turning on a completely nonsexy species. I felt a little seedy."

This time I can't hold back my laughter, and neither can Speio. "You're amazing, you know that," I tell him, wiping the tears from my eyes. "And you're right, I wouldn't last half a day without you."

"So anything happen at school today that I should know about?" he says.

"Not really. I was practically asleep all day." I make the turn into our driveway and collapse against the wheel. "Seriously, how can you look so chipper? I'm exhausted."

Speio smiles in sympathy. "You'll get used to it. You missed out on a lot. Don't worry, the first few days are always the worst."

A twinge of regret hits me as I think of all the missed time when I should have been training with Echlios and Speio instead of ignoring my duty. "Spey, do you think I'll be ready?"

Speio takes a long time before he answers, running his hand back and forth over his head as if he can't find the right words. "I think you'll be as ready as you can be. As queen, you can also name a champion in your stead. You don't have to fight."

"I could never do that!" I say.

"People fight for kings every day."

"That's people. We're Aquarathi. We fight our own battles," I argue hotly. I can't even stomach the idea of sending someone else to fight in my place. Ehmora's conflict is with me, not anyone else.

"And that is the pride that will get you killed. Sometimes you need help, Nerissa, and you don't think to ask for it. You can't do everything on your own. And you can't fight Ehmora on your own."

"Watch me," I snap, and walk away, our earlier cheer gone like dust in the wind.

As grateful as I am for what he's done with the jellyfish cover, Speio's superior attitude rubs me the wrong way. Is it because I'm female? Or a princess? We're not human, and we never will be. As much as I like humans, I know I can never be exactly as they are. I see that now more clearly than ever. I thought being human could be an escape from who I am, but instead I learned to appreciate being Aquarathi more.

In our society, it's true that the males are the fighters, but the females are the real leaders. We make the hard decisions. I refuse to let some male fight on my behalf just because that's the way of things. I need to avenge my father and save my mother. If the rules don't apply to Ehmora, then they won't apply to me, either. I'm not a coward, and if she issues a challenge I will face the challenger directly, win or lose.

I'll just have to change the game.

Because one thing's for certain…if I don't, I'll die.

14
Paper Walls

The marine center beach is crowded with people who want to see the amazing green jellyfish that showed up hundreds of miles from where they usually live. I have to hand the credit to Echlios and Speio—it's a brilliant cover. Biologists are coming up with all kinds of theories that the jellyfish migrated following cooler waters or a food source.

I didn't think my theory of them having the hots for a certain blond boy would fly so I stayed quiet and kept myself busy. It's the most action the marine center has seen in weeks, since a whale beached itself a few months ago. Echlios relented to let me do a couple volunteer shifts at the center, especially after I insinuated that people would ask questions if I didn't at least put in an appearance. It was a total lie, of course, but it worked.

Well, with Soren's help.

Echlios narrowed his eyes and stared at me suspiciously, but then caved when Soren gave him the look. She is quiet, but she has her ways of getting things done. I tried to tell her thanks but she only shushed me and said that I needed to have a breather away from the house—and her husband.

It's also been nice to see Jenna outside of school, and, of course, Lo, who has regular shifts at the center. He confessed to me during one of our late-night phone calls that he only agreed to Leland's suggestion for working there because of me and hadn't realized that he would end up liking it so much. It reminded him of the work he used to do in Hawaii with his foster dad. He's now a regular, although he isn't working today.

Which is why when he shows up at the front desk where I'm doing some filing to get away from the crowds out back, I'm baffled.

"Hey," Lo says.

"What are you doing here?"

"You're here. So I'm here, too." His words could incinerate ice, far less a girl with a definite non-icy heart. I'm hanging on by a thread not to be a puddle on the floor.

"Oh." It's the only word I can translate from my brain to my mouth. Everything else is gibberish. "But you don't work today."

"No, but you do." And…puddle.

Lo's dressed in board shorts and a plain black T-shirt. His sandy hair is a windblown mess that makes me ache to smooth it with my fingers, but I restrain the urge. "When do you get off work?" he asks me.

"Couple hours."

"What do you have to do?"

"Get more jellyfish samples," I say with a resigned look. "We've got an hour of daylight left so I have to leave now."

"Want some company? I'm volunteering my services," he says, bowing with a flourish. "It's your lucky day!"

We check in with Kevin, who is so totally bombarded by questions that he just nods insensibly in our direction, so we take that as a yes and load up the boat. I toss in our scuba gear and we're off to find Speio's harem.

Out in the bay, the sky is such a clear uninterrupted blue that I can hardly tell where it ends and the ocean begins. The wind is cool, whipping into my face as we make our way out toward San Clemente Island, an uninhabited island owned by the U.S. Navy. Kevin's been tracking the jellyfish patterns, and they've been moving steadily out to sea. I'm sure that Speio will be heartbroken that his little lady friends are leaving.

I'm so focused on getting us to our destination that I don't notice when Lo comes up behind me. His hands start at my shoulders and move down my arms to slide in over my fingers on the boat's steering wheel, and then back up again. I don't even know how I'm still standing. His simple touch ignites a flame in the pit of my stomach that spreads through my chest and into my limbs like wildfire. I'm not even breathing when Lo wraps an arm around my middle and pulls me against his chest. The boat jerks wildly the moment that his lips touch the indentation of my neck just above my collarbone.

With a shiver at the impression of his lips searing my skin, I steady the boat and slow to a stop, letting it rest in the middle of the open ocean where the slow-rising waves lap against its sides. I twist around only to find myself sandwiched between the steering wheel of the boat and Lo. His chest is a warm wall of muscle. Flashes of the time I'd seen him with his wet suit rolled down around his waist rise up to torture me. If my body can get any warmer, it does.

"Hi," he says in a husky voice, his hands falling to my hips.

I clear my throat. "Hi." I want to look anywhere but his eyes, those navy-colored eyes that make me feel so unhinged, but I can't. I'm drawn to them like water.

"It's nice to be alone."

"Yes." I can answer only in monosyllables. My hands are trembling so I shove them around my back, grabbing the metal of the steering wheel to steady myself. Being alone with Lo is exciting but terrifying. I'm more scared for him than I am for myself. What if I lose control and he sees things that he shouldn't see? What if I change?

What if I'm already changing?

"The jellyfish," I blurt out inanely, breathless. Tingles race outward from the place on my hips where Lo's hands are still resting. I swear his palms will be forever branded into my skin, with the amount of heat they're generating beneath them.

"What about them?" he says, kissing along my hairline to my temple.

I should push him away but I can't. I'm utterly helpless, at his mercy. Every touch of his lips burns into my skin, imprisoning me even more. I can feel the metal of the steering wheel behind me bending under the force of my fingers. It's the only thing holding me to reality even as every kiss threatens to pull me away.

My unexpected weakness makes no sense but I can put it down to only one thing…Dvija. It's starting, I can feel it—the tides inside of me rushing and receding, growing ready to find that perfect mate. In May I'll turn seventeen. Maybe Dvija isn't that far behind, so it's logical that I'm on edge and so responsive to Lo. No human could make me experience feelings as powerful as these.

Or maybe I've just never experienced what humans call being in love. Humans choose their mates, even if it's not the right choice. It's a matter of will versus genes. Bonding for us is more primal, more a case of genetic compatibility than something based entirely on feelings. Maybe this is a mind over matter phenomenon…a natural part of human life. Or maybe humans my age fall this deeply every time.

Lo moves his hands to my cheeks. "What are you thinking? I can see your mind whirring in there."

Flushing, I study the faint freckles bridging his nose. "Nothing."

"It's definitely something. You have these lines just here—" he rubs the space between my eyebrows "—that show up when you're thinking about something."

"They do? How do you know?" This time Lo's the one to flush darkly. "Oh, so Jenna is right. You do stare at me when I'm not looking." Lo smiles and rests his forehead on top of mine. A cool ocean breeze blows between us, lifting the hair off my face and fanning it into his.

"I stare at you all the time," he confesses in a whisper.

"Why?"

"Because you intrigue me. There's something so different about you. You're not at all like any of the girls I know."

"You mean like Cara? That wouldn't be a stretch."

Lo laughs at my cynical expression and leans backward. "Cara is just misunderstood. Underneath all of that makeup and bravado, there's actually a really nice girl."

I take advantage of the opportunity to disengage myself and check on the scuba gear. "We will just have to agree to disagree. We used to be friends once, you know, Cara and me. Until she decided that she didn't like anyone showing her up." Lo doesn't say anything, and I take a breath. "Now we're like oil and water. Some things never mix, no matter what's going on underneath. She puts on a front for you that you're obviously falling for." I don't know why my voice sounds angry but it does. I should never have brought Cara up.

"There's a lot you don't know about her," he says, and a shadow crosses his eyes. "And I'm not falling for her. I should think that would be obvious."

"Why is that obvious?" I snap, now irrationally angry and throwing scuba gear around as if taking my frustration out on them will help.

"Because I'm falling for you."

"Oh." That got me.

Lo leans against the side of the boat, his arms across his chest. "Why is that so hard for you to believe? You're smart, you're funny and you're cool." I snort and blush at the same time. "And you surf. That's just a bonus." He pauses, watching me carefully as if weighing what to say next—trying to find that middle ground of saying just enough without giving too much away. "You intrigue me because you're such a contrast of opposites. You're so aloof and uncoordinated sometimes, like you don't quite fit in."

"Thanks," I blurt out, laughing. "I think." But I'm left wondering whether he's just perceptive or whether I'm more of an outsider than I think I am. The princess versus the teenager… the metaphor of my life.

Lo shakes his head. "No, I meant that I don't really fit in, either. We're so similar, you and I."

I blink, savagely squashing my immediate negation. If only he knew. Lo and I are nothing alike. He's human…and I'm a giant alien monster. We are entire worlds—universes!—apart. He's falling in love with a mask, a fake human version of me that will only break his heart. As he will undoubtedly break mine. We are a romantic tragedy on an epic scale, doomed to disaster.

Literally.

So what? my inner voice argues. Is losing your heart so bad? You're both willing participants, and if it doesn't work out, it doesn't work out. That's life. Human life. It's what you signed up for. So live it. Who knows how much time you have left here? Or at all?

"Why does my inner voice sound like Jenna?" I mutter, but my decision has been made. I look up at Lo, who is still studying me from the other side of the boat. I smile at him, tremulous. Every beat of my heart is in that look, and I hold nothing back. "I think I'm falling for you, too."

"Well, then," Lo says with an unsteady smile of his own as he walks toward me. "If you'd gone the other way, I would have had to pull out the big guns."

"And what are those?" I'm completely unprepared when he flips up the end of his T-shirt to display his impeccable rock-solid abs, but I somehow manage to find my voice, ears aflame. "I'm not that shallow, but yes, those aren't bad."

"Not bad? Come on, I saw you checking me out the other day when we were surfing. You enjoy the Lo show?"

"The Lo show? Really?" But I can't help grinning at his over-the-top expression. "You are such an ass! Seriously, how do you go from saying the sweetest things to the most douchy things in the space of a breath?"

"Part of my charm?" he offers.

"Not so much," I say in a dry voice. I gesture at the gear now strewn all over the deck. "So you want to suit up or you prefer to stay out here?"

"Let's just go in."

"It's like fifty-eight degrees in there, and the sun's already set," I tell him. The cold water won't make a difference for me, of course, but I don't want him passing out from hypothermia or something.

"We'll be fine. It'll only be for a minute, anyway. Plus, it looks like both of us could use a cold shower," he says with a wicked grin.

"Maybe you do," I shoot back. "I'm immune to your charms."

"Oh, really, shall we test that theory?"

In answer to his mock threat, I strip off my shirt and shorts, grab a face mask and dive into the water. An answering splash tells me that he has done the same.

The sky is already a darkening blue, its edges tinged with pink and gold from the thin sliver of sun that is nearly sunk into the sea. All I can think is that Lo's eyes are the exact color of the ocean right now. Jellyfish surround me, firing at my touch. I spin my hands in a slow circle, watching as the spot where we've both dived into the water lights up with green star-shaped fireworks bursting outward.

Lo surfaces, his eyes lit with reflected green light, and dives underneath the surface. I meet him halfway as he grabs me around the waist and spins us both in the water, our movements causing a flurry of green lights to burst all around us. It is more than magical—our own private wonderland of lights, shimmering all around us at every touch of our bodies.

I break away and dive down into the mass of jellyfish, stretching my fingers outward, twirling my body and leaving a trace of vibrant emerald effervescence in my wake. Out of the corner of my eye, I see Lo doing the same, and I laugh underwater, throwing my head back and forgetting to breathe like a normal human.

I am foolish and in love and unhinged.

Lo's fingers catch mine, drawing me to him, fiery green light igniting all around us. The moment electrifies as Lo holds me close, my body wrapped against his. I let my hands slide over his shoulders and let the magic transport me to another world where Lo is like me, and he is the one I've been seeking all this time. The lights are mesmerizing, and I'm a willing fool, falling for my own lies as he turns me, weightless, in his arms and surrounded by radiance.

Our lips meet underwater and the fireworks inside match the ones on the outside, explosion for explosion. And everything inside of me falls into willing, hypnotized, beautiful silence.

For the rest of the weekend, I'm walking on air. Even Speio shoots me these random odd looks but I guard my secret closely, holding it like the prize it is. I know I will eventually have to tell Echlios and Soren about my decision with respect to dating Lo, but for now, I just want to pretend that the information is mine alone. I want to savor it and appreciate it just for myself, if only for a few days. Truth is, it has given me new strength because either I'm getting stronger or Echlios's training is getting easier. It's likely the former, but I know deep down that it is because of Lo. I feel alive, more alive as a human than I've ever felt. Being with him makes me feel invincible...untouchable.

As we're wrapping up our Aquarathi study session Sunday night, Soren shoots a censorious look across the table to note my wandering attention. Flushing, I stare at the scroll she has given me to study. Made from a superthin gellike material, it details the history of my people and the hierarchy of all the courts. With a finger, I trace my family tree back several generations to when it was the Gold Court. Nearly five hundred years ago, my great-grandfather won the challenge for rule against the Sapphire Court because the ruling Emerald Court had had no heir. For the past half a century, the Gold Court has been the High Court...a coveted rule that I almost handed over to Ehmora.

"Okay, I'm ready," I tell Soren.

She takes the scroll and proceeds to quiz me on the political structure of my kingdom. I answer each question in succession, watching as she makes little notes on a piece of paper. As much as Echlios is my trainer and protector, Soren's job is to make sure I'm appropriately groomed to rule. Which means studying endless historical scrolls and being tested to no end on said scrolls. On top of that, I'm officially enrolled in the Soren princess etiquette boot camp, where I learn the art of how to enter a room, how to entertain dignitaries, how to be graceful and how to do all manner of useless things.

"Why do I have to learn all this stuff?" I asked Soren once.

"When you are queen, you will be required to act like one, and it is my job to ensure that you do so."

"What if...I'm not good enough?"

"On the outside, you will be. Confidence will follow."

"What if I don't want to be queen?"

Soren stared at me with an unfathomable expression. "It is your duty."

A duty I'd chosen to run away from early on. Just as I had avoided training with Echlios, I'd avoided my lessons and anything to do with ruling the High Court. But now that our plan is in action for me to assume my rightful place, we've resumed my formal training with renewed vengeance.

"You did well," Soren says, bringing me back to the present. "Two incorrect."

I frown. "Which ones?"

"As Aquarathi queen, you must take the first bite before anyone else may eat."

"That's dumb."

"It is a mark of respect," Soren counters smoothly. "Second, a queen must wait for all lower-ranking Aquarathi to first extend their necks as a show of fealty before extending her welcome."

"I read somewhere that Queen Elizabeth has to extend her hand first."

Soren stares at me. "Humans don't have teeth and claws like we do, do they?"

"Touché," I say, and bite my lip to stop from smiling, watching as she gathers the scrolls carefully into her arms. Soren's sarcastic sense of humor takes getting used to, but she does have her moments.

"We're done for today. Have you finished your regular school homework?" she asks, stopping at the doorway.

I shake my head. "Still have art."

"Dinner is in an hour."

"Where I must eat first?"

"Gold star."

Grinning, I drag my art project to the middle of the dining room table and sigh. I stare out of the window to the sparkling ocean. I'd give anything to be out there instead of in here. Surfing. With Lo. Or doing other things, like kissing. The thought of that makes me breathless, and I shiver with the delicious indulgence of it.

Lo is still completely arrogant but there's so much more beyond the facade. He's caring and smart and his knowledge of the ocean is tremendous, which is a definite plus in my book. Anyone who loves the ocean as much as I do can do no wrong in my opinion. And he does. Not only is he volunteering at the marine center, he's also part of a national organization that supports global ocean policy and coordinates efforts for better conservancy laws.

He's so perfect that, for a moment, I wish that he weren't human. But he is, and that means that someone on his side is looking out for future generations and taking measures to protect the waters of our planet.

If I wasn't falling for him before, I am now.

Lo told me that he's always been interested in the ocean, and growing up near it his whole life made him sensitive to some of the challenges facing conservancy. He told me about his dad, but he also said that his mother was on some important governing board that made far-reaching decisions on federal funding for ocean protection. When I asked him about his mother, he clammed up and said that she was always gone and that he never saw her.

At least he still has a mother that he gets to see. Mine is being held captive by some lunatic usurper.

Of course, I couldn't tell him that so I just sympathized and said that she didn't know what she was missing out on. He laughed and said that he could never measure up, no matter what he did, so it was best for everyone that she wasn't around.

Lo's absentee mother aside—his biological father died when he was a baby—he seems to have everything he wants at his fingertips. He lives in a beautiful cliff-side house in La Jolla that has amazing views. I know it does, because it was empty for years, almost the same length of time that we've been here. Kids used to say that it was haunted but obviously that isn't the case since Lo lives there. We'd only ever talked about it once.

"Did your family always own that house?" I asked him during one of our many phone calls.

"Yes."

"And no one lived there before you got there?" He went so quiet on the phone that I almost thought we'd gotten disconnected.

"No." An awkward silence, and then, "It's my mother's, but she's never here."

"Wow, your own house and still in high school," I'd said. "That's pretty extravagant. Does she live with you?"

"Sometimes. She also has a house in Rancho Santa Fe." I was surprised that they didn't live together and that his mother lived in a very exclusive community, home to the likes of Bill Gates and Jewel, miles away from her son.

"So you live mostly alone?"

"I have a staff. Can we talk about something else?"

We dropped it, but it never really left my mind. The way he said "staff" sounded so empty. The more I get to know Lo, the more I realize that he's a loner, and he lives a very solitary lifestyle. The thing is, Lo chooses to be alone. He never talks to anyone at school—like voluntarily talks to them—except Sawyer when they chat about surfing, and me. Even with Cara, he tends to listen instead of talk. He doesn't hang out outside of school at any of the local haunts in town. He's a loner, a social observer, living more on the outside than on the inside.

He was right when he said that we were similar. Outside of my family, Jenna is my only real friend. I used to be interested in learning the social dynamics of kids at school, and what the humans have to teach me, but that all changed when I got to know her. Turns out, one true friend is worth far more than a handful of acquaintances.

"My lady," a voice calls out, interrupting my thoughts.

"What is it, Soren?"

"Come quickly! To the pool." The urgency in her voice sends wild alarms shooting through me. I toss my art project to the side and race out where Echlios, Speio and Soren are standing at the edge of the pool, staring into the middle of its depths.

"What's wrong?"

Echlios points in silence, his face a wooden mask. In the middle of the pool, lying on the bottom like a dot of blood, is a burnished ebony scale the size of a silver dollar. Ehmora has been here, or has sent one of her human henchmen to leave us a message.

"So what? We knew she was going to challenge me," I say, shrugging my shoulders. "Get that thing out of my pool and destroy it."

"Riss, there's more," Speio says in a small voice. I turn slowly, an ugly sensation prickling across the back of my neck. I can sense it's something terrible…something unthinkable. An ache fills my stomach and suddenly my legs feel like lead weights, refusing to take me back to where Echlios is standing with something in his hand. Ehmora wouldn't be so cruel. She couldn't have, could she?

But she has.

She's more than cruel, after all, and I'm just naive.

Echlios holds out a scroll that has been written in blood—Aquarathi blood—and a box containing a handful of scales and spines that look like they've been hacked off. I don't look at them. I can't look at them.

Instead, I read the letter inked in iridescent blood. There's a time and a date. One month from today—a few days after my seventeenth birthday—she will challenge me for the High Court. Nothing more. No ultimatums, no threats, no warnings.

"Give it to me."

"My lady—"

"Now," I shout, and then gentle my voice. "Echlios, please. I have to see it."

I open the top of the box and retch. Phantom pain slices into my head as I stumble backward, pressing my hands to my scalp. The scales are a pale bluish-purple color, oozing iridescent fluid along their edges. I recognize them as my mother's immediately. But it isn't just her scales in the box, it's her crown...the same elegant ridge of spikes and fins on her forehead that mark mine—the mark of an Aquarathi queen.

The entire thing has been flayed off her scalp.

I don't even realize that I'm screaming.

15

Secrets and Spies

"Nerissa, open the door, please. Please, my lady, you can't stay in there forever."

Pulling my pillow over my head, I wait for Soren's footsteps to recede. It's been three days, and I can't bring myself to come out of my room. I just want to stay in the darkness where I can drown my grief with silence. Because the truth is, if I open my door, I won't be able to control myself. I won't be able to hold myself back. I won't stop until I find Ehmora and rip her into shreds, challenge or no challenge.

I have to find my mother.

I swallow hard. The recollections I have of her are few but precious—a memory of memories—fragmented images of us lying together, a feathered voice against my temple whispering stories of Aquarathi past, a warm curl of tail winding protectively around me, jeweled eyes the exact replica of my own. So much time lost between us…and now, this.

I have to save her.

Lying in the dark, I stare at the slivers of moonlight streaking between the blinds across my door. Echlios said that Ehmora's spies are watching us. I wonder if they're watching us right now. Sliding out of my bed, I pull on a pair of black jeans and a black T-shirt before I slip through my glass doors to the back deck. The pool is glistening in the silvery moonlight but I can't even look at it without being consumed by rage.

"Figured you'd try to slip away unnoticed." I almost jump out of my skin at the whispered voice.

"Jenna?" I whisper back, peering through the gloom before I see her sitting in a chair at the far end of the patio. She's covered in a thick blanket and there's a plate of snacks on the table beside her. "What are you doing here? How long have you been here?"

"I'm your friend, that's what, and only a couple hours. You wouldn't let anyone in so Soren got desperate and called me. Plus, I had to cover for you at school. Again." She shoots me a glare. "Anyway, I decided to try a different tactic and just wait you out, hoping that at some point you'd just go stir-crazy in there."

"You know me pretty well for a human," I say.

I can literally hear the sound of her eyes rolling skyward. "How about, I know you pretty well, period," she retorts. "So where are we going?"

"We are not going anywhere. You are going home."

"Riss, don't shut me out, please."

"I'm not shutting you out. This doesn't concern you. I should have never brought you in because now you could be in danger."

Jenna's voice is gentle. "We can't turn back time, so that's that. I'm already involved. I can help, Riss. Let me help."

"I can't," I say flatly. "I can't lose you, too. Or anyone else." I ignore the feeling of agony bursting through my veins, as well as the green-and-yellow lines that are racing along my arms in furious response. Vinelike tattoos of gold curl up my arms and my neck, making my entire body glow. "She has my mother, Jenna. She—" My voice chokes on the last word, and my knees fail me. I sink to the ground, clutching my head.

Jenna jumps of the chair and runs toward me. "Riss…" But I shove her away almost viciously. If she won't listen to reason, I'll have to force her to leave.

"Get away!" I growl, pushing the spikes up out of my forehead and uncovering my eyes. We are fearsome in full form, but sometimes the half creature, half human appearance is more terrifying. Her eyes widen but she stands her ground, swallowing tightly. I feel the pull of my teeth lengthening into my human mouth and the ridges of my cheekbones pushing outward in sharp angles. I force myself to stop transforming so that I can still speak.

"GO AWAY!" I snarl, letting her see the hideous rows of razor-sharp fangs in my mouth. "You don't belong here." I snap my jaws together in her direction and she jolts backward. I can feel her pulse racing in uncontrollable terror from where I am.

"I'm not afraid of you, Nerissa Marin!" she yells.

"You should be," I hiss.

"You want me to leave, fine. I'll leave," she tells me. "But I'll be back. I'll forgive you because you're hurt, but if you pull any of this go-away territorial shit again, you and I are going to have a problem. Got me?"

The human girl in me wants to laugh at her fierce threats, but I'm too far gone to feel anything but anger. Plus, she's serious. As she leaves, my face relaxes back into its human shape and I fall back onto my haunches. Something wet whispers along the wind and I sigh.

"How long have you been standing there?" I ask my family.

"Long enough," Echlios says.

"I made a mistake with her. Now she'll never be safe."

"We'll keep her safe."

The fury rises like a volcanic tide. "Like my mother?"

Pain radiates across Echlios's face and I almost regret my accusing words. Almost. He's not responsible, but a part of me still can't forgive him for lying to me all these years, even at my father's command.

"Go back inside. I'm going out," I snap, uncaring of my rude tone.

"No, my lady, I must insist—"

I glare him into silence, pressing my will hard enough into his for his eyes to go wide.

He knows exactly what I can do—every day my strength grows. I'm already coming of age. I can feel it beneath my skin like a quiet unfurling storm at my center. After Dvija, my strength will be at its greatest.

"I must insist, Echlios, that you go back inside," I say quietly. He protests but I shake my head. "I don't want to force you to obey me but I will. I am going out. I will be back. I will not do anything foolish."

Soren steps forward from the shadows and places her hand on her husband's shoulder, her eyes watching me very carefully. Normally an open book, her face is unreadable. I stare back and lift my chin, daring her, too, to defy me.

Speio, watching from the sidelines behind his parents, is also quiet. He doesn't meet my eyes, and I'm glad. Because if he's the normal judgmental Speio, he's going to infuriate me, and if he shows any compassion, I will totally lose it. Either way, the outcome is better if he just doesn't look at me.

I walk out of the backyard without a second glance. None of them follow me, which of course, I'd know in an instant. Walking down the deserted beach to the water's edge, I sink my bare feet into the wet sand and curl my toes in. The moon makes the water look like black ink with silvery swirling patterns. I search for any evidence of the jellyfish but they've all gone back out to sea, and sadly, the only color in the ocean is an inky black capped with icy white crests.

I study the water, wondering whether Ehmora is somewhere out there, watching me watching her, but something tells me that she won't be that predictable. My insides twist. I've never hated anyone more. Remembering why I left my house, I step into the water and let it flow around my ankles and soak into my skin, turning to face the beach. Pulling the energy of the ocean into me, my eyes scan the area, all my senses alert.

I throw my glimmer out like a net, widening and widening until I feel it nearly separating the top layer of my skin from the flesh beneath. And still I push. They're there. I know it. I thrust the glimmer out even more, my alien eyes seeing the thin shadow of gold reaching farther than I've even gone before. I'm spread so thin that it feels as if I'm going to separate into the glimmer—I can barely hold on to it. I'm just about to give up but then I feel it.

A slight tug. Somewhere to my left.

Human.

Focusing all my water, I heave the glimmer-shadow to where I'd felt the pull and start running, letting the glimmer lead me like a fishing line. There are two of them. A brutish-looking ogre of a man and a woman built like a truck. She looks official, dressed in army fatigues, whereas he's more of a grunt. She is the one in charge—the one who will have the answers. She sees me coming but stands her ground, her fingers hovering over her sidearm.

Admirable, but stupid.

My glimmer jolts back into me in an electrifying rush, taking energy from the moisture in the air around me. I take a deep breath just as the woman draws her firearm and shoots. Dodging the first projectile, I catch the second in my hand, still running toward her. It's some kind of dart, one that is probably designed to put me out or to slow me down. I leap out of the way of three more darts and fling myself toward her midsection. Out of the corner of my eye, I notice the man taking off without a backward glance for his partner, and without thinking, I fling the glimmer out right at him, taking brute control of the water in his body.

He freezes, unable to move.

Flying onto the sand in a spinning tangle of limbs, I hold the woman down with one arm once we come to a stop and twist the gun away from her with my free hand. She bucks beneath me to dislodge my hold, but even with half my attention focused on immobilizing the second spy, she's no match for my strength.

"How many are you?" I demand. "Did Ehmora send you to spy on me?" She grits her teeth and struggles harder, kicking her knees up. I lean down. "Stop struggling, and answer my questions, or you will be sorry." Instead, the woman twists beneath me to give herself the leverage to smash her forehead into mine. Blazing greenish-gold light flares around us at the contact, but I barely budge. Her eyes widen as she falls back.

"You don't know what I am, do you?" I whisper as the lights wink down my neck and arms. "As you can see, I'm not like you, and you have no idea what I'm capable of." I draw my glimmer in, dragging its captive toward us until the man is just a few feet away. "Cooperate or he dies. Slowly." She stares at him for a minute but then turns back to me with a hard look in her eyes.

"What do I care about him?" she says.

"Because you're all hired guns?" I toss back. "Do you even know what you're doing? Who you're working for? What she's done? What she is?"

I've never killed a human before, but I've had more than

enough practice incapacitating prey bigger than me down in the depths of the ocean. I've numbed their reflexes with my glimmers, even put them into a comatose state. But what I'm about to do goes against everything I've been taught by my father—to never use my powers against humans.

My father is dead. And my mother is a prisoner.

The playing fields have shifted.

I push forward just as I did with Speio—only I'm not giving energy—I'm draining the water from his brain with savage force, watching as the man's face turns purple and visibly thins. He starts to gasp and clutch at his head, clawing at his scalp as if trying to get me out of him. Horrified, I stop and am completely unprepared for the fist that connects with the side of my temple.

The glimmer connection severs and the man crumples to the ground before dragging himself arm over arm in the opposite direction. Another blow jabs me in the stomach, and then I'm hitting the sand, vaulting onto my feet to face the woman. She's holding a knife in one hand, her face coldly furious. She's no novice.

She lunges toward me with the knife, dropping into a crouch and slashing at my waist. I lean backward nearly parallel to the ground and the blade manages only to cut through my clothes. Shaking my head to clear it of the disorientation from detaching the glimmer, I raise my hands in the air, calling her forward. My brain still feels cloudy, and she jumps in once more, slashing wildly as if to take advantage of my confusion. She's fast and well trained.

A hot welt braises my upper arm and I feel blood pour down. That strike was aimed at my neck but I spun counterclockwise at the last moment, deflecting it with my arm. The woman is backing away, staring at the glittery fluid on the blade of her knife.

"What are you?"

"Oh, so now you want to know?" I say casually, slapping my palm over the gash and applying pressure to stop the bleeding. "What do you think I am?"

She lifts the blade to her nose and sniffs in the darkness. "This isn't blood."

"No, it's not," I say. "Why are you spying on me?" The woman eyes me warily, her gaze dipping to the knife and back to me, then narrowing. She's smart enough to know that I'm not human but she's cautious, too. She's been a soldier for far too long. She doesn't have to answer but she does, still studying me.

"Standard surveillance operation."

"With tranquilizer guns? Really? What do you think you're surveying? Wild animals?"

"Looks like it." She raises her eyebrows. I have to admire this woman's gumption—she doesn't back down, that's for sure.

"She's just like me, you know," I tell her. "Your employer? Worse, probably. And you're dabbling in things you have no idea about. Do you even know who I am?"

She shrugs. "I work for hire. If the money's good, I don't ask questions. And it doesn't matter if you're a royal of Europe. Political espionage happens every day. You're just the mark today."

I glare at her. "You think I'm European? You just saw my blood on your knife, glowing an unnatural shade of the northern lights, and you think I'm a mark from Europe?" I want to laugh so badly, I can't even control myself. I snort loudly. "Look again. And remember your colleague. His brain didn't exactly collapse by itself, did it?"

Her eyes harden in the space of a breath. She shifts the

knife from one hand to the other. "Whatever you are, you still bleed. So you can still die."

Our stalemate is over. We circle each other like two predators, but I'm growing tired of the game. I don't want to fight or to extend this pretense that she's a match for me. With a vicious push of my glimmer, I force her to drop the knife. She glances at me incredulously, but I don't stop. I force her to her knees. Strangely enough, she's harder to control than the previous guy, but she's had a lot of torture resistance training, probably from her days in the military.

"How many of you are there?"

She sets her jaw. I squeeze harder and watch her eyes dilate. "Forty," she says under duress.

"Where?"

"Everywhere. At your home, at your school. Everywhere you go, we follow."

"Why?" I ask, wondering if Echlios knew of these spies.

"She wants to know where you are at all times. And who your friends are." Alarm swirls in my stomach. Jenna would be the first person on her radar. I grit my teeth—everyone's at risk.

"Who are the others?" But my question is too vague—and she won't give me names. She'll make me kill her before she does. I need to ask her nonthreatening questions that I can somehow put together for myself. "Do I know any of you? Are any of you in my circle of friends?"

The smile titling the corners of her lips is faint but chilling. She repeats her earlier words. "We are everywhere." Which means Ehmora has spies on the inside. I shudder at the thought. It could be anyone, people I trust, people I see every day.

"Where is my mother?" I ask urgently. At her blank look, I rephrase the question. "The other woman. Where is she being held?" I see a flicker of something in the woman's eyes but still, she resists, pressing her lips shut. I push hard, closing the glimmer around her mind like a net. Tiny blood vessels in her eyes are bursting red already from the pressure. In seconds I'll be down to yes or no answers. "Is she in San Diego?"

"Yes," she spits out, froth flecking the corners of her mouth.

"La Jolla?"

"No."

Time is running out. The woman's eyes have started rolling back in her head, but I can't stop myself. I have to know more, whatever she is hiding. My frustration makes me desperate. I shape the glimmer into sharp points and press into her body. She screams and falls to her stomach in the sand, her torso twisting into an ugly concave arch.

"Where is she?" I hiss. I'm in front of her now, so close that I can smell the fear of death clothing her skin. I don't care. Grabbing her convulsing shoulders, I pull her to face me in a rage-induced fog. "Tell me. Tell me now!"

"Nerissa!" someone shouts. "Stop. You're killing her!"

Rough hands rip me away from the woman, and the fog in my head clears as my glimmer slams back to me with a jolt. Deprived of my prize, the beast in me gnashes its teeth and my eyes focus on the owner of the voice.

Speio.

I scowl ferociously at him as the clouds above us thicken to make the night even blacker than it is, blocking out the moon completely.

"She knows where my mother is," I seethe. "I told you not to follow me!"

"We both know how well I respond to orders," he says. "And I couldn't let you kill her. Her blood would be on your hands."

A cold sense of reason seeps into me as thunder crashes above, responding to the call of my rattled emotions. Lightning splits the clouds, and the seas rise to meet the sky. "It's not like our people haven't killed humans before. And they want to kill us. They're all working for her. Her blood means nothing," I spit.

"Riss, this is what she wants. She needs to get under your skin to make you respond differently than your father taught you...with anger and rage, and without compassion. This isn't you. You know it's not." He glances at the woman lying on the sand, her chest rising and falling in faint motions. "Killing her would push you over the edge. You know that. You're too smart not to know that."

I fall to my knees, touching my head to the sand and feeling the first drops of rain pounding into my back. "You're wrong," I say bitterly. "Compassion? I wouldn't know the meaning of the word. I didn't do anything. All I did was run away like a spoiled little brat. And when my father told me to stay away, it was what I wanted, even though I knew deep down it was the cowardly thing to do."

Speio kneels next to me but he doesn't touch me. "I know you feel like it's all on you, Riss. But it's not. You obeyed your father's last wishes. What happened after that is not your fault."

"But my mother—"

"You thought she was dead. You had nothing to do with how and when she was taken."

"I could have helped her," I argue weakly.

"How? She was gone. Your father didn't tell you for a reason, Nerissa. Maybe he didn't want to hurt you."

"Why?"

"Need makes us do dark things," he says with a cryptic twist of his mouth, and then swallows hard. "We will find your mother, but you can't keep doing this to yourself. And you can't do it alone. You have to trust someone."

"Who, Speio?" I say, turning to face him. "Who can I

trust? Ehmora has spies everywhere, even among our friends. We can't trust anyone."

"You can trust me," he says. "And Echlios, and Soren. We want what you want. To return home with you as the queen. Now, let's go back to the house." Speio helps me stand, not that I need the help, but I like the gesture. He's not usually this gracious. The rain eases and stops, and the clouds separate to reveal a portion of the round white moon.

"What about her?" I ask as we walk past the woman that I'd nearly killed.

"I'll take care of it," he says, stooping down to check her pulse. I'm so focused on not staring at the woman's near-motionless body that I don't see the movement at first. All I sense is a blur of something barreling toward me.

Something huge, and powerful, and angry.

Curled thorns ring outward from its head, and its face is elongated into a ridged, fang-filled snout. Thick muscular arms bend downward into finned claws. The lower half of its body is still fully human, adding to its hideous mongrel appearance.

It's not human. It's something else.

The creature leaps over the woman and Speio, slashing out with a paddle-size talon to swipe first at his accomplice and then at Speio, knocking him senseless. The monster man clicks and pulses in my native tongue, and in the split second before impact, I recognize the second spy from earlier. So my glimmer hadn't killed him! Because he isn't even human. Shock stuns me into immobility. At the last moment, I dive and roll out of the way, sensing something oddly familiar. Yet not at the same time.

He's Aquarathi.

But that's impossible. Our laws compel him to reveal himself to me, but I sensed him as only human. I'm unprepared for the man's counterattack as his blow catches me in the side of the head, and I'm staggering backward. Hot fluid drips into my eyes and stars hover in my vision. Disoriented, I fall onto my hands, my mind reeling with doubt and question after question.

How is he able to survive? Or to transform? Or to not pledge obeisance to me, the living heir? Water sees water, doesn't it?

The creature advances and is nearly on top of me. "I am your queen, stand down," I command him. His eyes burn a putrid shade of yellow as his jaws open and unhinge with a series of furious clicks. His breath is fetid. I know he won't kill me—Ehmora needs me alive, after all—but I know contact is going to hurt like hell.

I brace myself.

The creature's bulk falls against me, his body shuddering as the smell of burning flesh fills the air with sparks flying all around us. Belatedly, I realize that he isn't moving, and I shove him away, confused and relieved. Speio must have taken him out.

"Speio? What'd you do?"

"No, it's not Speio, it's me," says a female voice. I blink twice just to make sure that what I see is real. Jenna is there like an avenging angel, holding a smoking device in her hand. "I Taser-gunned his ass."

"Didn't I tell you to go home?" I say, dazed.

"Yeah, I did go home. To get this." She taps the Taser gun in her other hand like a baseball bat. "Water and electricity don't exactly mix. And I've always got your back, no matter who or what comes after it." I'm still shaking my head in complete awed disbelief at her courage when Speio teeters over to us.

"What the hell was that?" he asks, rubbing his head.

"One of us."

His eyes widen. "But he should have revealed himself to you."

"I know. And he didn't. I only felt him as human. We have to talk to Echlios." We glance down at the man-creature that has slowly reverted to his full human form. "We need to take him with us. The woman, too."

"She's dead. He killed her," Speio says.

"Why would he do that?" Jenna blurts out.

"To shut her up? She was human, easy for us to break down," Speio says, barely looking at her. "They must be hiding something big to take out their own people. Any idea where they came from? Did he look familiar to you at all?" I shake my head, thinking hard. It's the first time I've ever seen anything that looks like him.

"What did he say to you?" Jenna asks me hesitantly. "He spoke in your language, right? I recognized it from the last time at your house." I lock eyes with Speio, who even after Jenna has saved both of our hides shakes his head. He still doesn't trust her.

But I do. She's earned it.

"He called me the false queen."

16
The Law of Natural Selection

Echlios's face is impassive as he studies the withered carcass. The wires from the Taser gun are still connected to the man's back, the areas around both entry points on his upper hip blackened and charred. The man's entire body looks like it has been drained of every drop of water.

"Is he dead?" I ask.

Echlios glances at me, then Jenna. "I'm not sure." He removes the sturdy pieces of metal gently from the thing's back, but still chunks of flesh flake away from the prods. Brittle remnants of hip bone are visible underneath.

I feel bile rising in my throat and look away. Jenna is still holding the Taser gun, her face as colorless as mine must be. "How'd you know that would work?" I say quietly, sipping some water out of a bottle.

"Salt," Jenna says. Her voice trembles a little, something she's trying valiantly to hide, but it's obvious that she's more than a little shaken up. "It's the mineral in water that acts as the conductor for electricity. You have a lot of it so..." She trails off.

"Aren't Taser guns supposed to be nonlethal?" Speio remarks in a prickly voice, glaring at Jenna as if she didn't just save his life.

"They are," she returns, obviously glad to focus on anything but the charred body beside us. "I modified the voltage and the metal conductors. They're silver." She shoots him a grim smile. "Turns out, not just for werewolves."

"Werewolves don't exist," he says sourly.

"But you do."

"Why?" I say, interrupting their heated exchange. "What made you modify it, Jenna?"

She stares at the ground, gripping the Taser gun close to her. She pauses, considering her words carefully. "After that night, when you told me what you were, I was scared. I didn't think you would hurt me, but others—" she breaks off, her gaze flying to Speio, who flushes red "—may not have been so inclined. I wanted...protection."

"Did you say something to her?" I ask Speio, not missing his guilty look.

"He didn't have to," Jenna says. "Everything between us changed after that day. Like he couldn't even look at me. It made me nervous...and I guess I just wanted to be prepared. I'm sorry."

"Don't be sorry," I say, standing and gesturing for her to follow me out to the patio. "I would have done the same thing if a friend of mine went all weird for no reason." Glaring at Speio over my shoulder, I nod at the weapon in her hands. "Well, you probably saved both of us tonight with it, so I can't say anything but thanks. Where'd you learn to modify a Taser gun, anyway?"

"YouTube," Jenna says, more color coming back to her face from the fresh air. "You'd be amazed at the stuff on there. There was even a video on how to turn a Taser gun into a teleporting device." She laughs thinly. "Yeah, if you want to teleport to deep-fried city." She stares at the device, hefting it. "I didn't even know if it would work. I wasn't even thinking when I shot it, but I'm lucky it went into the human part of him."

"You are lucky," I agree with a frown. "It wouldn't have pierced his hide anywhere else and he would have killed you in an instant if you had missed. Now that I think about it, what were you thinking?" I'm scolding her, gratitude falling by the wayside at the thought of her life being in danger.

"That my best friend was about to be crushed by the Loch Ness douche bag? What did you expect me to do? Stand by and cheer him on?"

I laugh so hard at her deadpan face that I'm snorting water through my nose. I concede defeat and raise my hands in surrender. The girl has a point. I turn back to look at Echlios, who is speaking in low tones to Soren, their clicking barely audible. They're looking at a DNA sample he just ran an analysis on, and their faces are grim.

"What are they saying?" Jenna asks me, following my gaze. I hesitate only an instant before answering. As much as I'm grateful to Jenna for her quick-thinking earlier, I can't put her in any more danger by involving her. So I opt for a milder version of the truth.

"They're trying to figure out who he is and why he attacked us," I say. Truth is, they are more concerned with him being able to conceal himself from me. Water calls to water—I should have sensed him as one of us in a heartbeat. "It's complicated."

Jenna nods as if understanding my sudden reticence. Always perceptive to social dynamics, she pulls me in for a hug. "Maybe I should go. It's late and my mom thinks I was studying over here. I'll see you tomorrow, Riss?" She pauses as if she knows it's unlikely she will see me. "There's a surf rally and a bonfire if you're interested. Lo will be there," she adds under her breath.

"Sure, I'll see how I feel," I say, flushing at the mere mention of Lo's name. I have a bunch of texts from him and several phone calls that I've completely ignored. He has probably gone back to thinking I'm mentally unstable. I make a note to call him once I have a free minute. "And, Jenna, thanks."

"Anytime," she says with a wink. "I've got your back, don't forget that."

Jenna hasn't even gotten a few steps out of the front door before Speio mutters something under his breath. I don't even have to call him out on it—Echlios gets there before me.

"She saved your life," he says.

"I don't trust her," Speio says sullenly.

"You've said that already. I think you're just mad because she did what you didn't do," I say as he turns an ugly shade of puce, but I don't stop, outrage for my best friend taking over. "And you don't like that I trusted her with who I am. She was there for me tonight. She was there for both of us. At least appreciate that." Speio snaps his mouth shut and turns away, slamming out of the living room to grab his skateboard and take off. Ignoring his theatrics, I walk over to Echlios.

"What did you find from the sample?" I ask him, trying not to let Speio get under my skin. Quick to temper, he's just as quick to cool off, but the constant mistrust of Jenna is grating on me. Hopefully, he'll be in a better mood once he comes back.

"You were half-right," Echlios says. "The man is Aquarathi... but his DNA is different, like he's some kind of a crossbreed." As I stare at him in horror, he continues. "There are elements in there that I don't recognize, ones that resemble human DNA."

"Human?" I say, looking from him to Soren. "But that's not possible, is it?"

Echlios clutches his nose between his thumb and forefinger, his forehead furrowed. "Anything is possible. It could be a mutation. Sometimes different species break off into others and evolve differently based on the laws of natural selection. It's the only thing I can think of."

"What are you saying? That Aquarathi were secretly living on land all this time and somehow they mutated?"

"Or made themselves evolve to be compatible with humans."

"But in human form, we are already compatible," I say. Echlios raises his eyebrows, waiting for me to make the connections. My brows snap together as I consider the possibilities. "You can't mean genetic compatibility? But that's—" I struggle to push the word out—*impossible*—but it sticks in my throat like a barb.

"Yes," Echlios asserts gently. "Any offspring will carry traits of their parents and adapt to survive. Like this one." He nods to the body of the creature on the table. "Which was why he did not have to yield himself to you. He's a hybrid...not bound to Aquarathi laws."

Soren's eyes are as wide as I know mine are but there's no disbelief there. She thinks it's possible, too. I still can't get my mind around it—everything I have been taught about procreation between our species is now obsolete. "So you're saying we can bond with humans?"

"It's not bonding. It's sexual reproduction and environmental factors."

"But I though we couldn't make...babies with them." Oddly, the thought sends a hot spiral curling into the pit of my stomach, one that I have no intention of analyzing.

"Nerissa," Soren says calmly, "think back to what you know about biology. The only two things that can change genetic characteristics are DNA mutation and sexual reproduction.

Once you incorporate either of these into an environment, like Earth, any species—including ours—can adapt to survive. It's the basis of natural selection."

"But it's not natural," I say.

"Nothing's unnatural, my darling," she says. "And Ehmora must have been planning this for years."

"She's a hybrid, too?"

"No," Echlios says. "She could probably mutate, but not to this level. My guess is she would have reproduced others. She is over a century old, you know."

"So you're telling me that there are hundreds of Ehmora's hybrid demon-spawn running around mating with the humans?"

Echlios shrugs. "I can only speculate about Ehmora." His voice grows quiet. "But it has always been possible. That is why procreating with humans was forbidden. Over the course of history, our people weren't always careful. Things happened, but it resolved naturally with the mothers. The offspring, more often than not, were unable to survive gestation."

"So there has never been a hybrid before this one?"

"Not that I can recall, my lady." He pauses, looking to Soren for guidance. Out of the corner of my eye, I see her nod. "But there were always rumors of ones that had survived because of some recessive gene mutation. It could never be proven so the rumors were never confirmed and they became urban legends—stories to scare Aquarathi children."

A hazy memory comes to mind of Speio telling me a tale when we were little about the monstrous creatures that stole children away from their parents if they ventured too close to the surface in Aquarathi form.

"So the stories are kind of true." I glance at the brutish body of the hybrid and suppress a shiver. In human form, he is ugly and misshapen. "How many of them do you think there are?"

"Not many," Echlios guesses. "Thousands would have died before one was able to survive. And even then, that one surviving child would have had to mutate further to increase genetic compatibility. It would have taken generations just to get to that." He jerks his head in the direction of the body. "And I checked, it has no gills."

"So it can't breathe underwater," I say.

"Right, and we don't even know that it can fully transform into our natural shape. You only saw a half form, correct?"

I nod and then frown. "I still don't get it. Why even go there? What's the point?"

"Think back to what Ehmora wants," Soren suggests. "She wants dominion of land and water. With a hybrid species that can make the best of both worlds, she can have that."

My jaw drops open. "So basically, you guys are saying that Ehmora is a huge ho-bag who has been procreating with humans for generations to build herself a secret hybrid army of Aquamen because she wants to take over the world?"

Soren smiles slightly at my tone. "Something like that, although not quite an army." I notice she doesn't say anything about Ehmora *not* being a giant ho-bag and I stifle a grin of my own. She's so proper most of the time that it's an anomaly to not have her correct me for my offensive word choices.

"That's kind of sick. And calculating. How long do you think she's been planning this cross-species experiment of hers?"

"A long time," Echlios murmurs.

If I had to guess Ehmora's age, I'd say she was a hundred and twenty, and still in her prime—some Aquarathi have lived close to two centuries—so about a century of scheming, give or take a few years. I hide my fear with a healthy dose of sarcasm. "So just to sum up, these hybrids don't have to show fealty to me, they have some of our powers but not all, they may or may not have gills and they are butt ugly."

"Language, Nerissa," Soren says. And she's back.

"Sorry. You know what I mean," I mutter, watching Echlios, who has gone back to prodding the hybrid. "So what do we do now? Is there, like, any silver lining in the dead thing lying in my living room? Any ID on him? Anything?"

"There may be," Echlios says, holding a piece of something in his fingers that looks nothing like a driver's license. "Can you smell that?"

I shake my head. If I breathe in any more dead monster, I'll be hurling chunks all over the floor. The only thing I can smell is charred meat, and it's not the good kind. I try not to focus on whatever he's holding. But Soren is suddenly on her feet and walking over to him.

"I smell it," she says, sniffing cautiously. "It's a scent."

"So he smells? What does that even mean?" I say grouchily, clutching my stomach.

Echlios shoots me a glare that doesn't hold back what he thinks of my deductive abilities. "It means we can track him, maybe to others." I perk up then, all thoughts of bile fading into the background.

"To where they're holding my mother?"

"Maybe."

"I'm coming," I say, anticipating an argument. Echlios's mouth thins to a white line and he crosses his arms.

"No. You are not." He glares at me. "This isn't a game, Nerissa. These creatures are not like anything we know, especially if there are more of them. We need to plan carefully and for any attack. I need to call in some of our people."

"So you're *not* tracking the scent now?"

An exasperated sigh. "Yes, but not to attack. To scout. And you are not coming."

"I want to go." There's no way I'm going to let my mother slip through my fingers now that we have our first very real lead. I glare back just as fiercely at Echlios, wary of using my Do As I Say trump card…again.

"I don't care if you force me to obey you," Echlios says, foreseeing my next move easily. "I will resist with every cell of water in my body. Your father's edict was to protect you and I cannot disobey my king. His orders overrule yours, my princess. So you are not going. Speio!" Echlios shouts to his son, hefting the dead body into a large black bag. I try not to notice as my simmering outrage overflows.

"Wait, what? Why does Speio get to go?"

"Because I need his help to dispose of this," Echlios says matter-of-factly, gesturing at the body. "And it's not exactly a job for a princess, is it?"

"I'm not afraid of a dead body."

Speio walks back in with a cynical smile cornering his lips and I want to punch it off his face. He's been listening all along from outside—I should have guessed or at least sensed his glimmer but I'd been too preoccupied. The mocking smile was payback for what I'd said about Jenna. He wouldn't even back me up on this one.

"I'm going because I'm me," he says, "and you are a royal pain in the a—"

"Speio!" Soren cuts him off. But we both know what he was going to say, and even with Soren's reprimand, I feel myself flushing red. My emotions are still on a precarious thread.

"Don't speak to me like that!" I screech.

Speio stares at me coolly, aware that he has the upper hand just because of how badly I don't want to be left out. He glances at Soren, who is still giving him the eye, but he shrugs, ignoring her obvious warning. "Or what? You're going to glimmer me into submission, too?"

"Enough!" Echlios roars, staring at the two of us in bewilderment. "What is with you two lately? Always bickering and fighting, and carrying on like two hostile strangers! We are on the precipice of a war that could destroy both land and water, and you two are fighting over trifles?"

"It's *my* mother," I shoot back.

"And *my* queen," he says, implacable. "Speio goes, Nerissa stays. End of discussion."

"Soren?" I try one last-ditch effort to appeal to Soren's maternal instinct. Totally wrong choice. Her expression is unbending and her words even more so.

"No, I agree with Echlios. Far too dangerous for you. And Speio is trained."

I snort out loud. Even with all Speio's training, I bet I could still take him. But Soren's eyes flare green fire, daring me to argue, so I hold my tongue. I back down, not just because I respect Soren but because I know that picking a fight with her will only end badly. She's also trained in Aquarathi battle arts—testing my mettle against her in anger is a bad bet in my current state.

"It's for your own protection, my lady," she adds more gently.

"Fine," I snap, and stalk off to my room, pacing back and forth and straining to hear the remaining conversation. But they know me too well. Peering through a crack in my bedroom door, I confirm that the living room is silent and empty. They've already gone out to the front and taken the body with them. Despite my earlier restraint with Soren, there's no way I'm going to sit in this room while Speio takes my place on the hunt.

My body bends outward into a glimmer. If I get too close, they will be able to sense me, so I hover near some bushes in the front yard and blend in to the drops of dew glistening on the leaves.

"Keep an eye on her," Echlios is saying to Soren. "You know how she is, willful to a fault. Speio, give me a hand here, and seriously, why are you pushing Nerissa's buttons?"

"I'm not, she's just so difficult lately," Speio says with a grunt as he hefts one end of the bag into the back of his truck.

So difficult? I'm not the one with the bipolar mood swings. He's Dr. Jekyll and Mr. Jackass personified. Everything starts to waver as I almost lose hold of the glimmer. Calm down, I tell myself. Figuring out where they're going is more important than griping about how much of a girl Speio really is.

"How long?" Soren is asking Echlios.

"Not long. We don't have much time before they discover him missing or, worse, go looking for him. If we don't move quickly, someone will track his scent here, and we can't have that happen. You know what to do."

They embrace and I snap myself back just as Soren enters the house. There's nothing I can do—she'll know the instant I leave. I throw myself onto my bed and pick up a discarded magazine that I stare at mindlessly. There are some bustling sounds before there's a soft knock on the door. I deliberate whether to answer and then decide to take the high road. Getting mad at Soren won't help anything.

"Are you okay?" she asks.

"Fine."

"It's really for your own safety," she says, coming in to sit on the edge of my bed. She rests a hand on my foot. "At least until we know what we're working against. I know how upset you are. Trust me, I know. But you can't help anyone by running in there unprepared and at a disadvantage. If your mother is Ehmora's only bargaining chip, she will be heavily guarded. You can't put yourself at risk."

"I know." I sit up, unable to look her in the eye. "I'm going for a swim."

Soren's grip on my ankle tightens. "Nerissa, just in the pool."

I pull my leg away. "Of course."

Sinking into the watery confines of the pool, I let the water and the salt drain into me and then I shift into Aquarathi form. I glance toward the house. Soren is still cleaning up inside but I can tell that a part of her is focused on me like a dog on its bone.

Taking a deep breath, I close my eyes, focusing the bulk of my power to follow Echlios and Speio. In minutes, I find them. They're on their way back from a secluded cove on a rocky beach, where I assume that they disposed of the body. They won't return to the house—Echlios won't let the trail disappear, not when it's so fresh. I'm already breathing hard by the time they get onto the highway, heading north, and my glimmer lessens the farther away they get. Even with my considerable strength, I lose them right before Solana Beach, my senses thinning like stretched neoprene on the verge of tearing.

The glimmer snaps back into me and I float in silence for a while, staring at the starlit sky. It's so quiet, almost as if the world has gone entirely still. There's not even a breath of wind in the air and the complete lack of sound throws me. I submerge, feeling the saltwater pass over my gills like a balm, as something strange unfolds like heavy wings in the middle of my stomach. Maybe I pushed myself too far with the glimmer.

But still, the blooming feeling stretches outward, tingling along my veins like a tiny electrical current, a hot awareness spreading like wildfire through me. And then the pain hits me in a wild roaring rush, clipping through my body with the force of a hurricane. I thrash backward in the suddenly tiny pool, my entire length lit up like a fireworks display. Every part of my exposed skin feels like it's covered in fire and then ice, the burnished scales along my hide flexing and vibrating with hot, pulsing light.

Soren bursts through the doors, her hand against my throbbing side. "Breathe, my darling. Breathe. Just let it happen."

"Just let what happen?" I gasp.

But as I ask the question, I already know. I feel it in the violent ripple of her skin against me. I feel it in the water from her body now desperately plastering itself against mine. I can feel it in the lifeblood of every single Aquarathi on land and in the deep waters below responding to the call of my Dvija. Embracing the raw power rushing through my veins, I open my jaws and scream.

A new queen has come of age.

17

Dangerous Deceptions

The beach is more packed than I expected, with guitar music strumming in the background and the faint murmur of people over the mellow sound of the surf. Jenna waves me over to where a bunch of our friends are sitting on the beach around a blazing bonfire. I say hi to a few of them and then move to the empty spot right next to her. Sawyer says hello, and tugs on a lock of my hair with the arm resting along the back of Jenna's shoulders.

"Hey, Wipeout," he teases, referring to the last time we hung out together.

"Wipeout, my ass," I shoot back. "Those were some freakishly large waves. Isn't that why you came in right after I cracked my board? I'll take you on any time, any place, surfer boy. How'd you do today at the meet?"

Sawyer picks up the bronze trophy at his side and hefts it over to me.

"Third, not bad," I say, tossing it back. I want to ask the question that's burning on my tongue and find out whether Lo placed, since I didn't make it to the meet. Some sort-of girlfriend I'm turning out to be. Lo's not in the group on the beach. I would have spotted him as soon as I walked down and a part of me is grateful. He must hate me. Again.

"Some kid from Bishop's took second," Sawyer is saying. "And Lo took first, but that was to be expected. That guy is a genius on the wave."

"Is he here?" I choke out, trying to sound casual and failing dismally. Even Jenna shakes her head at my obvious embarrassment.

"He went home after the meet. Said he had something to do but he'd be by later. Why don't you just text him?"

Sawyer's suggestion is as simple as it sounds. Only I can't text Lo to find out whether he's going to be at some bonfire on the beach, because I've ignored his texts and calls for days, or responded with one-word answers. Right now, I'm not even sure that he's talking to me.

"Yeah, maybe I will later. Congrats, man, that's awesome."

"Thanks."

Sawyer passes me a beer from the cooler behind him but I wave it away. I don't mix well with drinking because it's such a bad diuretic. Put it this way, one sip of alcohol and the effects on my system would be worse than a bottle of vodka on a full-grown man. So I stay away from the stuff. "No, thanks, I'm good," I say with a smile. "But I'll take a soda if you have one."

"I didn't think I'd see you here," Jenna says, and passes me a can of orange soda.

Throwing my sandals off and leaning back, I dig my toes into the soft crumbly sand. "Soren's in complete smothering mode. Speio's acting like he's king of the hill, and Echlios is Echlios. I'd rather be here than there."

"So you brought Speio, anyway?"

I glance to where he's standing awkwardly at the edge of the circle but there's no way I'm going to be nice to him. He can work it out on his own. With a frown, I notice that Cara, who's sitting on the opposite side, waves him over to a spot next to her. It makes no difference to me. They can have each other for all I care.

I shrug and answer Jenna. "Not much choice. Haven't you heard? He's my warden and my ride." I lean in, lowering my voice to a whisper. "Seriously, you come of age in my world and you go on lockdown. Shouldn't I get a sports car or something?"

"You did what?" Jenna's eyes are wide. I nod and her eyes widen even more as she eyeballs me up and down, looking for something. "You look the same," she whispers.

"It's more of an inside thing," I say, amused.

"Wow. That's cool."

"What's cool?" Sawyer asks, tucking his arm around Jenna's shoulders.

"Girl talk," Jenna says quickly, and shoves him away. "Menstrual cramps." At his horrified look, she kisses him to make up for it and then turns back toward me, whispering under her breath. "So any more news on that guy?"

"No," I say, uncomfortable at the lie. "Dead end. No pun intended."

Jenna's face drains of all color and I kick myself for royally inserting my foot in my mouth. "He died? I thought Echlios said he was alive?" Her voice is nearly a screech, and several other kids look in our direction. With a despairing breath, I remind myself that Jenna is dealing with things that a normal high-school kid should never have to worry about—dead people and alien creatures—all because of me. My regret is all consuming.

"He was alive," I amend unhappily. "In fact, Echlios took care of it…in case anyone came back looking for me."

Mindful of her emotional fragility, there's no way I can tell her that he had been killed on the spot by her home-modified electroshock weapon, so I lie again. I could have gone the route of the man not being an actual man but I figure that Jenna will be upset either way if she thinks she killed anyone, even if it wasn't human. I'm getting pretty good at making my lies convincing enough, because her face regains some of its normal hue and visibly relaxes.

"Oh," she says. "I'm sorry that it didn't lead to anything."

A part of me wishes I could tell her more. Having anyone to talk to would be better than a family who leaves you out of everything because they think you're some sort of fragile china doll. Plus, Jenna has a car and she's savvy in a pinch, if her handiwork with the Taser is any indication. And she's my best friend. But of course, despite all of the advantages to confiding my secrets, I can't risk it, so I say nothing. I'd rather have a live best friend than a dead one.

Instead, I shrug noncommittally and go back to staring at the flames and then at the people sitting around it. With a surprised start, I see that Cara and Speio have wasted no time and are practically making out in front of everyone. It's so out of the blue that I don't realize I'm staring until Jenna clears her throat.

"First Lo, now Speio, right? That's only a little creepy," she whispers. "It's like she wants to be you or something."

I don't answer, but the thought that Cara would do anything to get under my skin does rattle me a little. I shove it away, affirming that I don't care who or what Cara does, even if it is Speio. Averting my eyes to keep from being grossed out, I look past them to scan the shoreline. It's not as dark a night as the night before, and with the light from the bonfire, hazy shapes flit in and out of my peripheral vision.

The water is glassy with slow-rolling waves and barely any surf. Only tiny waves curl white in the shallows before breaking up into nothing. For a minute, I wonder with a pang why it's so calm and then chide myself for being so paranoid in the same breath. The most logical reason is because it's low tide. Plus, it's not like Ehmora is going to cause a freak storm that will kill everyone on the beach just to avenge her missing hybrid. A chill runs through me. Will she?

I shake my head of its heavy thoughts and peer over toward the rocky pier that juts out into the middle of the ocean. Just as the moon dips behind a cloud, I notice a lone figure sitting on the dock at the far end of the pier.

Lo.

Don't ask how I can recognize what is basically just a vague, indistinct shadow in the moonlight, but I can. I would know that boy anywhere—the shape of his profile, the curve of his back, the length of his legs. A chill of an entirely different sort runs through me and I get to my feet. Both Jenna's and Speio's stares converge on me in seconds.

"I'm just going for a walk. Jeez, relax." I roll my eyes in Speio's direction. "Don't worry, my ankle bracelet will go off if I leave the area, so don't let me interrupt you." Cara obligingly reglues her face to his after an oddly triumphant stare at me. Once more, I don't know what she thinks she's doing, but she can have Speio for all I care. If he's tied up with her, he won't be as worried about me. Little does she know, but she's doing me a favor, even if she's just doing it to push my buttons.

"Want some company?" Jenna asks. I nod to the rocks and raise an eyebrow. "Oh," she says, squinting into the darkness. "Have fun."

By the time I walk over to the rocks, the moon has come out of hiding, bathing the water and the rocks in a silvery glow. Even Lo's shape is outlined by silver, the moonlight flickering on his hair and making it gleam. I make my way up to the dock where he's sitting, his feet dangling over the side.

As I get closer I see that he's on the phone. His voice is slightly raised and I can hear the edge of frustration in his voice.

"I'll get it done, don't worry," I hear him say before snapping his phone shut and tucking it in his back pocket. He leans his head on the railing and sighs. He must not have heard me approach over the sound of the waves against the rocks and his phone conversation, so I hover silently for a while and then realize that my hovering is borderline creepy. I clear my throat.

"Hey," I say quietly.

"Hi." His eyes are surprised but not unwelcoming. "What are you doing over here? Shouldn't you be over there with the rest of your friends?"

"I saw you," I fumble, catching the tiny edge in his voice. He totally thinks I blew him off. "I mean, I was at the bonfire and saw you. Everything okay?" I ask, nodding to the phone peeking out of his pants pocket. "You sounded...stressed."

"It's fine," he says, frowning slightly. "Just my mother."

"Oh."

"She wants me to look at college applications."

"And you don't want to?"

Lo leans back on his elbows, watching as I sit with my back to one of the beams on the railing to face him. I cross my legs, my knee just grazing the skin of his thigh. The light touch has my body already heating up a few notches but I force myself to calm down. The coolness of the railing against my back helps.

"Not particularly," Lo says after a minute, turning his face away to stare out at the ocean. "I don't really think it's for me. I feel like my place is somewhere else, you know. I want to travel, experience different things...." His voice trails off. The expression on his face is wistful, almost longing.

"Where do you want to go?" I ask.

"Everywhere." And then, "Where no one else has."

"Who says you can't? Do that, I mean." Lo stares at me with a long searching gaze as if he's trying to see inside me. "What?" I ask nervously. The intense look in his eyes disappears and is replaced by something more shadowed and forced casual.

"Nothing," he says softly. "So are we going to talk about what I want to be when I grow up or are we going to talk about why you didn't return any of my phone calls?"

I'm torn between making up something outlandish or telling him some version of the truth as I'd done with Jenna. Lies can get you into a whole heap of trouble if you don't keep track of them. I opt for the latter.

"Lo, I'm really sorry about that," I begin. "Family issues. Speio and I had a big fight, and things got ugly. We were both grounded, and my phone and car were taken away." I shrug and paste an innocent look on my face. "So radio silence. I only got to come out tonight because Echlios is away for work—he travels a lot—and Soren got fed up of us." I peek at his face—he's totally buying it. "I'm really sorry."

"What did you fight about?" I opt for partial honesty again. "You."

A laugh. And just like that, I'm forgiven. If anything, I can see it by the lightening of his eyes and the slow smile that takes over his entire face. "He doesn't like me much, does he?"

"Protective," I say. "But we're not talking, and he's macking on Cara so you're safe. For the moment." I grin, nodding my head to the bonfire on the beach. Lo's eyebrows shoot into his hairline.

"Cara? Didn't see that one coming. Had no idea she even liked him."

"Probably has to do with me."

"Why do you think everything Cara does has to do with

you?" Lo says, his voice mesmerizing and drawing my gaze to his lips. I drag it away, short of breath.

"I told you, we have history," I confess. "Apparently I used to be a mean girl."

"You?" he teases. "Yeah, I can see that."

Grinning, I punch him and he grabs my fist in the same moment, pulling me toward him so I'm half-sprawled across his lap. I can barely move sideways, imprisoned by the railing on one side and warm muscular Lo on the other. His right arm cradles my shoulder and upper back. Holding myself perfectly still to not draw attention to my racing pulse, I try to stop breathing and stare at a button on his polo shirt. But even counting backward from one hundred doesn't detract from the moonlight dappling his collarbone or the pulse in his neck that's racing at the same speed as mine.

I lock eyes with his nearly black ones in the darkness and forget how to breathe. They are fathomless and deep, but I can see everything in them...everything he's feeling...everything he feels for me. No secrets. His hand weaves into the back of my hair and he pulls me against him in a warm hug. I breathe deeply. He smells like laundry detergent, ocean and salt, and something magical that I can't quite describe.

Incredibly, my heart rate slows to the tune of his, beating beat for beat in unison. I've never felt so at peace than I do at that moment with the sea crashing around us, and the only sound I can hear is that of our hearts singing the song of the other.

My cheek is pressed into the dip beneath his shoulder and his chest, and I tilt my head so I can study the line of his jaw. It's covered in a fine prickling of stubble that barely touches his cheeks. He has quite a nice nose, I realize—a slight bend in it suggests that it was broken at some point, but it suits him, balancing cheekbones that would be better suited to a supermodel. His ears are small, like curving seashells, and his eyes…are looking right at me.

"What are you thinking?" he says, a smile in them.

"Your ears remind me of shells," I blurt out, and flush as his smile widens. Couldn't I have come up with something a tad more romantic? Like, *You have a killer smile.* Or, *Your eyes make me feel like I can fly.* Okay, maybe not that last one. Lame.

Lo tightens his arm and tucks me into him. "I think you have nice ears, too." I laugh a little inside because my ears are pretty much the opposite of nice. They tend to gravitate toward the elf or bat species, depending on how you look at it. I prefer to think of them as the former—that's just me—but they're a long way away from seashells.

Silence falls around us like an old comfortable blanket. I like that we don't have to speak all the time. With Lo, there are no awkward silences. They're not empty, but full, if that makes any sense. Like we're still connecting even though we aren't talking. My skin is learning the surfaces of his, and my nose, his scent. My fingers learn that his pulse jumps rapidly when I trail them along his arm. Our silences are just as meaningful as everything else.

"You smell nice," I say, nuzzling into his shirt. "Like salt and sea and vanilla. I like it."

Lo smiles down at me. "I love the ocean. My father— I mean my foster dad—used to say that when I was little I would rather fall asleep, dead tired, at the water's edge than come in to bed."

"You didn't live with your mom there?" A vague recollection flits across my mind of the day that I read Lo's file in Cano's office. It seems like years ago when it had only been a few months.

"No," he says slowly. "They were friends of my mother. She was…busy and traveled a lot, so they took care of me when

I lived with them in Hawaii. She paid all the bills. I saw her once a year, and that was my life. Then the accident happened. And I came here."

It is the first time that Lo has ever spoken to me about the accident, and while I do want to know as much as he is willing to tell me, I don't want to push him. "What happened?"

"Electrical fire, the cops said, in our boat," he says so quietly that I have to strain to hear his words. "It was quick, they said. Painless, almost." I can barely hear him but he doesn't stop. "I miss them so much, Nerissa. Every day, it's a struggle to not see their faces or think of them. And my foster dad—he's the most helpless one of all and there's nothing I can do but see him wither in the hospital. My mom thinks she can help him, but there's no guarantee."

I don't realize I'm crying until Lo's gentle fingers wipe the tears away from my cheek. At his touch and the shine of wetness in his own eyes, my tears turn into a full-on waterfall. By the time my sobs subside, Lo's shirt is a damp soggy mess.

"Sorry." I sniff and rub my eyes, knowing they will be puffy and red and completely unattractive.

"It's okay. It's a shirt, and that's what laundry is for. You all right?"

"I'm so sorry. I didn't realize…your story…your family… and it's been a rough week…and I'm so tired of keeping everything in and together." I realize that I'm rambling and force myself to slow down and speak more coherently. "It's just that I lost my dad, too, before I could tell him, or show him, that I loved him. I mean I love Echlios and Soren, but it's not the same. And I just found out that my mom's…" I trail off, unable to find the words to finish my thought. Kidnapped? Taken? In danger?

"Your mom's what?" Lo asks.

"Missing." And then I kick myself. How do I explain a missing mother?

Lo turns me to face him, concern written all over his face. My breath comes a little more quickly at the attention but my brain is spinning with convincing enough lies to cover what I'd stupidly blurted out. I glance nervously toward the beach as if I expect Speio to come running any minute at my blunder. I make myself calm down, knowing that he— like Echlios or Soren—can sense when I'm agitated or upset. Thinking about baby seals, and breathing through my nose and out through my mouth in a rhythmic sequence, gets my heart rate back to normal.

"Since when? Why didn't you tell me?" he says. "Did you call the police?"

"It's complicated," I begin haltingly. "My dad died, and I thought that she was dead, too. But then, it turns out that she's alive. We have private investigators working on it." I can't believe how shaky my voice is, but deep down, I know it will give my words—my fabrication—more credibility. But despite a tiny twinge of guilt, a part of me does feel good to talk to someone about it, even if it's only a strung-together story of partial truths.

Lo's eyes are wide. "Do they have any idea where she is?"

"Maybe." I pause, staring at him. "It just never feels like they're doing enough, you know? They have a general idea where she is, but they're so slow. I hate sitting around and waiting. I just want to do something. Find her if I can."

"So let's do something. I can help." Lo's generous but dangerous words are like music to my ears, like kindling to a flame. Not only does Lo have a car, but also he's my friend, and I know that I can trust him with keeping this a secret between us. Even as the illogical part of me celebrates his offer of help, the sensible side of me argues that I should give him at least one out to walk away from something that could get him into a lot of trouble.

"Are you sure?" But my words and my eyes convey different messages. Inside and selfishly, my heart is begging him to say yes, but my mind wants him to say no, for his own sake.

"Yes."

"You could get into a lot of trouble."

"I know."

"And that doesn't bother you?"

"It's worth it." My heart leaps at his response and the look on his face. His expression is wicked as he winks at me. "Plus, trouble is my middle name."

I notice that the glassy ocean has turned choppy and the moon has disappeared into a bank of thick dark clouds. Pale streaks of lightning spiderweb the clouds into eerie, disturbing shapes. I swear that I can see the sharp angle of fangs in a giant open mouth, and I shiver a little. For a second, I wonder if the change in the weather is caused by my own guilt for involving an innocent boy in something that could get him killed, but I shrug that thought away. He won't get hurt, I tell myself. How can he, if he doesn't know anything?

"So why is it that we never seem to go on a normal date?" Lo says, and I laugh, my murky fears disappearing at his boyish question. "Surfing gone awry…supersecret spy activities… what's next? Synchronized swimming with robot sharks?"

"I didn't think you wanted normal," I quip back. "And I'll have you know, I'm a master synchronized swimmer. With live sharks."

"Whoa," Lo says with a lopsided grin. "Live sharks. That's impressive. So no trapeze with aquatic cobras? That's kind of my specialty."

I laugh out loud at the *Madagascar* movie reference and his ludicrous one-upping. "No, but tell you what. I'll teach you to swim with sharks if you teach me to trapeze with cobras. Deal?"

I stick my hand out and Lo takes it, only to pull me in close to seal the deal with a kiss. By the time he's finished, I'm breathless and would probably agree to skydiving with a boatload of flying rattlesnakes.

"Deal," he whispers against my lips, and kisses me senseless once more until my fingers are wound so tightly in his shirt that it'll take a crane to break them loose. He tips my chin up. "Jokes aside, I'm really sorry about your mom, Riss."

Despite my near-inability to function after his kisses, I can't help feeling like I've tricked him into agreeing to help me by not telling him the whole truth.

A strong gust of wind whips between us, lashing my hair into my face like a warning. But I ignore it. I'm torn between my selfishness and the cold sense of duty digging into my skull. It's all for the greater good. If I find my mother, I won't have to accept Ehmora's brazen challenge and all the scales will tip back in our favor. Lightning cracks in the distance and I close my eyes, ignoring what is another obvious warning. I pull Lo's face down to mine, letting his mouth erase any last bit of doubt from my mind. Spending more time with Lo and having his help to find my mother is the perfect combination.

Selfish? Probably.

Smart? Probably not.

But it's all I've got to go on, and without Lo's help, I'm stranded in a sea of nothing, unable to do anything useful. And the truth is, I'd rather be with him doing this than without him doing nothing.

What's the worst that can happen?

18
Love Makes the World
Crash and Burn

Turns out that the worst thing that can happen is pretty bad.

After a week of trying to spy on Echlios and listen in on conversations, I was still no closer to finding out anything useful. Unfortunately, one thing I did learn was that there was no way to track a day-old Aquarathi scent, which would have evaporated to nothing in the sunlight. So they had nothing to go on, which means I have nothing.

But that's not the worst thing.

Turns out that being secret superspies doesn't really help the image of Lo and me being casual friends at school, especially when our heads are practically glued together plotting, and the gossip mill is buzzing with rumors that Lo and I are a couple.

That's still not the worst thing.

The worst thing begins with C and ends with A, and hell hath no fury like one of those scorned. Apparently, she's only dating Speio to get back at me, and Speio's dating her because he knows I don't like her. It's like a Wonder Twins attack of epic proportions.

"Seriously, is she ever going to let up?" I mutter, staring at

Cara, who's trying to blow up my table with her eyes. "You know she's telling people I'm bullying her?"

"Want me to talk to her?" Lo whispers to me in study hall.

"Are you insane? That would be like going after a bull with a red flag." I glare at him and then sigh. Getting mad at Lo won't make things any better, and I refuse to play dirty with Cara. It's like she just can't let go. Sinking to her level isn't the answer, but I'm getting close to the edge of losing it. Everywhere I turn, she's there…always watching, always calculating. I sigh again and manage a small smile. "High-school girls are a curious breed. All the cattiness and backstabbing and general petty behavior makes for never-ending drama."

"You say that like you aren't a high-school girl," Lo says.

"Not like that, I'm not." Not anymore, I amend in my head.

Ignoring Cara and her entourage, I open my notebook to the hand-drawn map of San Diego that I've penciled and study it. The trail marked in blue pen ends at Solano Beach, with red pen circling the towns of North City and Rancho Santa Fe. That's where Echlios and Speio went that night I glimmered them.

My gaze moves from the paper map to Speio, who— surprise, surprise—is also pretending not to look at us. He knows where they went, but he'll never tell me. He won't go against his parents for me, not even if I beg him. Something has changed between us, and not just because he's dating Cara. It's almost like he doesn't trust me, which hurts something fierce. Whenever we are together, which is often, he speaks in monosyllables and disappears for hours at a time, with Echlios, I'm guessing. But we are nothing like we used to be, not anymore.

There is another way that I can get the information but it's far too horrific to consider. I can go into Speio's head to get it. But it's not like he won't know about it—after all, you can't access someone's memories without them knowing that you went in there in the first place…especially if they're Aquarathi. Speio will resist me with everything he has. And he will hate me, more than he does now. If I do it, it will be unforgive-able. But there's too much on the line now. I have to consider it, even if it's at the cost of losing him.

"What's wrong?" Lo asks, leaning over to wipe away the lines of worry creasing my forehead.

"Nothing," I say. "Just thinking whether we're going about this the right way."

"Like how?"

"Like whether I should figure out if anyone else knows something they're not telling us." I keep my eyes focused on the table, not wanting to give away who I'm thinking about. Despite his obtuseness with Cara, Lo can be quite perceptive when it comes to other people. "I sort of have a plan. I'll fill you in later, okay? We have a hockey game this afternoon so I'll call you."

Lo shoots me a weird look. "Riss, you know I'll be at the game, right? We talked about it?"

"Okay, I'll call you later," I answer distractedly.

At the bell, I grab my books and hurry to catch up with Jenna. We have a home game against the boys' field hockey team and a pep rally. It's our last one before the final in less than a week. The boys' team had been knocked out early in their tournament, so it's more of an exhibition game than anything. Well, that's the idea, anyway. But when boys and girls get on a field, things can get pretty competitive so who knows what will happen?

Once on the field, I stretch my legs next to Jenna and jog in place. I've missed a few practices but Coach Fenton excused me given the circumstances, especially after the fabricated doc-tor's note I turned in. Missing practice is not going to stop me from playing at my best, especially after all of Echlios's rigorous strength training.

"You okay?" Jenna says, stretching her arms over her head and twisting. "Haven't seen you all week. You and loverboy have been gone every day the minute school gets out. What are you guys doing, anyway?" She waggles her eyebrows suggestively.

"Not that," I say, flushing. "Or whatever it is you're thinking."

"What am I thinking, Riss?" she teases, puckering her lips and pretending to make out with an imaginary person.

"You're so lame," I say just as Cara runs past us with a scowl, chasing a ball that misses me by inches.

"Whoa. She's really out for you," Jenna remarks.

"Tell me something I don't know." I tell her about the bullying thing and her eyes widen, her mouth dropping open. "I mean, I can handle a prank as well as the next girl, but it's getting out of hand."

"Maybe you just need to say you're sorry," Jenna offers.

"Sorry for what?" Incredulous, I stop my warm-up to hear what she has to say.

She takes a deep breath. "Look, I'm your friend and I'll always be your friend, but you used to be her. And, well, you kind of ruined her life freshman year. Don't get me wrong—I'm not condoning what she's doing, but maybe it's a front for something else."

"Who are you? Dr. Phil?" I snap, resuming jogging in place.

"Do you want my help or not?"

I glare at her but grudgingly nod. "Yes."

"Cano's her uncle," Jenna says, as if that's the answer to everything.

"So? What does that have to do with anything? He's not going to fight her battles for her, is he?"

"People that damaged are that way for a reason," Jenna says, stretching her arms across her hockey stick and bending forward, twisting back and forth. "Maybe it was hard coming to Dover under the thumb of Uncle Cano. She wanted to be perfect, and you showed up." She stands, eyeing me up and down. "You were the epitome of perfect, and you didn't mind letting her know it even though you were friends. Then Cano told her to be more like you, and the rest is history."

I wince at the memory of freshman year. Empathy has never been my strong suit, or humility for that matter. "Whatever," I say. "She needs to get over it. That's water under the bridge."

"Maybe not for her."

"So what are you saying, Jenna? Grovel? To Cara of all people?" I grab my stick off the grass. "That'll never happen in a million years. I have nothing to apologize for."

Jenna shoots me a thoughtful look. "That's your call. But I think if you look deep enough, you'll see that you do. Apologizing to Cara isn't just for her. It's for you, too. Maybe you need to let go of all that negative energy. My mom always says that forgiveness is a choice. You control how you respond to something or someone. You can't change things that happened in the past, but you can decide how you let them affect you. And maybe she'll do the same." She shrugs. "Just my two cents."

"You really are Dr. Phil," I say.

"A leader leads by example. Take it or leave it," Jenna says, and grins, thumping me on the behind with the end of her stick. "Now enough daytime television drama, let's go school these boys and teach them a lesson that girls kick butt…off and on the field!"

After Jenna's eye-opening sentiments, I have no idea how I make it through the game, but I pass and shoot on automatic pilot. The boys, despite all their taunts, could hardly keep up with us and we beat them soundly fourteen to three. Even with my lack of practice, I managed to score four out of the fourteen goals. Jenna took three of them, and even Cara scored one in the last minutes. As far as pregame pep rallies went, we were more than amped up for the championship game. During the game, I looked for Lo in the stands but didn't see him.

I'm not sure that Jenna is entirely right about Cara, but she's said enough to make me take a long, hard look at myself. In my defense, all I wanted to do back then was to escape who I was, and no one really meant anything to me...not even my own people. I'd been euphoric to be so free of responsibility and pressure that I took the freedom too literally. Humans were things to be enjoyed and discarded, and Cara had been an unnoticed casualty of my teenage evolution.

I was wrong. I see that now.

But I have worse things to worry about than making things right with Cara.

Like Speio. And finding out what he knows because time is running out. The challenge with Ehmora is in less than two weeks. If we manage to rescue my mother before, I will still meet Ehmora's challenge and defend my throne. It's the only way that my people will be safe and the usurpers will be forced to bow to me once I've beaten their queen. And if I fail, at least my mother and my family will be safe. If Ehmora still has my mother by the time of the challenge, I will have no choice but to win. I'll have to be ready either way.

My preference, of course, is the former. But the days have been passing by with no success of discovering my mother's whereabouts. Echlios and his men have been searching day and night with nothing to show for it. I'm finding it more and more difficult to control my temper and frustration when he comes up empty-handed day after day.

"What happened to the trail?" I asked him during one of our twice-daily training sessions. "Of the hybrid?"

"It disappeared," he said. "I thought we had traced it to one place, but when we went back, it turned out to be a dead end. The house was empty with no signs of anything."

"So what have you been doing all this time?" I couldn't control the edge in my voice.

"We are searching every property in that area and we have twenty-four-hour surveillance over the perimeter."

"Where?" I said, knowing his answer before I even asked the question. Echlios explained that I would draw too much attention if I got involved, and I'd only put myself in unnecessary danger. I was getting sick and tired of being treated like a pariah.

"You know I can't tell you, my lady. It's for—"

I cut him off with a silent raised palm. "My safety. I know. I get it. I just don't understand how you had such a solid lead and you lost it."

"We are trying our best."

"Try harder."

That was two days ago, and I haven't spoken to him since. Even during training when I do see him, I remain quiet because I know that if I speak one word, I'm going to explode. And it won't be pretty.

Showering quickly in the locker room with my teammates' voices a murmur around me, I let my frustration at Echlios's efforts grow into full-on fury. He's leaving me with no choice. I will have to glimmer Speio and risk the consequences. They have all put me into this position by not trusting me, so the fault is theirs, as well. By the time I've finished getting dressed, I've worked myself into a fine rage and a self-righteous indignation—they've driven me to this.

"Hey, Riss," Jenna shouts, jerking me out of my thoughts. "You coming to eat with the gang?"

"No, I have to do something at the center. I'll meet up with you guys later." I'm becoming quite the consummate little liar. Although in my defense, I'm not exactly lying. I am going to the center, just not for work. On the way to my Jeep, I text Lo—whom I still haven't seen since class—that I'm following up on a lead and I'll see him later. A text comes straight back saying, Okay, call you later. Be careful.

If he only knew what I'm planning to do, he'd be shocked... alien mind-control taken to desperate extremes wouldn't exactly win me brownie points with any human, even if it's used against someone of my ilk. Jenna would be horrified, and Soren...I don't even want to think about what Soren would think of me mentally coercing her son. I take a deep breath and steel myself. They've given me no choice.

At the marine center, I park and say hello to Kevin, who's on the phone. I've been there so many times this week he doesn't even check the shift log, just waves me back. I make my way to the speedboat tied to the far end of the dock. It's nearly sunset and the water is a shimmery kaleidoscope of red, orange and gold. But I barely notice as I steer the boat at full speed past San Clemente Island, toward the uninhabited San Nicolas Island. The sun has disappeared into a melting smoky sort of darkness by the time I reach open water to the south of San Nicolas.

I shut off the engine and wait, lying on the front bow and staring at the stars. Speio and I used to come out here, away from everyone and everything, to transform and swim until our bodies were weary and our spirits were happy. We haven't done it in a while but it's still our spot. Squashing the tendril of nostalgia that makes my heart twinge, I take a deep breath.

"I know you're there, so you should just come on board," I

say. A splashing sound and then the boat rocking as someone climbs on board off the rails in the back. "There's a towel on the seat," I say over my shoulder.

Speio's eyes are glittery and the remnants of bluish-gold bioluminescence trails down his bare shoulders and chest, post-transformation. The towel is wrapped around his waist.

"Have a nice swim?" I ask him.

"What are you doing out here?" he says.

"Waiting for you." His face registers confusion and then an odd sort of bitterness. "I knew you would follow me."

"Nerissa, I don't have time for this kind of game," he growls. "Just answer the question—why did you make me come out here? I'm not interested in going for a swim for old times' sake. Or listening to whatever it is you have to say that will make everything better, because it won't. And I have plans."

I bend my head to the side, studying him. "I should think I'm a little more important than Cara. Surely she can wait." His face flushes deep red but he bites his lip in silence. "What happened to us, Speio? It feels like there's this huge wall between us and I don't know where it came from. What did I do? What can I do to make things better?" I say, echoing his words.

"You didn't do anything," he says after a while, with a deep sigh. "It's me."

"I don't understand. Why don't you like Jenna or Lo or even Sawyer anymore? They used to be your friends."

"No, they were always your friends. Not mine." Speio sits and puts his head in his hands, raking his fingers through his hair almost angrily. "I'm just worried that Jenna's going to crack under the pressure of what she knows. And then we're all in danger of being exposed and hunted like animals. Do you know what the humans would do to us if they knew what we are? And Lo, I know my father cleared him, but there's something about him that doesn't sit right." He stares at me. "And yet, you won't listen to me about either of them."

"What about Cara?" I shoot back.

"What about her?"

"Why are you even dating her? Is it to get back at me?"

Speio's mouth twists. "Turns out she's dating me to get back at you. I can't even have a normal relationship because of you."

"Cara's the furthest thing from nor— Never mind." I'm at a loss on how to respond to him or whatever misguided feelings he has for Cara. I've always trusted him over the years, more than anyone, but now everything about him feels so different. Even his fears seem unfounded, especially with respect to my best friend and my boyfriend.

"Speio, what is this really about?" I ask gently. "Do you not want me to have friends?"

"Of course not. It's about trust, Nerissa. You see with your heart, not with your eyes. Open them and look!"

"For what?" I nearly snap. "What am I looking for? What? Tell me. You think Jenna is the hybrid? Or Lo?"

"No, they're not," Speio says, surprising me. "It was the first thing Soren asked me to do, once we knew about the hybrids. I glimmered both of them. They're clear."

"So then, what is it?" I'm unprepared for the rush of emotions that flood into Speio's face, so quickly that I can barely separate each of them from the other, from fear to guilt to love to pain to anger and back to fear again. And then his face drops back into a wooden mask as if nothing had been there in the first place. Or maybe I imagined it.

"I just think you need to be careful."

I move to where he's sitting leaning against the silver railing of the bow, and grab his fingers. "What do you know, Speio? I need you to tell me. Where did you go that night with Echlios?"

He pulls his hand away and mine flutters in midair for a minute before it drops to my side. "You know what happened. We lost the trail," he says flatly.

"But you went somewhere. Where did you go? Which house?"

"I can't tell you."

I clench my jaw so tightly it feels like my teeth will shatter at any moment, and as much as my heart is breaking, I turn Speio to face me. His shoulders jerk at my fierce hold but I dig my hands in, holding him captive. My eyes slide backward, flaring iridescent fire, and his spark in automatic response.

"Which house?"

"What are you doing, Nerissa?" he asks, struggling against my fingers. For the first time, fear is sliding around like a dark shadow in Speio's face. But it's not fear of me—it's fear of something else. "You can't do this. Stop. What are you doing?"

"What I should have done a week ago." My glimmer spans outward, like a shimmer of golden fire hovering between us. I know that he can see it and the fear in his eyes spreads until his mouth is gaping open and his own fear is choking him. "What are you so afraid of?" I whisper. "It's just me. I won't hurt you, Speio, but I have to know. And if you won't tell me, then I have no other choice."

"You can't, Riss, please," he begs. "You can't see the truth of what I feel for you in my head."

I'm confused at his words and my glimmer falters, dimming slightly. "What do you mean?"

"You know what I mean."

"But you said you didn't...like me that way." Now I'm the one fighting to find the words, muddled by my own confusion. I shake my head to clear it—even if Speio is secretly in love with me, it doesn't change anything. I still have to know what he knows about the hybrid.

"I'm sorry, Speio. But it doesn't change anything. I have to know."

Speio gasps as the glimmer floats closer, his eyes like glowing round orbs. He struggles harder, jerking against me with every shred of strength he has. But it won't be enough. I am far stronger than he is now, especially after Dvija, and he knows it. His entire body is shaking like a leaf, bright lights pacing up and down his arms. I see the indecision in his eyes, and I act upon it.

"One last chance, Speio, before I take it from you."

"I'll never forgive you for this," he hisses, spit flying from his mouth.

"I know," I say gently. "But that's a risk I'm willing to take."

Speio stares at me with loathing and powerless rage marked all over his face. "Fine. Stop, I'll tell you. It was in Rancho Santa Fe. Cano's house."

19
What You Don't Know

My world is spinning. Principal Cano as one of Ehmora's pawns. Principal Cano holding my mother prisoner at his house. Principal Cano smiling at me and congratulating me on a game well won. Principal Cano lying through his perfectly veneered teeth.

I want to smash his face in.

Is he human? Or a hybrid?

He's been watching me all along. I feel disgusted and dirty, as if I need to take a long hot shower to wash the filth of knowledge now coating my body like grease.

Not to mention Speio's revelation, which still has me baffled. He's never been in the least bit interested in me. I remember the expression on his face months ago when I suggested that we should bond—he was revolted. And a boy who is in love with a girl wouldn't have that reaction. Maybe his feelings only developed when Lo came into the picture. It's so far out of the blue that I can't even process it, so I shove it to the side along with everything else, with the sole exception of Cano.

I have other plans for him.

By the time I drag myself out of bed for school, I have a

pounding headache. I haven't slept a wink between all my machinations for what I'll do to Cano once I find out where his house is, and wondering whether Speio has said anything to Echlios about what I did. I do feel badly at how I manipulated him, but he left me little choice. I change quickly into a pair of jeans and a sweatshirt and grab my car keys, slipping out of my patio door. Speio can get himself to school and I'm not in the mood to breakfast-talk with anyone. I'll take the fallout with Soren and Echlios if I have to. Gunning the Jeep, I'm flying as fast as I can within the speed limit to the high school. I have one sole purpose and that is to find Cara.

Cano, unfortunately, is only listed in the local directory at an apartment complex in La Jolla—where he lives with Cara—and not in Rancho Santa Fe, so my best option is to somehow fish any alternate addresses from his niece. That, or break into his office. Tackling a murderous high-school princess or breaking and entering? Tough call.

Taking a breath and heading down the hallway, I see her usual entourage standing near the lockers. Before I can chicken out, I hustle toward the group, bracing myself against the barrage of hostile looks coming my way. "Hey, Cara, can I talk to you for a second?"

She eyes me. "What about?"

"In private?"

"This is private," she says, waving a perfectly manicured hand.

I'd hoped to bring it up more naturally, but there's no natural in a conversation between Cara Andrews and me so I just blurt it out with a vapid smile. "You still live with your uncle, right? In La Jolla?"

Her eyes narrow. "What?"

"Look," I say, taking her by the elbow and drawing her off to the side. "I need your help with something."

"And I should help you because…"

I take another breath. Jenna was right—our past isn't water under the bridge for her, but I still can't bring myself to apologize, especially with our captive audience. "You're right. You have no reason to do anything, but I'm asking, anyway. I just need to know if your uncle has a second house."

"That's weird. Why?"

I force a bright grin. "It's just that Lo and I have a bet that he has one in…Carmel Valley," I fabricate wildly, hoping that the mention of Lo will soften her up.

"A bet," she repeats.

The lies barrel out like rocks. "Yeah, and he said I was wrong. Anyway, you're like the only one who can settle it."

Her eyes narrow even more. "Lo's been to both my houses. He knows where I live, so if he says you're wrong, then you're wrong." Ignoring the stab of jealousy in my stomach at that tidbit of information, I'm like a deer in headlights, caught smack-bang in the middle of the lie. Cara sighs and shakes her head. "Look, if you wanted to know whether Lo and I hang out outside of school, we do. We're friends, and if that bothers you, then you should take it up with him, but I really don't have time for this."

"Can I ask you one more thing?" I say, stepping right into her path.

"What?"

"Do you care about Speio?"

She smiles coolly and steps around me. "Now, that's *really* none of your business."

Watching as she walks away, I feel an odd sense of guilt. Not that I give a hoot about Cara, but if Speio meant what he said about not being able to have a real relationship because of me, then this is yet another thing that I've cost him. I have the sudden uncomfortable feeling that Speio's life here has been a very lonely one, more so now that things between us have become so strained.

Pushing my thoughts aside, I call Lo but he doesn't answer. The easiest way would be to get him to take me to Cano's house or at least give me the address. He isn't in English or any other classes, which means he's either surfing or sick. Jenna keeps shooting me weird looks but I brush her off with evasive answers. I won't involve her any more than she already is—there's too much at risk.

After Bio, I call Lo again and make my way to the front office instead of the cafeteria for lunch. No answer. Frustrated, I shove my phone into my pocket. There's no way I can wait now that I'm so close to finding my mother...not even another second. Then again, maybe it's a sign that I can't reach Lo. I'm going to have to do this on my own, which is safer for him, anyway. Darting into the nearby women's room as Cano walks past with Leland, I have to hold myself back from confronting him. But being reckless won't help me, or my mother. I stay silent.

I wait patiently until I see his receptionist head down to the cafeteria and slip into Cano's empty office. Taking a deep breath, I close the door behind me. The click of it is like a gunshot. Even in broad daylight, the silence is eerie and heavy, almost as if it has eyes, watching my every move. Before I know it, chills are running up and down my back with every breath. I glance at my watch—I have about five minutes until the receptionist comes back. Not wasting any time, I search all the desk drawers in a methodical fashion, starting with the ones closest to me. Three or four times, I'm interrupted by the murmur of voices or strange banging noises but no one comes into the office. I resume my search, moving on to the file cabinets on the side of the room. And I freeze.

My file is at the very top.

But it's not the only one. There are five other files beneath it—Lo's, Jenna's, Sawyer's, Speio's and Cara's—marked with a yellow Post-it note with "Known Associates" written on it in red ink.

Known associates?

It makes me sound like the kingpin of a weird undercover drug ring or something. I can understand the first four but definitely not the last one. My fingers draw it out from the pile and open the manila cover. Not sure what I was expecting but Cara's file looks the same as any other student file. A couple notes draw my attention. She's a volunteer at the local Children's Cancer Hospital. The snarky thought that she'd do anything for brownie points rushes through my head at the exact second that I see the second note. She lost her mother to the disease and grew up in foster homes for her entire childhood until she came to Dover. She's done such a good job hiding her secret and pretending to belong that I never even guessed that she wasn't born and bred here. I don't think anyone did.

Maybe Lo was right when he said that underneath it all, we didn't really know her and that she was a nice girl. I think about the events of the past week and shake my head. Maybe if hell froze over, she'd be a nice girl. Still, knowing about Cara's childhood goes a long way to mollifying some of my hostility. Maybe that's why she and Lo are so close. Technically, she's been an outsider all along. I put the file gently back on top and keep searching. I find what I'm looking for in a thin drawer right under the lip of the desk. It's an old magazine, likely junk mail, with Cano's name and Rancho Santa Fe address typed into the corner.

Sierra.

An exclusive gated community that requires advance notice to access. Rumor is that it's patrolled by armed security, mostly because of its high-profile residents. And no doubt

Cano will have security of his own. There's only one person I know who has access to that particular community because his mother has a house there.

Lo.

My stomach sours. I thought it'd be better to do it on my own and not involve him, but it looks like I'll have no choice. Time to ditch school. Twenty minutes later, I'm parked outside of Lo's house and banging on his door. He answers, his face still bleary with sleep. His hair is sticking up in all different directions and he's dressed in ratty jeans and a T-shirt, as if he's just rolled out of bed. No shoes. Scruffy. I've never wanted to jump someone's bones more.

"You do realize that it's the middle of the day, right?" I say with a gulp. "And you have a thing called school that's mandatory?"

He rubs his face. "Yeah. Went night surfing. Swell was epic. Bertha called in that I had a doctor's appointment." His "staff," I presume.

"That's convenient," I say, glancing at my watch. "I need your help."

"Sure, what's up?" he says, his brow furrowing. He doesn't question why I need his help, and it makes a tiny burn ignite somewhere in the pit of my stomach. He leans over to kiss my temple. "Everything okay?"

"Everything is fine but I need you to do something for me. Take me somewhere."

His pushes a stray lock of hair out of my face and grins at me with a knowing look. "And you're sure you want to go there right this minute? Since you're here and breaking all kinds of school rules, why don't you come back inside with me and we'll just go later?"

As much as his suggestion makes the tiny flame in my center nearly explode into something uncontrollable, I shake my head. "We need to go now."

"Where to?" he says, and pulls the door shut behind him.

"Sierra." Lo's dark eyes turn to me, his eyebrow raised and all traces of sleep gone. "I know your mom lives there, and I need to get in. I'm sorry to ask, but I don't have anyone else." I don't know why I still don't tell him whose house it is—maybe it's some last-ditch effort to protect him. Once we're in, I can do the rest on my own.

"Is this about your mother?"

"Maybe. She may be there, but I'm not sure."

"In Sierra."

"Yes," I say, exasperated. Didn't I just say it five times already? Lo raises his palms in surrender and then jumps into the driver's side of my Jeep, his hands gripping the steering wheel. He starts the engine.

"Only asking because it's not exactly the type of neighborhood that's amenable to runaways or missing people, unless they want to be missing." I glare at him and he stares at the road, muttering, "Just saying."

We remain silent for the rest of the fifteen-minute drive. I shouldn't be upset at Lo—normal people who go missing probably wouldn't show up in Rancho Santa Fe, either. But my mother isn't normal. And neither is Cano.

Lo makes a turn down a curving road and pulls up to an ominous-looking security building. The security guard is the size of a Hummer. I can't help but notice the weapon clipped to his belt and I frown. This is one of the richest communities in San Diego—it's not like they are going to be the target of low-life scum from other less affluent areas. Or maybe I don't know anything about crime. Maybe people pay for protection in communities like these so that they don't have to worry about anyone breaking and entering. At the thought,

I hunch down in my seat and try not to make eye contact with the guard.

The security guard takes Lo's pass and inserts it into some kind of metal scanning device before handing back to him. I notice the second guard checking the underside of the Jeep and then peering through my window to stare at my face. He nods grimly to his partner. I get the feeling that even in the middle of the day, we've narrowly avoided being strip-searched.

The gates open on well-oiled hinges and we drive through on a long, unmarked, perfectly paved road that is lined with precisely spaced green pine trees. Everything is like a well-executed movie reel, with all the trees the exact same height and the road like oily black glass.

"Once we get past security, I can just get out," I tell Lo, trying not to feel like Alice entering Wonderland.

"No way I'm letting you go doing bad things in here. You'll get arrested in seconds. See up there?" He points to a camera positioned on top of a streetlight. "The security here is like Fort Knox, the gate guards are only the tip of the iceberg. That's just one that you can see but there are many others that you can't."

Okay, I'll have to rethink my plan.

"What's the address?" I tell it to him from memory, and he shoots me an odd expression, his fingers tightening on the wheel.

"What?"

"That's Principal Cano's address."

It's my turn to stare at him as he makes a right-hand turn down another wide, unmarked street. "Cara mentioned that you've been there," I say tightly.

"Nothing to do with Cara," he says with a shrug. "Cano lives next to my mother. I only see Cara there once in a blue moon." Well, that's a surprise. I didn't realize that his mother and Cano were actual neighbors. Lo grins. "How do you think I got into Dover midyear? It wasn't because of my stellar academic record. So you think your mom is at Cano's house? Isn't that a little weird?" Lo pulls to the side of the street and turns off the engine. "What's going on, Riss?"

Even thinking about it makes it seem far-fetched. *Um, we found a creature that's some sort of weird human and alien hybrid and tracked its scent back here. I think it may have been working with a vigilante alien hybrid school principal who is holding my mother hostage in his house. Oh, and I'm an alien, too, and so's my entire family.*

Probably not.

"You know, if you wanted to see where my mother lived, you could have just asked me," Lo says.

Spluttering, I want to punch him so hard that my teeth hurt. "I don't care about your mother, you ass. I care about mine."

"And you think Cano's got her in his house." Lo falls silent, watching me. "In the middle of the day. In the 'burbs. You do know how crazy that sounds, right?"

"Trust me, I know how it sounds. I think she and Cano know each other. Maybe there are clues to where she is. Will you just check with me while he's still at school?" I glance at my watch. It's nearly one o'clock, which means we have a couple hours before Cano comes home.

Lo puts the car in Drive and takes a few more turns on some more glassy roads before he pulls up to a large stone archway over a narrower driveway. He drives straight up for a few more minutes and then pulls the Jeep just in front of a detached four-car garage. "My mother's house," he tells me, getting out. I follow. "It's the easiest way to get next door without being picked up by the community security."

"What about your mother?"

"I think she's out of the country."

Lo takes my hand and leads me nearly half a mile through

some bushes where we can see a clear view of Cano's driveway. My stomach sinks. There's a car with some kind of maid service sign painted on the side parked in the driveway. My watch says a quarter past one.

"Don't worry, they'll be gone soon," Lo says. "They come the same time every week." He sits on a rock and chews on a twig, studying me. "So for argument's sake, what are you going to do if she's there?"

I answer honestly. "Take her with me."

"And what if she's not?"

"Then at least I'll know that my best friend betrayed me," I whisper, lowering myself to a rock to Lo's right. We have time to kill, after all, and my legs are already starting to ache. I draw my knees up to my chest and prop my elbows on them.

"Who? Jenna?"

I shake my head. "Speio." For an instant, a shadow clouds Lo's face at the mention of Speio's name but it disappears as quickly as it comes. "My best friend, my brother and a lot more by the sound of things."

"What do you mean?"

I can't quite hide the blush that rushes to my cheeks. I hadn't realized that I'd said the last part out loud. "He says...he's in love with me. Can you imagine, of all things?"

Lo smiles, a slow sexy smile that makes my toenails rattle. My blush heats up and I lean forward so that my hair falls into my face. "I can imagine lots of things like that and more. In fact, I can't imagine why half the male population of Dover isn't in love with you."

"Stop, you're being silly."

"Am I?"

I take the bait just as he knows I would. "Why would they be?"

"Because there's just something about you. You're strong but you're fragile, too. You could probably whip my butt if you tried, and then you'd care if you hurt me. You're an amazing surfer and athlete. You have a kind heart, you're interesting and you're beautiful." Lo sticks his foot out so that the heel of his touches my toe. His feet are still bare but all I hear are his last words. The sound of it is like music, making my heart race and my blood thicken in my veins. "But it's like I can't quite figure you out, like there's this shell around you. And sometimes I see glimpses of what's inside, and it's...magical."

"You don't speak like any seventeen-year-old I know," I say for lack of anything else, still staring at the ground, embarrassed but flattered. "You sound like a poet."

"It's true. And I'm eighteen." His teeth shine white in his face. "Got held back because I skipped classes for surfing way too much. Teachers didn't like it, and they got immune to my boyish charm."

I laugh out loud at his mock-resigned look. "I turn seventeen on Friday."

"I know," he says. At my look, he clarifies. "Jenna. Are you having a party?"

"No. The school dance is that night. Plus, we don't do parties out here. We do social gatherings that people turn up to, should they be so inclined. Last year I had a bonfire gathering on the beach with fireworks. It was amazing. Then we all went skinny-dipping at midnight."

Lo's eyebrows shoot into his hairline. "Skinny-dipping? Wow, what I wouldn't give to have moved here one year earlier." His blatant flirting is charming. So to pass the time, I do the one thing I have zero experience in doing. I flirt back.

"That could be in your future if you play your cards, right, Mr. Seavon," I say in a low, what-I-think-is-sexy voice. I try to bat my eyelashes, but probably only manage to look like I have epilepsy. Lo bursts out laughing, which he quickly stifles at the injured look on my face. But I can't keep my face straight, either, and I start giggling so hard that I'm snorting.

"You're cool, Nerissa Marin."

"You're pretty cool yourself."

"Go to the dance with me?" Lo asks, so softly that I barely hear him. "I know it's your birthday but it might be fun." The question takes me by surprise. I hadn't planned on going to the dance, not with the challenge so near, and trying to find my mother, and everything weird that is going on with Speio. School dances seem trivial. Even school is no longer a necessity.

But now that Lo has voiced the question, all of a sudden, I do want to go. I want a piece of normal in this tornado of crazy. I want to experience a school dance with a boy whom I actually like being around, and one who likes being around me. I want to have a real date before things take a turn for the worse…because there's a very real possibility that I could die. Ehmora is strong, and she's the queen of her court. She's been ruling for more years than I've lived and I can't underestimate her. As confident as I am in my own abilities, I can still lose.

And for that reason, the simple question from this boy sitting on a rock while in the middle of a stakeout in front of our school principal's house is like a lifeline.

One moment of ordinary in a sea of chaos.

So I take it, I take it and I run with it, because it's the only thing I have anchoring me to the teenage version of me… the one that has been suffocating to death under the stress of Aquarathi politics.

Without my teenage self, I know I will lose.

"You have exceptional timing," I say with a smile. "I definitely won't forget being asked to my first dance while spying on Principal Cano."

"Come on, I'm sure you've been asked dozens of times," Lo says.

"Contrary to what you may think, boys my age have a hard time approaching me for some reason. So you're the first," I say. "Must have to do with your advanced years."

"Ha, ha. Very funny, but I prefer to think of it as maturity. And the boys at school are all idiots, well, with the exception of Sawyer, who seems to have it all worked out despite his clueless moments."

"Sawyer's a keeper," I agree. "And so is Jenna. They're a great couple."

Silence falls between us. I tie my hair into a ponytail using the spare elastic on my wrist and stand to stretch my legs. I'm as tense as a coiled spring, basically running on adrenaline. Spinning my arms in a slow windmill, I breathe in and out slowly.

"You okay?" Lo asks.

"Fine. Just tired." I glance down at his feet. "Don't you own any shoes?"

A smile as he stands to said bare feet. "I don't like them. Or clothes, either, for that matter. If I had my way, I'd be running around nude all day."

I bite my tongue so hard that my eyes water, but I'll bite harder if it will make the image of Lo with no clothes on disappear from my brain. I windmill my arms even faster, thinking of the grossest thing I can imagine…which is Cara and Speio making out. Until Lo's face merges into Speio's and Cara becomes me. Now I'm making out with Lo and he has no clothes on. Gah!

"What's wrong?" Lo asks innocently. "You look strange."

"I'm fine. Just a cramp in my shoulder," I lie.

"Need a hand?"

"No, thanks!" I say hastily, and put a few steps of distance between him and my suddenly overheated brain and body. I'm sure he's good with massage—he's good at everything—but the last thing I need is Lo, clothed or unclothed, touching me while we're waiting to break in to someone's house. I clear my throat. "Anyway, Lo, thanks for doing this with me," I say. "I know it's out of the blue and totally weird, and you probably think I'm some kind of paranoid freak already."

The teasing moments gone, Lo glances at Cano's house, which we can see the tip of in the distance. "I just want to help."

"Well, thanks. Look," I say, pointing to the driveway as one of the garage doors opens up and the soft tenor of voices waft out. Lo and I peer through the bushes, our faces nearly touching. My entire body freezes as he blows a feathery kiss against my ear. "Stop," I tell him breathlessly, wanting him to do more than just blow kisses at me. Lo grins with a knowing expression, but then his smile fades as he jerks his head to the sound of a car starting. We both duck as the blue car zips past.

"It's now or never, Spy Kid."

"You are such a child," I say, sprinting past him to the garage door that has started to close and ducking underneath it. Lo rolls by just before the door clicks shut on its smooth automatic hinges. The three-car garage is wide and spacious, and unlike Lo's mother's garage, it's attached to the house.

Everything inside is silent.

"What if he has alarms?" I whisper.

"Why bother with all the mob security outside?" Lo says. "You take downstairs, I'll take upstairs, you know, just in case you throw up all over the bed at the thought of the magic that happens there."

"Ugh. I'm going to throw up right now."

We separate in the large open living room. The space is masculine with dark furniture. It has no personal touches whatsoever as if the person living here is a ghost. I've never thought of Cano as someone without any personality, but as I think about his plain gray prison-cut suits, I see that his colorless house fits him perfectly. There are some gorgeous black-and-white landscapes on the wall, but other than those, the room is bland.

The kitchen is more or less the same. Pristine with dark cabinetry, looking like a kitchen out of a food magazine. The entire first floor is clear but there's one door I haven't gone into and it's at the far end of the house. My breath catching, I push open the heavy door to see steps leading downward into darkness. There's a light switch on the side so I turn it on before heading downstairs. The fluorescent lighting is bright, making the white walls seem almost neon. Basements are uncommon in California, but Cano obviously has the money to build some kind of reinforced dungeon beneath his house.

I stop at the bottom of the narrow staircase, my jaw dropping to the floor, and scream as a hand grabs my shoulder.

"It's just me," Lo says quickly. "Upstairs is clear."

"Don't do that again," I tell him, my pulse racing. I didn't even hear him behind me. "Are you seeing this? What is this place?"

We both look at the spotless white space in front of us, lined with metal tables and all kinds of shiny, expensive-looking equipment. At the far end of the room are what look like animal-size wire cages. A swirl of black wires line one of the other walls like a huge black coiling snake. The room is empty but it feels ominous. My eyes are drawn back to the electric cables.

What would Cano need mainline electricity for?

Torture? Experiments? I take a deep breath and engage all of my senses. It's useless—if there was ever anything alien, hybrid or human in this room, it's gone now. There is no trace of anything—not one spot of blood, hair or fluid. Stepping backward, I nearly crash into a desk on the back wall. A thin computer tablet is lying faceup on its surface. I glide my finger over the black screen, and it turns on to show a bunch of files that look like video logs.

I press Play.

My brain swings into slow motion, every second elongating impossibly. Pain pulls at my cells, nearly dragging them from my body at the images on the screen. My mother...with her arm around Cano, and another dark-haired woman in profile who I can only assume is Ehmora, talking about genetic permutations. My mother...smiling coldly with something like triumph written all over her face, chattering about DNA and coding, in the very lab we are standing in right now. My mother...alive and well.

A traitor.

"It's some kind of lab," I hear Lo saying from behind me on the other side of the room, but his words fall into a black hole as I stare at the video record. My heart is collapsing into nothing. "Looks like Cano has some unresolved mad scientist issues," Lo says.

At Lo's words, I remember that Cano used to be a molecular biologist, and my heart beats so fast that it feels like it's going to jump out of my skin. Jamming my finger onto the pause button, I back away slowly. Every hair on my body is raised in warning as Lo inspects one of the shiny knives on the counter closest to him. "Let's go. Don't touch anything."

"What about your mother?"

"I was wrong."

"How do you know?" Lo says as we shut the basement door.

I don't speak until we are back outside. Surprisingly, my eyes are dry. The only thing I feel is a wide net of nothingness spreading inside of me, numbing everything it touches.

The betrayal is dull, as if I'd expected it somehow…as if I've always known. My father knew. He'd tried to protect me.

"Riss?"

"Because my mother died thirteen years ago."

20

Broken Bones and Dreams

The sky is blue and melting. Floating in the middle of the ocean, I feel nothing but the waves rocking me in their wide, emotionless arms. Even though I feel as heavy as a stone, I'm weightless. Countless fins spin around me in a wide circle, attracted by whatever bitter feelings are being leached from my body. I sink lower, pulling them closer until I'm surrounded by the silver glitter of scales. It's oddly beautiful in a mesmerizing sort of way. A huge gray nurse shark swims past, its mouth open and full of razor-sharp teeth, so close that I can touch it.

I do, and watch as the swirl of bluish-green iridescence from the ragged cut in my human palm diffuses into the water like ink. The peaceful dance explodes into something feral. The fish swarm into a frenzy as the bigger fish rip apart the smaller fish, and I'm surrounded by a floating array of bones and flesh—a graveyard of the strong defeating the weak.

It makes me feel less broken. I feel my skin snapping as webbed fins span between my fingers and along the sides of my face. The sharks eye me, never coming too close but never straying too far, either. I'm worse than they are. They want me but they fear me.

As they should. As they all should.

With one thought from me, they scatter and I push myself to the surface, feeling my body return to normal like molding clay. As I break the surface, I see a shadowy figure on Lo's balcony watching me. But when I look more closely, there's no one there. Lo is still on the beach, lying on a blanket next to his surfboard. It must have been a trick of the light or one of his strange, silent staff.

After surfing for a few hours and a picnic on the beach, Lo decided to enjoy the sun for a while. I decided to go for a swim instead. Sleeping makes me dream and doing nothing makes me think, and neither of those were things I wanted to do. We've spent the past two days at his house, skipping school and surfing. I didn't want to face my family or Cano, and Lo didn't mind being a complete school burnout with me.

After the fiasco at Cano's, he'd asked me what I meant about my mother being dead but I wasn't ready to talk about it. Not with him…not with anyone. But in my head, all of the pieces were coming together.

My mother started it all.

Floating on top of the waves, I think back to the video I'd seen at Cano's house. All of the work was hers. The voice was hers. But the most damning evidence was seeing her face—her human face—on the video log, with Cano on one side of her and another woman on the other. The woman I can only guess is Ehmora.

My mother didn't look like a captive. She looked like a leader.

And Echlios must know. Otherwise, why would he try so hard to keep me away…to keep me from finding out the truth that my father tried so hard to protect me from? I can't face Echlios with what I've learned. His pity will break me more than I'm already broken.

I'm not quite sure how the pieces fit together, so I'm speculating, but my mother must have been branded a traitor. So she went to the only person who would take her in—my father's enemy. And with me out of the picture, Ehmora could be next in succession by right of challenge. A vision of my mother's body parts in the box that Ehmora sent me along with her challenge spins through my mind. The cruelty of it takes my breath away.

Not Ehmora's, but my mother's.

How could she have sent a barbaric message like that to me, her own daughter? I lied to Lo that she was dead, even though she's very much alive in breath and in body. After what she's done to me, she may as well be dead. And if I see her, I will kill her myself.

Swimming in to shore, I lie next to Lo on the blanket on my stomach and rest my face in the crook of his arm and chest. His skin is warm from the sun, and I let the feel of him chase my simmering anger away.

"Your phone buzzed a few times," he murmurs, kissing my wet hair. With a sigh, I grab it, wishing I could toss it into the ocean, but I check the messages instead. I already told Echlios where I was staying, with curt orders for him to stay away. Not that he'll listen—I'm sure he's already checked in on me in secret a few times. As long as I don't see him, that's all good. I also told him to not tell Speio, which I hope he listened to.

The text messages are from Jenna, with increasing usage of exclamation marks. She's freaking out, I can tell. The last one has some particularly offensive comments about me being holed up with Lo, which makes me giggle.

"What?" Lo asks sleepily.

"It's just Jenna. She thinks you've kidnapped me and are forcing me to go all *Fifty Shades* on you."

"It wouldn't be forcing, would it?" Lo says, and I elbow him in the side, blushing.

Lo has been a total gentleman the whole time I've been here. And despite my throwing myself at him on the first night, when we came back to his place after I downed a wine cooler, he sent me to have a nice long shower and then put me to bed.

In the guest room.

The next day at breakfast, Lo told me that it was the hardest thing he's ever done, saying no to me. But he somehow knew that I was an emotional wreck despite my exterior indifference, and that my booze-induced advances were just that. I, for my part, thanked him and let it drop. I'll never admit to him that, drunk or not, I knew exactly what I was doing.

"I guess I better text her before she and Sawyer start staking out the beach," I say, tapping on the screen and hitting Send. A text comes back before I can even close my phone.

Knew it. You are such a tramp

It's not like that, I text back. Explain later.

When later?

I smile at her tenacity and lean over to poke Lo in the stomach. "What did Bertha tell Cano about you being absent?" Bertha, a fierce-looking Scandinavian woman, is Lo's cook slash housekeeper, and she always has the best excuses for when Lo misses school, which is often.

"That I had food poisoning."

"Darn, that's a good one." I sigh. "I'm out of excuses. If I show up to the dance tomorrow, I'm toast. With everything going on, I didn't even tell anyone I was out of school. Again.

And I'm sure they've already called Soren." Lo props himself up on one elbow, his eyes glittering in the sun.

"Don't worry. I took care of it." I stare at him incredulously. "I had Bertha talk to Soren a couple days ago, letting her know that you were doing an extra credit kelp care project at the marine center for this week. School's covered."

"And that worked?"

Lo nods solicitously. "Bertha can be very convincing. Soren called here, too, to check on you."

That gets my attention in a heartbeat. "You spoke to her?"

"Don't worry," Lo says, blowing sand from my temple. "I only told her that you were staying here and that you had already talked to Echlios. It's all good. I didn't say anything about anything." Relaxing almost immediately, I pick up my phone and text Jenna back.

"Assume that means we're still going to the dance tomorrow?" he asks, nodding at what I've typed on the screen.

I grin and hit Send. "Well, it *is* my birthday." My phone buzzes and I laugh out loud at Jenna's return text. It's a smiley face with about fifteen exclamation marks. "What's the theme again?" I ask Lo.

"Under the sea, last I heard."

I laugh. "Are you kidding me?"

"I thought you liked the ocean?" Lo asks, bending over me to drop tiny kisses from my jawline to my ear that are making me see white starbursts.

"I do," I manage, breathless. "It's just... Never mind. I can't think while you're doing that."

"Doing what?" Lo asks with a wicked grin.

I raise an eyebrow—two can play at that game. I flip over onto my back and run my fingers across the rounded curve of his shoulder to the sleek bulge of his arm. His blue eyes turn dark and storm-tossed in the space of a second. My hand glides back upward on his side past his rib cage. A trail of goose bumps bloom on his skin at my light touch and I smile as I slide my fingers down the muscular planes of his stomach. Lo grabs my hand in his, stalling my movement just at the waistband of his swim shorts.

"Coward," I tell him.

"Maybe so," he says, silencing me with a kiss. "But I'd rather be a coward than get arrested for getting busy on a public beach." Bringing my hands to his lips, he kisses my knuckles. "Plus, I can't be held responsible for my actions while you're doing that."

"Getting busy? People still say that?"

"Only in the coolest circles," Lo says with a straight face.

I kiss his mouth and then his nose and jump to my feet. "Okay, then I'll race you inside and we can get busy in private." I've never seen a boy jump to his feet so quickly, but I'm already off and running up the trail to Lo's house, giggling like mad.

He catches me just as we round the back door—actually, I allow him to catch me since I wasn't putting much effort into staying ahead of him—and lifts me clean off the floor. I can run almost as fast as I can swim, and after all of Echlios's training, I've never been more physically fit.

We both freeze in the living room at the person sitting on the couch, his face expressionless as he sees me covered in sand and in Lo's arms. My grin fades and I lower myself awkwardly to the ground and dust off my arms.

"Mr. Seavon," Grayer, Lo's butler/valet, intones. He unnerves me as much as Bertha does. They're both cut from the same grim, silent cloth. "Ms. Marin has a guest, her guardian. He insisted on waiting. I was just about to call down to get you."

"Thank you, Grayer," Lo says, walking forward to stick out

his hand. "Echlios, always a pleasure." They shake hands, but I remain standing where I am, motionless. Half of me wants to grab Lo and run back the way we came and the other half knows that I have to face Echlios sooner or later.

I sigh. "Let's take a walk."

Excusing ourselves from Lo, we walk back down to the beach almost to the water's edge, where the crashing sounds of the surf will keep our conversation private.

"I told you not to come," I say in a low voice.

"I know, but I had to see for myself that you were all right."

"You've seen that I am," I counter. "I know you've been watching me."

Echlios amends his earlier statement, conceding my words with a nod. "I had to speak to you in person. It's still not safe for you, my lady. And this boy, we know next to nothing about him."

"You cleared him."

"Because he wasn't a threat. For all we know he could be a hybrid."

I laugh. "He's not."

"How do you know?" It's not like I can explain to Echlios that I've played tongue twister with the boy in question and know his scent so intimately that there is no biological way he could be anything but human. Lo smells delicious, perfect. The hybrid had been so pungent that every predator instinct inside of me had been alerted. It isn't a smell that I'd be slow to recognize, now that I'm familiar with it.

Instead, I just say, "I know what the last one smelled like. I came face-to-face with it, remember? And Lo smells nothing like that one did. Just trust me on it."

"Speio doesn't trust him," Echlios says quietly.

"Did you tell him where I am?" I ask. Echlios shakes his head. I study the waves, contemplating my next words. I decide to be honest. "Speio is jealous of Lo, that's why he hates him. Do you know that he told me that he is in love with me?"

Surprise crosses Echlios's face. "My lady, Speio loves you for certain, but as a brother. I am sure of it. Soren and I would know."

"Then why would he lie?"

"I don't know. Speio—" Echlios rakes his hand through his hair "—has changed. He has become so moody and discon-nected, disappearing for hours at a time. We thought he was with you, but the other day I found him in the ocean near San Clemente in the middle of the night. When I asked him what he was doing there, he told me that it was the only way he could think."

I try to make myself care, really I do. But I don't. Speio has made his bed or whoever's bed he's crawled into. I turn gla-cial eyes to Echlios. "Did you come here to talk to me about your son? Because I really can't help you. And you're wrong, Speio now hates me more than anyone else."

"No, he doesn't—" Echlios begins, but I cut him off with a silent, raised hand.

I study the waves, watching the white eddies froth into the darker water beneath them. The demons in my head are clam-oring for answers. "Why didn't you tell me about my mother? That she was a traitor?" I ask softly. "You knew, didn't you?"

Echlios looks pained. "We suspected."

"Did you know, back then, that she hated my father?" His pained expression turns into something so dark that I flinch. He shakes his head just once. "Tell me."

"You were too little, and they never fought in public," he says. "But they disagreed often, and sometimes violently. She always agreed with Ehmora. Did you know they used to be best friends...?" He trails off, staring at the sand beneath his boot as if the sting of the memory is too great, but I can't let it go that easily. Not now, when he's finally talking.

"Tell me everything, Echlios. Do not lie to me," I tell him.

"There were rumors that they were more than friends," he says after a while. "Bonded."

"But my parents," I gasp. "They were bonded."

Echlios shakes his head sadly. "It was their biggest secret, and one that I was tasked to protect at all cost. Theirs was a politically arranged alliance from the start. Your mother bonded with Ehmora the night before they were united, and the day she turned against your father, all the others knew. Because a true bond is one that can never be broken. So your father cast her out and told you that she was dead."

I want to laugh, because the rumors were that my father had something with Ehmora when all the time it was my mother, but the truth hurts too much to laugh.

"Why did he stay with her?" I ask. "If he knew about her indiscretion?"

"Your father loved her. And she convinced him that she felt the same, but of course, her heart—and her loyalty—were always elsewhere."

"With Ehmora."

"Yes."

"Did they plan it from the start?" I say, trying to keep my raging emotions in check, but it's useless. The clouds are already rolling in, dark and thunderous, blotting out the sun's light. "For the throne?" Echlios nods, his hand reaching toward me. I step away in the same breath. I don't want to be touched. Lightning cracks in the distance. "She never loved either of us, did she?"

"She wanted different things, Nerissa. That doesn't mean she didn't love you."

Suddenly Echlios's eyes narrow and he shoves his arm out to

push me to the side. I glare at him but he's staring into empty space at something behind me. "What's wrong?"

"Nothing. I thought I saw a glimmer." When I glance behind me, there's nothing there but a shimmer of sunshine trickling through a gap in the thunderclouds.

"That's not possible. Both of us would have sensed it in seconds," I say. "It must have been a trick of the light or something." I shrug, glancing around just in case, but there's no one there, not even any movement on the balcony of Lo's house. "Or maybe it's Speio, spying. Did you tell him I was here?"

"No," Echlios says. "But he already knows. Either he followed you or someone at school told him. He knows." But it doesn't even matter to me anymore. I take several deep breaths and watch the rays of the sun dancing across the tops of the waves.

"Echlios, I need some time. Time away to process everything," I say. "The challenge with Ehmora is soon—"

"You don't have to accept," Echlios interrupts.

"That's just it," I say calmly. "I do. I have to prove myself now. My mother orchestrated my father's death so that she could be with her lover. I have to fight Ehmora. I have to do it for my father, and you know that. Don't you?" Echlios doesn't say anything for a long while but I can see it in the set of his face. He knows I'm right. He nods just once and bows slightly.

"Two days. That's it, Nerissa. I will come for you on Saturday. Then we will resume our training. And you will fight. And we will return to Waterfell."

"Agreed."

"One more thing."

"Yes?" I ask.

"Have a happy birthday, my lady."

I watch as Echlios walks along the beach to the road. He doesn't need to go back to the house, but I see him stop and look up at it all the same, a thoughtful look on his face. I stay at the water's edge until he's barely a speck in the distance.

The next three days will decide the rest of my life. Whether I live or whether I die.

21
Gods and Goddesses

"Ugh, I look ridiculous."

"You look gorgeous." Jenna's mom doesn't mince words as she tugs on the hemline of my jewel-toned satin dress, which is the startling color of green sea glass. I tug back on the sleeveless bodice, only to encounter a tittering sound on her part.

Seriously, when Lo told me that Bertha had already gotten our costumes for the dance, I assumed it was something simple, not this extravagant. I stare at myself in the full-length mirror in Jenna's bedroom. My hair has been roped into intricate braids under a gold net and wound with brilliant green tendrils of fake seaweed. Gold-and-green glitter is dusted across my brow and cheeks, accentuating the greenish tones in my human hazel-colored eyes. The glitter continues its trail across my bare shoulders and down my arms.

"Who am I supposed to be again?" I ask Jenna, who's smoothing her own outfit on the other side of the room. She's dressed in a mermaid costume, complete with a sparkly emerald dress that turns into a mermaid's tail at the bottom. She looks great, while I look and feel weird.

"Salacia, the Roman ocean goddess," she says. "Lo's got good taste."

I can appreciate the irony of my costume, only I'm no goddess. In fact, staring at my reflection, I look exactly like a phony human version of my other self, green-and-gold fake bioluminescent glitter included. It's a little off-putting. My choice would have been to go as Ariel, the Disney mermaid, but that's Jenna's costume. She makes a far better mermaid princess than I ever could.

"Roman mythology," I mutter, tugging at a stray piece of plastic seaweed.

Jenna's mom stops at the doorway. "I'm going to get my camera. The boys are downstairs already, so hurry up."

"Sure, Mom," Jenna says, and makes sure the door's closed after her mother leaves. "Omigod, I've been dying for her to stop hovering for, like, two seconds. So seriously, you've been shacked up with Lo this whole time?" One thing about Jenna, she gets right to the point. Her blue eyes are intense, brooking no escape on my part. I tug the skirt of my dress over a swatch of bare leg.

"Sort of," I say. "Things with Speio have been shaky, ever since…you know."

Jenna nods, agreeing. "So what happened?"

Grabbing some blusher off the dresser, I deliberate just how much to say and decide to tell her most of it. Chances are, in a few days, this will all be over…and I'd rather she knows than not know that Cano is a complete two-timing slime ball. Pulling her to sit beside to me on the bed, I take a deep breath.

"Remember that creature thing from the other night? Well, I traced it back to a house. Actually, I forced Speio to tell me, which is why we're not talking. He pretty much hates me, but I can't help that. Anyway, the house the trail went to was Cano's."

"Cano?" Jenna gasps in a hushed whisper. "As in Principal Cano?"

"One and the same."

"You think he's one of them?"

"No, but I think he's working on some kind of genetic DNA thing. He has a giant lab in a facility under his house and a whole bunch of research on genetic mixing."

Jenna's eyes are the size of saucers. "You're saying that he's mixing our DNA and yours?"

"That's what it looked like. Is that even possible?" I ask her.

"I'm not sure," she says, "because we're two different species with different DNA." She stares at me so hard that I can see the wheels in her brain turning through her eyes. "Although...I'd have to see what your DNA looks like, but since you can take human form, I'd assume that there must be some similarity."

"Like hybrids?" I ask softly.

Jenna is nodding thoughtfully. "Technically, a hybrid would already have combined DNA strands from both species, and he could be trying to introduce nonnative genotypes to increase genetic variability."

"Speak English, Dr. Who," I say, frowning as my mind tries unsuccessfully to keep up with the genius speed of hers.

"He's introducing new alleles, or specific genes with specific DNA codings, so that he can cultivate or grow distinct traits, human or alien...like the best of both worlds."

"Still Swahili."

"Sorry, sounds like they are trying to make the hybrids better." Jenna's eyes narrow. "It's like that one we saw, remember? It was nothing at all like you. It had bits of you but was bulky and beastly like a monster." She grabs my hand and leans in, her voice low and urgent. "Wait, have you told Lo what you are?"

"No, of course not," I say. "You're the only one who knows. Well, besides the ones I never knew about, like Cano."

Jenna leans back with a sigh on her pillows. "I wonder if that's why..."

"That's why what?"

"Leland told me Cano wanted me to keep an eye on you," Jenna says. Her cheeks redden. "That's why I had to go see her so often weeks ago, to report in that you were fine and not on the edge of some kind of inner teen collapse. I had no idea this was the real reason."

"Did you tell them anything?" I ask, my own voice urgent.

"Of course not! I just told her what she wanted to hear, normal teen stuff," Jenna says, shaking her head as if in complete disbelief. "Holy crap, I still can't believe it. Freaking Cano, this whole time. That's insane. You know he used to be some kind of famous biologist, right?"

I nod. "Tell me about it. We can't trust anyone.

"Jenna," I say quietly, pulling her arm so that she's facing me on the bed. "Whatever happens, thank you for being my best friend, and for always looking out for me. And thanks for not freaking out when I told you my secret and for not calling the *National Enquirer*." We both smile, but my voice chokes up. "I'm serious. You're everything a girl could ask for in a best friend." I pull her into a tight hug, saying my own silent goodbyes. "I love you loads."

"Love you, too. Why are you being all weird like you're never going to see me again?" she says, hugging me back and frowning. "You know I've got your back. Always. Everything okay?"

I paste a grin on my face and blink away the tears pooling in my eyes. "Yes, it's fine, I promise. I just wanted you to know. Now let's go downstairs and get our dates, and rescue your mom from their clutches."

Jenna giggles. "More like rescue them from her. Sawyer's used to my mother, but Lo may be ready to call 9-1-1."

"I just need one minute, okay?"

"Sure," she says with a long look at the door. "You really look great, Riss."

"Thanks, so do you."

I stare in the mirror after Jenna leaves, studying the girl standing there. She doesn't even look like me. She looks like a pale imitation of the real Roman goddess of the ocean, with her vulnerable sad eyes, who knows that her time on Earth is at an end. A soft knock on the door has me spinning around.

"You look beautiful," Lo breathes from behind me. I catch his appreciative eyes in the mirror and smile. It's amazing how three words from that boy can make me forget that my bodice is too tight, or the skirt is too long and too flouncy, or that Salacia's heart underneath this dress is breaking into tiny, unrecognizable pieces.

Instead, I feel like a girl…a girl going to a dance with the boy of her dreams.

"You look good, too," I begin automatically. Turning around, I try not to choke on my own drool. "More than good," I amend. Dressed as Neptune—my mythological counterpart—Lo is every inch the god of the sea. I try not to stare at his gold-dusted bare chest and instead focus on the huge golden trident in his hand. "Nice spear," I murmur, breathless.

"Thanks."

A twisted wreathlike crown is on his head, interspersed with bright fiery bits of coral, and a cream toga-style cloth is hung low on his hips, and thrown over one shoulder. The gold dust meanders down his long legs and I gulp past the sudden knot in my throat. His feet, as expected, are bare.

"Is that all you're wearing?"

A wicked grin. "Well, Neptune was historically pictured as naked, so I can do that if you prefer." I can't even speak as a blistering flush makes its way through every bit of skin on my body at his teasing words.

I hide my body's wild reaction with sarcasm. "You have nudity issues, you know that?"

"Don't worry, I have shorts on." They must be the tiniest shorts ever because I can see the bulging muscle of his upper thigh through a gap in his loincloth. A stifled giggle bursts out of my lips.

"Ready?" Lo asks me, sticking out his arm. I nod.

This is going to be an interesting night.

After posing for photos with Jenna's mom and piling into my busted, rusted Jeep with the top down, we're off. It's only a ten-minute ride, but by the time we arrive the dance is already in full swing. The gym has been decorated with crepe streamers hanging from the ceiling in various shades of blue and green. Underwater scenes, painted by the art club, litter the walls of the gym. A bright, colored disco ball is hanging from the middle of the ceiling and bubble machines off to the side are blowing a constant stream of multicolored bubbles into the middle of the dance floor. A band at the far end completes the scene.

I have to admit that it looks magical and exactly what a high-school dance should look like. I grin at some of the costumes floating past us—various kinds of fish, shellfish and mer-creatures. I even spot a giant octopus at one point. Kids have gone all out, and for a minute, I thank Bertha under my breath because I was initially going to show up in jeans and a T-shirt. At least Lo and I look pretty original. But it's Sawyer who steals the show in his bright yellow-and-blue homemade Flounder fish costume.

"How come you didn't go as Prince Eric instead of Flounder?" I ask him.

Sawyer grins. "Jenna wanted me to, but I'm more of a guppy myself."

"Well, you're my guppy and that's all that matters," Jenna says.

"Rissa! You look amazing!" the goalie—Sarah—from our hockey team screeches from across the dance floor. "Awesome costume, Sawyer, and I'm loving the mermaid thing on you, Jenna," Sarah says, and then turns to go completely speechless at Lo. I bite back a smile. "Nice costume, Lo," she eventually chokes out, obviously embarrassed, and we all burst out laughing.

"What? Roman gods didn't wear clothes," Lo says, puffing his chest out and making us all laugh even harder at his affected expression.

"I think he looks fabulous," a familiar breathy voice behind us says. I don't even want to turn around, but good breeding demands that I do. Cara is standing with Speio in tow and waves hello. Her arm is wrapped around his waist but he doesn't even look in our direction. He's dressed in as revealing a costume as hers. Maybe worse. I have to look away.

"Thanks, Cara, so do you. Nice costume," Lo says.

Cara twirls, showing off her—surprise, surprise—very revealing outfit, if it can even be called that. She's clothed in black-and-yellow spandex that is draped artfully across her chest, stomach and hips. She's completely covered, but the outfit fits like a second skin and doesn't leave much to the imagination. Her dark hair has been looped in shiny curls down one shoulder and intertwined with gold ribbon. I have to admit it's a striking costume and, with her figure, she totally pulls it off. Not that I'd tell her that, of course.

"So what are you guys?" I ask. She answers my question but looks at Lo.

"Isn't it obvious? We're electric eels," she says in a supercilious tone. She smiles and flutters her eyelashes at Lo. "Anyway, a little bird told me that the god of the ocean was here and I wanted to pay my respects. So here I am at his service."

"That's only a little creepy," Jenna mutters, earning herself a death glare from Cara.

"Why, thank you," Lo says in a fake gallant voice that makes me want to kick him right in the loincloth. I try not to let my irritation show. I don't want anything, not even Cara, to ruin my one night of freedom…and quite possibly my last.

I glance at Speio, who's smiling at something Sawyer's saying. They're in the middle of a heated discussion about board size to wave height, and while it would normally be a conversation that I'd toss my two cents into, something holds me back. A twinge of regret slides through me at how ruthlessly I'd manipulated him.

Jenna loudly announces that she's going to get some punch, and Cara and I are left staring at each other in awkward silence. On her way to the drinks, Jenna turns around and jerks her head toward Cara, raising her eyebrows.

"It's a great costume," I say to Cara.

"What?"

"I said you look great."

"Thanks," she says with narrowed eyes.

I take a deep breath, feeling the weight of Jenna's stare, and take the plunge. "Look, Cara, I'm sorry about freshman year. For my part in it, I mean. And I'm really happy for you and Speio. He's a great guy. Just wanted to say that."

"Glad you got that off your chest," she says after a while, and turns away. She pauses and then looks back at me as if she has something more to say.

"What?" I ask.

"It's too bad none of it was real. I only became friends with you because my uncle asked me to," she says loudly. "Let's just say you made that impossible, too."

A tumult of emotions fills me at her revelation, even though it doesn't surprise me that Cara would have been one of Cano's unknowing spies. No wonder she always stayed close even after freshman year. It must have been hell for her with Cano on her case to get closer to me.

"Well, I'm sorry," I say lamely.

"Whatever," she says and walks away.

"Well, you can't say I didn't try," I mutter, and join Jenna over at the punch table, leaving Lo, Sawyer and Speio to Cara's mercy.

Jenna hugs me and hands me a glass of neon-colored punch. "I'm really proud of you."

"Told you it wouldn't work," I say.

"It's not for her," Jenna says. "It's for you." I gulp down some of the punch she's given me and nearly spit it all over her. "Spiked?" she asks.

"Way spiked. This could knock over a linebacker," I say, putting the glass onto an empty table. Cara laughs loudly at something one of her friends says, and walks past us with Speio in tow. They both ignore us.

Jenna sighs loudly. "Just remember, you took the high road."

"If you say so," I say sourly. Speio's silent treatment is grating but I refuse to let him get under my skin, and Cara...well, she's just being Cara. Despite Jenna's brave words to the contrary, I'd have no illusions about her. "Where'd Lo and Sawyer go?" I ask, peering past Jenna into the throng of gyrating bodies.

"They did not go dance without us!" Jenna says, snapping her fingers in a Z motion across her body. I snort out loud at her theatrics and drag her into the crowd. We find the boys in the middle of the dance floor showing off for a bunch of adoring girls.

"Hi, Neptune," I say. "Nice moves."

"Where have you guys been?" Sawyer says, doing some kind of weird *Saturday Night Fever* sashay that makes me bite my lip to stop from laughing. The kid cannot dance for the life of him.

"Drinks," Jenna says, and claps her hands gleefully. "Oooh, what's the band doing?"

The lighting in the gym twinkles and lowers as shades of green and blue spin in a slow circle. Lo walks me to the center of the dance floor and a space clears around us. The band singer looks directly at me and grins, then winks at Jenna, who is standing right beside me. She nods and I stare quizzically from her to him.

"From your friends here at Dover Prep, happy birthday to the one and only Salacia, Miss Nerissa Marin!" The singer leads off into the opening chords for "Happy Birthday to You," and practically the entire gym—with the exception of Cara—sings along with him.

Thank you, I mouth to Jenna, and her smile is so bright, it makes me choke up.

The band fades into a cover of Plumb's "Sink 'n' Swim," and Lo pulls me into his arms. The lyrics of the song are so poignant that I bend my head to hide the stabbing sadness that sweeps through me. My life is all about swimming or sinking. Lo's fingers grab a gentle hold of my chin, turning my face up to his. His navy eyes are liquid, flickering with the glow of the spinning lights all around us.

"Are you okay?"

"Fine," I manage. "I'm just lucky to have such good friends, that's all."

"And me?"

I smile. "Especially you."

"Have I told you how lovely you look tonight?" he murmurs into my hair. "Like my very own."

"Your very own what?"

"Just mine," he says.

"Oh."

We twirl in silence, Lo's hand around the curve of my waist and my hands wrapped around his shoulders. I can't imagine having a more perfect moment than what I'm sharing with Lo right now. But it's bittersweet because I know it will be one of the last moments I will have with him, or with Jenna.

It's one of the last times I will be a human teenager, here on my seventeenth birthday. I was always meant to return. This isn't my life—it's a borrowed one.

But borrowed or not, it is mine with all my friends surrounding me with love and secret pieces of themselves. I belong here, too. Burying my face in Lo's neck, I've never felt so torn. All I want to do is to stay in his embrace forever. I want to forget about Ehmora and everything else that will pull me away from this world.

I want to be like them.

But I can't. Once tonight passes, everything will change forever. For now, for these brief precious seconds, I can enjoy the feel of a boy's arms holding me tight...of shared secret glances with Jenna that only two best friends can share...of the magical feel of the music around me...of the beauty that is my life alone without the threat of it disappearing.

"What are you thinking about?" Lo asks. "You're far away right now."

"I'm here. Just thinking about life and getting older."

"Jeez, Riss. You're seventeen, not seventy-seven. You still have a long way to go before worrying about adult responsibilities. Take it from me." He grins and pokes me in the side.

I roll my eyes at him, letting him chase my sadness away. "From you? As in the full-time slacker with the professional staff at his beck and call? Some of us aren't so lucky."

"Hey, I'll have you know I take my slacking responsibilities very seriously." He purses his lips and throws his hands onto his hips. "I am a god, after all."

"A pretend god," I remind him.

"But one nonetheless. Now, grovel before me, woman."

In response I punch him in the arm and leave him stone cold in the middle of the dance floor. I'm still giggling by the time I reach the table with the drinks. One thing I can say for Lo is that he can always make me laugh even when I'm flailing in equal measures of joy and sadness. He always knows exactly the right thing to say.

"Having a nice time, Ms. Marin?" A slimy sensation crawls across the back of my neck and I shiver. The voice is the same as it always is, but now that I know what he is, there's an oily undertone of slyness. Cano is dressed in a dark suit. I remind myself that he doesn't know that I know who he really is, so I smile with my usual grace.

"Of course, sir."

"How's that project you've been working on? At the marine center?"

"Great, thank you." Taking a sip of my water, I'm trying to figure out how to tactfully extract myself when Cano takes my elbow, making me cringe inwardly.

"I see you have been spending a lot of time with Mr. Seavon," he says. I freeze at the awkward touch of his fingers squeezing my arm. He steers me out of the gym into the hallway where we are alone. For a second, I feel nervous until I remember exactly who Cano is—a threat to my people, not just a school principal. I'll defend myself if I need to. "And you two have been getting quite close."

"I don't know what you mean," I say, taking a slight step backward.

"He's not the best influence on someone like you."

"Someone like me," I repeat slowly, his tone setting off all kinds of creepy alarms in my brain.

"Principal Cano," says a honeyed voice from behind me. I glance over my shoulder. It's a woman I've never seen before, dressed for the occasion in a flattering red gown. She has glossy dark hair falling around her face in soft dark waves, with high cheekbones and smoky dark eyes. "Allow me."

"Ms. Marin," Cano says smoothly. "I don't believe you've met Emma Seavon. Lotharius's mother."

Lo's mother?

She smiles. "So nice to meet you, Nerissa. My son has told me so much about you."

"He has?" I say, at a complete loss for words. Lo's mother is nothing like I'd imagined. For one, she looks nothing like him and she's got none of his unaffected warmth. Now I get why he prefers to live with Bertha and Grayer.

She smiles again. "Of course. What Principal Cano is trying to say is that my son makes…rash decisions when it comes to personal matters."

"Shouldn't you be having this conversation with him, then?" I suggest.

Cano clears his throat. "We are only trying to protect you, Ms. Marin." The image of his lab flashes through my brain and I shiver. His voice may sound normal, but I know the words are a little more than a heavily veiled threat, and I don't do well with threats. "It's really for your own good to stay away from him."

Straightening my shoulders, I say, "Or what?"

"I'm sorry?" Cano's eyes laser on me like black ice. Keeping my back to Lo's mother, I focus all of my attention on Cano.

"It's for my own good or what?" I repeat, meeting his gaze with an icy one of my own. I move to walk back into the gym and Cano grabs me once more by the arm. This time his touch is not gentle. His fingers are digging into the flesh of my arms with far more pressure than even a human can take. And he knows that. It's time for me to drop the pretense, too.

"You do not want to cross me," he growls softly so that no one but me can hear.

"And you," I murmur in a low whisper, stepping in and letting my true eyes flare, "do not want to cross me." Cano smiles, a dark ugly smile full of everything horrible he has ever done. I try not to let it penetrate me but it does. I can barely hold back the chills racing along my back and raising the pores on my skin in warning. "Now, release my arm," I say, nearly ripping my arm out of his grasp.

I turn around, my eyes slipping back to normal. "It was nice to meet you, Mrs. Seavon," I say. With a breath to steady my shaky nerves, I open the door to the gym and nearly crash into someone pushing it outward into me.

"I was just looking for you," Lo says, staring from me to Cano to his mother, his eyes narrowing. "Mother? What are you doing here? I thought you were in China?"

"I was," she says. "But I'm back, and Principal Cano asked me to chaperone."

"Chaperone? That's new for you," Lo says almost rudely, and then glances at me. "Everything okay?" he says to me, his voice low.

"Yes. I just want to get back inside," I tell him, and pull open the heavy gym door. "You coming?"

"Enjoy the dance, Ms. Marin. And happy birthday," Cano says, watching me carefully and lowering his voice so that only I can hear. "Your mother sends her regards." His eyes are knowing and cruel. He takes Emma Seavon's hand and walks past us down the hallway. I don't miss the long measured look that Emma throws at Lo, nor the half-bitter expression that crosses his face when she does.

"You sure you're okay?" he asks me.

"Fine."

But I can barely control the fury simmering inside of me at Cano's parting shot. I want to run into the gym and throw him against the wall, demanding why he said what he did. Over the past few days, I thought I'd gotten her betrayal out of my system, but it seems it's as fresh as it has ever been. I realize I don't really want to punish him.

I want to punish her.

"Let's go," I say to Lo.

"Already? We just got here. And what about Sawyer and Jenna?"

"They'll survive. I just need to get out of here. Please, Lo, just take me home."

In the Jeep on the ride back to Lo's house, I stare out of the window, preoccupied with my thoughts. I don't want to think about my mother being alive, but just the idea that she is, and the fact that she and Cano have discussed me, makes me want to scream. She betrayed my father, me, all of our people, and still thinks she can have control over what I do.

I glance at Lo. His gaze meets mine, his eyes melting. "You okay?" he asks again. I nod.

"Cano knows…knew my mother." My voice is flat, monotone, but Lo still reaches his hand across the gearbox to clutch my numb fingers in his. My cold hands suck the warmth from his greedily, and his slow rhythmic squeezing helps to banish some of my tension. We pull into Lo's driveway and he parks the car, turning to face me.

"I'm sorry, Riss."

"So that was your mom?" I say haltingly.

"Yep. I get my sparkling personality from her," he says, obviously trying to make me smile.

"You're nothing like her," I tell him. "She's cold, and you're warm. She's unreadable and I can see everything you feel right there in your eyes." Lo kisses my fingertips, making the breath catch in my throat. "Cano thinks you're a bad influence."

Lo laughs again, the warmth in his eyes overwhelming. "Little do they know it's the blind leading the blind." Grinning, I start to protest, but Lo leans across the console between us and silences me with a long slow kiss.

A kiss that quickly turns into something else, the warmth in his touch becoming fiery and demanding. Glancing down at our intertwined fingers and breathing heavily, I realize that the intensity isn't Lo's.

It's mine.

It's overtaking every part of me, my body shaking from the sensation of falling so fast that I can barely breathe. I've never felt such overwhelming longing for someone. And even if nothing comes of it, and I never get to see Lo again...I know. I know that I don't want to leave without sharing this part of him. Without leaving him a part of myself.

"Let's go down to the beach," I say, grabbing a blanket from the back of my Jeep.

"You want to go to the beach now?"

"It's the perfect time," I shout, racing down the hill.

By the time I get down to where the waves are breaking, with the moon high in the sky, I am breathless. I don't even wait. In the water, my green dress swirling around me with a magical frondlike life of its own, I duck under the breaking waves and strike out to the calmer water. Lo breaks the surface at the same moment as I do, gasping and laughing.

"Where's your toga?" I ask him, swimming toward him

and throwing my arms around his neck. I kiss his ear and then his cheek.

"My robes are on the beach," he says, wrapping his arms around my waist.

"Where mine should probably be," I say.

"I can help with that." He hesitates, as if waiting for my permission, so I nod, swallowing past the tightness in my chest. This is the point of no return. I take a deep breath and hug him tightly, letting my face press against his as Lo's fingers unbutton the tiny clasp at the top of the back of my dress and draw the zipper downward.

He smiles at me. "Now you are truly the goddess of the ocean, and I'm just some poor boy at your mercy."

"Really? That's how it is?" I tease back, and kiss his neck, letting my legs slide against and between his. "I thought you were a god?"

"Yes," he says, his voice thick. "Both yours." His arms tighten around me. His eyes are dark and silver at the same time as the moonlight plays across our faces, shimmering in the water. His mouth meets mine and everything disappears, and we're floating in space, weightless. I'm anchored to the salt on his lips, the taste of his mouth, the warmth of his body against mine. Every drop of water inside of me is begging to break free, pressing against my skin and surging toward his.

"I'm at yours, too, you know," I whisper into his ear when we finally break apart.

His eyes meet mine, and the only word in them is *yes*. I bend my arms around his neck as he lifts me effortlessly into his arms and wades us both in to shore. Surf crashes around us, and we both laugh as he struggles to keep his balance. Lo lays me gently on the blanket and lies next to me, his hand trailing against the bare skin of my stomach.

"Are you sure?" he whispers, kissing my shoulder.

"I'm sure."

As Lo's mouth and hands make everything but him disappear, the only thing I can think of is my green dress, floating free and unfettered in the ocean.

The goddess of the sea, returned.

22
Lies Are the Root

"Harder!" Echlios pulses. "Faster."

My heart is throbbing out of my chest and I want to scream with the pain racing like fire up and through my limbs. We've gone from diabolical football drills to mixed martial arts to ten-mile runs, and everything in between.

"This is torture," I tell him, aware that he's been pushing me more because of how little time we have left.

"This is the difference between winning and dying," he says grimly. "Again."

In the depths of the ocean, I come at him again, fast and furious, swimming as if my life depends on it and jabbing at him with my claws. But Echlios anticipates my moves and ducks easily, hitting me on the back of the head with his tail. The blow makes me see three of him but I shake it off. Gnashing my teeth, I dive toward him, spinning at the last moment and ripping my back claws down his hindquarters.

"Better," he says. "Do not be predictable. Ehmora has fought many battles against many stronger and smarter than you." He sees my look. "Yes, you have speed and some skill, but a misplaced strike can be the difference between life and death."

"I get it."

"Again," he commands.

We fight and spin and repeat until I'm weary, but still Echlios pushes me. And I let myself be pushed because I know he is right. Already, I can feel my muscles responding and healing, readying themselves for another bout. I let the ocean seep into them, taking its strength like fuel. I am focused and I must be strong.

I haven't even let myself think about Lo even though the minute his name pops into my brain, it's like minifireworks explode all over my body. The thought of him makes me feel calm but wired at the same time. I've never experienced anything like it. Even Speio has been giving me weird, mystified looks but I'm too content to be bothered by him. Jenna had been over the moon for me. For once, all her plotting and scheming over my love life worked out.

I haven't seen Lo since the day before yesterday, that night after the dance, even though we've spoken often. I've never been with a boy whose hold on me has been so much more than physical. It's like we're joined mentally and emotionally in addition to the physical part of it. The thought of that makes me feel like my stomach is made of fluttery wings, and my limbs made of jelly. Without thinking, my bioluminescence kicks in and the water around me lights up with a greenish-gold glow.

A whack to the head catches me off guard, and I growl fiercely at Echlios. "You're distracted," he accuses, his eyes narrowed.

"It's because I'm starving! We've been here all day."

Echlios stares at me frowning, and then nods. "Fine, let's head back."

At the house, I shower and change into a pair of shorts and a T-shirt. Lo has left me six texts, and each one of them makes my heart beat a little bit faster than the one before. But I don't even have time to savor any of them before both Echlios and Soren confront me. I tuck the phone under my leg and raise my eyebrow at their serious expressions.

"We need to talk," Soren says.

"About what?"

She doesn't skip a beat. "Have you bonded with anyone?" I almost choke at the blunt question, my eyes darting from Soren to Echlios.

"No!" I gasp, flushing. And then, "Who would I bond with, anyway? Why are you asking me this?"

Echlios stares at me. "I noticed you today. You were distracted."

"Yes, I said I was hungry."

"So thinking about food made you illuminate?"

I flush, knowing exactly what I'd been thinking about. "I like food."

Soren sits beside me on the bed, her face gentle. "Nerissa, it's not just today. We've both noticed your behavior, and we know the signs."

"Guys, trust me. I haven't bonded with anyone! The only person I can actually bond with is Speio, and believe me, he's happily distracting himself with one of the girls from my hockey team." I pause, wringing my hands. "But I am with someone else. A boy."

"Did you—" Echlios begins.

"Soren!" I beg with a beseeching look. I really do not want to have this conversation with him. She gives Echlios a look and he leaves the room with a lingering worried glance at me. I take a deep breath and meet Soren's eyes. "The answer to his question is yes. Two nights ago, after the dance," I say in a rush to her, wanting to get it out. "I really like him, Soren. He's different from other boys."

"Is that why you've been so happy?" Soren smiles, and I cave completely. I've wanted to talk about Lo to her for weeks, so I give in.

"Yes. I mean, I see how Jenna is with Sawyer, and it feels like that. As if I'm giddy and I want to see him every single second of the day. Sometimes, I feel as if I can't breathe if I don't talk to him. And he feels the same way about me. You'll like him, Soren, just as much as I do." My words are shaky, flowing out of me like music. "I think I may be in love with him. Like how the humans fall in love, I mean."

"I can see that," Soren says with a hint of relief on her face.

"It's all in my head, isn't it? Just like how the humans love?"

"Yes, and no," she says. "Your feelings are real, but unlike us, there is no real bond linking you together. In time, your feelings for him will fade. And when you find your own mate and the bonding is complete, he will be a distant memory, if that." She pats my face and my hair. "Enjoy it, but he cannot be a distraction in the coming days. Do you understand that?"

"I do," I say, the happiness leaching out of me at her grim expression.

Soren's words are like knives, tearing into me and ripping apart my fragile joy. But she's right. I'm a queen who has to fight for her throne, not some girl who only has to worry about being in love. I wipe away the tear that meanders down my cheek with a violent swipe.

"Your responsibilities outweigh whatever fleeting emotion it is you are feeling. I don't mean to be cruel, please know that. But I'm here to guide you and to educate you." She pauses and takes a deep breath. "It may be better to start making your goodbyes now. Sever anything that can be used against you by your enemy—including the humans you love. Whatever happens with Ehmora tomorrow, we will all be returning to the sea."

"I understand."

Soren kisses my hand, and leaves me to my thoughts. I stare at the phone and, with my heart breaking into pieces, I delete all of Lo's texts. I knew that this moment would come. The moment I would have to say goodbye. Retrieving my laptop from my desk, I open the drafts of letters I've written to both Jenna and to Lo, and scroll down. The one to Jenna is considerably longer—I've told her everything. She deserves it all.

But the one to Lo is barely a page, barely a sentence.

How do you explain to someone you've given every part of yourself to that you're going away and never coming back? How do you break someone's heart when yours is already shattered? How do you say goodbye when all you want to do is do the opposite?

Before I can second-guess myself or start rewriting them for the hundredth time, I hit Send on both, and lie back on my bed, staring blindly at the ceiling. I close my eyes and clear it of everything but Ehmora. She's my focus now. She's the only focus.

I wake to darkness and the sensation of someone looming over me. The weight of a body presses down into the bed just as a pillow crashes into my face. Instinctively shoving upward with all my might, I throw my attacker across the room, and lunge forward to stop at the last minute, my eyes widening.

"What the hell, Jenna? I could have killed you!"

"What the hell to you, you asshat," she says, wincing as she pulls herself to her feet. "You can't send me an email like that without consequences! Horrible, deathlike, best-friend-will-go-ballistic-with-pillow consequences!"

"Jenna, I'm sorry," I say, raking my hands through the snarls in my hair. "I don't have a lot of time, and I didn't want to just disappear."

"You could have told me in person!"

I stare at her, a wild enraged virago, her red hair a mess and her hands on her hips, not in the least afraid of me. I can't possibly love Jenna more than I do in that moment. "I didn't think I could handle seeing you," I say quietly, falling back to the bed, my head in my hands.

"Oh," she says, thinking for a minute and glancing at my open computer on the bed next to me. "Did you send one to Lo, too?"

I nod, meeting her eyes with my wet ones. "It was a lot shorter."

"So I guess I got here first. Did he write you back?" I shake my head—the only email is the response from Jenna before she'd sped over here to beat me over the head. The subject line is filled with F-bombs and exclamation marks.

"Just you," I say. "He probably hasn't gotten it yet, which is for the best. A part of me hopes I'll be gone before that happens."

"What did you tell him?" Jenna asks, sitting next to me.

"That we're moving to South Africa."

"That far?"

"It has to be far," I say. "And remote, with no internet. And it has to be a clean break with him. I couldn't take it if we were just email buddies…not after we…" I trail off, leaning on Jenna's shoulder.

We lie back on the bed, staring at my fake Waterfell ceiling. I let the tears come as she whispers that everything is going to be okay just as a best friend should. We lie quietly for a few minutes, with my occasional sniffs breaking up the silence until Jenna props herself up on one elbow. Her eyes are puffy as I expect mine are, too.

"So after you beat this Queen of Wannabe, then you're going back home?"

"Yes."

"Will I ever see you again?"

"I hope so." I smile through my tears. "It's not like I'm on a different planet. I'll always be here, just not *here*."

"You're going to miss the hockey final," Jenna says with a wry grin. "We're never going to win State without you."

"You're going to do a lot of things without me." Leaning over, I reach into a jewelry box on my bedside table and pull out a necklace. I hand it to Jenna. "I was going to ask Echlios to give this to you. It's one of mine, so you never forget."

Jenna's eyes widen at the shimmering iridescent yellow scale that's the size of a silver dollar, hanging on a thin gold chain. "It's beautiful," she says in a choked voice. "Thank you, Riss. I don't know what to say."

"You don't have to say anything."

"Why, oh, why couldn't my best friend in the world have been normal instead of some shape-shifting alien who has to leave?" she says, burying me in a hug. "It's not fair! In the movies, you guys always take a human with you. Can't I go with you?"

"Not in *E.T.*," I say. "And even if you could come with me, what about Sawyer? You wouldn't leave him in a million years."

"Girl, boys come and go, but best friends are forever." She grins. "But yeah, if I left him, he would probably pine away to nothing." Jenna puts my necklace on and gets up to admire it in the mirror. "I'll never forget the day I saw you change," she says to me. "Are you happy to be going home?"

"Happy to go back, sad to leave here. Double-edged sword." I shrug. "And I could die, too."

"Are you kidding me? You're Nerissa Marin! Get that thought out of your head or else I'm going to get in a boat myself and come find you."

I stare at her, horror on my face. "Don't do that!"

"Relax, I may be crazy, but I'm not stupid," she says. "You know what I mean. You kick that skank's ass, you hear me?"

"When did you get such a potty mouth? You've been watching *Jersey Shore* again, haven't you?" We both crack up just as my phone buzzes. It's a text from Lo.

We need to talk.

"What does it say?" Jenna says, peering over my shoulder.
"He wants to talk."

"You going to go over there? Or is he coming here?" I shrug again and Jenna pulls on my T-shirt, staring at something on my back. "Wait, when did you get a tattoo?"

"What? No. What are you talking about?"

Jenna tugs at the collar of my shirt as we both stare at the blue swirls marking my skin at the base of my neck. "It's really pretty," Jenna says, tracing one of the patterns with her fingers.

"Must be something to do with Dvija."

"Dee-vee-what?"

I pull back on my shirt. "Remember, that coming of age thing I told you about on the beach?" I ask. Jenna slowly nods after screwing up her face for a second. "Probably has to do with my coming of age and becoming a queen. Royal thing, I guess."

My phone buzzes again.

Meet me at my place.

Can't, I text back. Soren would flip if I went over there.

Marine center? 10 mins?

Okay.

"He wants to meet at the marine center," I tell Jenna. "I have no idea what I'm going to say to him."

"Just tell him the truth," she says. I blanch and she grins. "You know, that Echlios got a job in South Africa and your whole family has to go. Don't embellish, just keep it simple. It will be okay."

"Thanks, Jenna," I say, and hug her.

"Call me the minute you get back, okay?"

"I will."

After Jenna leaves, I let Soren know that I have to pick up a couple things I've left at the marine center. Speio, who is sitting at the dining room table, looks up with an odd look. I'm getting really sick of his strange expressions every time I open my mouth. I ignore him and grab my car keys.

The marine center is deserted but I unlock it with the spare key I carry on my own set of keys. I know Lo will already be inside. Without turning on any lights, I walk to the back of the first floor, where there's a giant aboveground saltwater tank. The tank connects to a larger outdoor pool. We use it when we find injured marine animals in the bay but right now it's empty. The dolphin that had been in there a week ago has been rereleased into the wild.

Lo is standing on the other side of the tank, the bluish water making shimmering light patterns across his skin.

"Hey," I say.

"Hi," Lo says, putting his arms around me and inhaling deeply as if he hasn't taken a real breath since he saw me last.

I feel the same way. We stand that way for a few minutes, letting our bodies reconnect in the silence. My heartbeat aligns with his within seconds.

Lo shifts against me, his breath warm on my temple. "I got your email. So, South Africa?" I can't speak so I just nod against him, trying to etch every curve and bend of his chest into my memory. "It's not that far away."

"It's on the other side of the world, Lo." I feel the pressure on my nose bridge already from the tears building up behind my eyes. "It may as well be at the bottom of the ocean." It's the closest I've ever come to admitting anything like that to him, but of course, Lo won't know the truth. Lo chuckles softly.

"If it were, I would still find a way to be with you."

"How?" I whisper, giving in to the false fantasy for one brief moment. "How would you do it?"

Lo places his hands on either side of my head and kisses my lips in a soft, melting kiss that does little to stop the burning of my eyes. It only makes it worse. "Don't you remember?" he says, brushing my hair off my brow and kissing there, too. "I'm the god of the ocean. I can make anything happen."

"Anything? Can you make me stay here?"

"Is that what you want?"

Suddenly the conversation has taken a serious turn, and we aren't playing anymore. Lo's eyes are shadowed, his expression inscrutable. I can't read him or anything he's thinking, but I can't shake the feeling that his question is double-edged somehow.

"I…want so many things, Lo," I whisper. "I want to be with you. I want to be with my friends. I want to stay here. I'm going crazy with all the wants bubbling inside of me, because everything I want, I can't have." My tears have broken free now, running down my face like an unstoppable tide.

"Then stay," he says in a thick voice, kissing my cheeks

so that his lips are wet with the salt of my tears. I step away from the haven of his arms because I need to think. When I'm in there, it's too easy to say yes to whatever Lo wants… what I want more than anything. "Run away with me, just the two of us."

"It's not that simple. I have responsibilities. My family… people are counting on me. They need me to be there for them, and I can't just run away anymore. You don't understand." I turn away to stare at the empty tank—a metaphor of who I am, a caged animal in a pool. The thought of running away with him is nearly my undoing. "How could you understand?" I say almost to myself.

Lo embraces me from behind, wrapping his arms around my torso and threading his fingers through mine against my stomach. "I understand more than you know."

"You don't."

A strangled laugh that sounds like it came from the bottom of Lo's throat. "You think I don't know about responsibilities? About having to do things that someone else wants you to do, even though you don't agree with them? About never being free to be who you are…who you want to be? About never being able to say no because you're always afraid—" Lo breaks off, his chest heaving on my back as if he can't breathe.

"Why are you afraid, Lo?" I ask, turning around to face him. His arms fall to his sides and he steps backward, staring at the ground. I step toward him. "Look at me, Lo." When he does, his eyes are so full of pain and regret and something else I can't quite place that the force of it makes me gasp. "What are you afraid of?"

"I'm…" He rakes his hands through his hair and slumps backward against the side of the tank, holding his head in his hands. "I lied to you, Nerissa." I crouch down beside him, my heart pounding. I've never seen this side of him before—so vulnerable and broken that it scares me. Lo's always the one who keeps me together, not the other way around.

I brush away the single tear on the side of his face. "You aren't the god of the ocean?" I ask, tremulous. Lo's shoulders jerk with a choked laugh and his fingers find mine, squeezing tightly.

"Yes, that, too. I lied to you about everything. About who I am." He leans toward me, his head against my brow. "And I'm so afraid that she'll hurt you, too."

"Who'll hurt me?" I say.

"She hurts everyone to control me. My foster dad is on life support because she allows it. His life is in my hands. If I don't obey her, she pulls the plug and he dies. I do everything she says...on the promise that she'll help him." Lo is sobbing now, little sounds coming from his mouth between his smothered words. "She hurts people, and says it's to teach me how to be strong. How to lead."

"Your mother?" I ask, thinking of the cold impervious woman I'd briefly met.

Lo nods. "And you...all I had to do was get you to fall for me. And I did everything she said. Then, I got to know you and everything changed. I'm in love with you, but it doesn't matter, you're still going to hate me."

My alarm bells are ringing like crazy but I want to believe him. I want to believe that he's everything I thought he was...my Lo. "I could never hate you, Lo," I say. But my voice is breaking with doubt, falling apart already at the truth in his eyes.

He turns toward me, his face earnest. "I didn't plan on falling for you," he says. "But I did. And now, for you, I'd do anything. I didn't think I could love someone so much that I'd be willing to risk it all. But I do. Everything about you is beautiful. Your face, your heart, your glimmers—"

"What did you say?" I whisper, the water inside of me like beating wings.

"I'm so sorry, Nerissa. I'm so sorry...."

The fluorescent lights in the poolroom turn on in blinding brightness. We both scramble to our feet. "Get the hell away from her, you asshole!" Speio shouts. He's wielding Jenna's homemade Taser in one hand and has a wild look on his face.

"Speio, what are you doing?" I scream, rushing toward him in the moment and forgetting all about what Lo had begun to say.

"Don't you know what he is, Riss?" Speio pleads with me, his eyes tortured. "I'm sorry. I wanted to tell you but I felt so cornered by what I'd done. I felt so alone, and then after the dance Cara told me what you said to her. I've been so stupid. I'm so sorry. You'll never forgive me, and I know that. But I couldn't let it happen."

"You're not making sense, Speio. Let what happen?" I say, looking back and forth at the two boys. Lo hasn't moved, but he doesn't look surprised at Speio's accusations. The expression on his face overwhelms me because it's the same expression I couldn't place before. Guilt. "What the hell is going on?"

"He knows, Riss," Speio says, his voice harsh. "He knows about you. They all do."

"They?"

The world feels like it's spinning at my feet and all the air has been knocked out of my body. I'm spiraling with it, uncontrollable, like a feather in the middle of a storm. Lo and Speio are fading into two black hazy shadows, and I close my eyes, dizzy.

"He's one of them, Riss," Speio says. "He's Aquarathi."

And I'm spinning again but, this time, in furious denial. I turn to Lo, remembering his recent words. "Is it true?"

His face is pleading, begging me to trust him. "I tried to tell you—"

A slew of images rip through my brain in cold, cruel succession. The glimmers I'd felt at school all the times Lo was looking through me. The glimmer down on the beach with Echlios in front of Lo's house. Lo's expert skill in the water and with a surfboard. Lo going with me to Cano's house and pretending not to know who he really was. Lo kissing my hair and telling me to trust him.

"When did you try to tell me? Just now?" My voice rises with every word.

"Riss—"

"Don't," I snap, the tides building inside of me and spreading like acid through my veins. More images, torturous. Surfing…flirting…swimming in an ocean of jellyfish…our first kiss. The pain of it is like lava flooding through me. He'd kissed me after he'd pulled me from the ocean floor, after the snakes. "Was it you? Was it you that time at La Jolla Cove? Did you save me?"

"Yes."

Something unfurls in the pit of my stomach at his simple admission. Something ugly and violent and powerful. I feel the bones on the crown of my head pushing outward and flexing through the barrier of my skin. The pain is hot but welcome as razor-sharp fronds pierce their way in a semicircle as the pieces of truth come together in horrifying detail. I see Lo's eyes widen at my appearance but I don't care. He knows what I am. He's always known.

"Are you a hybrid?" My voice is cold, flat.

"Not exactly," he says. I hiss in his direction at the evasive answer. "But I have hybrid genes."

So Lo was the big secret all along. He was the Aquarathi

with the hybrid blood. No wonder he hadn't had to reveal himself to me.

"Show me," I growl, nodding at the pool. With a long look at me and without any protest, Lo slides into the pool and transforms. My breath hitches in my throat and all I can think about is the last time we danced in the gym.

Thick muscular shoulders elongate into a burnished gold curved neck the color of wet sand. Electric green-and-yellow patterns swirl through his scales in a mesmerizing outline. He is bigger than I am but not by much. His fins are navy—like his eyes—and shimmer with different shades of blue, from midnight to cobalt and every shade in between.

Lo's alien eyes meet mine, his heart in them. My nails dig into the soft flesh of my palm, my heart nearly derailed.

He is beautiful.

And I'm still in love with him.

23
Light and Stone

"Riss, we need to go. The others are coming," Speio says urgently.

I turn glacial eyes on him as Lo drags his human body out of the tank and pulls his shorts on. I feel nothing but a deep simmering fury at Lo's betrayal. Everyone I know has lied to me—Echlios, my mother, Speio and, now, Lo. Either I am at the epicenter of an epic deception or I have an exceptional ability to attract liars.

"What others?" I snap at Speio.

"The ones he told where you'd be," a female voice says. Speio freezes in his tracks as we both turn to see a bald, striking woman walking into the tank area from the entrance leading to the outdoor pool area. The raw and jagged scar across her brow does little to mar her appearance. She is savagely, achingly beautiful. My recognition is immediate but my breath still hitches as she comes closer and my blood rises to the tide of hers. This night cannot get any worse.

"Mother," I say.

"That's your mother?" Lo blurts out in a low whisper. I glance back at him to see if he's speaking the truth about not knowing who she is, but it's written all over his face. He looks genuinely surprised. I don't deign to respond. Right now, Lo doesn't deserve anything from me.

"Speio, you've done well," she says to him. His face is stricken as he looks toward me. The Taser drops to the floor as he holds both palms up in a supplicating gesture, his face beseeching. Of course, just add the worst liar of all to the mix. His own guilt at what he did drove him to follow me, to try to save me. But it's a little too late.

Like Lo, he has betrayed me all along.

"Riss—"

"Save it," I seethe. "Don't come near me, Speio. You'll regret it."

"No, please, you have to believe me," he begs, but doesn't move any closer. "I was so mad after you made me tell you about Cano, and I wanted to punish you for that. But I never meant for any of this to happen. I felt so alone. I just wanted to go home, and she said that I could, if I just helped her to get you and Lo together."

"But you hate Lo," I say, wondering why I'm even engaging. But a part of me wants answers. "You never wanted me with him."

"If anyone told you not to jump off a cliff, what would you do?" Speio smiles a little sadly.

I stare at him, a horrible thought occurring to me. "That's why you made up all that stuff about liking me. You didn't want me to glimmer you and find out what you'd been doing behind my back…plotting against me all this time."

"It wasn't like that."

"What was it like, Speio?"

"I just wanted to go home," he repeats brokenly. "Then things started getting out of control with the hybrid attack. That wasn't meant for you—it was meant for me. She knew I was wavering. I'm sorry, I'm so sorry. I wanted to tell you. I wanted to fix it. But then you started getting so close to him, and the other day, I knew it was over."

"What's over, Speio?" I say, alarmed at his nearly nonsensical rambling.

"Look at your hands," he says sadly. "It's done."

I look down at my palms. Thin blue swirls are shimmering along my skin, similar to the thicker ones Jenna had pointed out on my neck. With everything going on, all I can think is that they're the color of Lo's eyes. "What's done?"

"He means that you are now bonded," my mother chimes in cheerfully. My palms tingle, and for a long moment I think of the yellow-green swirls I saw on Lo's Aquarathi body. My colors. Lo's face is inscrutable, his eyes dark and shadowed, watching me. All the breath in my body steals out of me at the similar marks I can still see on his shoulders. I drag my eyes away, ignoring the magnetic pull I feel toward him. Now I understand why. The dark swirls are not royal Dvija marks, after all. They're *bonding* marks.

I've bonded with someone. I've bonded with Lo.

"You planned all of this?" I ask my mother weakly. "This was what you wanted? So I could bond with someone?"

"He's a prince. Of royal blood, just as you are." I blink, frowning as if that should make any difference. They—he—tricked me into bonding myself to him, prince or not.

My fists clench at my side. "So what? You think you know everything there is to know about bonding, don't you?" I say to her. "But you know nothing of love. You murdered my father." I lurch forward in a rage but freeze at my mother's warning look and follow her gaze to where Jenna is lying motionless near the exit doors.

"What have you done to her?"

"Nothing," she says. "Yet. She's just sleeping. She's an insurance policy so that you won't do anything rash."

"She's human," I say, tightening my fists. "Involving her against her knowledge is against our laws."

My mother eyes me coolly. "But you chose to involve her so the fault—if any—lies with you." My gaze collides with Speio, who hangs his head guiltily. I can't believe he told her about Jenna, when she'd stuck her own neck out for him!

"You must understand what we have to do, Nerissa," my mother says, drawing the fire of my anger. "I am sorry about what happened but your father was stuck in the old ways. He refused to change. The humans will destroy us without thinking twice."

"The humans are trying," I fire back. "If we give them half a chance, they will do what they need to do to protect the oceans. I've seen them." I wave my hand. "Here and other places. They care. But Ehmora," I say through clenched teeth, "does not. She wants to destroy them before they can threaten our existence. How is that the right way? It was their planet before it was ours."

"So you would sentence us to a slow, highly probable death? Millions of us died on Sana because of the choices of the land dwellers. We can't afford to let that happen here. Like you, your father still had faith in the humans and refused to see that we were becoming just as trapped as they were. I had to do something for the sake of our people."

"Your people? Whom you abandoned to go to her, your lover?" I snarl, and watch her eyes widen. "Oh, I know your dirty dark secret. That's why you wanted me to bond with him, isn't it?" I jerk my head toward Lo and claw at the skin of my palms, iridescent streaks of my blood marring the telling swaths of blue. "Well, it won't work. Because it's a lie."

"You don't love him?"

"No." The lie is as painful as the raw welts on my hands. My waters rush against me as if furious with what I've said. Even now, they strain toward Lo with overwhelming strength, and it's all I can do not to run to him. I close my eyes and steel myself. "I reject him. I reject the bond."

My mother lips part in a cold, chilling smile. "You, my darling, cannot undo millions of years of evolution. The bond is unbreakable. And you know that as well as we do."

"What does Ehmora even get out of this?"

"The High Court," she says.

"She will never have control of the throne, not while I'm alive," I say. "My father died defending it from her, and from you. You think some false bond with a lower-level prince will change any of that? He has nothing to do with you."

"He's not just some prince," a deep voice says from behind my mother, followed by a long mocking laugh, as another person comes into view. "He is my son."

Emma Seavon.

I'm in the twilight zone. First of all, doesn't anybody realize that this center is closed and it's private property? Why is she even here? And why is she holding my mother's hand? Confused, I remain mute, staring at her face in dumbfounded silence as she steps forward, a smile on her face, her alien eyes flashing crimson fire. This time, the pieces click together with dizzying succession.

"Ehmora," I breathe.

She smiles again. "Surprised?"

But I don't even hear her as the final piece of the puzzle snaps into place—suddenly my world is splintering into a million pieces, and I am a stone sinking to the bottom of the dark, empty ocean.

Emma Seavon is Ehmora.

Ehmora is my mother's lover.

Ehmora is Lo's mother.

I start laughing hysterically until the tears are pouring from my eyes. I turn to Lo, who hasn't moved from where he was standing next to the tank. His face is anguished but I ignore it, fighting against the terrifying demands of the bond nearly dragging me toward him just from that one glance.

"Ehmora is your mother?" I say, ripping my eyes away and mocking his earlier words. "That's just priceless, isn't it?" I laugh again and throw my arms into the air, looking at my mother and Ehmora in turn. "Come on, you have to find this a little funny? I fall for the boy who is the son of my mother's girlfriend and my father's killer, who wants to assume my throne for her own?"

Ehmora nods, amused at my theatrics. "Lo was your mother's idea," she says. She glances at her son, distaste written all over her chiseled face. "Neriah insisted that an...alliance would unite the courts, and make it easier to gain their trust. I told her it wouldn't work. Lo has always been too caring...too weak."

"You mistake weakness for strength," I say. I have no idea why I'm defending him but I can't stop myself. "Compassion is something I've learned to appreciate during my time here. Perhaps your son did, as well."

"Is that what you call it?" she sneers, and then studies her immaculate manicure. "Nonetheless, a union between two of the most powerful courts in Waterfell would have been an acceptable plan, until my son decided to grow a backbone for the first time in his life. Sad, really, that it won't work, after all."

"What do you mean?"

"He didn't tell you?" She glares at Lo, who is staring at me with his heart in his eyes. "Imagine my own progeny turning his back on his own mother. Shameful, really."

My gaze flutters to my mother. "Well, the bond is unbreakable so you kind of set yourself up to fail. But you two would know about that, wouldn't you?" I paste an empathetic look on my face. "Just my two cents, but I say good for him."

"He'll face the consequences of his actions sooner or later," Ehmora says mildly. "Just as you will."

"Is that a threat?"

"Just a fact." She smiles coldly. "So let's not beat around the bush, then. Do you accept my challenge, little princess?"

"Nerissa, you don't have to do this," Speio says from behind me. "You're the rightful heir. You don't have to accept."

I stare at him, with furious eyes. "Oh, like I'm going to take advice from the very one who set this all up because he didn't believe in me in the first place? Go crawl into your hole, Speio, and pray I don't find you later."

"Riss—" Speio begs.

"Stop, Speio. Just stop. You sold me out the first chance you got." I jerk my head at Jenna's still-inert body. "The only one I can trust is her, and she's human. She's better than all of you put together."

I can't let anything happen to Jenna. I won't. If Ehmora wants a fight, she's going to get the fight of her life. Gathering my strength, I pull my water into me, readying myself just as Echlios has taught me. Even though it's dark outside, I can already feel the night air brewing and responding to me. I'm still the heir, regardless of any bond with Ehmora's son. I can't even think of him as that and as Lo in the same breath without my insides feeling like they're rocks. To me, they are two distinct entities.

Lo, the boy, and Ehmora's son, the Aquarathi prince.

The air in the center is thick and nearly solid with tension. Ehmora and my mother are silent, anticipating my response. I lift my chin and square my shoulders. The gauntlet has been thrown and the cards have been dealt. I've decided to fight, instead of hiding from my responsibilities. In the end, I'd rather stand for something than fall for nothing. But we won't fight here. Our fates will be decided on the gray sands of Waterfell.

But first, I need to know what they know.

"Tell me about the hybrids," I say with steel in my voice.

"What about them?" Ehmora says.

"I don't want to play games with you."

"What games?" She laughs. "You have no cards to play. I am holding them all."

But she's wrong. I do have one card. Without thinking twice, I dive toward Lo and grip his neck in a backward chokehold. He doesn't struggle even though I can feel his pulse racing below my forearm.

Grimacing at the feel of my Aquarathi bones cracking beneath my skin, the fingers on my right hand extend into curled, sharpened claws. They press into the soft center of Lo's human throat. "Bond or no bond, you underestimate the power of vengeance," I say.

"You wouldn't," Ehmora says, but I can see the tiniest flare in those crimson eyes. Maybe she does care about him, after all. He may be a disappointment to her but he's still her perfect hybrid specimen. That has to be worth something.

"I can. And I will."

My voice is unwavering even though every cell in my body is pressing through my skin to melt into Lo's. I know that he can feel it, too, but he remains silent, his own water pressing against mine, submissive. We are bonded, and our bodies know it. Our minds know it. Every living part of us knows it. Touching him is the worst thing I could have done because all I want to do is stay there.

But I fight it with every shred of willpower in me because if I appear weak for one second I know that Ehmora will take immediate advantage. My arm tightens—but gently—against

Lo's neck. "Tell me about the hybrids," I repeat, directing the question to my mother. "Why did you make them?"

Ehmora's eyes burn red but she nods at my mother to comply with my request. "We were working on a way to combine the strengths of the different species. But pure Aquarathi rejected the genes of the humans. We need to combine them at a genetic cellular level first."

"Offspring," I interject. "How many actually lived past birth?"

"Only two," she says. "From that point, we harvested their genetic material and started the process to introduce new alleles into our own DNA. It's why you couldn't recognize either of us and why Lotharius didn't have to yield to you." She pauses, looking to Ehmora for confirmation on continuing. "He's the firstborn with the new genes, inherited from his mother in utero." She stares intensely at me. "Lo is the future, Nerissa."

I stare back at her. The plot she is describing goes back years, before Lo or I were born, before either of us became pawns in their little game. "Did you ever love him? My father? When you were planning all along to betray him? Did you ever love me?"

"We don't operate on love," she answers, and something inside me dies just a little. A tiny part of me had hoped that despite all her machinations, I would still mean something to her. "Love is a human condition, my darling. An illusion. Just like compassion and all those other useless human traits."

"You are the illusion," I tell her. "You're nothing more than a liar and a traitor." I deliver my next words to Ehmora. "Release Jenna, and I will release your precious son," I say to her, but she shakes her head with a cold, calculating expression. I understand immediately. Jenna is going to die, anyway, because she knows too much. They won't risk it.

I have to save her.

There's no way I can do it alone, so I cast a glimmer toward Speio in a last-ditch effort. *Still want to redeem yourself? You're the closest to Jenna. Get her out of here. If you ever felt any loyalty to me, do this. You owe her. You owe me.*

Uncertainty plays across his face but he nods once, imperceptibly. I take a deep breath and pull my water into my center. Bending my head toward Lo, I murmur into his ear. "At least you'll be good for one thing now that we're bonded, my love."

And I glimmer his energy into me so hard that I'm gasping with the force of it. Lo's body arches against mine but he doesn't fight me. If anything, he pushes it out of him, like reverse Sanctum. I don't question. I just take. I take until I feel him bending into me like a bow. His body slumps against mine and, in a smooth motion, I lift him and toss him into the saltwater tank. The water will help him heal and restore some of his energy. I don't know why I did it, but despite his deception, I couldn't just let him lie there, vulnerable and defenseless.

Barely a second has passed and, before anyone can react, I am running toward them in a sprint. I roll once on the floor to collect Jenna's fallen Taser that Speio dropped. Ehmora snarls but she isn't my target. My mother is. Out of the corner of my eye, I see Speio scramble to scoop Jenna up and disappear with her through the exit, just as I reach my mother.

Kicking off of Ehmora's torso with all the force I can muster, I complete the spin kick by twisting back toward my mother just as Ehmora flies into the side of the tank with a sick crunch. Water sprays everywhere as the sealant cracks. I crouch on top of my mother, staring down into eyes that are the mirror image of mine.

"Nerissa," she begins. "I'm your mother. I'm doing this—"

"My mother is dead," I say, and jam the Taser into her side. "This is for my father. Tell your lover that I accept her challenge."

Her tortured shrieks echo against the walls but I'm already running out the door to the dock and transforming with each step. I can hear Ehmora's cries of fury behind me and the thump of something huge following in my footsteps. The skies are ripe with lightning. Crashes of thunder break all around me, and the sea is churning with the rush of a thousand emotions.

Mine and hers combined. The perfect storm.

Already the dock beneath my feet is shaking from the force of the waves crashing against it in violent, primal rage. I embrace my power as I've never done before, letting the sea's energy fuel me. My bones push outward through my flesh, lengthening and snapping as my body morphs into its natural shape. My skin burns, sliding over new bones and hardening into place, thickening with sinew and strength. Everything feels more fluid and more visceral as the creature inside reclaims control of me.

At the end of the dock, I dive into the black water, spinning at the last moment to see a gigantic beast of fury racing toward me on the dock with blood on its breath and fire on its tongue. Its scales are ebony with bloodred fins spanning its length. Its eyes are crimson and full of hatred.

And it wants to kill me.

I swim as fast as I can out to sea, cleaving through the water like a torpedo. The sane part of me knows that I need to get as far away as possible to limit any human casualties—and of course, to protect Jenna. Grateful for Echlios's training, I feel my muscles eagerly leaping to the demands of my will until I'm nothing but a blur in the water.

Racing past San Nicolas Island with every ounce of speed

I can muster, I dive deep, down and down and down where the water is nothing but a vortex of cold and darkness…where only the monsters live.

24

Crown of Bones

My father's face is kind, his beautiful silvery white fins floating around him like a halo. Everything about him is as I
remember—vibrant and warm and full of life. He's not alive,
of course, but he couldn't be any more real at this moment. If
I try hard enough, I can just reach out to feel his tail curl protectively around me and bury my face in the feathery fronds
beneath his glossy auburn neck.

I managed to reach the safety of Waterfell even with Ehmora hot on my heels, and the first place I went was my father's
grave. Now I press my body onto the headstone that marks
his resting place in the deepest part of Waterfell, connecting
the waters in my body to the remaining elemental essence
of his. The connection is but a shadow of the one we shared
when he was alive, but I can still speak to him in a sense. Part
of our royal legacy, the secrets of Aquarathi rulers have been
passed down this way for centuries.

"What if I fail?" I whisper to him.

You won't.

"How do you know for sure?"

Because my blood runs in your veins.

My tears are hot, dissolving into the cooler water around me. "She's stronger than I am. And experienced."

But you are young, fast and smart. She won't see you coming. He smiles then, his silver-colored eyes like shards of mirrored glass. *And you are fighting for something bigger than she is. You fight for your people and for love. She fights for power. Never underestimate the fire inside of you, my Nerissa. It was always there. You just had to see it.*

I rest my head against the darkening headstone as the vision blurs and dissipates, my father's essence fading like an echo. Movement behind me makes me turn. It's Echlios and Soren—loyal to the very end, no matter the outcome.

"They're ready for you," Echlios says.

I nod, holding my father's words close. I glance at the two of them, swallowing hard. "Thank you. For training me, for taking care of me and for bringing me back here. Everything I've become is because of you."

"It is our honor," Soren says in a voice that makes me choke up even more.

"Is Jenna safe?"

"Yes," Echlios says.

"And Speio?" I ask.

"He's here. Now, come. It's time."

We make our way out of the royal burial chamber into the throne room and out of the main halls of the underground fortress. A dozen or more of Echlios's men join us—my royal guard. Subconsciously, I know where we are going but I trail behind Echlios and Soren on automatic pilot, my mind curiously calm. I'm thinking about my friends—the human ones like Jenna, who had given her friendship in spite of the risks. I think of Speio, who'd fallen prey to the gilded promises of my mother a couple months ago. I think about Lo and how he'd tried to stand up to Ehmora, for me. I think about what

Jenna had told me about Cara and forgiveness, and only now I truly understand what she'd been trying to tell me that day of the pep rally.

Forgiveness releases the forgiver.

"Where's Speio?" I blurt out, halting the small procession.

"I'm right here," a small voice says, swimming out of the shadows near the tail end of the guards.

The rush of emotions at the wretched look in his eyes nearly kills me. "What you did was messed up, but I get it. I messed up, too. And I'm sorry you felt like I gave you no option but to put your faith in someone else. I'm sorry I made it worse with Cara—and made it impossible for you to be with her. I'm sorry for not being a better...friend. Someone worthy."

"You are more than worthy, Riss," he whispers.

At his words, like magic, a weight lifts off my shoulders. Looking at the proud faces of my family, I've never felt so strong as we swim into Waterfell's arena—a desolate wasteland of sand, spines and bones. It's bigger than I remember. Speio and I had once joked that if you combined the arena from *Gladiator* and the quidditch fields from *Harry Potter,* you'd have the Aquarathi challenge arena. All the Lower Court witnesses are already there as well as the bulk of our people. Although there've been many feuds resolved here on the sands, there hasn't been a royal challenge in centuries, not since the first years when our people fled here from Sana. No one wants to miss this.

I take my place in the middle of the arena, all eyes converging on me, some with interest, some with contempt, others with pity. I swallow hard, refusing to let fear swell within me. I've never given them a reason to trust me with their lives, so their response is only what I deserve. With a shaky breath, I address them in our native tongue, my words strong and unwavering.

"Many of you don't know me, but you knew and trusted my father for many years. The Lady Ehmora wishes to rule Waterfell, but she will go against everything my father has built. She wants to change the core of who we are." I leave off the part about the hybrids, considering I'm now bonded to one, and focus instead on the inherent values of what our people know. "We are an ocean species and this is our home. If you let me, I will continue to build upon the legacy of my father. We will guide the humans and help them to protect this planet, as has been the Aquarathi way for thousands of years. This I promise you."

"Spoken with such naïveté."

Slow, mocking laughter ensues as Ehmora enters the arena, her eyes like red death. Graveyard silence follows in her wake. Not even the ripple of a fin of the spectators in the stands disturbs the water around us. My eyes fall on the pale gold swirls shimmering along her neck and I almost snarl. I think of the corresponding red bonding marks on my mother's body—everyone had assumed they'd been my father's, but we'd all been duped. They'd been Ehmora's.

Ehmora circles me, crimson lights glowing along her scales and her fins like lines of blood. In response, gold-and-green lights come to life along my body. She eyes me, her expression full of loathing. "If Neriah dies, you will pay, that I promise you," she pulses at me more quietly.

"She's my mother. If she dies, it will be for her crimes against my father and all of her people," I say.

"You are a silly child."

"If I'm such a silly child, why force your only son to bond himself to me? You could have just left it at the challenge and been done with it. So why did you? Because Neriah told you to? I'll destroy your perfect weapon the first chance I get."

Her face ripples with rage. "The time for talk is over."

And then she's plunging toward me so fast that I barely see her coming. I dart out of the way just in time but not before her barbed tail catches me on the side of the face. Thick iridescent liquid spills out like colored ink into the water as pain flowers along my jaw. I hear a cry behind me that I recognize as Soren's but I block it from my mind. I need to focus on the enemy right in front of me. Locked in a battle that is as much mental as it is physical, I know that one moment of hesitation can cost me my life.

Swimming upward and putting distance between us, I take a breath and remember my father's words. I'm better than she is. Be unpredictable. Be swift. Be aggressive. My time in the human world has given me something that she has long forgotten—the sheer ingenuity of youth. This is nothing more than a hockey game and she's my opponent. Only there are two players instead of eleven, and she's trying to kill me instead of getting past me to score. Life-and-death hockey, then.

Game on.

I smile and crook the finned end of my tail, whipping it back and forth in a taunting gesture. Ehmora snarls, baring rows of sharp curved teeth. She lunges again, but this time I'm ready. Instead of dodging her attack to the side, I dive and twist upward to snap my jaws on her tail, my teeth tearing off the deadly barbs at the end. Her claws smash into my side, trying to push me off her, but I hang on until I feel my teeth rip through flesh. She crashes into me head-on and we death-spin to the sand until we collide with the ocean's floor. All the breath is knocked out of me upon impact, the force of it wrenching us apart. But Ehmora is already on her hind legs and charging toward me, pummeling me with her tail. Pain rockets through me as scales rip away like paper.

She's nearly on top of me, her face triumphant. "Ready to die, little princess?"

Catapulting myself out of her reach, I face her, both of us swimming in a slow circle. Ehmora charges again. This time, I avoid her attack with defensive movement, ducking down and darting to the right as if I'm charging up the field with my stick and ball. Turns out you don't need a stick to show off your stick skills. My heart is pounding as she chases me, hot on my tail, but I double-back in a reverse cutback, whipping my legs out so they catch her in the side on the rebound movement. She goes flying into the side of the rocks, right at the base of the Ruby Court.

"Yes!" someone yells, registering through the haze of adrenaline. It's Speio. For the first time, I sense the Aquarathi in the stands, some foe and some friends, I expect, but I can't make out anyone enough to recognize them. Two queens battling it out for succession would be the event of the century. I search for Echlios, and even though I don't see him, I know he's there…watching and waiting.

Be unpredictable.

"Looks like they're happy I'm winning," I tell a seething Ehmora. Brackish fluid from the wounds in her side spirals upward. We circle each other again but I try a different tactic as the noise around us reaches thunderous heights. "Beating me won't gain you a crown, you know. They loved my father. They love him still." I need to rattle her, get under her skin. She's too clever, too seasoned in battle, for me to beat with strength alone. "And what do you think your son will do once he knows what you've done?"

"Lotharius will do as he's told. It is what he was bred for."

"Bred for?" I say, disbelieving. She speaks about him like he's nothing more than a means to an end, a thing that was created for her benefit—a pawn.

"Yes," she says through her teeth. "He will obey me."

I cock my head to the side, feeling my body come alive as

tingles rush along my skin in a wild rush. I almost gasp at the strength of the bond—Lo is here. I lift my chin. "You sure about that? He defied you earlier by coming to tell me the truth, didn't he? Didn't seem like he was obeying too well." Her lips gnash together, her eyes narrowing. My strategy is working. "Maybe he has a mind of his own, after all."

"Perhaps. But my son's puny acts of defiance are of little consequence to me. Lotharius knows the cost. By defying me, he has lost the one thing that matters most to him."

"What have you done?" I gasp, seeing the truth in her eyes.

A cold smile breaks across her face. "Such is the price of disobedience."

I don't have any time to respond before a dark gold blur rushes past me to smash into Ehmora with furious force. The blur kicks and swipes and punches, but still, he is no match for the cold efficiency of his mother. And he is angry, which makes him a predictable target. Ehmora captures him easily, holding him down on the sand with her talons raking across his soft underbelly.

"Back!" she commands the guards, including Echlios, who'd followed Lo onto the sand. Ehmora presses down into Lo's body with her claws and I gasp, raising a shaky arm.

"Do as she says," I say to the guards. They stop advancing but don't leave the arena. I'm grateful for that, because I have no idea how I'm going to save Lo and defend myself at the same time.

"How could you kill him? You promised that if I did as you said, you'd let him live," Lo is screaming. "My father was innocent. They all were, but they had done their jobs, right?" Ehmora's burning red eyes are unfeeling. "Nerissa was right about you," Lo says, jerking his head toward me. "You feel nothing."

"You see?" she says, addressing the now-silent crowd peering down from the stands. They can sense that Lo is one of theirs but they know he's different, too. "This is what the humans do. They make us weak. They make us bend to silly emotions, turning us into insipid colorless versions of themselves." Her voice hardens. "They will be the death of us."

"You're wrong," I tell her.

"Am I?" she says, and presses down with her nails. I'm not prepared for the agony that follows as her sharp claws pierce the skin of his stomach. She eyes me viciously, doubled over and clutching my belly, even as her son does the same in writhing agony.

"Feel that?" she says. "That's because you're bonded. You will feel everything he does. Pain, like love," she spits out, "is something to be shared." Turning her forearm, she presses the spikes into his face, and then Lo is screaming and I'm screaming. My eye feels like it's being gouged out with a hot stake.

"Stop!" I cry. "You're killing him."

"I'm killing you." Her voice is so matter-of-fact that, for a minute, what she's said doesn't register. And then it hits me with the force of a sledgehammer even as her hind legs slam into the side of her son's chest. I gasp for breath, the pain excruciating, and I understand that Lo, like his foster father, is merely a means to an end. A means to me, and the one thing she's always wanted. The throne.

I stare at Lo and the blood pooling out of him, and make my decision. "Stop, and I will abdicate my rule to you in front of everyone here." It's enough to make her freeze, eyeing me carefully and the Aquarathi surrounding us.

"And why should I believe you would do that for me?"

"Not for you. For him," I say.

And then she laughs, the sound of it like clanging chains echoing in the water. "Thanks but no thanks. I'd rather do this my way. Him first, and then you. Two loose ends, removed."

"You'll kill your own son?" I whisper.

She shrugs. "When you threatened to kill him before, I had an epiphany. He is not irreplaceable. Surely you know by now that nothing thwarts me," she says mildly. "Lotharius is no exception, especially now that his fealty is to you, as he so emphatically displayed. I guess I should have trained him to fight instead of flirt, but at least I know he was good for one thing."

"What thing?" I say before I can help myself.

"Getting you to fall for him, hook, line and sinker. Just like a silly little girl." She laughs then. "Still think love doesn't make you weak? Look at you. Ready to give up everything to save him, even after everything he has done. It's pathetic."

Ehmora bares her jaws and leans into Lo's exposed throat. I want to move but I'm immobile with fear as the seconds tick by and her teeth sink closer. And in those seconds, I realize that Ehmora is right. I am ready to give it all up for Lo, and regardless of what he has done, he will always be mine...and I will always be his. I can't just let her kill him, not even if it costs me my life...or a throne that sits on blood and bones.

And then I feel it—strength from the Aquarathi around me pressing into me, pledging their loyalty, court by court. I haven't won them by blood. Somehow, I've won them over with heart. Emotions may run deep in my people, but that doesn't mean we don't have them. I see that so clearly now.

"Stop." Something in my voice makes Ehmora meet my eyes. "I forgive you for breaking my family apart and for murdering my father in cold blood," I tell her softly. "Most of all, I forgive you for everything you've done to put our people at risk. Everything," I add with a meaningful glance at Lo. "Including him."

"You stupid bitch," she snarls.

"A bitch is a dog, and I'm far from that."

Suddenly with newfound purpose, I'm darting forward with immense speed to hit her head-on. The brutal strike hurls her body several feet away. One of my spines has broken off into the side of her neck. I bare my teeth and attack again, this time catching her in the mouth with the barbs on my tail before she can get up. I strike again and again, each time my strength growing and growing, and my speed getting faster and faster. I don't stop until she is lying twitching on the ocean floor, until there is nothing left in me but fire and fury.

I swim over to Lo. He's still alive, but I can sense his pain through his broken bones and the welts all over his body. I touch him gently with my mouth and we're connected by a jolt of energy that leaves me breathless. Engaging Sanctum, I offer back the strength that I took from him earlier, and I can feel him healing. Through the connection, I can also feel everything that he feels for me. It's so raw, so visceral, that I have to pull away.

"Nerissa," he whispers. "I'm sorry I didn't tell you. I'm sorry for everything. But I love you, and that has always been true."

"I know," I say. I want to tell him that I love him, too, but the words are buried like rocks inside of me. So instead, I nod. The words will come later.

I'm so dazed from his emotions that I only see the black shadow hurtling toward us when it's too late to do anything but react. I brace, taking the powerful blow on my left side and staggering backward. After giving so much of myself to Lo, I'm not at full strength. But Ehmora is weakened, too, and isn't quite as quick to come back with a counterstrike. Echlios rushes forward but I shake my head, keeping my eyes on Ehmora the entire time.

"It's over," I tell her.

"It's over when I decide it's over," she growls. I respond by throwing out a glimmer that stops her in her tracks. Imprisoned, her eyes are wild and savage. "That's impossible. You cannot control me."

"They've chosen me, our people. Can't you feel it?"

Bend, the waters in my body command. Her eyes go wide as her body struggles futilely against my will, a new queen replacing the old. For some inane reason, I think of Cara and our hockey game against Bishop's, and I hesitate for a second. It's not an attack of conscience; it's more a stab of delayed understanding. Giving someone a chance isn't a show of weakness…it's one of strength. Knowing when to pass the ball is half the battle on the field.

"What are you doing?" Echlios says.

"Something I may regret." I step forward, palms spread. "Swear fealty to me and I will let you live out the rest of your days quietly, here in Waterfell. You will not be exiled or executed for your crimes, but you may never return to the human world. That is all I can offer you."

Her laugh is cold and brittle. "You think you can keep me here?"

"The alternative is exile."

Fear slinks across her face before it is erased by a stormy, dark rage that she conceals behind a compliant smile. She hoped for execution—a swift death, and exile is far from swift. But it's only her pride that is hurting, and in time she will realize that. I'm giving her a chance…a chance to live, and maybe to redeem herself. It's more compassion than she would have shown me, had our positions been reversed. But that makes no difference—I don't control her actions. I control mine.

"Do you yield?" I ask her.

"Never!" she shrieks, and leaps for me again, a long shard of discolored bone in hand. A flame-red shadow barrels in from the side to collide with Ehmora, pinning her to the ground as the weapon falls harmlessly to the sand. Wrenching out of

Echlios's grip with near-inhuman strength, she comes at me again, claws extended. Froth and blood fleck her lips. But this time it's Lo who darts forward to retrieve the broken length of bone. Ehmora's mouth opens into a soundless scream as the forward momentum impales her on the edge of the bone shard that was meant for me. She stares at her son, her dying eyes wide with surprise and something oddly resembling pride.

"Now, it's over," Lo says in a dead voice, the piece of bone slipping from his fingers. "None of us would have been safe if she had lived."

"Lo…your mother…" I trail off.

"She wasn't my mother. She was my maker. Big difference."

Amid the suddenly deafening cheers in the arena, Echlios grins and hugs me fiercely. His voice is quiet but proud. "All hail the new queen of Waterfell. Well done, my lady. Well done."

But I can barely process what he's saying or any of the other voices cheering around me. Somehow, I've won back my crown—the very one that I'd thrown away. In the end, my people have chosen me…because I chose to fight for them. Ehmora lost because she didn't even realize what was really worth fighting for, or that our people would see right through her. From Jenna to Cara to Lo, I have experienced the gambit of human emotions, and that only made me stronger. Not weaker.

After all, love favors those who are receptive to it.

And that is a universal truth.

25
Endings and Beginnings

"So do you still have to go?" Jenna asks. "I mean, now that the big bad is gone?"

We're sitting on my back patio around the pool, cross-legged on the cool flagstones. All of our furniture has been donated to local charities, and the house is empty with the exception of a few treasures that I'll be taking back with me.

"Yes. I'm the...queen now." Getting the word out is tough, considering saying "princess" used to be hard enough. "And the big bad isn't really gone with Cano and my mom still out there. We've just cut off one of its legs. My people need me."

"I know," Jenna says. "I am really going to miss you."

"I'll miss you, too, but I won't be that far away, and I'll come visit you." I laugh. "Plus, I read that James Cameron recently did an expedition to the Mariana Trench. What's to say you couldn't come visit me one of these days?"

"Count me in." Jenna fingers the scale necklace I'd given her with a thoughtful expression. "So what happens with Lo? I mean, he can stay here if he wants to, right, because of the gene thing? But he's your...boyfriend or king or what?"

Flushing at the thought of Lo, I say quickly, "The correct term is *royal consort*. But yeah, *boyfriend* works, too."

"So is he okay?"

"He's fine, apart from a few bruises and broken bones that will heal eventually," I say.

Echlios had told me that the emotional wounds would probably take a lot longer to heal than the physical ones. He and Soren had been pretty cool about everything when they found out about Lo. Well, truthfully, Soren had freaked out a bit at first, but she has since spoken to Lo and she approves.

"Wow," Jenna says, shaking her head. "I still can't believe that this all happened. I mean, it was so surreal. You left to go meet Lo and then Lo's mother showed up at my house looking for you guys. I didn't even think twice about letting her in." She stares at me. "So the other lady was your mom?"

Ignoring the stab of pain at her words, I nod. "Yes."

"I know you probably don't care, but she was actually nice to me in the car. Emma Seavon terrified me, but your mother was...kind." She trails off awkwardly.

"She's a liar. I should have killed her instead of just knocking her out."

"I'm sorry."

"You have nothing to be sorry for," I say, shrugging off any thought of my mother. "It was my fault that they came for you...and Speio's."

The thought of Speio is a bittersweet one. He already went to Waterfell with Soren. I forgave him because I couldn't not forgive him. After all, he was seduced by my mother's words of a better life and a way out, and he'd been so unhappy and lonely that it had been an easy thing for her to convince him. Maybe if I'd made more of an effort to repair things with Cara, he would have been happier here with her and less susceptible to my mother's promises. Things could have turned out far differently. But I'll never know. The truth is, I couldn't have saved Jenna without him so he did sort of redeem himself in a roundabout way.

"He told me he was sorry, you know," Jenna is saying to me. "Before he left. He came to apologize for not keeping my secret and for telling them about what I knew. I told him it was okay but that he owed me one…which I'll probably never collect."

"You were right, by the way," I say. "About Cara. I should have been a better person. A better friend. Maybe if I'd made the effort with her, Speio could have been happy. He wouldn't have been so lonely and craving to return to Waterfell so badly."

"You can't blame yourself, Riss. Hindsight is always twenty/twenty. At least everything worked out in the best possible way. Well, except for the worst part ever. I really hate good-byes." She raises her hands with a dramatic sigh. "I can't believe you are all leaving! Seriously, what am I going to do?"

"You're going to do everything that Jenna does so amazingly well. And you're going to win that hockey championship for your best friend. Or else." Jenna laughs and I make a mock-stern face. "I'm serious. I want you to score at least three goals for me."

"You got it."

Jenna's blue eyes are teary. We stare at each other in silence, so much history between us and so many other things we both wish we could share in the years ahead. Saying goodbye for the last time is harder than I ever thought it would be.

But I know I'll see her again.

I squeeze her into a hug and place her hand on my heart and mine on hers. "I will always love you like a sister. And I will never forget you no matter how many years go by. Always know that you made me better— A better friend and a better leader." We break apart and she's full-on crying now. My face is just as soaked. "One more thing, look out for Kevin for me, will you? The marine center's going to need a lot more volunteers to keep the ocean safe."

"I will, Riss. I promise. You be safe, and take care of Lo, even if he was an idiot. I've never seen anyone in love with someone so much... Well, except for Sawyer, of course." Her voice breaks and her smile wobbles. With one last lingering look at my backyard, where we spent countless hours swimming, goofing around and talking hockey, boys and school, Jenna waves. "Love you."

"Love you, too."

After I watch Jenna's car drive away until it's nothing but a speck in the distance, I sit at the edge of the pool and stare into its glittery surface. I meant what I said to Jenna—I owe so much of who I've become to her and to this place. Humans have something to offer, too, and they have the same, if not more, invested in this planet. We have to have faith that they will do the right thing, and just like my father, I believe that they will.

I sit at the edge of my pool with my feet dangling in the salt water, watching the ocean in the distance until the descending sun turns the surface a brilliant sheen of red and orange. It's nearly time to leave...to say goodbye to this chapter of my life.

"My queen?" Echlios says from behind me.

I can't help grimacing. "Echlios, can you stop calling me that, please? It's only, like, just a little bit weird."

"Sorry," he says with a tiny smile. "Old habits."

"Any news on my mother?" I ask him.

His smile fades and his all-business expression returns. When his people went back to the marine center, there'd been no sign of her. She'd escaped. Maybe a tiny part of me had even wanted her to, despite everything. "She's gone into hiding," he says. "And Cano has disappeared, as well. All of the equipment in his house is gone."

"Are they a threat?" I ask him. With their knowledge of the hybrids—and especially Lo—they could be dangerous. And Jenna will still be at risk with them out there.

"I don't know," he answers. "They have taken all of the genetic research, and that could pose a bigger problem in times to come. We will continue to look for them, but with her genetic mutation, she can survive farther inland than we can."

"So basically, you're saying we'll probably never find her," I say.

Echlios sighs and stares out at the ocean. "Either we will find her or she will find us. You will be safe in Waterfell, but I have a feeling that it's far from over." Echlios studies me and I can feel the weight of the question hovering on his tongue.

"Just ask me."

"What about the boy?" he says.

"What about him?"

An exasperated huff. "Do you trust him? Or better yet, can I trust him with you?"

"Yes, Echlios, you can," I answer softly. "He killed his own mother for me—you can trust that he won't betray us."

There's a lot still unresolved between Lo and me, especially following his deception. After all, he was tasked with making me fall in love with him under the guise that he was a human boy. It was the lowest form of trickery. But Lo didn't count on falling in love with me as hard as I fell in love with him. What I felt from his entire body in the water and what I saw in his eyes had been nothing more than truth. And so I forgave him.

That doesn't mean I'm going to let it go that easily, because forgetting always takes time, and so does rebuilding trust. And now we are linked forever...tied to each other for better or for worse, literally. I'm not sure how I feel about the whole being-bonded thing—it isn't something I'd thought about or been prepared for, partly because I'd thought Lo was human, so falling for him would have minor consequences. Turns out the consequences are slightly bigger than I expected.

Soren told me that she had just known it was Echlios from the day that they met. It was something immediate, primal. With Lo, there've been so many other layers—human ones— blended into the Aquarathi ones that things are not as clear.

"Soren told me you fell in love with him," Echlios says hesitantly, interrupting my thoughts about Lo, "as the humans do. Before the bond."

"Yes."

"Does that make it easier?" I can see that asking the questions are hard for him, but I know he asks because he wants to protect me. I owe him an honest answer.

"No," I say sadly. "It only makes it harder."

"Why?"

"Because bonding occurs at the basic core level for us. You know and you accept it once it happens. With Lo, I gave him my heart and then everything else. Almost like I chose him before the bond chose us, if that makes any sense." I lean backward and stare at the deepening twilight sky and the first hint of stars on the purplish-blue background. "And now that I will be queen with him at my side, we need to navigate a life that we've both lost touch with, somehow together. It's just…overwhelming."

Echlios places his hand on my shoulder and squeezes. "You will be a good queen, my lady. Your father would be very proud." I hear the tremor in his voice and raise my hand to grasp his fingers.

"Thank you." I pull myself to my feet and embrace Echlios.

"I'll just be a minute. Just want to say goodbye. We'll be right behind you."

Walking down the beach, I see a bonfire in the distance and wonder if my friends are sitting around it. A sense of nostalgia fills me as I think of Jenna and Sawyer and wonder if they miss me as much as I already miss them. The beach is empty even with the rising moon. In the distance I can spot figures walking along the edge but they're still far away. The sand feels velvety between my bare toes and I dig them in, enjoying the feeling. There's nothing like it in the world. I smile to myself. No wonder Lo is so obsessed about walking barefoot all the time.

I push my glimmer outward and sense him at the end of the pier. It's so easy to sense each other now. All I have to do is push outward while thinking about him, and I will find him in seconds. Apart from what I already learned—we can give or take strength from each other and communicate mentally over great distances—there is still so much to discover about bonding and each other.

Lo stands as I approach. "Hi," he says, his voice husky.

"Did you say goodbye?" I ask him.

"I don't really have anyone to say goodbye to," he says. There's a trace of sadness in his voice. "Bertha and Grayer were both my mother's staff."

"What about Cara?" I say, fighting my smile. "She's going to be a mess without you, you know. And when the fact that we've eloped hits the rumor mill on Monday, you'll have no hope of ever returning to this town."

Lo smiles. "I emailed her."

"Good."

We stand next to each other, looking out at the inky black water glittering under the light of the moon, silence stretching between us. Only this time, it's not our usual comfortable silence—this silence is full of unsaid things, colored by lies and dishonesty…not just on Lo's part, but also on mine. I wasn't honest with him, either.

"Lo," I say after a while. "Are you sure this is what you want?"

"What do you mean?"

I hesitate, glancing back toward my house and the beautiful stretch of moonlit beach reaching as far as the eye can see. "You could stay here. You don't have to go to Waterfell. I mean, you've never even lived there—it'd be like starting all over again." My words are rambling now, falling out of my mouth unchecked. "Won't you miss this?"

Lo's eyes are unfathomable. "Yes. I'll miss it. But I would miss you more." My lips clamp shut but the more I think about it, the more it makes sense. The idea grows with shape and form and purpose.

"What if you did? Stayed here?"

"You don't want me to go with you?" His voice is aching, and I feel the pull of it against my breastbone like a deep tenderness.

I lick dry lips and take a deep sustaining breath. "Of course I do. But I think you'll be better off staying here. My mother is still out there, and Jenna is vulnerable, at least in the short-term. And with what happened between us, maybe some distance will be good at first." I grasp his hands but his fingers remain slack against mine, unresponsive.

"Distance," he repeats dumbly.

"Lo," I say, grabbing both his hands. "I love you, please don't think otherwise. We are bonded for good now—that will never change. But I think you need this, and I need this. And Jenna needs our protection. I can't just leave her alone and I don't have anyone else I can trust who can stay land-bound and protect her."

"What does Echlios say?" he asks in a tiny voice.

"He doesn't know I'm asking you. No one does. I just don't know who else to turn to, and I believe deep down that this is the right thing to do. You and I will still be able to speak, and I will get here as quickly as I can if anything should happen. Please say you'll do this."

Please, Lo.

In my heart, I know that it's right. Lo and I still need some space to deal with our own baggage, and Jenna needs someone she trusts to look out for her. And I know that Lo will be happier here for a while, figuring out who he is without standing in the shadow of his mother and walking right into another shadow—mine. He can learn to live for himself again. Last of all, I will be able to assume the mantle of my responsibilities without having to worry about whether Lo is fitting in or whether he and I are okay.

The truth is, we both need time to grow up.

And I think Lo knows it, too.

"Okay," he tells me in a quiet voice. "But just until the end of the summer, until things settle down. Then I'm coming to find you...with or without your permission."

I throw my arms around his neck and bury my face in his chest, inhaling his unique smell of sea and salt and warmth. His lips find mine and I'm lost in the desperate heat of the kiss, every emotion caught up in that single moment between us. Lo kisses away the tears on my cheeks and brushes the hair out of my face, his fingers excruciatingly tender.

"I love you, bond or not," he says. "Always." And then I'm clutching his chest and sobbing as if my heart is breaking into two from his words and his touch and the broken look in his eyes. "Go," he tells me gently. "I'll be here. Waiting."

"Lo," I say, pressing kisses on his cheeks, his nose, his eyes... every part of him, I'm desperate to memorize. I want to remember the feel of him, the taste of him on my lips, the way his hair slips through my fingers like velvet sand, the weight of his eyes when he looks at me. "Will you transform with me?"

He nods and we slip into the water, still hand in hand. Raising my palms to his, I watch the blue swirls in mine line up with the greenish-yellow swirls of his. We will always have that piece of each other. We swim out to deeper water. I touch his face with my hands and pull him toward me for one last human kiss.

And then his bones are shifting, elongating, pointing through the human skin that transforms into shiny hard scales. I feel it in my body but see it in his. We transform in unison but experiencing it through each other's eyes is so intimate; it makes every part of me ache. His bronze neck is long and beautiful, curving around the golden green hide of mine. The colored swirls that mark our bonding nearly merge into each other as Lo's body coils against mine. Even my iridescent fins bend toward his blue ones, until our bodies are nearly one.

Lo's eyes are deep blue with electric blue lines like lightning forking in the middle of the ocean at midnight. They are beautiful. I commit them to memory, too, and the entire Aquarathi shape of him, just as dear to me now as his human one is. Resting my brow against his, I repeat the words again and again in my mind until I know he knows...and he's sure.

And then I say it for real one last time before I release him and submerge.

I am yours forever.

★ ★ ★ ★ ★

Acknowledgments

There are so many people I have to thank who made this book possible. First of all, thank you to the tireless and talented team at Harlequin TEEN for all their brilliant work on *Waterfell*. From the editors to the designers to the publicity team to the digital media team—Tashya, Annie, Erin, Gigi, Lisa, Amy, Michelle, Fiona, Mary, Larissa, Siobhan—thank you! I must admit that when I saw the initial pages of revisions, I balked, but as someone once told me—*a great editor is worth her weight in gold.* In this case, the indomitable Natashya Wilson is worth hers in platinum. Through all the drafts and revisions, I cannot thank you enough for your insight, your enthusiasm and your expertise in making this book exceed my expectations. Thanks for taking a chance on *Waterfell,* and on me.

To my fearless warrior princess agent, Liza Fleissig of the Liza Royce Agency, and her partner in crime, Ginger Harris-Dontzin, thank you, thank you, thank you! I'll never forget that phone call when you told me this book had been sold—thanks for finding me such a great match! Above all, thank you for enduring my panic attacks, for being my champion, for all the laughs, for your unwavering support and for being completely and positively dauntless. That is all.

To the incomparable Kristi Cook, who has seen me through several books, including this one, I owe you a mountain of cupcakes. Not only are you a great critique partner, you're a trusted friend. Thank you for all your guidance, advice and encouragement over the years, and for keeping me sane pretty much every day. I wouldn't have been able to make it through the countless rounds of brainstorming, writing and editing without my wonderful writing retreat mavens, the HBK Society—Kristi, Cindy, Danielle, Kate, Angie and Ariane. Thank you for all the cookies, motivation and inspiration. Huge thanks to Damaris and Wanda from *Good Choice Reading* who have been so generous in their support and friendship over the past few years. It means so much to have you in my corner. A big shout-out to Julie and Marissa from JKS for all the help and publicity—thank you! To my ever-faithful first readers—my mom, Nan Ramsey and Pam Sullivan, what would I do without you? Thank you for never saying *no* when I ask you to read anything I write, even if it's the first or hundredth time you've read it. First drafts can be brutal—thanks for your honesty.

Last of all, but certainly not least, my family. To my three wildlings—Connor, Noah and Olivia—I love you loads. Thanks for all your impish smiles, sloppy kisses and unconditional love. I am so blessed to have you in my life. To my wonderful extended family and friends all over the world who are my biggest fans no matter what, thank you for your continued love and support. It means so much. Finally, to my husband, Cameron, who sticks with me through everything, who makes me laugh every day, and who fills my life with love, thank you. You are my rock, always.

Nerissa has won her crown.
Now she must keep it.
Don't miss the next book of

THE AQUARATHI

OCEANBORN

coming in 2014.
Only from Amalie Howard
and Harlequin TEEN!

Prologue

We are savage. We are proud. We are the dark rulers of the sea.

Deep in the ocean near the earth's core, I survey the Aquarathi people—a firestorm of color—as the three lower courts come to pay homage to their new queen. The Blue Court is flamboyant in their tribute. The Green Court, more demure. But the Red Court, I watch with cautious eyes. Weeks before, they supported a rival queen in her bid against the High Court, and she almost won.

Almost.

Today we celebrate my coronation as heir to the High Court. The crown of bones on my brow pushes forward like a fan of finely webbed coral. Echlios, my handler and captain of my royal guard, is beside me, his body rigid, but I can see the approval flashing in his glowing silver eyes. He nods and extends his long neck, his dark red scales glittering, as he bares it to me in a gesture of submission.

Golden-green lights shimmer down the length of my body, mirroring the deep ruby of his, and I click fiercely in my native tongue to my people, calling water to water and blood to blood.

Bend, I will them silently.

Power ripples along my spine, making my golden colors flare so brightly that every finned head dips in deferent succession. Green to blue, and finally to red in a wave of molten crimson.

I rule by strength now. Not by love.

Trust is a luxury, and the time for compassion in Waterfell has come and gone. If I don't control my people, all of the humans will all be at risk. And everything for which my father fought and died will be in vain.

I arch my neck, my tail curling through the water, and freeze as a violent stab of pain lances through me. It wraps itself around me like a wave, closing over every inch of me, inescapable. My lights flutter and die. I can feel the startled pulses and the clicks of the courts, but I can't even focus on them.

All I know is pain…deep, shattering, all-consuming pain, as if a thousand blades are carving into me at once. The navy swirls on my body deepen like ink, sinking into me. Everything disappears and all I know is the pull of the bond…and the one on the other side of the bond calling to me.

In that moment, I know. The threat isn't here.

It's there.

1

In seconds, Echlios is glued to my side, the rest of his guards surrounding us in a protective circle. "My lady, what is it?"

"Lo," I gasp. "Something's wrong. I have to get back to La Jolla—"

"I'll go."

"No," I insist, nearly doubling over. "He's in trouble. I have to go."

Echlios bares his teeth in frustration. His wife, Soren, joins us, her eyes flashing gold fire. Something in them tells me that I'm not going to win this argument, even if I am their new queen and can overthrow whatever she says. It's a look that I've seen many times before, and after four years of human conditioning I'm still not immune to it.

Her voice is gentle, as is the pale green tail fin circling me in a protective manner. "Breathe, Nerissa. Try deep calming breaths. It will help with the pain. Let Echlios go. It is his duty to protect you...and the prince regent."

I do as she says, letting the salt water enter through my gills and breathing out the sharp pulsing pain until it resembles a dull throb. Nodding weakly to Echlios, I watch as Soren dismisses the courts that have come to pay their respects. I don't even care what she's telling them or what they're saying behind my back, but I have to imagine that seeing their new queen incapacitated on the day of her coronation has to be cause for concern. Still, that anxiety pales in comparison to the urge I'm feeling to take off in a mad rush for the mainland.

"I need to get out of here," I pulse to Soren.

"Go," she says to me and then frowns, her eyes narrowing. "Not far, Nerissa."

She knows me too well. I nod ungraciously and make my way out of the throne room into the tunnels beyond. There are two silent shadows behind me—my royal guard—whom I'm aching to get rid of, but pulling any kind of disappearing act will only cause more trouble than it's worth for a few minutes of solitude.

"Stay here," I click to them at the entrance of our undersea fortress. "I'm not going far and I don't need you two right on top of me."

I swim away from Waterfell with a few short, powerful strokes, but stay within watching distance of the first tunnel. The guards' forms are indistinct, cloudy shapes, which means they can still see me and that's all that matters. I close my eyes and stay perfectly still, clearing my mind of everything but the feel of the water against my skin and the soft muted sounds of ocean life around me.

For a heartbeat, floating in a sea of space and nothing, it's easy to pretend that everything is okay. That my parents are alive and in love. That my people aren't living in fear for their very existence. That the one who has my heart isn't a million miles away…and that he hasn't been hurt, or worse.

Lo…the prince regent. My mate.

A flush winds its way through me at the thought of what that means; we are bonded for life now and bound by an unbreakable tie. We belong to each other in a way that only lovers can know. My eyes fall on the bands of navy shimmering through my golden-green scales—the Aquarathi marks of our bonding—and green bioluminescent lights tingle along my sides in automatic response. The longing for him is as demanding as ever. But I was the one who insisted we be apart. I told him to stay in San Diego, to try to find his place alone instead of being in the shadow of someone else. But the truth is I needed to figure out who *I* was. I wanted to process everything that had happened and my fragile fledgling feelings for Lo and, most of all, I needed to separate the truth from the lies.

I try to push the thought of him—and the thought of his blue-black eyes so like the heavy darkness of the ocean surrounding me—from my mind, but it's like trying to separate my skin from my body. Every breath I inhale, he inhales with me. As if in response, the tug from before becomes more insistent, less painful now but still sharp. I can only hope that Echlios finds him safe.

As I drift deeper into the coldness, the current tugs at me with unrelenting force and ushers me into a more vicious swath of blue. I'm not afraid. I can handle the ocean at its worst, control it even, but I let it take me, enjoying the feel of not having to be strong for just a moment. I don't care that I've lost sight of my two guards or that there's nothing around me but pitch-black murky gloom. I'm the worst predator out here; it's not like I have anything to fear, especially with Ehmora being dead and her allies in hiding. Those whom Echlios hunted down have either sworn fealty to me or were executed.

Despite my effort to not think about him, my thoughts inexorably return to Lo, the son of the very one who had tried to kill me and usurp my throne. Sure, he killed her—for me—but our relationship is still delicate at best, and even at the core, a bond isn't the only thing that would hold me to him. I'm not sure whether it's because of the human acclimatization time I spent on the mainland but, illogically or not, I want to *choose* the one I'm meant to be with, as the humans do.

Then again, it's not like I *hadn't* chosen Lo. I'd given myself to him fully in every way when I'd thought he was human, before the bond was made. I loved him. I still love him. The fact that he hadn't told me the truth of who he was doesn't change any of that. But if it doesn't, then why do I feel so splintered inside...as if everything between us is hinged on a lie?

Would I have chosen Lo if I'd known that he was Aquarathi?

Or worse, would I have chosen him knowing he was a murderer's son?

THE GODDESS TEST NOVELS

Available wherever books are sold!

A modern saga inspired by the Persephone myth.

Kate Winters's life hasn't been easy. She's battling with the upcoming death of her mother, and only a mysterious stranger called Henry is giving her hope. But he must be crazy, right? Because there is no way the god of the Underworld—Hades himself—is going to choose Kate to take the seven tests that might make her an immortal...and his wife. And even if she passes the tests, is there any hope for happiness with a war brewing between the gods?

Also available:
THE GODDESS HUNT, a digital-only novella.

The Steampunk Chronicles

Available wherever books are sold!

Enter an alternative Victorian England where automatons and magic are the norm and one strong heroine will battle not only a criminal genius but also the darkness within herself.

Harlequin TEEN invites you into the
spellbinding world of the TWIXT,
a darkly beautiful new fantasy series.

**Some things are
permanent. Indelible.
And they cannot be
changed back.**

When Joy Malone notices
a boy no one else can see,
her life is forever altered
as she is drawn into the
mysterious—and dangerous—
world of the TWIXT.

DAWN METCALF

INDELIBLE

· THE TWIXT · BOOK ONE ·

Available wherever books are sold!

Enter Tudor England in 1554, when there has never been a more dangerous time to be a witch. The only punishment for branded witches is to be hung or burned at the stake.

Meg Lytton's existence becomes more dangerous every day, with the constant threat of exposure by the ruthless witchfinder Marcus Dent. And things are only made more complicate Spanish priest, Alejandro de Castillo, to whor despite their very different attitudes tc

Thrilling and fast-paced—this is the begi Tudor Witch Trilog

Available wherever boc